PHANTAMMERON

BOOK ONE

MITCHELL STOKELY

First Edition, 2015

ISBN: 978-0-9970375-1-7

Printed in the United States of America

Published by: GiantIsland LLC

Contact: phantammeron@gmail.com | www.phantammeron.com

Phantammeron "Luffa" cover design by Mitchell Stokely

— *for Simon*

TABLE OF CONTENTS

Three there are that undying dwell,
the tree, the mist, and the ancient well
They alone in dreams are cherished,
three that long ago had perished

THE ESSENCE ETERNAL

There was nothing in the beginning. No darkness or light. For the black Wings of Night had yet embraced the starless Heavens. Only a silent fog floated upon the ruin and waste that filled the cold and empty space. Like a pale shroud, that solemn cloud lay upon the fallen corpse of the world. Its hollow husk then collapsed back into dust and the dreams from which it was made.

But the dreams that ebbed and flowed beyond that shattered world had returned to fill the empty gulf with its ethereal seas. And the Great Mother, whose spirit bore its sleepy tide, washed clean again its celestial shores. Thus began the Anakra, the Dreamtime of the Great Mother, whose broad and hopeful vision was born again in this world.

From out of that yawning gulf rose forth the Essence Eternal, he who was made from the Spirit Divine. He had come from the old world, rising up from its ashes, until his argent wings unfurled and stretched forth across the barren waste. Like a beacon shining out, clear and bright from the depths of night, his radiant wings cast their sanguine light down upon that fearful world. The hidden splendor and glory of the shining Heavens was then revealed to him.

Descending into the depths, the Essence Eternal filled the hollow spaces of those valleys with the brilliant lights of his shining spirit. He commanded the mighty Mountains of Heaven to rise up from the firmament before him, until their towering heights pierced the Heavens and rent its roof asunder. Sublime in their majesty, the shimmering peaks stood proudly against the sky, looking down upon their sister-valleys below. The Heavens then rejoiced. For the shadows of the night had retreated back into the depths from which they were spawned.

But there were two that had lain hidden in the darkness of that decrepit world. The sinister twins, Emptiness and Nothingness, had long dwelt unchallenged in the gloomy spaces below, slowly consuming the last of the shadows and lights of Heaven that had remained. But those terrible twins fled in terror. For the light of the Essence Eternal shone forth with great force, blinding and burning them with its insatiable flame.

Driven forth from that illuminated world, they fell into the unending abyss that lay in the farthest reaches of the Great Beyond. There they dwelt concealed, far from the radiant beams of dawn that wrapped about the world, and lapped the wounds wrought upon them by that angel of light. Their foul pit soon became their prison. And they were bound to it, though it was of their own making.

The Essence Eternal now began his greatest works. For there burned within his spirit the Creative Flame, which ever consumed him. And there flowed within his heart the Sacred Waters, which had bestowed within him the gift of life. With strong hands wielding mighty tools, he carved out the hollows of the Arch of Heaven, like waters weaving their way and wearing upon the rocks. And with his spiritual fire, he forged from the mountains the Pillars of Heaven upon whose weight the Arch would rest.

He too built the silent Halls of Time, which stretched endlessly into the immeasurable depths of space. Within their hollow hallways he made the wide Corridors of Darkness, upon whose great gates he hung the black Veils of Night, beyond which no light would shine. For they guarded the Lands of Midnight, that wicked realm of boundless gloom that stood between the Heavens and the Great Beyond.

When his work was done, he climbed the shining Mountains of Heaven. Standing upon their summit, he looked down with wonder upon the sublime grandeur of all he had wrought. Weary from long labor, he rested his spirit in the shadow of the mountains. But as he slept beneath the twilight Heavens, a tiny ray of light shined forth from beneath the roots of the mountain. The secret fire of the Sacred Light had awakened once more, shining out its golden beams from within the hollows of its grave.

Thus, in the Dreamtime of the world were the Heavens remade and forged anew by the noble spirit that had come to dwell therein.

The Essence Eternal awoke from sleep. For he heard voices echoing up from the depths of that which he had made. They were the lonely cries of his children, calling up from the dark waters that lay hidden within the heart of the world.

Reaching out, he held their tiny lights in his hands and breathed into them the fire of his own spirit. They were now cast from the Spirit Divine, of which he too was made, taking form and shape as sons born unto him. Yet were they also of him, as his divine immanence, through them, took form incarnate. So would he, forever after, remain whole and inseparable in all his children. Through their various forms and works would they be known to each other, while through their spirits would they be known to him alone.

Many children were born unto the Great Father. Yet, only five came to him in this world. These were the Primordial Ones, who now gathered before him in his mighty halls. He revealed to each of his children the cherished gifts he had granted unto them. For he had known of their coming and had prepared their various forms and powers, which were once his own. These he had equally divided among them. They knelt before him and were thankful. The Great Father then looked upon his children with love and joy. For of all that he had made, they were his greatest creations.

He then told them that he would soon perish and depart this world, never to return. For he had planted his flame within them, desiring only that they work in harmony as one to finish what he had wrought. Upon its completion, they would return to him and dwell in a house prepared for their keeping. His sons then wept for him. But he comforted them, telling them to go forth and begin their various labors. For through their creative works alone would they find salvation. His sons then departed for their given domains, which he had prepared for them long ago.

But discord soon rose between them, born of the jealousy, greed, and desire for power that had grown within their darkened hearts. For their own secret passions, borne by their gifts, soon consumed them, driving them against each other in vicious and violent conflict. The world their Father had created fell into ruin, and much that he had made was undone.

Within the gloomy Halls of Time, in the secret chambers of his house, the Great Father grew weak until the time had come for his spirit to leave that troubled world. The Creative Flame that once had burned bright within him was now nearly spent. From within his empty halls, his voice cried out, calling for his children to come to him. For he desired to speak to them as one. But none answered his call, nor came to him in his time of need. For they were blinded by their burning hatred, and deafened by the clamor of continuous war.

Upon the eve of his passing, one of his sons came to him at last. For beyond the Mountains of Heaven, deep within the secret realm in which he had dwelt, the gentle child had felt his father's sad heart beating within his own.

With woeful eyes, the child sat beside his father, telling him of the many sad deeds which he had committed against his siblings. The Great Father looked upon his son's doleful face and saw in him a shattered spirit. And he saw too the sorrowful fate that would yet befall his son, born of the fruit of the dark seeds he had planted within him. For his son's spirit burned bright with the Creative Flame, a presence wild and untamed, which he too possessed. And he knew that soon all his children would be consumed by the fires of their own passions.

But as he lay dying, compassion and mercy filled his heart. He felt the humility and love that yet remained in the heart of his child, and gave unto him the last of his essence, whose silver waters he now held in his aged hands. These, the Sacred Waters of the world, were all that remained of the Great Father. These hidden waters alone had sustained him with their hopeful presence. And yet the memory of something dark dwelt within.

He told his son that in those waters would the fates of the children of the world now lie. For in his hands swirled the waters of an ancient pool—the spiritual waters cast away from some other world destroyed long ago and forgotten.

These he gave to his son, who took them as a treasured gift, though he knew not their meaning or purpose. The child then looked into those strange, twilit waters, seeing only faded lights and shifting shadows. He then looked upon his father's eyes, one last time. But as he did, he saw hidden in their shining depths the shade of a darker spirit he had not seen before.

His father's face now faded from view, and the last of his spirit drifted away. The Spirit Divine of the Essence Eternal fled forth into the night, beyond the heights of the Mountains of Heaven, until its distant light disappeared beyond their peaks. His son then wept bitterly for his father.

THE TROUBLED SONS

The golden dawn of the new world had returned to dusky gray. And the Primordial Ones, now dwelling far apart, hid in their own dim realms which their father had given them long ago. In their dark and twisted minds their hatred for each other grew ever stronger, which in turn spawned poisonous plots of deception and darkest treachery. For many ages they had waged war upon each other, brother against brother, for dominion over that world, until the Heavens had fallen, once again, into waste and ruin from the savagery of their struggles.

With the fading of the lights of the Spirit Divine, the Heavens became trapped in the gloom of the fogs that had once filled it. The Primordial Ones then saw the last gleam of Heaven dim before them, and the memory of their father hung heavy in their hearts, his words echoing in their minds again. They then abandoned their wars against each other. And the wrath wrought upon the world waned for a time, though the guiding light of hope would never again shine brightly upon it.

Beyond the distant fringes of the shadowed Heavens, past the Veils of Night, which hung like ragged drapes before Time's war-torn halls, there stretched a vast realm of darkness and dolor called the Lands of Midnight. Beyond the Corridors of Darkness, within a fortress forged of pitch and might, the first-born son of the Great Father had dwelt, he who is named the Endless Night.

Most blessed was this child of shadows. For the Great Father had given his son a divine gift bearing great purpose and design. By the Wings of Night given unto him would the faded sky be born anew under the satin sheet of midnight, and bound unto the stars of Heaven, yet unborn. In that black mantle would the light of a million suns come to dwell, and within its black cloak the Children of Heaven shine forth in all their glory, joined as one to that single shade in purposeful union. This had been the one labor the father had given his shadowy son to fulfill.

But even before the death of his father, the Endless Night had succumbed to his own dark and decadent desires, seeking to envelop the world in his vile shadow, and devour the last of his father's lights that yet gleamed in the Heavens. For he proudly wielded his father's ebony flame, that which now burned brightest in him. This fire was of the Glourun, a dark glamour whose enchantment masked all things by its black beauty. But the Endless Night had remade this dark power so that he might hide, by their seductive shadows, his lies and deceptions from his brothers and the all-seeing eye of the Spirit Divine.

With the Wings of Night he had corrupted, he drew them about his form like a cloak. He then cast their black veil over the dying light of the world, so that only the feeble glow of Heaven remained unconcealed.

With his new powers he then summoned forth sinister servants from the lands beyond. To him came many evil spirits that had lain hidden in the shadowy pits and pools of the world. Mightiest of these was a strange monster called the Nightmare Unending. It had been birthed from the depths of the Endless Night's own perverse mind. Yet it had grown from a seed unseen and planted by the hands of a sinister source that dwelt beyond the fringes of this world.

A servant to the Endless Night, this foul spirit had been created to fulfill a more malevolent will. For in that being dwelt the inner shadow that pollutes the heart and mind in endless heartache and anguish, dimming the light that shines from within the living. A depraved creature, it had the penetrating eye that sees that which the heart must hide. Feeding off the suffering of the living, it sought those trapped in the unending agony of life who, struggling to find the will to defy temptation, must endure or fall to their heart's unbending darkness.

And so the Nightmare knew more than any other being of the secrets that lay buried within the hearts of the children of the world. This creature the Endless Night carefully nurtured. For through its dark powers and treachery, the Night had sought to pollute the minds of his brothers, perverting their dreams and destroying their hopes until, weakened in spirit, they would serve only his will.

The Endless Night sent the evil essence of the Nightmare Unending into the world, deceiving and corrupting the minds of his brothers until they fell into a frightful sleep. Black seeds of terror were then planted within them, growing freely within their clouded minds, until its dark roots had pierced their hearts and drank the sacred lights of their spirits. Trapped in fear and tortured by terror, they cowered in their own beds, bound to the will of their brother and his conniving servant.

The Endless Night then summoned forth his bat-winged children, driving them from the Lands of Midnight, and sending them flying forth into the Heavens. His armies beat the skies with their ebony wings, until their dark forms stretched across the heights of Heaven, drowning the valleys of that once-shining realm in utter darkness. Their endless streams, like long black vines, stretched beyond his realm, entangling his brother's lands in their boundless shade. The Endless Night then opened forth his wide wings until their terrible shadow enveloped the very Mountains of Heaven, cloaking every corner of the cosmos in darkness. The dark lord watched with perverse joy as the last lights of Heaven faded from view.

He then looked down upon that bleak, broken, and baneful world with a contemptuous eye. For the mighty spheres of Heaven were now bound to his will alone. Completely clothed in his grim shade, to him were its children now enslaved, hiding in terror under the gloom of the horror-filled skies. Then was realized by all whom dwelt under him, the true nature of the Glourun, his cursed shade. For the infinite silence of the sinister night had drowned the very spirit of their lives, suffocating the sound of every last beating heart in its great shadow.

The Endless Night stood proudly upon the summit of the Mountains of Heaven and proclaimed, "Come, my children, and bow before me. For I am the Lord of Darkness, overlord of all that dwells under the shadowed Heavens." To his many black servants, he then decried, "In this world, no dusk shall ever fall or dawn ever rise, no star ever dwell or sun ever shine."

The world would have remained bound to his eternal shadow. But the vile servant of the Endless Night, the Nightmare Unending, had come upon its master unseen. It watched as the Endless Night had lain with a witch-queen most foul, whose spirit and form the Endless Night had summoned from the dark waters that billowed up from beneath the world.

By his seed, in secret, she had brought forth a son and daughter, the Shadow and the Shade. To these children the Endless Night then bestowed his greatest gifts and powers. For he had conquered this world for them so that, like him, they might make it in their own image upon his passing.

But the Nightmare Unending saw that within its master's dark heart had grown the faint glow of love's undying flame, fostered by a father's unfaltering hope that its enduring light might someday shine bold and bright again within his children. Enraged, it fled from his master as one betrayed, its vile spirit departing from those he had enslaved in the unending horror of their dreams. It then found the Shadow as he slept, the first-born Child of Night, and placed within the eldritch son its own corrupted spirit, so that the fate of this world and its shadowed child, forever after, would be bent towards its secretive will.

For the Nightmare Unending had no hope for itself or this fallen world. And within that precious child it had seen a truer source of this world's hopelessness and despair than in the father. From within this fallen son would soon arise a greater evil, whose hateful violence and wrath would be inflicted upon this world. By its vow to leave behind its cursed spirit, the Nightmare Unending was now free from its long servitude to the Endless Night. It fled into the gray fog, returning to the hateful hollows from which it was spawned.

Free from their night terrors, the Primordial Ones rose from their troubled sleep. Seeing their world wrecked by the great shadow that lay about it, they gathered as one to destroy the

Endless Night. They wrought great wrath upon him, casting his dark armies back beyond the Veils of Night that guarded his lands. The Endless Night then fled forth from the fray, beyond the walls of his great fortress, disappearing into the catacombs that lay beneath it.

There he dwelt alone, crying out in pain and tending to the terrible wounds inflicted upon him. But his brothers came and cruelly stripped his own troubled children from him. They in turn were imprisoned in the pits of the world, far from his knowledge and reach. So was the Endless Night and his kind banished from this world, and his dominion over it broken, forever.

The Endless Night climbed forth from the black labyrinths below his keep and stood upon the edge of his battered lands, his black claws clinging to the crags that hung above its shadowed shores. He wrapped his ragged wings about him, and with eyes glowing like red embers, looked down upon the remains of his ravaged realm.

Weak and in despair, he vowed never again to bathe his father's domain in darkness, nor consume the last of the feeble lights of that world. Nor had he sought revenge upon his brothers for their cruel acts. For he was now weakened by war, and weary with regret. But in the silent hours, he thought upon the fate of his lost children and the mystery of their imprisonment.

Yet, unknown to him, evil had been sown in his son's heart by the hand of the cruel Nightmare Unending. For that creature had planted a secretive seed into the Shadow, whose own hate, like a dark tree, would soon grow forth and bear foul fruit.

* * *

Beyond the Veils of Night, past the gloomy Corridors of Darkness that wound their way through the Lands of Midnight, there lay a wrecked and ruined region called the Realms of Oblivion. Chained to the unforgiving shade, this sad realm lay permanently stained by the ever-lengthening shadows that crept into it from the neighboring domains of darkness.

Here, countless menacing mountains stood, rugged and savage, their horned peaks thrusting up like daggers of obsidian through the belly of a tumultuous sky. Bound by black ice and pelted by frigid rains, their unrelenting winds chewed away at the weathered rock that lay exposed upon its heights. Their barren crags and cliffs looked down with pity upon bottomless pits and chasms of blackest night, whose unknown depths, cloaked in a cold gray fog, no living thing had ever seen or fathomed.

Here lay a domain much maligned, spawned by the mind of a being born of ultimate destructive and evil intent. By its crushing hand had that land become a place beyond all measure of cruelty fashioned—a world of blight, famine, and pestilence which had risen forth from the violence and destruction that had eternally plagued it. The gloomy valleys of this ominous realm had long remained imprisoned in the grip of the dead and the dying. For about its expanse remained the wreckage of a vast and unending war, whose fierce conflict, unleashed over many eons had nearly consumed it.

Yet upon the slopes of the shadowed mountains slept the sparse remains of a once-divine city, rising up from a vast graveyard plain below, about whose foggy tombs of the dead trailed away countless stone stairways, down into the dizzying depths of its yawning pits. Above those ruins the remnant battlements of a mighty keep now stood, with walls of steel and stone, the last victim of some forgotten siege from which forceful fists had rent a brutal justice upon its many shattered walls and spires. For the Primordial Ones had bent all their might to fell that fastness and drive its malevolent creator from its hold. The fortress had then fallen with its defenders in a final crushing blow, so that a tangled wreckage of crumbling rock, twisted iron, and earth were all that remained.

Below those haunted battlefields of horror could still be heard the tortured screams and moans of the dying and the ghosts of the slain, their fallen enemies, continually roaring up from the cold depths of the shattered cities below. Only their pitiful cries of suffering now challenged the wailing winds in the peaks above.

Countless carved tombs and crypts of colossal stone had arisen from the rock, strewn about the pits and valleys to honor the fallen in a great City of the Dead. Forgotten by the living, the shattered city and its sister necropolis now stood empty and abandoned. Only an oily, black mist crept about its crumbling walls, curling about the stony streets, and crawling down and around the roots of dying trees, whose twisted trunks hung bent and broken into the valley below.

But the red and glowing eyes of sleeping beasts still blinked and rolled in the shadows of the haunted cities. For a few demonic beings crept there, lying hidden under slabs of stone, within cracks of walls, or under rocks and piles of rubble. These leaderless offspring of evil, the demonic enslavers of this land, had dwelt there in hiding for many lost ages. The last of their kind, they lay curled within the dark corners and spaces, bloodstained and blackened from ages of endless war.

Others had perished, but only in form. For their spirits had remained behind to haunt the desolate landscape. Though their phantom spirits were now cleft from their bodies, their ghosts had remained imprisoned in the trees and rocks until the time when they would be reborn into this world. These sad specters would wait for their master's return, when they would rise up again in flesh even more frightening, unleashing their wrath upon the children of the world yet to come.

Within the darkest depths of this fallen realm, a vile being had lain hidden, imprisoned in the bottom of its deepest pits. This was the cruel lord and callous ruler of that realm, he who is named the Limitless Void, the sinister second-born son of the Great Father.

The Lord of Destruction he was called, a colossal being of uncontrolled power and might, who had for ages ruled over this vast domain of death. Like the Endless Night, his older brother, he was a cursed spirit who had succumbed long ago to the temptations of his own evil designs and delusions. For he had sought to defy his father and take his brother's lands for his own. But the plotting of this cruel brother was more malevolent. For his villainous and violent mind was ever turned towards the utter destruction of the Primordial Ones and their children.

In the youth of this world, the Essence Eternal had given the Limitless Void a most sublime gift. Through him was bestowed power over the dead and their consumption. And by his great appetite could he devour the waste of the world, returning all things to the primeval dust from which they were made.

He was the eater of the Vatar, the flesh-of-the-earth that is the body. Yet, by his will alone were their spirits spared utter annihilation, as through death could they yet live again. And so by his hand were they born anew. For the Void alone had been granted the power to devour the endless train of the dead that wound its way to him, unbinding both light and shadow from their forms, and sundering their spirits from their flesh with his shining sword Vatavandr. Thus, the Limitless Void could return the spirits of the children of the Primordial Ones back to the world as a gift most precious. In flesh renewed could their spirits then be recast, as through death had the spirit of the world thus been remade. For this purpose alone had the Limitless Void been born.

But long ago, the Limitless Void had in secret sought to defy his father and destroy his brothers in both flesh and spirit. He first set about building his arsenal and armies of might to defy them. By the hand of his swarthy smiths were fashioned dark swords of death to cleave their spirits in two. Cursed relics of black magic and strange enchantments were also forged, which he used to bind the lost spirits that dwelt within Oblivion to even more frightful forms of dread. And so were the black hosts of Oblivion first summoned forth from the infernal pits of the underworld by that sinister son.

Within his lands he gathered his vast armies of might, commanding them to prepare for war. Great throngs of monstrous beings came before him, giving him their full obedience. His forces then flung wide the gates of Oblivion, creeping forth in one black mass to assault the neighboring lands of his brothers.

But in the fray they were cast back, again and again. For they could not match the strength and power of the Primordial Ones, or the will and might of their noble sons and daughters. And so hatred and vengeance against them grew ever stronger in the black heart of the Limitless Void.

Then was heard by the Limitless Void a strange and agonizing cry, echoing up from the depths below his cities. Beyond his father's knowledge, he had travelled in secret to find its source—to the forbidden realms of the Great Beyond that lay upon the farthest fringes of his world. In that gray and infinite space, the evil twins, Emptiness and Nothingness, had lain hidden in their unending domain of death. For by their fear of the Sacred Lights of Heaven had those dire enemies of his father lain imprisoned in the sunless abyss of which they themselves were made.

The Limitless Void summoned them forth. Their terrifying forms then appeared before him. And he saw that his own empty spirit, like a cup, would be filled with the dark draught of their mighty powers.

Standing upon the edge of their grim abyss, the Limitless Void spoke bold words to the evil twins, saying, "Come before me, pale spirits. I alone know of your nature and of your secret desire for the world. If you will aid me in my war against my brothers, I will destroy the lights of Heaven wherever they might shine. And by their destruction shall you be free of your prison."

But the black storms of the evil twins boiled and blistered before the Limitless Void, ever-changing and most loathsome. Their booming voices then spoke, saying, "We will assist you in your time of need. But we do not as yet desire the death of the Sacred Light of the Creator. We seek only to devour the spirits of the living. When the last child of this world is consumed shall the Spirit of the World then perish and the light with it. My brother and I shall then be free to feed upon its lifeless corpse, as we have done many times before."

They then demanded he now sacrifice his own children to them. Only then would they grant him their many powers and servants of might.

Hearing this morbid demand, the Limitless Void recoiled in horror. For he saw their true nature—that they were conceived within some vile womb of violence, decay, and death. And so was revealed to him their appalling evil most foul. But his desire to destroy his brothers burned like an insatiable flame that would never cease, so that he succumbed to their will, surrendering his own children to the black mouths of those vile beasts.

Before their doom, his frightened children had tried to flee, flying beyond the peaks of Oblivion. But they were soon sucked down into the vortices of the many vile servants sent to find them, the last of their kind crying out to their father, begging for mercy. Their flesh was then ripped from their bones, and their spirits obliterated forever from this world, devoured by the gaping mouths of the Emptiness and Nothingness.

With the annihilation of those spirits, the vile beings that dwelt within the Great Beyond rose up with even greater force, renewed and replenished by that grave sacrifice. Their frightening storms grew beyond their prisons, bursting forth into the world, defying the burning lights of Heaven.

The Limitless Void, seeing the immense power of their storms, climbed upon a peak and spoke to the Nothingness, saying, "The time for you to devour the world has not yet come. For though the lights of Heaven have begun to fade, the lights of the Primordial Ones and their children still shine brightly."

He then commanded the Nothingness and his brother to come into his form and dwell therein. By his guiding power, he would take them to the lands of his brothers so they and their children might be consumed by them.

The Nothingness rose up, and with his great gray face, smiled upon the Limitless Void, saying, "We shall now enter your flesh and become one with your spirit. But should you fail, you shall suffer the same fate that has befallen us."

The clouds of the evil twins then came into the mouth of the Limitless Void. Within him surged the unbridled strength and power of the evil twins, which they now bestowed upon him. By their powers, the Limitless Void could now obliterate all things in this world, if he so desired. And so in his prideful and devious mind, he plotted unbridled destruction upon his brothers and their kind.

In a vicious assault, the Limitless Void unleashed great wrath upon his brothers, so that their children fled before the ruin of his hateful carnage. From his monstrous mouth billowed forth storms and violent winds of savage destruction. For he had summoned forth the full powers of the evil twins, whose vast vortices could annihilate all who stood before them in futile defiance. Many of the last and greatest works of the Great Father then fell into crumbling ruin before the violent onslaught.

The Primordial Ones' many servants and shining armies fled before the frightful forces that the Limitless Void had now unleashed, until many of their own children fell before that evil, consumed into the gray mouths of the Nothingness and Emptiness, never to be seen again.

His brothers, in terrible fear and despair of the Limitless Void's vast and unlimited powers, seeing his alignment with the monstrous horrors that had long dwelt in the abyss, faced the full force of their brother upon the battlefields of space and time. For the Primordial Ones had risen up as one force united to challenge him. By their unity were they victorious. But not without great sacrifice had they won. For many of their strongest and bravest children had perished in that frightful war.

They then took the Limitless Void away in shackles. Chained to the bottom of his own pit, he now lay imprisoned. There he wept, tortured by unfulfilled desires and uncontrolled hungers, which he could no longer satiate. Within the rocky depths of that chasm he cried out in endless suffering, agony, and isolation.

With the fall of the Limitless Void, the terrible twins of the Nothingness and Emptiness fled forth from his weakened form, out into the Heavens, seeking vengeance upon the living that yet remained. But the Primordial Ones, seeing those mighty horrors rising forth before them, awakened the Sacred Light, which one among them had found hidden on the slopes of the Mountains of Heaven.

As they cast its mighty beams down upon them, the Nothingness and Emptiness were burned and blinded, once more, falling back into their prison, never to rise again. For as long as the children of this world yet lived, and the lights promised to them still shined, the evil twins would be bound to the abysmal depths of the Great Beyond.

The Limitless Void now slept alone in the pits beneath Oblivion, anchored by long black chains to the rocks below. But in his misery, there remained in his heart the desire for freedom, and revenge upon his brothers.

But in the corners of his misty cavern, he came upon a strange pool filled with weird waters, black and poisonous. About that decrepit well stood a dark husk of a great tree, the dead and bent limbs of which hung, like long dark fingers, down into its silent waters. In his frustration and anger he took Vatavandr, the spirit-sword his father had given him, and cast it into the pool. His eyes burned with a vengeful light, as he watched the shining sword sink beneath the waves.

The Limitless Void stood before the putrid waters of the silent well, thinking upon all he had lost, when he saw the image of a dark spirit shining dimly upon its surface. There then appeared the ghostly image of a dark queen, who revealed to him strange visions of future events and tidings of things yet to come. But as those images faded before him, a dark object shone forth from the depths of the pool.

Pulling it from the water, the Limitless Void saw it was a ring carved of darkest jet, whose great stone shined forth with an eerie light. But for fear of it, he would not wear it, as he sensed something cursed and baneful about it. But through his touch was his spirit strangely bound to that malevolent band.

He returned to sleep, where in dreams mysterious and haunting, there entered into his mind the image of the ring again. From his prison, he awoke, as in a sweat, crying out for the last of his winged servants, who soon came to him from the dark Realms of Oblivion above. One by one they flew to him in his prison. They then tried to free him, but could not. For those black chains were enchanted by an unbreakable magic. He then sent servants into the world, commanding them to bring news of his brothers' plights and the many secretive plots they had made against him.

To the Limitless Void then came the secret knowledge of his brothers' works and the labors of their last children in this world. This knowledge he gathered to himself, so that in time he could use it to his own benefit. By the dark works of his servants, he then placed before his brothers many traps born of their own temptations and carnal desires, which in time he knew would bring doom upon them. For by their own decadence would they plant the seeds of their own destruction, and by these acts, his freedom.

But the Limitless Void could not escape his prison. And in those terrible depths was he doomed to dwell alone for many ages, far from the Great Father's guiding lights, which still shone faintly upon the Mountains of Heaven.

This world now was spared the cruel hands of darkness and destruction. And the designs of evil's vile benefactors were stayed. Its two troubled sons now restrained, that embattled world fell into a certain, yet fleeting peace, once more.

THE DREAMING SEAS

For many ages there dwelt alone, under those quiet Heavens, the sad and solemn third-born son of the Great Father, he who is named the Twilight Mist. That wayward son had mourned for his father, alone in the depths of a dark and rocky abyss that lay beneath the vast Arch of Heaven. For this was his domain, a land born of haunted mists and evening's shade, whose lavender clouds perpetually drifted out over the rocky firmament, filling the lonesome spaces beneath the bosom of the mighty mountains.

His were the powers of the dewy mists, which the Great Father had granted unto him so that this world might be fed by his life-giving rains. But it was the gift of his mysterious twilight glow, the Avara or shining mist, which alone had remained to brighten this doomed world. For its dim and dusk-filled lamps ever burned upon the surface of the waters of his sad heart. And therein would shine the last light of hope that peace would dwell again in the hearts of his brothers.

Embattled with his siblings, having suffered by their endless wars and treachery, the Twilight Mist lay weary and broken in the valleys of his distant lands. There he remembered his father's words, spoken to him so long ago, and looked with bitterness upon the lightless peaks where now only a faded glow of his father's lights had remained. He had held in his weathered hands the strange and mysterious waters given him by his father, looking into them at times for solace, and the blessings of his merciful spirit.

As he wept for him, he saw the light of his father's face shimmering upon its surface. But as he looked deep into the pool, the ghost faded from view. The Twilight Mist turned and looked away in bitterness. But as he did, a new shining vision appeared upon its surface. He saw within those waters a dim glow cast from some strange forest. In its midst grew a golden tree, high upon a hill, which looked down upon a shining pool of silver. And he saw that the twilit aura cast forth from the mingling of their lights was much like his own.

But as the vision faded, he cried out to his father in frustration and confusion. For he knew not the meaning of that vision, nor the purpose of those waters given to him so long ago.

The Twilight Mist then took shape as a thick fog, gathering before him swirling clouds and tumbling mists born of his anger, fear, and frustration. Up from that vast gulf he climbed, high into the Heavens, curling and twisting in a savage display, until drowned in his own dew, he fell back upon himself, dripping down his waters into the empty waste below. Like endless tears his waters fell, the first tender rains of the world, down into an unfathomed pit, until there rose up from the dismal depths a dark ocean, rolling and raging in the twilight gloom.

The Twilight Mist then lay calm, drifting out upon the face of the waters he had made, casting his dim lights upon the surface of the seas. For the beauty of the waters, and the doleful song of those seas, drew him down upon their bosom. As the secret waters of the seas and the dews of the mist embraced, the Twilight Mist felt his Father's love burning bright within him. And the power and purpose of all he had made filled his spirit at last.

And so was fulfilled the making of the Dreaming Seas that the Great Father had foreseen. For this was the one labor he had given his son.

In that wild ocean there lay entombed in their watery womb a sleeping dark-haired maiden named An. Her divine form now lay silent and serene in a secret sepulcher in the shadowy depths of that brine. Wrapped in the raiment of her dreams, untouched by time, there fell upon her quiet mind faded images of a past and future yet to be. Like the rough waves that rolled above her, she tossed and turned in tortured slumber. For she was cursed to bear alone dark dreams, born of that cruel and unending sleep, where fleeting phantoms without forms or faces, spawned from some black night of the mind, haunted her with strange visions she could not yet fully fathom.

As the ages passed away, this lonesome child of the seas lay bound in the loving embrace of her mother's swelling waves. Yet none could find her there in its depths, nor disturb her fright-filled sleep. For the Dreaming Seas, like a fortress around her, lay unassailable, with boundless cliffs of water, foam, and spray. So this Child of the Mist and Sea lay guarded and unseen.

But An's parents had placed within their sleeping child a special heart, whose magic waters it alone would bear. For with the gentler generations yet to come, these waters she would someday share. But in their wisdom, they determined she should remain undisturbed and inviolate, ever after. In her watery prison was she so chained, never to depart or awaken again. Yet, the haunted waters that had filled the fair maiden's time with the nightmares of her timeless mind, the world's fateful future, uncertain and unknown, she and those waters would decide alone.

* * *

Deep in the blighted and black Realms of Oblivion, there had come another into this sad world—a lonely child named Agapor. He was born of a cold and cruel mother, and conceived by the seed of a father, yet unseen. Within the fearful and forbidding hallows of Oblivion was he born, crying out for the hands of comfort and compassion. Yet cradled in the cold arms of that being called the Nameless One was he cruelly kept. For no love was shown him as he slept.

Within the frigid halls of her fallen fortress, the mother had heard the cries, not of her wailing child, but of a monstrous being hiding in the chasms that lay deep beneath her keep. It long had cried for the bastard child whose father had departed long ago. The aged mother then cruelly ripped her son away from her, casting him from her mountainous halls, down into the roaring depths below.

Into a hidden land, bathed and bound in relentless fog, Agapor was thrown. Past the Gates of Eventide he fell, beyond whose portal neither dark nor light might tread, down into the timeless Not-World called Wendalia. Through the shifting shadows of gray mists, whose dim light cast a somber glow upon that formless space, he drifted, down into the cold and silent waste, until at last his little body fell upon the rocks below. There, he clung upon the lonely lip of a barren precipice, overlooking a yawning chasm, whose dark ether ebbed and flowed.

Alone and abandoned, the frail child cried upon the windswept ledge. A frigid fog flowed down and around him, wrapping the child in its cold embrace, until it was itself ripped away from the face of the rock. Its vapors were then sucked down into the monstrous mouth of a violent vortex, which slowly spun about itself in the gray depths below.

Here Agapor lay, cast away by his mother, forgotten by the world. His tears dripped down into that storm, until a black spirit awoke in the gloom about him. That being saw the suffering child and took pity on him, until at last it reached up with its great black hands and took the crying child with it into the chasms below.

There in its dark bosom was Agapor nurtured, feeding upon the waste and refuse that fell from above. For many ages was he nursed within the black arms of that being, until in time he grew with strength and power, and awoke as from a dream. At last he opened his eyes, and looked into the terrible face of that grim spirit whose dead orbs stared down at him like shaded suns eclipsed by shadowed moons.

The sinister being then spoke to Agapor, with words dark and yet divine, saying, "My child, the hand of cruel fate has delivered you unto me. For long ago your own loveless mother, who dwells in the hateful lands above, had cast you away into this lonely pit so you might perish alone in its cold prison. And so I found you as a baby, frightened and abandoned, taking you into my arms, and loving you as my own."

The spirit spoke again in a softer timbre, most beguiling, saying, "But my child, I too am a prisoner of this forgotten realm of Wendalia. In ages past, I was bound to the bottom of this chasm by the powers of another. Black manacles, forged by the forces of darkness, entangled and entwined within them, were placed upon my wrists. By unbreakable chains was I then bound to these rocks so I might be kept, ever after, from the fulfillment of my dreams.

And so, like you, I have suffered, but with unending and torturous hunger and thirst, crying out in pain and agony, trapped and hidden from the lands above where once I dwelt among my kind."

Agapor then saw the full suffering of that being and took pity on him. He climbed out from the icy breast of that black beast, and rose to his feet upon the jagged rocks of Wendalia. He found the dark manacles of iron that bound the being to its prison and broke them. For unknown to Agapor, within his own hands lay the source of the strength that could unbind them.

The vile spirit was freed at last, and rose up into the dark skies above, forming a vast and angry storm that filled the air with thunder and lightning. Agapor then heard the terrible roar of violent winds, and the malevolent cackle of laughter from within its great black orifice. Agapor climbed upon a rocky summit, and seeing his master's monstrous force, called out to it in the gale. But the beast in truth cared not for the child, and came down upon him to consume him. For that being was evil and deceptive, and had used the troubled child to free it from its prison.

Agapor stood fearlessly before it and spoke with bold words, telling the spirit that he too sought to escape his prison. He desired only to find his mother in the lands above, and to unleash his anger upon her for his cruel abandonment. He told the spirit he would also seek his father in that realm. And he too would know of his anger. By his own hand they both would suffer. Such was Agapor's sinister plot, conceived by pride yet birthed by vengeance.

The prescient spirit looked upon the face of Agapor with his callous eyes, and saw reflected within the boy's spirit his own dark heart. And yet in the boy it saw too a strange fate, only partially revealed to it through the child's words. For it had seen in a strange vision borne by haunting dreams that their two fates would be joined as one, and that through the boy would its will be done. And great evil against his brothers and their kind would be unleashed into this world by this child's own hand.

The dark being then spoke to the boy, telling him it would help him find his mother, if he would destroy yet another. For unto it had come many servants, telling it of a terrible ocean that lay beyond the Lands of Midnight, within whose cursed waters a creature of misery now slept. This creeping monster that dwelt beneath the seas had been born to command those strange waters, and by its powers drown this world in its dark and decadent seas.

Agapor stood upon the rocks and listened to the spirit and its tale, until he at last vowed to help it consume the seas and slay the terrible creature that lay within it. The black spirit then told Agapor he desired to possess his form. And so could he travel to the lands beneath the Arch of Heaven unseen. But first he must place upon his wrists the manacles of iron that he had broken. For they contained fearsome spirits, which had been bound to them by the dark magic hidden within their metal. And the spirit of his own being could only be contained within Agapor by those dark bracers.

Agapor thought upon the creature's words, and the powers that would be bestowed unto him. By them alone, would he finally fulfill his vengeful desires. But he hesitated. For he heard in those black manacles strange whisperings from the spirits of the night that yet hid within their iron.

As he placed the evil bands upon his wrists, the dark breath of the storms above him were drawn into his body, so that he and they were now bound as one. The energy of that spirit then flowed like a mighty river into Agapor's veins, so that his eyes turned black as jet, and his heart pumped and burned with the same cruel passions and all-consuming desires it possessed. Into him had come an everlasting hunger and unending thirst, which no force created under Heaven could now satiate. He thirsted for the waters of the seas. And he would not stop until he had made them his own.

Agapor fled the fringes of Wendalia, travelling its hidden paths about the bloodstained cliffs, until he found the twisted stairs that led up to the Realms of Oblivion. Upon their summit, he came across his mother's ghoulish chambers. For their high-walled hallways were built of the bones and skulls of the children of the

Primordial Ones who had fallen in the countless wars waged in those dark lands.

Hidden in the depths of her mighty mausoleum, sitting on her ebony throne, Agapor found her. About her sat many vile servants, dire children born of her many lovers. From above, the twisted faces of the undead looked down from their shadowed heights, grimacing and snarling at the brave boy.

This was the home of the Nameless One, the queen of that unliving land, who for many ages had ruled over the gruesome host that crept there. She had a twisted mind, born of madness and cruelty, most depraved. For she wielded her bony fists of iron such that none would challenge her. Nor could any being enter her house, living or dead, which was not soon perverted to her will and thrown into everlasting servitude to her. For she alone now ruled that horror-filled domain, its former lord having long ago been ripped away from it.

At the first sight of the boy, she recognized him as her long-forgotten son. The cruel queen then smiled and walked forth to greet him. With knotted and aged arms outstretched, she sought his embrace.

But Agapor came upon her swiftly, like a black cloud cast down from the Heavens. With the fearsome forces that now dwelt in him, he bore his full vengeance and wrath, rising up with inky and billowing clouds of shade and shadow, bearing the full tempest of his own black and betrayed spirit down upon her. Agapor then wrapped his misty tendrils about her throat and drew her form into him.

In terror, she called out to her son, pleading for her life. But in her anguish, he only smiled down at her with cold and remorseless eyes. Yet, in the throes of her demise, she looked upon his face once more with a cold and cruel visage and laughed.

Agapor then stood aghast at the words she spoke to him.

"In you, my son, now dwells the spirit of the Limitless Void, he who was once ruler over this savage land. You are now bound to that vile spirit. And though by your own hand has he been freed, nevermore shall you be free from him," said his mother.

She told him that the Void was her creator and lover. He had drawn her evil spirit from his own, long ago. He had then given her a gift that altered her hideous form, making her desirable in the flesh, so she might go forth and seduce her master's brother. By their jaded and carnal union was he, Agapor, conceived—a bastard child, born and abandoned by the parents of two worlds. He was thrown into the cold pit so that her master might find him and be freed by his hands. For by his birthright could he alone break those chains. And so, for this one purpose alone, was he conceived.

Agapor looked deep into his mother's eyes as she spoke. Into his mind now came many unanswered questions. Agapor then raised his fists in rage, shouting, "Who is this father who hath willed me into this fallen world, then abandoned me to my own doomed fate?"

Then from within Agapor's own spirit came billowing forth the great storms of the Limitless Void. The mouth of that all-devouring tempest, which had sprung forth from the boy, now widened and began to spin before them as a monstrous black storm.

With a booming voice, it spoke boldly to the Nameless One, saying, "Surrender to me, my servant. Your labor is now complete. Yet, for your ignoble deeds must you now pay the forfeit of your life."

But the Nameless One cried out to the terrible spirit, saying, "Why, master, must I perish? Have I not served you as you wished? Have I not given you the child of the one you sought?"

With swirling clouds and shrieking winds, the Limitless Void opened wide his great black orifice before her. Looking upon her with his dark and sinister eyes, he said in a booming voice, "Come to me."

The dark mother then closed her eyes and obeyed, walking forth into the darkness to meet her doom. As she was sucked into its depths, she cried out for her son. But her form and spirit were quickly consumed by the powers of the Limitless Void. Agapor could only look on in horror, and yet fascination, at his mother's terrible fate. Her cries echoed out into the night, as her spirit disappeared into the depths of the Great Beyond, where awaited the evil that had crept there for all eternity. Like the deathless realm from which she had been conceived, nevermore would she be known in this world.

So was the will of the Limitless Void enacted. The Void now sought to destroy the Dreaming Seas by the hand of the child he possessed. And the great eye of his storm turned towards Agapor. Seeing its wrathful shape gathering about him, Agapor knelt before the cursed spirit. The cloud of the Void then gathered into himself his true form, taking the shape of a noble man with a tangled beard upon his gray face, and a bejeweled crown upon his head, whose massive stone shone dimly its ghoulish light down upon their faces.

He came before Agapor, saying it was done. His mother was dead. He then commanded Agapor to go forth under the Heavens, seeking the Dreaming Seas, so they might destroy them. Agapor obeyed. But as he looked upon his master's face, he saw a mysterious and unspoken fear within the eyes of the Limitless Void. And he saw a hesitation he had never seen before. For the Limitless Void had sensed within that watery domain an unknown and mysterious power he could not yet comprehend.

The Limitless Void then formed himself into a streaming cloud once more. And Agapor received his spirit back into his flesh. The icy veins of Agapor again flowed with the spirit of the Void. But he also held in him the cold spirit of his mother. He felt the curse of her blackened heart within him, as he thought upon her cruel words. But so too, an unbridled passion for revenge against his father still burned within him.

As Agapor turned to leave his mother's halls, a glint of something caught his eye. As he looked down he saw below in the black dust of his mother's ashes a large ring carved out of blackest jet. By its dark enchantments, the Nameless One had tempted Agapor's father with her seductive form, though it had devoured any love between them long ago. Enamored of its strange form and glow, Agapor placed the evil ring upon his right hand. And a spirit within it vaguely stirred.

The baneful children of his mother's house now fled before him in terror, back into the depths of the endless and twisted hallways. Agapor wrapped his dark cape about him, and climbed out of his mother's cold halls, past cloud-covered chasms, and over the cragged cliffs that bordered that dire realm. Through the Halls of Time and past the Veils of Night he travelled, where the darkness that guards the Lands of Midnight break free, until he saw the dim twilit mist of the ocean before him. He then stood in awe of the beauty of the silver lights of the Mountains of Heaven as they shined down upon the seas.

He gazed down from a windswept and rocky rim, looking with wonder upon the vast and limitless, watery waste of the Dreaming Seas below him. The ocean had slept undisturbed and quiet in the dim light of that twilight realm for many ages, filling the vast and limitless abyss, whose dark depths no eyes had yet seen. For the embrace of the impenetrable mist refused to reveal its secret child. And the Dreaming Seas' gentle waves, though calm, were yet wild, hiding within their monstrous mass a vast morass of secretive waters which, conceived from some other world, had been thrown like him coldly into this crueler one.

Their monumental presence appeared to Agapor both threatening, and yet strangely calming and familiar. Agapor knew not the measure of their immense power, nor the limit of their form. When he looked upon that ocean, he saw only the wind upon the waters. And he heard only the whispers of the waves. Yet within that boundless ocean he suddenly felt a presence of something mysterious hidden within their waters—something that stirred within him some elevated feeling of hope and happiness, yet whose source he could not see, only sense. For the abiding spirit of its being was concealed within its darker depths.

He then heard within those waters a heartbeat now stir, pounding with a living force he had never felt before. But Agapor's mind could not wonder upon its mystery for long. For the evil spirit of the Limitless Void that hid in him rose forth again. It now filled him with its great thirst and hunger for vengeance.

The Limitless Void then spoke with its black tongue, saying to Agapor, "The secret beast of the seas lies beyond this shore, in the darkest depths of these waters. You have made a vow to find it and destroy it, Agapor. And to this vow are you still bound. With the powers I grant unto you, go forth and part the seas and slay the creature in its tomb. Then shall the oceans falter and fall before you. Nevermore shall they be free to fill this world with their cold and wasteful presence. For I shall summon up from the abyss great evil to consume them. And with their fall, I shall break the heart of their creator, and obliterate the blasphemous being who hath dared to make them."

Agapor obeyed. Yet within his secretive heart there remained great doubt.

The Limitless Void now summoned forth, from within Agapor, his violent storms and winds to assault the seas. Agapor felt those forces rising within him steadily, as a river flowing before a mighty cataract. He wrapped himself in his dark cloak, which swirled about him as he stood upon the rim of the world.

The forces of the Limitless Void gathered as one within him. Then from Agapor's own mouth billowed forth a terrible storm of dark clouds, booming thunder, and raging winds. Rising up from the depths, the towering thunderstorms gathered, black and foreboding above him. The peaceful seas trembled on the shoreline, until the surf grew still in fear under the growing shadows of the clouds.

But the Arch of Heaven, in its quiet majesty, shuddered as it looked down upon the shadowed seas and saw within their quiet mass a malevolent force take shape.

With the powers of the Limitless Void, Agapor summoned up frightening black mists and tumultuous clouds from out of the pits of the world. The mighty storm climbed up into the Heavens with great gusts of winds and spinning gales. From on high, he then commanded the storm to descend upon the ocean, assaulting it with wild winds and pelting rains.

But the Dreaming Seas, seeing the approaching storm, gathered their watery might within them to meet the approaching tumult. Rising up from their twilight depths, their waves rocked and swayed in violent defiance before the storm. They then threw themselves against the mighty maelstrom, wherein the wind and water clashed in a fearsome display. The ocean's waves were slung about, torn by the terrible winds and rains of Agapor's wrath, until they summoned forth great powers born of some secret source, unseen within. They then drew the black clouds from out of the sky, down into their waves, so that Agapor himself was sucked into their dismal depths.

Agapor was thrown about the waves until, nearly drowned, he was flung upon the black shores of the ocean's rocky rim. Wounded, Agapor bled great billows of cloud and fog, until in his utter exhaustion he lay there alone, broken, and beaten upon the rocks. The troubled seas lay calm once more, as the storms retreated into the distant horizon.

Agapor clung to the rocks of that forbidding shore, looking down with rage at the swirling dark waters below him. The sea had not parted, nor was revealed the sinister creature the Limitless Void had said would be found hidden therein.

But as his dark eyes looked upon the surface of the seas, the ocean was cast aglow by the twilit mists that descended upon it. He then saw in their depths a distant light, beautiful and seductive. Like a silver pearl in the confines of a tiny shell, it shined with a warm and loving light. Within his black heart something new was now awakened.

With curiosity, Agapor stood and walked to the farthest rocks of the shore and saw, hidden beneath the rolling waves, a creature of enduring beauty. There the lovely maiden An lay, her dark tresses unconfined, flowing freely in the brine. Like a tiny flower she seemed to him, which, blossoming forth in the dark corners of some hidden glade, shines forth clear and bright from within the shifting shadows its rare and radiant beauty upon some privileged eye. For the waves wove steadily her warm colors across the shadows of his cold and hardened heart, until it softened and fell away like the waves that now drew themselves apart.

Yet Agapor's passion for her was soon eclipsed by a dark obsession, born of the perversions of his mother's lustful heart. And, like his father, he now succumbed to some strange temptation he could not resist. And the ring upon his finger seemed to dimly glow and burn upon his hand, as it had done when his parents had fallen to their own sordid desires.

Agapor called to the child of the seas. But she remained silent. Nor would she be lulled from that dream-filled slumber by his calls. Her darkened eyes opened not, nor could he sense upon her lovely face what her inner mind outward wrought. So it seemed to him the cursed seas, like a prison, held her fast within their grasp. He could not part the maternal waves that bound her, nor break the spell of fateful slumber wrapped about her.

Yet to him alone had the secret of the seas been revealed. She was not a monster but a maiden, whom the seas had long coveted. For this lonely child of the ocean seemed much like himself, enslaved to the will of a greater power, and tortured by it. He would free her. He would rip that precious pearl away from its watery prison and take her far away from it. His eyes grew black, and his dark lips twisted with a sinister smile from the lustful designs that now filled his mind.

But his thoughts were soon broken again by the deep and booming voice that rose from within. The Limitless Void spoke to Agapor once more, reminding him that by his hand alone must the sleeping siren of the seas now die. And with her death would the seas then falter and fall before them, so that he, the Limitless Void, might have vengeance upon their maker.

Agapor then felt within his chest the Limitless Void's penetrating hunger. And the unquenchable thirst burned upon his tongue. Agapor fell to his knees upon the rocks, trembling. The Void then turned Agapor's frail mind against the seas again, so that his possessed eyes glowed with a pale and ghostly cast.

"Thy will shall be done," Agapor said. But hidden in Agapor's heart still burned a secret desire for the child of the seas.

The Limitless Void granted to Agapor the last and greatest of his powers. He would summon the might of Oblivion's greatest demonic armies. And to him would now be granted the evil servants of the Great Beyond, which the Limitless Void had once commanded as his own.

Agapor rose to his feet again, and with renewed strength, called forth colossal servants from the bottomless spaces of the world. In endless streams, the Void's most loyal servants came forth, riding the dark winds cast forth from the catacombs of Oblivion. Ghostly spirits and dark denizens of the underworld soon appeared, driven forward by black behemoths of monstrous force and might. Beyond these armies rose up vast storms of destructive power, summoned from the depths of Wendalia, so that the hands of their streaming fogs stretched their slate-gray fingers over the phantom armies, shrouding their masses in its smoky blanket.

The undead servants of his mother's house also heard his cry, rising up from the foul craters and chasms of the land in which they long had hid. They were abominations of form and flesh, born of some sinister creator whose sickened mind had at last surrendered itself to the horror of its own imaginings. They came in countless numbers, bubbling up and slithering out from the mindless unknown. These were the forms of the fallen flesh of corrupted demons—the bastard children of the Realms of Oblivion, whose lost and forlorn spirits had been denied the path to the Lands of the Afterlife.

They flooded through the haunted Corridors of Darkness, past the Veils of Night, driven by the crackling sounds of barbed whips slung forth by grim lords of might, bound together as one by chains of ebony and iron. Agapor commanded these mindless flocks to gather upon the rocks below, until as one mass they throbbed and moaned beside the foaming and sloshing surf.

Of all the beings the Limitless Void summoned, most feared were the servants of the Emptiness, the violent storms called the Magra. These were the spinning vortices, the Gray Ones, whose strange and monstrous forms now slowly spun up from the pits of Wendalia. They had come into being before even the birth of the world, formless and ephemeral, first collecting themselves into great gray clouds born of the very breath of the dying spirits of former worlds now lost. For they had gathered into them the pale dust of the cosmos, ground down from the bones of many worlds prior, which the Nothingness and Emptiness had themselves long ago consumed.

The Magra were the devourers of dreams, which the Emptiness had cast out from the corpses of those countless worlds. They had hung themselves upon the corners of this universe, where their jaws eternally chewed upon its roots. Like their evil creator, they drew forth all form and matter into their blackened maws, such that none could avoid annihilation. The true Lords of Emptiness were they, such that by his will they alone could unbind the lights of the Spirit Divine from the Heavens, and thus return the Great Father's many forms to formlessness.

These huge beings now gathered before the grim spectacle, beyond the Mountains of Heaven, looking down with their many malevolent eyes upon the shining seas below. The oceans trembled as the Magra gathered their howling winds and twisted clouds about them, drawing forth into their black mouths the silver lights from out of the Mountains of Heaven, until only the Twilight Mist remained to shine down its somber light upon the trembling waves of the sea.

Agapor looked upon the dire armies that had gathered below and was pleased. But as he stood upon that cliff, he gazed upon the black manacles on his wrists. And he heard from within them weird whispers, and the flickering of mysterious lights. For in those forged manacles had been placed the spirits of the children of the Endless Night, the beings named the Shadow and the Shade.

Agapor called forth the spirit of the Shadow from the black manacle upon his right wrist. And he called its sibling spirit, the Shade, from his left. Their dark and sinewy clouds streamed out from his hands, climbing forth into the skies, until the winged forms of those two dark angels stood before him on the black rocks that lay above the swaying seas. Agapor then looked with curiosity at their strange forms.

The Shade was the daughter of the Endless Night, and beautiful beyond words. For she had her father's noble face and form. And so the power over the nighttime skies and airs were hers alone. Her long sable hair wrapped about her voluptuous form. And her hypnotic eyes of jet none could resist. But her crimson lips could only smile, as she drew her black feathered wings about her seductive form, and looked at the frail figure of the pale boy that stood before her.

But the towering form of the Shadow, her brother, was black and threatening. Of these twin spirits, the Shadow was most powerful. For he was the first-born child of the Endless Night. Into him had been cast the spirit of the Night's infernal darkness, whose shadows first stretched out from the feet of the Mountains of Heaven. His powers were of the lightless mantle of Midnight, which his father had placed within him. Yet he held not his father's greatest gift, the Glourun. Nor had he the Wings of Night. For they yet remained with the Endless Night, his father.

The Shadow's ebony skin drew all light into it, as his long and muscular form stretched its leathery, bat-like wings above Agapor. The Shadow grinned and bore his black teeth to him, as he looked upon his small frame. And his large red eyes burned with a secret fire born of an ancient hate, which caused Agapor to step back from him.

Agapor looked again upon their towering forms with fascination. He then said to them, "The lavender lights that lie upon the oceans before you must be extinguished. And the skies above must be turned to blackest night. Go forth and do as I command."

The dark angels looked at their new master, with faces cold and unmoving. They then turned away, flying up into the Heavens. Before their master their darkness took shape as a huge ebony dragon, whose great wings stretched across the skies, gathering beneath it a vast sheath of impenetrable darkness. The monstrous form cast its dark shadow down upon the seas, so that where the mist had gathered, its dim light was now hidden from its surface.

Agapor laughed with delight, as he saw the last lights of the seas diminish, and the gathering of the Magra grow near. He then sent the Behemoths from the Realms of Oblivion to drive the infernal armies down around the shores of the seas, so that the oceans, now separated from the paternal lights of twilight, grew grim and fearful. For they could not see, only sense, what terrors gathered about them in the darkness.

Agapor gathered the Void's vast storms above him in the Heavens and, encircled by his demonic host, descended upon the seas again. Fearsome winds and the boiling rage of that tremendous storm slung the waves of the seas back against themselves, so that its waters were thrown up into the clouds of Heaven in fits of foam and sea spray. The embattled waves at first resisted the seething mass, drowning many of their denizens in its dark waters. But in the fray, the waters of the seas were thrown back by the fuming ire the armies had unleashed upon them.

Storms of savage winds and sheets of rain then beat down upon the ocean from all sides, until they and the shadow armies enveloped them in their mass. The giant hammers of the black behemoths then smote the waves, flinging their waters away from the rocks and shoreline, sending them bleeding away, back into the more distant hollows of the rocks. Demonic armies of great strength and might threw the remnant waters back before them with their brutal blows, until the very ocean split in two and was rent asunder.

Dark demonic sorcerers, summoned from the underworld, then gathered as one to cast the waves before them with their spells, while the storms from above blew down upon the waters with their violent gusts and gales. There then came forth from the depths of Wendalia a vile gray mist. Before it fled the ocean in terror. For all it touched was devoid of spirit. The vast armies of Oblivion then drove the remaining waters before them, until the seas were beaten back at last, crashing down below, and falling away into the rocky abyss which the waters once had filled.

Agapor called out to the Magra who, forming great whirlpools and cyclonic clouds within the Heavens, drew forth the waters of the crying seas from out of the darkness. The seas were then drawn up into the wide maelstrom mouths of the Magra Lords, and sucked down into the fathomless spaces that lay within the Great Beyond. For there the Emptiness had long waited to devour them in its colossal jaws.

But the remnant waters of those Dreaming Seas would not entirely surrender themselves to that awful fate. For what remained of the seas had bled away in horror, down into the hidden depths of the chasm which contained them. For its rocky cup, like a wide cauldron, held the last of their doomed waters still in its grasp.

As a silent fog drifted down into the darkness, the forces of evil descended into the muddy depths of the waterless canyon. Agapor, with a wary eye, looked upon the destruction he had wrought, and climbed down into the misty gloom. At the bottom of that chasm he drank deeply from a solitary pool of water that yet remained there, so that his own cursed thirst was vanquished.

Then he saw, upon the ocean floor, the muddy tomb of An. He smiled with perverse desire as he approached its dreary opening. But as he entered it, the dark ring upon his hand glowed with a cold gray light. Down the tomb's slimy stairs he descended, until he saw at last the guarded maid of the sea, lying upon her lonely bed. Beautiful and serene was she, just as she had appeared from above.

Agapor removed the pale pall of the sea that had been wrapped about her gentle form and face. And he saw with his own eyes the true beauty of her countenance. She lay still, in deep repose, neither waking nor stirring. Agapor then removed his dark cloak, and lay with An in her hidden chamber. And with a passion that within him burned, he took her for his own.

As he rose from her bed, he looked upon his lovely prize. He then reached down to take her in his arms. He would carry her away from her prison, and keep her as his own. For soon the spirit of the Limitless Void would come for her and seek to slay her.

But as he reached down, he saw something strange shining from within her chest, something unforeseen reflecting out from deep within her like a light cast from the mirror of a pool. He reached down to touch the shimmering form that shone upon her breast. For he desired to know of it, and to possess it.

The last of the storms and winds had chased the remnant waters away from the rocky cliffs above. In the rising sea-fog, upon a lonesome precipice, stood the Shadow, his oily wings wrapped about him. Below him hid his faded sister, the solemn Shade.

Watching the destruction below with eyes of burning coals, he looked into the depths of the chasm, until he saw the form of his master beside the creature that slept there. With the inner eye of the Nightmare Unending that dwelt within him, he saw now the cursed temptation of his master by that child of the Dreaming Seas. And he grimaced with disgust and loathing.

For he now knew the true heart of Agapor. And the source of his own doom was revealed to him. He and the Shade then fled away on their ebony wings, back beyond the drapes of night, deep into the Lands of Midnight. For the Shadow alone saw that soon the vengeful sea would return to inflict its full wrath upon them.

As Agapor reached down to touch the heart of An, she awoke, startled as from a dream. Then was heard in the farthest corners of the world, a pitiful cry—the screams of the waking An. From the ravages of the savage passions unleashed upon her, she awoke in terror from her tortured sleep. Her cries of pain and suffering echoed out into the seas' cauldron, until they shook the firmament of the very Heavens. And the waters of that wide ocean trembled in the darkness, as the black armies and storms in the skies were stilled.

But the paternal Mist had heard his child's pitiful cries. He then gathered his violet clouds upon the summit of the Heavens, sending down upon the host below great torrents of rain, born not of tears, but of anger. They fell into the depths, where the fearful waters had gathered to collect them. For the Dreaming Seas' heart was now broken, seeing the suffering of her only child. She then was freed from her own nightmares, such that they were now released upon the world.

The ocean, now wide awake and fed from the mist above, gathered and grew once again in the quiet gloom, seeking to save her daughter from her doom. For as a child of the seas, separated from her mother-ocean, would An soon perish.

An opened her eyes and looked into the face of the heartless Agapor. But Agapor, meeting her gaze, felt within himself a strange pity for the girl, born of compassion and shame. And yet there was something more.

Agapor spoke to her, saying, "Look upon me now, but do not fear. For I desire to free you from your watery prison and the curse of this strange and endless sleep which haunts you."

But as An looked upon Agapor, she called out in fear, "Father…why, why have you returned? I see your face…the face of the Twilight Mist. Is it you?"

Agapor then recoiled in horror. But as Agapor looked upon her again, he saw his own visage therein. And like her, he too felt her spirit somehow connected to his own. Within his corrupted mind then returned the cold words of his mother. Agapor now knew who his father was. This maiden of the sea was his sister. And the Twilight Mist his father. He then realized that she, like him, had been thrown into this world, imprisoned by some cruel fate, in which they were but pawns of a higher power.

With fearful and yet knowing eyes, An looked upon her brother's face one last time. She then fell back into the swoon of her dark slumber, leaving Agapor alone in horror and shock to think upon their strange fates. The black ring upon his finger glowed with a savage light, fierce and bright, and screeching with a sinister delight.

Hearing the cries and cruelty inflicted upon their daughter, the Twilight Mist and Dreaming Seas gathered their forces again, as one. The Twilight Mist descended from the skies, his torrential rains falling down into that hollow abyss in widening sheets and wind-wrapped columns. The Dreaming Seas that had hid in the depths drew her remnant waters to her breast again. Fed by her lover's rains, she poured her widening ocean into the empty gulf, flooding it with her wrathful waters.

The angry seas, ravaged and raped by the servants of Agapor, drew all their might and force against Agapor's violent host, flinging their waves upon them from below with great foaming ire. Monstrous walls of waters of unequalled force soon gathered about the fleeing hoards, so that they were pushed back towards the rocky rim of the chasm above.

Within the tomb of An flowed the seas again. For the rising waters rushed in from below, flooding her bedchamber, until their icy waves shook Agapor from his trance. He was then awakened to the truth of his horrid crime. And he fled from that tomb in terror, leaving An behind, as the waters embraced their precious daughter, once more.

But the waves soon encircled Agapor. Alone, in the cavernous bottom of the ocean, Agapor struggled to escape. But he was caught within the ocean's watery grasp. Thrown about in their cyclopean waves, he cried out in terror, as he was no match for the raging seas.

The waters grew quickly, as the rain poured down from the skies, until even the skies were pushed up and out, and the walls of Heaven itself were drawn in and drowned in the mist and rain. The last of the shadows that had clung about the surface of the oceans had flown away, so that the shining mists again cast their mottled beams about the ocean floor. And the storms that had beat down upon the seas, flew forth high into the skies to escape them. But the waters quickly rose up to drag their trailing clouds down into their depths.

The last of the great Magra, the horrid children of the Great Beyond, descended upon the terrible seas with even greater force and strength. Their wide mouths, now agape, began to suck the seas down into the cyclones and whirlpools which they had spawned. Their coal black mouths cast up a sickly gray fog, as they devoured the raging seas into them. The oceans groaned and moaned as they fought to defy that horrible fate. But the Magra were all-powerful and unstoppable. For their vast orifices were joined to the devouring will of the Emptiness, whose many mouths no matter, living or dead, might ever escape.

As he drew himself out of the sea's deadly grasp, Agapor regained himself upon the shore. Climbing out upon a rocky peak in the midst of the crashing waves, he rose to his feet, commanding his demonic host to assault the oceans and drive them back. But as he looked below, he saw no sign of his armies. He then looked to the oceans and saw no sign of his sister beneath the waves, or her shimmering sepulcher in the depths. And he cried out to her.

The returning winds and storms of the Limitless Void now gathered, black and ferocious, swirling about his head. But the rains of the Twilight Mist had poured down with even greater fury, so that the seas rose ever higher, filling the abyss with towering wave and foam to defy his brother.

As the Magra sucked down the seas from every quarter, the pillars about the very Arch of Heaven shook, and the rocks of the abyss themselves trembled with the great rocking of the embattled seas. Agapor looked, and saw with horror that the ocean's waves had nearly reached the summit of Heaven's heights. Then before him, he saw in the fog a towering wall of water, rising up from the angry oceans below.

Agapor stretched out his arms, summoning forth the remaining powers of the Limitless Void. He called forth vast storms of thunder and lightning from out of the skies, whose bolts splintered the waves about him, tossing their foam and spray high up into the skies. But seeing the massive wall of water approaching, he cried out in the confusion.

In one great mass of water the seas crashed down upon the rocks, pouring their swelling volumes over the rocky rim of the abyss, breaking through its lip, and crashing down into the bottomless pits of Wendalia. The seas poured through the Lands of Midnight, and into the Realms of Oblivion, flooding its many bottomless chasms and pits, and casting up a dense cloud of salty mist and spray.

As the ocean's waves collapsed upon them, the last of the servants of Agapor fell before the seas, thrown to their watery doom. For they were hurtled into and over that mighty cataract, until their broken bodies disappeared into the depths below.

The force of the falling wall of water cast up great clouds of sea-smoke and fog so that nearly all of the land and sky were consumed by water and mist. It seemed that water itself would devour this world. But Agapor had remained. For he had clung to a rocky prominence that yet stood above the seas.

Enraged, the Limitless Void drew his dark spirit out of Agapor. And the terrible gray face of his cloud hovered upon the heights of Heaven, looking down with boiling fury upon him. With a commanding voice that shook the ocean, the spirit of the Limitless Void then commanded the Magra to descend into the very heart of the ocean, telling them to devour the maiden that lay there.

The violent Magra Lords now turned their black orifices down upon the bulging seas, as Agapor called out to the spirit of his master, crying in pity for his sister, and begging for his mercy upon her.

But the mother-ocean would not surrender up her beloved daughter so easily to that evil. For the Dreaming Seas had now borne fully the suffering of her child, whose pain none might know but her. She then drew all of her waters about her into one great towering column, until they filled the skies and broke through the very Arch of Heaven.

With vengeful violence, fully unleashed, the oceans crashed down their tremendous mass upon the Limitless Void and his Magra servants. The Gray Ones were then drowned in that vast mass of cursed water, until they were thrown back down into the cold and empty realms whence they came.

But in that last great tumult of sea and spray, the broken form of Agapor had also been drowned. For he was washed over the rim of that chasm, cast down past the ruins of his mother's house, and into the silent spaces below, where he as a child had once been thrown. Past the gates of Eventide again he fell, through the dim shadows of that land, until he lay again upon the precipice of his former ruin. For in Wendalia he had long ago been imprisoned, bound to that cursed pit. And once more to it was he so enjoined.

In those lonesome depths, no sound was heard, nor voice cast forth, save the roar of the waterfall that now cascaded down into the haze and smoke below. From within that sad place was then heard the wailing and crying of Agapor.

As he slept in that hollow space, endless nightmares came to him, born not of the wreckage he had wrought, but of regret for the evil he beget. Like his sister, he awoke in fits of terror and despair. For in his dreams he saw the face of An, hidden forever beneath the waves. And he thought upon the father who had abandoned and forgotten him so long ago.

He too thought long upon the lies of the Limitless Void, and how so many in that cursed world had used him. But his own savage acts upon the maid of the sea had fashioned doom upon himself. He cried out in the throes of his suffering, until his pitiful voice echoed out across the skies, and through the Lands of Midnight.

No one heard the cries of Agapor, save one. For that being, alone of the dark hosts of Agapor, had survived the tempest and turmoil. He was the Shadow, that foul angel of darkness, who had returned to the lands of his father that lay beyond the Veils of Night. In a secret cave upon the edge of that land he sat unmoving. Like a grim phantom, the Shadow cloaked himself in his own dark dreams, embracing them wholly, as he had done many times before.

But upon hearing his master's cries, his gruesome eyes now opened, and unblinking, stared into the dusky gloom of the twilit Heavens. Long did he listen to the sad wailing of Agapor from afar, and the howling of the vengeful seas below, which had now sought to drown them out.

The Shadow then climbed upon a lonely perch. There he looked down with jaundiced eyes from the roof of Heaven, and saw the wreckage wrought by those merciless seas. He thought upon the ruinous fate of Agapor. And his disdain for his master grew within him.

But no greater was this scorn than that which he now bore for the Dreaming Seas and their terrible temptress, the child named An, who lay hidden once more in the seas' now impenetrable depths. Yet strangely, the seas now seemed to shine forth anew, like the poisonous wine from some cup of death, brimming with a sinister delight. And the meaning and purpose of its cursed waters even the Shadow's own penetrating mind could not yet fully comprehend.

THE FOREST OF TWILIGHT

The Dreaming Seas now lay calm and peaceful again. For they slept once more, returning to the enduring dreams in which they had long been immersed. Across a wide abyss, this vast ocean seemed to stretch forever, having filled the empty spaces of this ravaged world with its cold and watery waste. Torn by strife and violence, the wreckage and ruin of this world's former splendor would now lay entombed and forgotten, buried beneath the timeless waves.

It seemed as though this doomed world would be utterly consumed by the savage seas. And in its ocean grave it would have remained. But by a strange and incomprehensible force was its flood restrained. For the wild waters that now filled it were somehow bound within a rocky cup, whose wide cauldron the Great Father had forged to contain them. By the mighty grail of his merciful heart were its tides now held back. For he alone had known this time would come.

Upon the farthest shore of that sea stretched a rocky rim, whose shattered cliffs looked down upon a gray and gloomy pit. Here the seas could not flow. And so a part of the realm of Wendalia had yet survived. Upon its rim the ocean waters had gathered, until with great force they flowed forth as a wide waterfall, over the lip of the canyon and down into its yawning chasm. Its waters fell forever into the darkness of that endless space, until the roar of the falls above was heard no more in the showering mist that fell below.

Such was the power of the seas that its great cataract ever after flowed ceaselessly into those terrible depths, crashing down onto the heads of the dark beings that now clung to its cliffs. For its falls, fog, and spray held at bay the dark denizens of that foul pit. Yet it was the memory of their former ruin that would ever after haunt them, such that the powers of darkness and destruction would never again challenge the supremacy of the seas.

The rumbling tempest of the skies, which had torn the seas in two, now departed. For the winds had died as the clouds drifted away. Above the fringes of that watery waste there now appeared a lonely prominence, whose solitary and shining presence stood proudly against the angry torrents of darkened sea and sky. Its phantasmal form in the half-lit mist stood like a solemn and silent specter, unmoving, above the tranquil sea.

As the pale sea-clouds melted away, its black head pierced the skies above and looked down from the dizzying heights of Heaven upon the gray waste below. It then reflected its dark shadow upon the cold waters in rigid defiance. This isle of gloom, alone among its rocky brethren, had survived the violent tumult of sea and storm. For when the oceans had broken through the ancient rim of the world, there remained a small piece of its rocky cliffs and peaks that had yet survived.

This was the last of the noble earth and rock, which long ago had been imparted to the Immortal Clay, fourth-born son of the Great Father. For the Immortal Clay, in both form and spirit, had been made from the very Mountains of Heaven. And by the great hands of his father had his mighty mold been cast.

Over the rocks of the earth was he king, the sacred realms of the Impenetrable Depths. And in a second land under these was he lord, the Darker Deeps of the underworld. But yet was he ruler over a mysterious third realm which lay beneath the Dreaming Seas, who alone guarded its one mysterious gate. And this, his one true labor, would be granted to him by the Great Father, yet only revealed to him upon his death.

The Immortal Clay had stood strong and defiant before his troubled brothers, until their wars had unleashed great fury upon him. There upon the heights of his realm, beyond the Arch of Heaven, he had fled with the last of his children to the safety of his mountain halls. For though he had proudly withstood his brothers' endless wars, and alone remained victorious at the end, he was most harmed of all his siblings by their violent struggles.

Much had been destroyed by them. And great were his losses upon those battlefields of sorrow. For in those terrible wars, all his children had perished, but two. With great despair, he finally turned away from bloodshed and violence. And the hatred he felt for his brothers was replaced with deep regret for that which he himself had done.

Of the children that had survived, first of these was the proud son, he who was named the Rock Eternal. From the mountains that lay roofed above the Heavens had he been cast. A handsome child of great fortitude and strength, he alone had stood as guardian of his father's fiercest lands. But in the terrible wrath the Limitless Void had wrought upon that world, were all his siblings lost, save one. From that final conflict had he alone returned to his father victorious. But seeing his son bloodied and beaten, the Immortal Clay hid his son away from the world, for fear he too would perish.

The Immortal Clay then spoke in secret to the Rock Eternal, saying, "My son, I shall place within you my own mighty heart, so that you shall know of my love for you the rest of your days. With it shall be given unto you alone the many hidden treasures of the earth, so that you might gift them to the children of the world, yet to come."

But he told the Rock Eternal, "The time will soon come for me to leave this world, my son. Yet shall I remain in the Lands of the Afterlife to guide you. Go forth now, into the dark world that remains. Do not wage war, but forge anew its fading spirit with your gifts of earth and rock. For many children, both in flesh and spirit, will soon come to dwell therein. You shall then be bound eternally to them, not by chains of iron, but by the bonds of love. And so shall you remain in this world, alone ever after, to guide and protect its many children, until the time of your own passing and the passing of the world."

And so the Immortal Clay gave his only son as a gift unto this world. But so too had he sought to spare his son the terrible pain and loss which he had suffered. The Rock Eternal bowed before his father, saying, "Father, I am grateful." And they embraced. For his son's respect and love for him was great.

But there remained another child of the Immortal Clay, the girl-child who is named the Secret Spring.

She was born from the Rock of the Well of this world. For within her dwelt the crystalline waters of the earth. And the blood of her father's noble essence flowed in her. She was of the water cast forth from the rocks, and which flows throughout its many forms. And so was contained in her the earth's life-blood, and the springs of the Eternal River which flows throughout.

But so too was her spirit born of a kind and loving heart. She would give forth her waters unto the earth, freely, surrendering her own life for it. For unlike her brother, her own essence could not flow forever and would in time be depleted. Like the mortal children of the world would her essence then be spent. And so, because of this, were her gifts more precious.

Yet her father had given her another strange gift. For in his youthful days, the Immortal Clay had roamed the Mountains of Heaven, upon whose slopes he had seen a strange glow. Within a mound of earth and stone had shone forth the bright beams of the Sacred Light, which had for many ages lain hidden from the eyes of evil.

But its source none now knew. For the Immortal Clay had found the light beneath a mighty stone, which marked the grave of an unknown spirit that had perished there upon the mountain. The Immortal Clay had kept it burning within a shining lantern upon the summit of his mountain, so that his brothers could see and feel its candle of hope reflecting upon their faces, long after their father's loving fires had ceased to shine within their hearts.

Seeing the evil twins rise from their prison, the Immortal Clay had turned his golden beams upon their spirits, burning them, and driving them back down into the hollows of the world. And so, by its spectral flame had the world been spared a terrible fate.

Fearing its final abrogation by the servants of those sinister spirits, this light he took and gave to his youngest daughter, the Secret Spring, so she might carry it, hidden within her hair, and surrender it unto the world at a time of her own choosing. For she would someday grant its warm spirit to her own children, and thus the children of the world, which the Immortal Clay had long foreseen would come into it.

Only the Rock Eternal and his lonely sister, the Secret Spring, had stood with their father in that dire age of the world until, unseen by them, the Dreaming Seas had risen up to wage war against Agapor and his terrible armies. They were then sundered from their father, tossed about by wind and wave, storm and sea, until thrown upon that ravaged shore they stood apart from him.

Trapped within that boundless ocean, they dwelt alone in their fear and grief, separated from their loving father by the Dreaming Seas that wrapped about their desolate isle. Their father, the Immortal Clay, had called out to them from his peaks, with pitiful cries, loud and mournful. But the spiritual lights of the silver summits of Heaven had long ago dimmed, so that nevermore could the Immortal Clay find his children in that dark and dismal world of rain and mist.

But the brothers of the Immortal Clay had heard his cries, and so were awakened. However their servants could not find the last children of their hated brother, nor even the lonely isle where they now dwelt. For they were now secreted away, deep within a new and unknown land, hidden from their all-seeing eyes.

Yet the Immortal Clay had given his children the last of his many gifts and powers to guide them in this world. So was contained within them, the indestructible spirit of the earth, and the ephemeral spring of the rock into whose forms had been left the last burning cinders of their father's Creative Flame. And so by these would they endure.

Weak and sorrowed by the loss of his children, the Immortal Clay was near death. He climbed to the summit of his mountains, and there laid his giant form within a tomb he had long ago prepared for his keeping, deep beneath the highest peak of Heaven.

But his spirit would not completely leave this world. For he now dwelt in the Lands of the Afterlife, the Avredd, whose ethereal plane the Great Father had created under the Arch of Heaven for the spirits of the fallen children to dwell therein.

By the Great Father's own tears, drifting down into the great gulf of the world, had that undead realm been formed, until the Dreaming Seas had poured forth over its rocks, hiding it forever from the world. The Great Father had then granted the Immortal Clay lordship over the spirits of this ghostly realm. And so, as Lord of the Dead, was fulfilled by him, his one great labor. So was he to remain bound to this strange realm between rock and sea, long after his brothers had departed that world.

Over Avredd was the Immortal Clay now lord and king. Upon his own death, he travelled to the lands beneath the Dreaming Seas, where he prepared this unliving land for the spirits of the children, yet to dwell there. So were all the children of this world, born of the earth of the Rock Eternal, now made his own in spirit. And so both father and son would become their stewards. For they now sought to protect and guide the spirits of the children from the devouring evil that had come to dwell therein—the Nothingness and Emptiness who had long sought to annihilate their spirits, and devour the flesh of the rock of which they were made.

By their own choosing, upon death the children could now safely return to the Lands of the Afterlife by way of the Dreaming Seas, where the Immortal Clay would await their return. And so were they freed of the curse of flesh, and of the cruel undying destiny that awaited their spirits at the hands of the Limitless Void. For by the powers of that evil being had so many of the children of the Primordial Ones been denied their spirit's release, becoming lost in his pathless lands. They were then cursed to be his demonic slaves, bound to his evil will and trapped in the ill-fated Realms of Oblivion forever.

The Immortal Clay now held the keys to the many secretive gateways of Avredd. There, within the three planes of his realm would he keep the spirits of the world until, through their own willful incarnation, they would seek their return. Yet, by the loving hand of the Immortal Clay would the spirits of the children be held apart from it, until such time they would be gifted back into it by him.

Their memories were then stripped from them, and their spirits washed clean. They would then set sail through that ethereal realm, borne by ghostly ships sailing upon a silent sea, until they returned once more to the phantom shores of this world, to live again. They were thus reborn in new raiment at a time and place of their own choosing—their spirits now housed in flesh anew, and through his son's earth, revived, refreshed and renewed.

None would ever know why the dead should return to the tragic stage of life, nor what part the risen spirits would have in the great play of the world. For these secrets would remain with the Spirit Divine, until such time as the last of its many acts had been played, and the final curtain had fallen.

After many ages, the assaulting oceans retreated from the rocky isle that had stood defiantly before them. Yet, deep within its rocks had hid the Secret Spring, safe within the heart of her brother's lands. She then had walked out upon the shore and knelt upon the rocks. And there she wept alone for her father, and for the fate of her siblings who had perished long ago.

But far across the ocean the Twilight Mist had awakened, hearing her cries. And so he had gone to find their source. It's then he first saw the golden lights of the Secret Spring, her beautiful face and hair, shining from afar. And he felt sadness for the wreckage wrought upon her by the wrath of the unforgiving seas, which he himself had made from his own anger and sorrow.

The Twilight Mist then formed a great cloud upon the summit of the isle. It first gathered as a peaceful mist, and then a soft dew, falling as rain about the isle's many peaks and valleys. Small streams and rivulets then formed, carrying those waters down through its rocks. They gathered together in raging rivers, pouring over the cliffs in great floods, and falling away into the gloom of the seas that splashed about the feet of the lonely isle.

And so the Twilight Mist had given the Secret Spring the last of his rains, casting them down from the Heavens above, to feed and sustain her. These were the waters she would long covet, gathering them in her dress, her tears becoming one with the rains and rivers of that land.

Up from the dismal depths of the abyss, beneath that island mountain had risen the waves of the raging seas in anger. Hearing the clamor of the streams and their cataracts falling from above, they gathered about the rocks to assault them. Surrounding the isle, the jealous seas roared below the rugged cliffs, crashing down upon the rocks with ferocious surf and spray, until the island's feet were buried beneath the waves.

Yet the towering cliffs above stood defiant before them. For the form of the Rock Eternal would not be destroyed. Within him lay his father's great heart and spirit. And so by his will did the last rocks of that earth stand resolute before the envious tide.

For many untold ages the seas swirled and churned, grinding away at the rocks and clay, until their mountains of stone at last gave way. The rugged heights, now battered and worn, tumbled down into the sea and surf. A gentler tide then returned, until all that remained between the two realms was an endless beach of sands and sea-gravels, which ever rolled beneath the rhythmic waves.

But not all of the sands that were stripped from the rocks had drowned beneath the waves. Nor had the last of its rocks given way to the might of the seas. For much of its earth had been thrown back upon itself, forming a vast mass of soil and clay. There between the two lay a limitless shore. So was first formed the uneasy truce between land and sea that for eternity would bind them as one, and remain unbroken.

For an age, there remained above the sands an endless landscape, mysterious and proud, that would not weather, nor wear away. This new land stretched back into eternity, beyond the reach of the seas and shadows. For the lonesome isle was now an immense and impenetrable mass of earth, one whose strange domain filled the empty spaces that the seas had forsaken. Its dark earth had pushed beyond the misty spaces, until it tumbled forth into the narrow Halls of Time itself. And so for many eons had the lands of the Rock Eternal slept in peace beside the rolling seas, whose mournful cry could yet be heard in those distant halls.

But within the heart of this land still hid the Rock Eternal and the Secret Spring. After many ages, the Twilight Mist returned, seeking to find the golden maiden who still slept deep within the rocks. His lavender mists had drifted out from the darkened seas across this strange new land, to find the beautiful damsel he had seen standing beside the shore. Her golden hair had beamed forth in the dark of night, like the shining of a thousand suns. For within her hair had dwelt the Sacred Lights her father had given her.

But it was the warm light of her heart and the aura of her youth that had glowed upon the surface of the seas. And by her shining presence was renewed within the heart of the Twilight Mist an abiding and sustained hope for this sad world, which had long ago faded within him.

The silent fog of the Twilight Mist had drifted, deep into this dark land, seeking to find the Secret Spring, until his mists stretched far beyond its borders. But not finding her, he had become lost in its wild expanse. And so he was sundered from the seas. It was then he found his father's mysterious chamber once more, hidden within the Halls of Time.

Deep in the heart of this land, the Secret Spring had felt the presence of the Twilight Mist return to her, and had risen from her earthen bed to go to him. For the loving rains he had given her so long ago she still held close to her heart. Far from the cold shores of the seas, she now walked alone to look for the Mist in the depths of that new realm. But there had appeared above her spring, perched upon a high rock, a dark form, shadowy and unseen.

This was the Endless Night. Long ago, upon black and decrepit wings, he had flown into that realm, where for many nights he had stood upon a lonely cliff beside the Mountains of Heaven. His wide wings had carried him beyond the Veils of Night, seeking his lost children in the farthest corners of the world. Still bleeding black blood from his war-wounds, he had sat alone, peering into that strange new realm of rock and clay, pondering its mysterious nature.

He had then seen a strange light cast from afar, which had nearly blinded him. Yet he wore upon his shoulders the sable Wings of Night, which no light could touch, save the stars of Heaven. Seeing the radiant and golden form of the Secret Spring walking upon that lonely shore, he became enamored of her. He followed her to the heart of her lands, where she lay hidden in a rocky grotto. He then called out to her in his shadowy tongue, professing his desire to see her, and to know of her.

Hearing a voice calling in the shadows of the rocks, she climbed out from her bed, thinking it was the Twilight Mist calling her from afar. But as she came before his presence, she looked in horror at his dark and grotesque form. She then ran in terror from him, hiding far away from his shadows, which had fallen upon the cliffs and rocks that lay beside the sea. There she roamed, forlorn, for many ages along the shore, until she became lost upon its farthest cliffs, wandering far and away from her brother, who still dwelt within the heart of the land.

For many ages the Endless Night had remained in that barren realm, seeking his lost love, the Secret Spring. He then returned to the barren hill where once the golden maiden had roamed, until his shadow stained the very rocks with its shade. But the Secret Spring would not return, and he grew weary. He flew down upon the mound, seeking the place in which she had slept, until he found her dry and empty well, lying dark and cold, before him. Seeing now that all he had loved had finally left him, he thought again upon his lost children, and of the Essence Eternal, his generous and loving Father, whom he had betrayed so long ago.

In the depths of his despair, the Endless Night then fled that place. But as he did, the tears he shed for his forsaken beauty fell upon the base of the great hill where she had slept. From his tears grew forth the black roses that are called the Murgala. These dark buds would be the first seeds sown in that strange land. And by their presence would this world be cursed to remember the sorrows of the Night and his unrequited love for its golden spring.

But there also came into those sickened roses a part of his own shadowy spirit. For by his dark blood were they also sown. Through their enchanted blooms would the Children of Darkness know of the Glourun and be healed by it. By those black roses might they also seek to find their way to the strange well of the Secret Spring that would soon come to dwell beneath the hill. And so, like him, were the Children of the Night forever after drawn by mysterious forces to the Murgala, following the many dark paths that would lead them to the ghoulish roses growing within the heart of this new land.

Yet to all others, but the Children of Night, were the thorns of the Murgala poisonous and deadly. Those that smelled of their sweet fragrance would be bound to a wicked sleep of unending nightmares and terrors from which they might never awaken. This was the hidden curse left by the Endless Night upon that hill and on all that would come to dwell therein.

Alone and fearful, the Secret Spring had roamed far and away from her abode of rest, far from the heart of that land. For she had become frightened of the shifting shadows that had come to haunt it. But the Twilight Mist, in his many forms, had left a trail in the form of purple mists for her to find. These now snaked their way through the barren land. By his twilit fogs he had hoped she might be guided, and so eventually find her way to him.

She had seen his alluring cloud floating above her as she slept. And so she followed the mist, as it floated beyond the fringes of her brother's realm, deep into the grim Halls of Time where the dark earth had poured forth into its crumbling hallways. She wound her way within their corridors, until she found the Twilight Mist kneeling beside his father's bed in the lonely chambers of the Essence Eternal.

There, in that hallowed place, the Secret Spring first saw the handsome form of the Twilight Mist. But she also saw great sadness borne upon his face, as he had knelt before his father's barren bed. But as her presence neared, the golden light of the Secret Spring glowed forth into the room, so that he looked up and saw her beautiful form standing before him.

He then ran to her and she to him. And she was overtaken by his gentle heart, as they kissed and held each other in a tender embrace. But as the Twilight Mist looked into her eyes, he saw reflected therein the miraculous glow of her golden light, cast upon a relic hidden in the depths of the chamber. The Golden Hourglass of Time had shone out from the corners of the room. For it had long ago been hidden there by the Great Father for his son to find.

The Twilight Mist held it in his hands. And they both were drawn to its strange and radiant beauty. But he saw that its sands shined but by her light only. And so he gave it to her as a gift. They then walked forth together, hand in hand, through that land for many ages. Their bodies lay entwined in the hollows of the world, so that they as one burned bright with the undying lights of their shared passion. Their hearts now beat boldly with the Birth of Love, abiding and true. So was this world renewed by their sacred and loving union.

The Twilight Mist then shared with the Secret Spring the knowledge given him by the Essence Eternal, his Father. For in its tale lay some hidden truth he had at last discovered. He told her of the prior world through which the Great Father had passed. And he spoke to her of the new world they must now prepare for the children, whose blessed spirits would soon come forth into it. She treasured his words as a gift granted unto her, most sacred and profound, as she now knew the purpose of all things and that which was to be.

But the Twilight Mist looked with sadness upon the Secret Spring, saying, "I must leave you now. For my Father hath given me one last labor, which I must now fulfill."

The Secret Spring then came to him and held him close to her. And she said unto him, "Let me return with you. For my heart desires to be with you, always. Take me to the seas or the skies, wherever you might go. But do not leave me to suffer here alone in endless longing."

The Twilight Mist then kissed her gently. "You must return to the heart of your brother's realm, my love", he said. "For a tree shall soon be planted there. And beneath it a silver pool shall issue forth. But to you shall come a brave child of the oceans, one who shall bless this fallen world with an enduring gift. You must prepare a place for this child in the heart of your brother's land. For in her alone shall reside our renewal and the hope of a better world. But do not fear, for in time I shall return to you."

The Secret Spring understood, yet knew not the meaning of his words. But to her love for him was she still bound. And so her heart was conflicted by his departure. They embraced one last time. She then wept as she watched the Twilight Mist leave her side, walking forth into the darkness, and disappearing beyond the shores of the Dreaming Seas.

The Secret Spring returned to the great hill of her brother where she had once slept, carrying the hourglass given her by the Twilight Mist. She then laid herself in a sepulcher beneath her brother's mound, which lay in the heart of that land. And there she dwelt for many ages, undisturbed, in peaceful solitude.

But within the depths of that mound the Secret Spring bore children of her own, twin daughters, born of the bonds of love with the Twilight Mist. To these children were then given the gifts of their mother and those things given to her by her father so long ago.

To her first child she gave the waters of her essence and the mighty rock of her heart. And so by this child's spirit would the rivers of the world always be guided, and the mythical voices of the rocks and earth be known to her.

But to her other daughter was bestowed the Sacred Light, which she had closely guarded. For through its radiant beam, like a guiding light, would its signal fire shine forth to chase away the encroaching shadows of the world, and bring new life to the darkened lands where only death and decay had once been known.

But unknown to all others had one of the Secret Spring's two daughters died at birth. This child she carried forth to the top of the hill, where she buried her in a secret grave upon its height. And there grew many poppies about its grave, born of the tears she had shed for her fallen child. There its spirit dwelt, forsaken and alone.

Strangely had the Sacred Light once more rested within a hollow grave, awaiting some unknown fate. But with that child's death would the golden heart of the Secret Spring shine no more. And so this world again returned to darkness and gloom.

But as the Secret Spring sat beside her grave, the spirit of the fallen child returned to her, bearing strange words, saying, "Mother, I have returned to you. Do not be sorrowful for my passing, for I bring good tidings."

The Secret Spring then looked in amazement at her child standing before her, saying, "My beloved child, you have returned to me!"

But as she reached up to touch her face, she saw that she was but a ghost. Smiling, but with tears in her eyes, she said, "Know that my love for you endures, my child, though your form has left me in this world. I had feared your spirit had been taken by the evil that creeps about the fringes of the world. And so, in my deep sorrow, is my heart also overjoyed. For your loving spirit has returned to me."

The smiling child then said to her mother, "Mother, know only that it was not my destiny to remain here. For it was my will, and fate, that I should perish and leave this world. With my passing, I have left behind the light of my own spirit, and the light of the world, within my grave. These twin fires the children of this world shall someday find. By their many graces will this world soon be saved. And by their guiding lanterns, shall all those born anew within the world be granted the power to chase away the darkness that fills it, and the shadows that fill their own hearts, if they so choose."

She then looked into her mother's tearful eyes, saying, "Mother, do not cry for me. Nor be fearful for my spirit. For I shall now go forth to the Lands of the Afterlife, thy father's house that lies beneath the rocks and sea. For the dead may easily follow the ethereal paths that lead to him, should they not stray. I hear him, even now, calling for me, as he blows upon his mighty horns.

For there he has waited with great patience for my spirit to return. It was set by our Creator, long ago, that I be the first to dwell in the house of the dead. Upon those solemn shores I shall now stand for all eternity, welcoming the many spirits that come to me upon their deaths. I shall be their guide, as they board the many ships that set sail for those timeless lands. And so I must now depart. But know that we shall meet again."

As the child disappeared from view, she reached out to touch the hand of her mother. The Secret Spring cried as her child's spirit fled away into the night.

In her anguish the Secret Spring had fled to her hidden chambers within her hill. There she mourned for many nights, until in her suffering a great flood of waters rushed forth like blood from her form. And so were released the springs of the world, to feed and nourish its earth. These crystal waters rose up from within the rocks. But they also carried her surviving daughter, the river-child that had yet resided with her in that tomb.

The brother of the Secret Spring, the Rock Eternal, seeing his sister's child floating in the flood, guided her and her waters through the rocks, until bursting forth upon the surface of the mound, they fell away, down into the landscape. Here, upon the hill of the Rock Eternal, had the first waters of life bubbled forth from his sister's silver spring. Plundering the warm soil about the hill, her waters had spilled over its lip, down into the valley below, where its wide river wound through the somber landscape, making its way towards the awaiting seas.

So were released the waters of the Secret Spring, born of her sadness and loss. Yet were those waters clear, bright, and pure. For in time would they feed the many living things born into that world. But when the Secret Spring had fallen, the Golden Hourglass had been shattered. And so were the Sands of Time released into this world, carried forth by her waters, and spilling into the valley below. They would then become both a blessing and a curse.

As the mighty river formed beneath the hill, the Secret Spring's last living child was carried upon its waters, cascading down its many waterfalls, and into its pools, where she disappeared beneath the waves. There she would remain in hiding, unknown and unseen, for many ages.

The river that had formed in the valleys below was now one with the flesh and blood of the land. With its unceasing ebb and flow it had withdrawn the Golden Sands of Time from out of the timeless rock. It then had deposited those temporal sands about its muddy banks in great heaps and hills of soil. Filled with those strange sands, Time would now shape the destiny of that land and the rhythm of its life.

But the river had also worn down the lands of the Rock Eternal, its waters made from the tears of the Secret Spring. By her sorrows were her brother's lands thus reshaped. Its rushing waters had sculpted the land, such that it alone bore the mold upon which it was cast. And so was that land's fate intertwined, ever after, with the wild and wandering river. Yet no one saw or heard the strange child that now hid within its depths.

Yet the river was not like any force known in this world. For it was not born of timeless dreams, like the seas. Nor was it entirely bound to the mother-spring that rose up within the rocks above it. It flowed free and untamed, bearing the Sands of Time within it. Yet as a living being, it remained wide awake to the knowledge of its mortal and aging nature. Its own waters slowly trickled away with the ticking of time, flowing through the hidden halls from whose sands that house was yet conceived. Thus was created the River of Time, whom some named Avalyr, the shining waters. For the golden grains that hid beneath its waves were, ever after, borne upon its timeless tides the sparkling sands which the Essence Eternal had made in the youth of the world, to measure it's ebb and flow.

Never ceasing in its endless march, the noble river flowed valiantly onward through the eons. Gathering its liquid essence from distant realms, it drained the watersheds of those vast lands. Forming one great artery, Avalyr travelled downstream, carrying the shining sands within its flow, until rushing forth with great force and power, it fell headlong into the timeless waters of the Dreaming Seas.

By waterfalls tall and proud, the river then cast its noble seed, the golden sands borne by its wild waters, into the drifting and shifting sands of the seas. Falling away into that widening gulf, the Sands of Time filled the boundless beaches that stretched before the seas. And so the long-denied dreams of love—of joined destinies and of time's passing, long shared between the two troubled realms of land and sea—were finally consummated and made whole upon the shining shore of their joyous union.

The great cataracts of Avalyr's crystal-clear waters would, ever after, pour into those sleeping seas. The Dreaming Seas, fed by those waters of Time, drew those golden sands into her bosom. Continually fed by it, they had then grown to know the rhythmic beat of Time. And so were spawned the time-filled fates of this world's children, who would be woven into its sacred loom of sleep.

Yet that ocean would never know the true boon or bane, blessing or curse, of Time itself. For the Dreaming Seas, though bound by Time, were in timeless dreams still entranced. And so the seas could never awaken to the glory and the grandeur that is life. Though the lands above the seas, bound to those cursed sands, could birth and give flesh to the living children, their destinies the seas still controlled. For though the river's own turning wheels had foreseen their troubled fates, their lives the mother-seas alone had dreamed and destined, long ago.

By the slow turning of the timeless tides, it seemed the living and their immortal spirits would yet live on, forever. But the River of Time would thrust cursed age upon all that would be born into the living lands that lay above the seas. For it had been the design of the Spirit Divine that the sands and waters, borne by their flesh, should return again upon their death to the sea's cold embrace. And so, like its sands, the river would slowly drain this world of its life, until all things that had come to dwell therein would someday perish.

And yet, in the youth of the world, had the earth of the Rock Eternal remained untouched. Avalyr had flowed fresh and vibrant within it, such that no living thing could come into this realm that he alone now nurtured. The purity of the river and the beauty of the earth had thus remained untarnished. Fed by the river and guarded by the seas, this solemn land of life and death, of earth and clay, had lain hidden beneath a blanket of shadow and mist until after many lonely ages, long forgotten, there grew upon its shores a vast forest called Phantaia.

None remember when the towering trees of that timeless wilderness first sprang forth from the blackened soil. For in the midst of its youthful splendor, the thirsty roots of Phantaia had first pierced the mold of that primeval earth, drawing up from below the waters of the Secret Spring that flowed throughout. The trees had also penetrated the warm earth of the Rock Eternal until, drawing forth his nutrients, the towering trees thrust up into the sky, thick with trunks of leaf-laden boughs.

The groan of time moaned on into the countless ages, until Phantaia's great elder trees grew hoar beyond their time. Black and bent, many fell back into the earth, crashing before the feet of their brethren, and leaving an empty place against the sky. Here, in time, the saplings born of the children of the dead would gather again upon their parents' fallen flesh. Growing forth from the rich decay of their rotting logs and corpses, their dark trunks clamored and crowded within that lonesome space for the empty light of a black and vacuous Heaven.

Yet many of the greatest trees could not, or would not, die, but lived on into the ageless night as pale, twisted, and hulking phantoms, standing side by side like sentinels in the lonely depths of that wilderness, undying and immortal.

These ancient trees of Phantaia had themselves come from a secret source, which none had known. For in ages past, before the seas had fully formed, there had fallen into this world the Sacred Seed, the fifth-son of the Great Father.

But this seed had come into this world, not from him entirely, but from another–the last child of an unknown tree, whose primeval form none had seen. The Sacred Seed had hung upon the dying branches of that timeless tree, in the gloomy emptiness of space, hidden within a dying world unseen by living eyes, until the foam and waves of the Dreaming Seas had drawn this last child of that aged tree down into its waters.

This final seed was cast about in the waves and foam, until it found its way to Phantaia, thrown ashore onto the warm sands of that hidden realm. There it lay dormant for an age, until the breezes of the mother-ocean, by her breath, woke it from its shining dreams.

Before the birth of the river itself, that lonesome son of the Immortal Clay, the Rock Eternal, had roamed the shores of that land, until he had come upon the Sacred Seed hidden in the sand. He carried the golden seed into his realm, on a sojourn most mysterious, until he had come to the secret hill where he and his sister had dwelt. There he planted the seed atop the golden mound, beside his sister's shining pool.

From within its rocky depths, the silver waters of his sister's spring had poured forth, feeding the Sacred Seed, until its tender sapling took root in the warm earth and rock. It grew in time into a towering tree. Its first fruits then fell down about its feet, where they were carried by the waters of Avalyr, far and wide. And so from these seeds was birthed the forests of Phantaia. The dense growth then spread out across the land, filling the hills and valleys with countless forest children, whose voices filled the endless glades with the laughter of their swaying boughs.

But the mighty tree that had grown upon the mound had sent its thick and thirsty roots into the grave atop the hill, piercing the corpse of the fallen child of the Secret Spring that had lain buried at its feet. The tree then fed upon the Sacred Light that dwelt within her heart, transforming its own life-giving force, so that the great tree's leaves and bark shone forth with a mysterious new radiance.

Its warm beams then drifted out across the landscape, brightening the very edge of the shining shores that stretched before the seas. The many hungry children that grew about the hills and dales fed upon its enchanted light, growing ever taller and more magnificent in their beauty, until Phantaia was but a mighty forest fortress of colossal trees, impenetrable and vast.

The shining light of the tree then turned its salient fires upon the black eyes of the dark servants and denizens that had crept there. And the monsters of the Limitless Void that had come to haunt that realm in the youth of the world fled before its blinding light in terror, fearful to enter its domain ever again.

So by powers of the great tree, and the sacrifice of the fallen child, were the merciful beams of the Sacred Light reborn. And they shined through the depths, revealing as the Great Father had done, the hidden beauty of the Heavens once more.

The Sacred Seed was the first Vatar to be conceived in this new world. For all others before had dwelt but in spirit alone. By that living form was this youngest child of the Spirit Divine given the greatest of his gifts. For the tree's purpose was to renew the life-giving force of the world through its flesh and spirit, its many seeds sowing a new heavenly forest, and its merciful light nourishing the spirits of those born from it.

But with its fruit-laden limbs, the tree would also sustain the true children of the forest, the Manna, yet to be born. And by its sweet ambrosia would they be drawn together, given the strength to endure many trials, and forge anew the great works of their Creator.

Yet another mysterious seed did this tree now bear. A curious child had come forth into this world from its great golden acorn. He had been sent to guard the tree and the vast forested realms over which he was now lord. But few would know of the purpose or meaning of this hidden guardian, the great Son of the One Tree, until the last shining age of the forest was spent.

But the Sacred Seed and its source would remain hidden from the eyes of many. For the seed had come from a tree beyond this world, one which the evil twins of the Great Beyond had sought. They had tried to find the seed and destroy it, so that a new tree would never grow in this world, nor a light shine in it. With its death would this world and all others finally perish, withering away and falling into unending decay and rot, never to rise again.

In time, the Nothingness and Emptiness had found them all. Yet the last seed had been cast into this world and somehow survived. And so had Phantaia been born anew, with a new tree, and thus a fresh hope.

For many distant ages Phantaia had grown, alone and apart from the eyes of that evil, beyond even the Dreaming Seas, whose waves roared in the darkness along its forbidding and forgotten shores. Wild and free, the forest had thrived over many eons, tangled, cobwebbed, menacing, wrapped in mist, and drowned within the darkness of its own shadowed past, until its massive trees of tremendous girth and height, growing splendidly within their solemn shade, at last pierced the inky skies. Their twisted boughs had scaled the heights of Heaven, with crowded and haughty umbrage, until they looked down with a menacing scowl upon their sister seas below.

The trees of Phantaia had clustered upon that shore until, forming a great bulwark of trunks, they stood like bearded warriors, guarding the dark gateways to the tangled glades and secretive lands that lay beyond them. No sea or storm, light or dim glow of night, would or could now enter there. So Phantaia remained a timeless place, a forest paradise, forever free of the waxing and waning of seasons, the changing rhythm of moons and suns, the churning and turning of the stars and seas, and the lights of Heaven, which had yet been born to brighten the lonesome depths of that wilderness.

Nothing could ever enter or leave Phantaia. Nor had any being known its secretive paths, save one. For the vast forests of Phantaia had stretched far beyond the shores of those seas, back into the farthest spheres and mazes of eternal space and time, into an limitless landscape of black boles, twisted roots, shattered stumps, and shifting shadows whose reaches none could ever grasp or fathom.

Past the Lands of Midnight, beyond even the echoing Halls of Time, that unending wilderness had grown, until Phantaia's tangled and rugged waste, nightmarish woods, and maddening mounds and mountains of thirsty growth had spread themselves throughout the farthest fringes of this world. At their farthest frontiers Phantaia's ghoulish trees seemed to disappear, into an unknown realm filled with strange blue fog and yawning catacombs of darkening depths. There upon a misty and rocky precipice, Phantaia's black and hulking trunks, trembling with terror, clustered upon its farthest cliffs, and looked down into the frightful gulf that fell away, into the hate-filled abyss of the Great Beyond.

But unseen by all, one had returned to haunt the dark woods and gloomy glades of Phantaia. For he had come on a mission most mysterious, seeking to protect the secrets of the forest from the terrible powers that yet hid in the shadows of the world. For the forces of darkness and destruction had awakened within the fringes of that wood, seeking to do Phantaia great harm.

The Twilight Mist had seen the anger and violence of his son against the seas. And by Agapor's works, he had seen the wrath and evil of his dark brothers return to haunt the lonely woods of Phantaia, seeking to obliterate the last living works of their Great Father.

He had seen Agapor's storms boiling within the skies, gathering about the fringes of the seas. For their ghostly specters and winged shades lingered still within the darker corners of the world. So had the Twilight Mist remained behind to protect the sea and land, and guard the precious secrets that yet hid within its hollows.

But the Twilight Mist had felt, within the world, a new and unseen presence come into it. With his thick mists, he had drifted out across the fringes of Phantaia to hide the hidden wonder of its birth from evil, and prepare a path for its blessed arrival. He would covet this secret as long as he could, hiding it away from the world, until such time as sinister forces finally discover it, rising up from the dark depths, seeking to destroy it.

The Twilight Mist had left the skies above the realm where An, his daughter, slept in peace, seeing her and the seas now safe from harm. He descended from the Arch of Heaven onto the silent shores of dark Phantaia, where once he had roamed in search of its golden child. There his spectral mists silently collected above the roots of the trees, taking refuge near to the shore, and fleeing the remnant storms born of that earlier war.

Hiding there among the limbs, he stretched his violet tendrils out into the silent canopy, wrapping about the boughs above, and curling around the dark trunks of trees. His lavender mist, like a ghostly shroud, filled the haunted woods, until they lay entombed within his dense, purple cloud.

But the Twilight Mist had also come to dwell beside his love, the sleeping Secret Spring. Seeing her sad fate, he wept for her beside her pool. Then was heard by him a strange song, rising from the river below. It is then he first looked in wonder upon the river-child, his lost daughter, seeing her from the river's bar as she played within its wild currents. He made his presence known to the shy and secretive child, guiding her in her course by his mists and fogs, and singing to her softly as she slept in the depths of that emerald river.

Eventually, the fatherly Mist had embraced the entirety of the woods and rivers of Phantaia, filling every corner of them, and hiding their hidden beauties from all eyes but his own. With his dense cloud, he now guarded the last of the lonely gates and gloomy paths leading into that paradise, so that none could ever enter or leave it, seeking to hide the precious child that now lay hidden within its depths.

But he had cast the forest aglow with a strange spectral light. For his pale glow was not of the boundless and perpetual darkness of the nighttime skies, nor of the bright light of the shining sun. His light was of the preternatural glow of dusk and dawn combined. And so the shifting shadows of his changing mists gleamed with an eerie light that burned from within its fog. By way of his dripping dews and gentle rains, the trunks and leaves of Phantaia were now transformed, glazed over with a soft lavender sheen. And the somber shade of his purple mists shined down upon the earth and sea below with an almost ghoulish light.

Ever after were those woods named for his mist, the Forest of Twilight. For his lavender clouds and fogs would remain there, curling about the trees and valleys of Phantaia, bathing that weird wood in his protective mists, long after his own spirit had left it. By his essence, Phantaia would be a foreboding and fearful place, trapped in the strange space that exists between sunlight and shadow—an alien world where the translucent mantle of Heaven's sheen and midnight's shade had once dreamt and crept.

Yet neither light nor shadow had dared to dwell in the Forest of Twilight, or ever would again. Only the somber glow of his perpetual gloam, cast by his phantasmal fogs, would yet remain behind to haunt the gloomy forests of Phantaia, long after its brighter days had past.

It was in this misty forest primeval that the strange imaginative will of the Twilight Mist would, ever after, hold sway. So unlike the undreaming thoughts of the awakening river, the forest in perpetual but broken sleep would lie, awakened by light, yet still dreaming by night. And so was it cursed, a domain locked in unfulfilled and half-seen visions, trapped between land and sea, the living and the long-dead, the undying and the undead.

The wilderness of Phantaia, now bounded by sea and bathed in mist, lay quiet for many ages after, save for the soothing sounds of the roaring surf, where the Dreaming Seas and the Mists of Imagination mingled upon their endless beaches. For where the wilderness met the sea's broad belt, the peaceful dreams of the forest and the ever-awakening seas had mixed. And upon those beaches the lurid visions of An would soon be made real.

Phantaia now slept undisturbed. But upon an overlook, above the seas, the manly form of the Twilight Mist had taken shape. The crowned prince of that land looked down from Phantaia's lonesome cliffs, into the gray ocean abyss below. For in his heart he had felt the presence of his lost son, Agapor, hidden in the gloomy realms that lay beyond his own. He knew that soon his son would awaken and come looking for him.

THE RISE OF AGAPOR

The wooded gateways of Phantaia had remained guarded from all eyes, encircled by the seas that raged below their windy cliffs, and bathed in the ominous mists and dews that had enveloped them. Unmarred by the violent hands of wind and wave, Phantaia had remained pristine, its dense trees standing in sublime grandeur before the silent shore.

But the darker woods, which had lain beyond them, had for many ages slept in their quiet shade, dreaming alone. Even the winds of evil had not yet stirred their virgin leaves. For no one but the Mist had penetrated Phantaia's strange and haunted pathways, nor walked within its gloomy and tangled wood. The aging wilderness had thus endured, long after the quieting of the warring seas and storms.

But far away down the beach there lay about the sea-bound shores a line of black cliffs, whose broad waves, cold and gray, still crashed against the barren rocks. For the storms of older conflicts continued to ravage both land and sea upon that shore with their angry clouds and whipping winds.

Beside those misty cliffs, where the seas themselves met the land, there poured a glorious waterfall from high above. For untold eons, the river of Avalyr had carried the shining waters to that shore, drawn themselves from an idyllic source that none had seen. By shining streams, swift and bold, deep and cold, twisting and turning through the interior of that land, the river had swiftly carved itself a great vein within that realm. Gathering all its waters together from distant arteries, it slowly drained the land of its waters until, upon those stony heights, it at last poured its plunder, with great fury, down into the Dreaming Seas below. This mighty cataract then cast up great billows of fog and dew upon the damp cliffs and trees high above it.

But beneath these falls, upon the troubled shores of this broad borderland, lay another cataract, the wide waterfall of the Dreaming Seas. Here the oceans had gathered before its rocky cup where, like the river, they themselves at last fell away, over the rim of the world in one last monumental wall of sea and spray. Down into a bottomless pit the waters fell, into the gray depths, until all sound had been silenced by its monstrous roar.

In the fog-enshrouded caverns of Wendalia, Agapor had slept, broken in spirit and body by the vengeful violence of the seas. The dark forces he had amassed within himself had long ago diminished. And the servants he had summoned from the hollows of the world had fled far and wide. He had lain broken and battered, for untold ages, trapped in dark nightmares born of his anguish and anger. Yet somehow he had survived.

Many unanswered questions and visions had entered his awakening spirit. He thought about his sister An, who now lay imprisoned in the depths of the seas. The sound of her cries continually echoed in his mind, like the cursed continuum of a nightmare he could not escape.

It is then he had a vision, in which he saw his father, the Twilight Mist, looking down from a cliff, high above. He was a dark figure, tall and proud, with a crown upon his head, and a great beard trailing from his face. With shadowy eyes, his father stood staring at him, surrounded by a dark, lavender mist which seemed to hide the outlines of his face and figure.

With his angry fists held high, Agapor cursed his father from the depths of the sea. He hated him for the tortured life he had given him, and the heartless imprisonment inflicted upon his sister. But as he looked upon the dark cliffs where his father had stood, Agapor saw only a silver cauldron, floating in a dark fog. Its rim was lined with pearls. And its surface was bejeweled, reflecting many colors.

A mysterious light rose from its inky waters. And the Heavens above seemed to open up, as a golden light cast from that cup was thrown down into the slate-gray waters about them. Within the lights he saw reflected upon the rolling seas the form of a baby floating upon its surface. He reached out to take the child into his arms. But as he did, a black spirit cruelly erupted within him. And Agapor awoke from his tormented sleep.

Opening his eyes, Agapor called out to it in his suffering, "...Father..."

But its black cloud had begun to climb forth from his frame, until its gray fog hung about the caverns above, casting an eerie light upon its walls and floors. Its vast vortex began to encircle him, its center forming a great black mouth that wafted a hot and putrid breath upon his face. Huge eyes then opened from within the cloud, and looked with anger upon the frail boy.

But the Limitless Void now spoke with furious and fuming ire, saying, "You have failed to slay the child of the sea, and denied me my rightful prize. By her death would the Dreaming Seas have perished at my hand. And its creator would then have fallen before me, heartbroken, and in despair. By your failure, they have secured themselves a permanent place in this world, dwelling apart in the depths of the sea. Their unyielding spirits now lie permanently hidden and protected from harm, such that no force in this world will ever challenge them again."

But Agapor said in defiance, "You have deceived me, foul spirit. For you withheld from me the knowledge of my father, the Twilight Mist. And you used me to try and destroy my own sister."

But the Void only laughed, telling him, "It matters not, as your father never loved you. He abandoned you in this pit, just as your mother had done. You have now forsaken your own sister, leaving her alone in the depths of the seas. So has your family fallen by their own wickedness, widening the rifts that now divide you."

Agapor thought about his sister. And he felt great sorrow and shame. Yet by his act alone had she been spared certain death at the hands of the Limitless Void. For she now lay safe in her tomb, far from harm.

The Limitless Void then looked upon Agapor with his black-rimmed eyes, saying, "Never again will you see your sister. For no power under Heaven can now penetrate the cursed seas. She will lie entrapped for all eternity, bound to the watery prison that is of her own mother's making. And there she shall remain, forever tortured by the memory of her brother's cruel and savage acts inflicted upon her." Agapor fell to his knees in despair, hiding his face from that truth.

Yet, unknown to them both was An now bound to a strange and twisted fate. To a vast Wheel of Time was her mind now chained. For that wheel now turned about her in the seas, fed by the waters of the mighty River of Time, and bound to the turning of the world's future events, which she alone now controlled. No force under Heaven would stop that wheel from turning. Nor would any power wrought upon those seas divide them, until their last drops had been spent.

Agapor saw within the Limitless Void's lies many truths too painful to bear. But they fueled within him even greater anger. And he stood before the Limitless Void in defiance. With arms outstretched, Agapor raised his manacled hands, commanding the spirits of the Shade and Shadow to rise forth from them, and drive the Limitless Void back into his prison. Agapor would then refashion the black chains that had once bound his spirit to the rocks of that chasm, remaking that which he himself had unmade.

But the spirits of the Shadow and Shade had been released from those irons long ago in the war with the seas. And so had those dark angels betrayed Agapor, fleeing from him in his time of need.

The Limitless Void then laughed at Agapor, telling him that those black servants had returned to their hateful father's realm, where they now slept within its darkened catacombs. He told Agapor that his own father, the Twilight Mist, had forged those black manacles in ages past, so that the Children of Night might be bound to them for a purpose most foul. For in ancient days, the Twilight Mist had taken the children of the Endless Night from their father, imprisoning their spirits in those shackles, and enslaving them to watch over that which his cowardly self could not confront.

Yet, unknown to Agapor, by the hidden powers that lay within the Shade and Shadow could the Limitless Void alone be bound.

For the nightmare forces within them had enslaved his mind to their will. And this truth the Twilight Mist had somehow seen.

But the Limitless Void told Agapor that, by a dark pool's vision, he had seen how his brother's own bastard child could be used to undo that which his brother had done. And with the rending of those shackles by Agapor, had the spirits of those bracers finally departed, and the son undone all that his father had made. With a wicked grin upon his face, the Void said that all he had plotted and planned was now complete.

Weak and near death, Agapor collapsed to the ground. Hearing these words, he saw that he was but an actor upon a stage of a larger play. And in the bigger design, he had glimpsed his tragic part in its final dramatic end. He no longer cared to live in a world where all that he had hoped for was but an illusion designed to fulfill the will of a malevolent mind.

The Limitless Void then gathered its clouds about him, and took form as a towering lord again, with a shining crown upon his head and a thick, gray cape that stretched forth behind him. Agapor then recognized the face of his master, as he had ages ago in the house of his mother. For this was the true form of the Limitless Void, which he had taken long ago when the world was young, and before the Nothingness and Emptiness had corrupted his form and spirit.

Looking into his rugged face, Agapor beheld in the coldness of his eyes the callous spirit of the Limitless Void. Yet, just as An had seen in him, he saw a piece of himself reflected therein. The Void knelt beside Agapor, saying, "My son, I was freed by your hands. And for this am I most grateful. I will soon be the last of the Primordial Ones. For my brothers who still remain in this world are weak and near death. This world shall soon be mine alone to rule. For I shall go to the evil ones that dwell in the depths to reclaim my promised powers. By their merciful will and judgement, shall I be then granted kingship over the remnants of this fallen world. My unfinished works will then be completed. And by my dominion over this world shall it be remade in my image. Then shall I eat away at the roots of the sea and forest, until they are sucked dry of their essence. The last of the children of my brothers shall then come to me as willing slaves, before they themselves are sent to the evil ones, whose gaping mouths wait for them even now in the Great Beyond."

"Your role in the fate of the world now has passed, Agapor," said the Limitless Void in a calming voice. "Your spirit shall be drawn into me, and sent before the Nothingness and Emptiness that dwells in the pit below us. There your spirit and flesh shall be obliterated from this world, forever. For I cannot lie. I have dreamt of the day I would see the last son of the Twilight Mist perish before me."

The Limitless Void placed his cold gray hands upon the boy's face. But as he did so, the Limitless Void hesitated. For a part of him truly cared for the child, which he had raised and nurtured. And there had dwelt in his evil heart a tiny piece of the compassionate light of his father.

With icy breath, he began to draw forth the dark spirit out of Agapor's body and into his own. Agapor screamed in agony, as his ghost was slowly sucked into the mouth of the Void.

But from the skies above there descended two dark and ominous forms. From the Lands of Midnight had returned the Shadow and the Shade, the dreaded Children of Night. They had fled forth from this world when the seas had risen up to destroy it. But they were still bound as servants to the cursed manacles upon Agapor's wrists. For Agapor's father had made them strong, and yet enduring, knowing the Children of Night would seek to free themselves and release their terror upon the world.

The Shadow and the Shade had heard the cries of their master from beyond the Veils of Night. As they flew down into Wendalia, an ominous darkness was cast about the pit by their beating wings. With great vengeance, they dove down upon the figure of the Limitless Void, so that he was blown back by the force of their wings. Their gnashing jaws and teeth of shining jet then lashed out at him, driving him back from the boy, so that the Void cowered before their might.

But the Limitless Void feared the Shadow most. For in him had been placed the spirit of the Nightmare Unending, which he had used to imprison the Void with the illusions of his own mind's innumerable horrors. And by those night terrors had his shattered spirit been chained to Wendalia. Blown down and lying vulnerable on the ground, the Limitless Void looked up at the Shadow in terror. For he saw in his menacing eyes the many horrors that had haunted him before.

Seeing the Limitless Void cowering before his servant, Agapor rose to his feet. With renewed energy, he went before the cowering Void, and said to him, "Your time in this world has passed. With the Children of Night, I shall now bring the powers of your world and theirs under me. No more shall the Night and the Void dwell apart. For the time of darkness and destruction united has come at last. By their powers shall I take what is mine in this world. I shall then go and find my father and, with these twin forces, destroy him, which you yourself have failed to do. Then shall the seas falter and fall before me. And at last, my sister shall be free from her cruel bondage."

Agapor flung his fist before the Limitless Void, saying, "Never again shall her life be threatened by you!" Agapor then looked upon that broken being with his own empty eyes, as he had looked upon his unloving mother, so long ago.

But the Limitless Void pleaded with Agapor, saying, "Agapor, do not trust yourself to such a fate as this. These fading powers shall not last. For there dwells within this world an even greater evil, which yet haunts and tortures the Son of Night. This sinister being, which has long hid from the world, shall soon be unleashed, rising up through his servant to torment his heart and mind, until he is driven towards an even crueler destiny."

"Look upon the face of the Shadow. Do you not see the evil that stirs within him?" cried the Limitless Void.

At these words, the Shadow looked upon Agapor's fearful face and laughed, saying in a deep voice, "Master, he lies as a coward who stands before the doorway of death."

But in the depths of the black heart of the Shadow had dwelt such a spirit. For in the Shadow, the powers of the Nightmare Unending had grown unhindered, spawned by a sinister desire to pollute the children of the Primordial Ones. The Shadow had not sought to use such powers to pervert the minds of others, but to slay them by his own evil designs.

So had the Shadow desired, more than Agapor himself, the death of the Limitless Void. Yet Agapor was unsure. But the Shadow could not hesitate. For he advanced quickly upon the Limitless Void, wrapping his ebony claws about his neck, strangling him. Agapor looked on in horror as the Limitless Void cried out in the anguish and suffering of his last breath, until he fell to the floor, pale and lifeless.

The Shadow then laughed as he released the Limitless Void from his claws. Agapor looked upon his own hand, and saw the strange ring of his mother throbbing with a sinister blue light. The spirit of the Limitless Void then rose forth upon a dark wind, drawn up and out of his body, until it filled the cavern about them with its black tendrils, and encircled them with its eerie fog.

Then was heard from the depths beneath Wendalia, the groan of the waking spirit of the Nothingness, rising forth from the bottomless depths. For it had sought to devour the spirit of the Limitless Void.

But Agapor saw that the ring upon his hand now glowed with a fearsome white light. As he raised the ring before him, the light seemed to blind the Shadow and Shade, who hid from it in fear. With a great gust of wind, the spinning cloud of the Void was slowly drawn into its burning crystal, as Agapor was blown back by its gale.

Opposing powers were at war over that spirit. For great clouds of dust and rock had spun about them, until those swirling winds were sucked down into the pit, then back up and around the black ring and its fog. Agapor saw the gray cloud of the Limitless Void flee before that power, as it was quickly drawn into the shining stone of the ring.

The moaning and wailing of the winds from the depths beyond the cave finally died away, until the hollow groans of its sinister spirit were all that could be heard in the distance. As quickly as they had come, the winds were gone. And Agapor beheld the dark ring of jet resting, black and lifeless again, upon his hand.

The dark servants crawled out from the corners of the cavern. Agapor then looked upon the curious face of the Shadow, whose evil and envious eyes stared at the ring upon his finger. The Shadow rose before Agapor, as darkness rises upon a storm cloud in the Heavens. He then demanded, "Give me the ring..."

But Agapor, in fear, raised the right manacle that lay upon his wrist, commanding the Shadow to back away from him. And the great black beast fell to the ground, cowering before his master. The Shadow and the Shade were now his alone to command. And seeing them bowing before him, Agapor renewed his power and drive to use them to his advantage. But he also saw that they could, by their sinister nature, turn against him.

Agapor looked down upon the sad form of the Limitless Void. Only the husk of his body now remained, a hollow corpse made of stone, appearing as a fallen figure carved from ashen stone. But Agapor could only look away.

But as he did, the Shadow walked up to his statue and, with the terrible force of his angry fists, shattered the empty remains of the Limitless Void. The rocks and dust of the once-mighty Void now lay broken upon the cavern floor. Agapor looked back at the Shadow in fear, and yet anger. For he had done this terrible act though his own powerful will. But the Shadow could only smile, seeing with evil delight the final demise of the Limitless Void by his own hand.

Agapor walked away, deep into the cavern, until he stood upon the edge of the pit. He looked into the mysterious depths below, knowing now a dark evil crept therein. He then looked about the cavern, remembering how once the cruel Void had held him as a child. Agapor thought upon the fate of the Limitless Void, and of his own life, seeing a new destiny for himself born of the terrible choices he himself had now made.

He noticed a light cast about him, and looked with fascination at the strange ring upon his hand. For its large dark crystal had begun to dimly glow, burning with the phantom flame of a hidden spirit. Or was its strange light ebbing and flowing with the thoughts and emotions that now filled his conflicted heart? As Agapor's mind calmed, the crystal of the ring also dimmed, glowing with a paler color, yet flickering and smoking with the strange essence of the Limitless Void, whose cursed spirit remained trapped within its crystal. Agapor felt hypnotized by its lights, as he watched their ghoulish wisps and shadows play upon the cavern walls.

Agapor sat upon the rocks and pondered the ring's many mysteries. He then rose to his feet and returned to the Shadow and Shade, who stood alone in the midst of the pale fog that wrapped about them. Their evil eyes glowed with eerie red embers as their master approached.

Those black beasts seemed to have grown bolder and more prideful. For with the death of the Limitless Void, they had tasted their long sought freedom. Yet had they known they would remain enslaved to Agapor, and by his strength of will alone, his to command.

They were terrible to behold. For they stood like great horned and black-skinned demons, bearing upon their broad shoulders powerful ebony wings. The Shade's wings opened to Agapor, as he approached. The black feathers of her gossamer wings shimmered as they fluttered in the winds of the chasm, revealing her dark and sensuous body. Yet it was her charcoal eyes that deeply penetrated his own. But her brother, the Shadow, was monstrous and tall, towering over Agapor, bearing shiny black skin that drew the pale light of the cavern into it, such that the illusion of his lightless presence seemed to shift about in the dim glow.

They knelt before Agapor in servitude. The Shadow then looked with envious eyes upon his master, saying, "What you have long desired is now done. The Limitless Void is destroyed. But his spirit and his powers yet remain in this world. For he now dwells in the ring that lies upon your hand. By his great cunning, the

Limitless Void has avoided eternal damnation and death at the hands of the Nothingness. For he must have fashioned it long ago for his spirit's keeping, fearing his essence would be devoured by that which he had served."

Agapor turned his gaze upon the ring, as it cast its hypnotic glow upon their faces, saying, "He could not have fashioned such a thing as this. For it does not seem to be of this world."

But the Shadow looked upon Agapor, with eyes set aflame by the passion of his words, saying, "The spirit of the Limitless Void is now yours. For his powers are given to those who wear the ring. You may now summon the destructive storms of Oblivion, or command the wracked spirits of the dead to rise again. By your instruction alone, shall the directionless hosts that yet roam the wastes of Oblivion take flesh again, gathering as one to fulfill your dire will in this world, and inflict untold agony and suffering upon its children. For you are now their undisputed Lord."

Agapor's eyes glowed with a fearsome light. And he thought upon the words of the Shadow, as he stared deep into the fading light of the ring. But the Shadow gazed upon the boy with a hatred that yet stirred deep inside him. For unknown to Agapor, the Shadow still looked upon him with much malign. This truth the Shadow kept from him. For Agapor was but the son of his enslaver. And the Shadow would bear, ever after, great animosity for his new master, who had so cruelly enslaved him like his father had done.

But the Shadow had seen how easily Agapor could succumb to temptation. And he knew that he, like his father, would soon be consumed again by his heart's yearning desires.

Agapor looked at the remains of the form of the Limitless Void, as they lay scattered about the cavern floor. He bent down and picked up his bejeweled crown and placed it upon his head. And so was Agapor given the sovereign powers of the Limitless Void.

Agapor had a renewed strength and determined will. He turned and looked upon the angels of darkness that stood before him and smiled. Agapor then summoned forth the magical powers of the black manacles upon his wrists. And the Shadow and Shade, still enslaved to those irons, bowed before him, their heads held low to the ground.

Agapor said to his servants that he was now the Ruler of Oblivion, the Lord of Destruction. And his voice roared up through the pits of that hollow earth as he spoke. With the sacred crown he now wore, he would reign over Oblivion, casting the shadow of his hand like a dark cloud across those barbarous lands. Unto him now would the demons of Oblivion bow in obedience, serving only him.

Agapor then commanded the Shadow and Shade to carry him to the Realms of Oblivion. There would they seek the cavern in which stood the ghoulish throne of the Limitless Void. For it had stood idle and unused, alone in darkness, too long.

The Shadow and Shade, with expressionless eyes, only listened, unmoving. They then obeyed.

Taking Agapor in his black claws, the Shadow flew up and out of the cavern, the Shade following close behind. He carried him out of the pit and across the rolling seas, through the vast skies that lay beneath the Arch of Heaven, and past the Veils of Night that hung within the Halls of Time. Through the hollow Corridors of Darkness they flew, past vast arcades of arched alcoves, which hid in their towering heights the bat-winged servants of darkness. For these had once filled the skies during ancient wars, long forgotten. Through those shadowy and forsaken hallways they travelled, past dusty and rubble-strewn corridors, within whose dizzying depths no light or air ever stirred.

Beyond the bleak Lands of Midnight they travelled, until they came to the borderlands that lay before the rocky remnants of the Realms of Oblivion. Below them, Agapor saw the sad and gloomy ruins of his mother's keep, whose twisted and teetering towers and castle walls trailed off into the dreary valleys below.

On they flew, between maddening mountains of jet, whose cliffs thrust up into the skies with rocks of obsidian, sharp as razors, then down into the fringes of Oblivion, which stood before the empty spaces of the gray and grim Great Beyond.

Before that dire waste, there rose up from the mountain slopes a giant stone stairway, which some huge hand had carved in ages past. For the Essence Eternal had fashioned these stairs for the feet of his sons, before they had destroyed through their relentless violence the noble house that once stood above it on the mountainside.

Down they flew, over the massive stairs and through the stagnant fog, until below him Agapor saw the ruins of a colossal city, rising up from a vast network of caves and caverns. Over the wreckage of that gloomy metropolis they flew, down into its frightening catacombs, and through its crumbling city of the dead. Its entangled causeways and towering archways had once connected a great matrix of cavernous tombs and towers in an enormous maze of decayed and rotting stonework. Long abandoned, that sprawling city of countless crypts now appeared as a never-ending cobweb of frozen rock and black ice.

In the middle of that decrepit city lay a giant orifice, whose wide mouth stood before them like that of a great fish of the deep that tempts into its aching belly a long awaited and unwary prey. Into those trembling depths they plummeted, floating upon the cold and cavernous winds, until at its bottom Agapor saw a new dread suddenly rise up from the gloom before them.

Beyond the shadows, a monstrous chasm stretched off into the infinite darkness. About its shores lapped a slimy sea, upon whose oily surface hung a vile green and gray fog that disappeared into its fathomless frontiers. Within this underground sea's unknown depths slept horrors unseen by any eyes since the birth of the world.

As they flew over its silent waves, Agapor thought he could see the amber glow of a gargantuan eye, lazily staring up at him from the slimy gray depths. Beneath the gray waves squirmed the lustful flesh of countless writhing bodies and perverse lovers, who in one orgiastic mass of strangers, seemed to pulsate as one in the depths of that great debauchery of the seas. Or were they but pale sea-worms, feeding ravenously upon the corpses of the dead?

Through an eerie fog they floated above that phantasmal sea until, upon the farthest shores of that colossal chasm, there appeared a mammoth cave opening within a sheer wall of towering rock.

Into its monumental heights stretched massive cathedral-like pillars, their twisted columns supporting the endless galleries, gothic hallways, and forgotten walkways that stretched back into the depths of that gruesome underworld. Towering statues of demonic lords, cracked and crumbling, peered with stony eyes, through the salty mist at the lonely travelers as they flew past. Upon the dense surface of every wall and railing had been carved entangled figures, grotesque faces, and the last carnal embraces and sufferings of the tempted, tortured, and dying. But though the macabre architecture had portrayed some perceived heroic time, it yet belied a tragic end.

Great rusted cages bearing the monstrous skeletons of creatures, long dead and dust-covered, hung in the gloom from the vast ceiling above them, their bodies having long ago rotted away after unknown ages of torture and suffering. Giant tangled chains, collapsed ironworks, machines, fallen stonework, shattered pillars, and the skulls of beasts and strange behemoths rose up in great heaps and piles from the shadowy depths below them. Agapor then saw how ages of ruthless and decadent violence had transformed the majesty of this world into one of madness.

From out of the decay and dust climbed a huge set of colossal stairs, upon whose dark heights lay a massive platform of rock that stretched back into the shadows of the chamber. There in its midst, sat a towering throne made of the ancient bleached bones of the dead and the long-suffering flesh of slain beasts, who yet had fallen in some forgotten and ancient war.

This was the throne room of the Limitless Void, who in ages past had ruled this broken land of death and decay by his merciless hand. But from his perverse desire for complete and total power over the world had death come to his own kind, so that only the tragic remains of his former struggles had now remained.

Unto Agapor had the Limitless Void's haunted lands and legacy now been bestowed. And with the power and might of the corrupted Children of Night, and the possessed ring upon his hand, would he now be lord over this shattered and horrific domain of death.

Agapor walked slowly towards the ghoulish chair. But as he sat upon the evil throne, Agapor looked down through the empty waste below and smiled. For though no armies knelt before him, he knew that this was now his domain. Soon would he forge it anew. He would keep to himself, hidden from the world, quietly plotting his revenge upon it. But in the catacombs of that vast underground city of secrets had yet been hidden much evil, still undiscovered, and even greater truths waiting to be unearthed.

The Shade, sister of the Shadow, Agapor had summoned forth to tend to his wounds. But the Shade in secret had desired Agapor. Through his beguiling power over her, she became drawn to him. So tempted, she selfishly desired to possess him, and keep him for her own. Her grim shade fell upon his mind. And for a time, she drew away the shadows of his hardened heart, filling him with visions of her own body and form, its sensuous curves and salacious delights.

But Agapor was wary of her affections. For his heart was still with An. So by false pretense, he used the Shade for his own purposes. He demanded she watch over the Shadow, her brother, and hide his wary heart and mind from her brother, so that the black servant knew little of his plans. For Agapor now looked upon the power and might of the Shadow as a threat to him. He was a force that had grown in power and knowledge beyond even his own.

Through his sister's prowess did Agapor control his own mind still, so that the Shadow remained unsure of his master's motivations. But the Shadow had, long ago, looked deep into his master's heart and saw that his secret love for An had yet remained true and undying. And this revelation stayed within his plotting mind.

In time, Agapor was filled with renewed strength. He gained greater power over the Shadow and Shade, such that his own spirit was imbibed with new powers over Oblivion's many dark denizens as well. To him came the lost servants of the Limitless Void, who had walled themselves away within the countless crypts and bedchambers of that forgotten underworld. And by the iron crown upon his head, and his stern presence upon that throne, was Agapor revered by those dark servants as their lord and king.

But through the use of dark enchantments, bound to the ring and manacles, Agapor's own body became corrupted and changed into a fearsome form. His face grew distorted and wide. His skin became as a hide, thick, pitted, and scaly. His knotted arms and shoulders grew strong and wide. And his black-rimmed eyes ever burned in their sunken hollows with bewitching fires.

Upon his head grew a short but tangled mass of horns, which grew more threatening and bestial over time, until they appeared as a woven crown of thorns, encircling his head. And so, by the powers that had come into him, was he a most formidable and fearsome lord, ruler over all the darker realms as he had vowed he would be.

Sitting upon his throne of the fallen house of the Void, he continued to fashion in his mind a dire plan to destroy the seas. But he had begun to doubt that he alone could penetrate, or harm them, ever again. Yet in his silent hours alone, upon his throne, he still longed to know of his sister. And he thought long into the night of the odd disappearance of his father's twilit mists, which once dwelt above the seas. But unknown to Agapor, his father now dwelt far away in the dismal woods that lay hidden beyond the farthest shores of the ocean. And so his father's whereabouts had remained a mystery, which tortured him day and night.

The Shadow had returned to Oblivion after completing the errands on which he had been sent. But learning from the Shade, his sister, of Agapor's new designs upon the world, he bellowed with laughter to his sister in secret. For he knew all these machinations were bent towards the same futile desire to see his sister again, and rescue her from the ocean's grip. And the Shadow saw that Agapor's flawed desire still burned within his foolish heart.

The Shadow then came before Agapor, and spoke bold words to him, reminding him that no force in this world would ever penetrate the Dreaming Seas again. For its daughter now held a strange power within its watery depths, which no force could discover or destroy. And she and her mother-ocean would be guided and protected by its sway, until the end of time itself.

Over many nights Agapor thought upon the truth and wisdom of his servant's words. He then called the Shadow to him once more, telling him he must now go on a new mission, into the mysterious lands that lay deep under the Arch of Heaven. He must fly far and wide, seeking to find the Twilight Mist, his father. For he perceived that his father lay hidden within the valleys of his lost and unseen lands, which lay beyond the edges of space and time.

Agapor's desire for revenge against his father had not diminished, but had grown within his heart. And he thought that through his father would he gain knowledge of the mystery of the seas, and his sister's strange enslavement to them.

But the Shadow told Agapor he knew not where his hidden lands lay. For though his eyes could look deep into the mind and hearts of many in that world, he could not penetrate the heart of the Twilight Mist, nor know of his secret dwelling place. For the Twilight Mist was a Primordial One, and a being of great power.

But unknown to them, the Twilight Mist had hidden his heart and mind from all seekers, dwelling within the strange realms of Phantaia. For by his mists, he guarded those who dwelt there from the sight and knowledge of all others.

But the Shadow bowed before Agapor, his master, and obeyed, flying out into the night on his strange mission of discovery. On he flew with his mighty wings, into the gray depths, seeking to find the homeland of the Twilight Mist, which was said to lie beyond the Mountains of Heaven. But this secret crystalline land no other being but the Twilight Mist had ever seen, or would ever find.

But unknown to Agapor, the Shadow had in secret begun to plot his escape from the servitude of his master. For the Shadow had returned to the black Lands of Midnight, seeking his own father, the Endless Night. Yet the Shadow had not sought love or revenge, only to take from him the last of his noble powers that still remained. For his father had hidden the Wings of Night with which he had conquered and ruled the world in eons past. And by his father's corruption of their powers, he had finally turned them against their truer purpose, using them to bathe the world in boundless darkness, and so consume it. These wings the Shadow now greatly desired.

But the mystery of the fate of his father, the Endless Night, had not been revealed to the Shadow. Nor had his presence been felt by him, so that the Shadow now thought him dead. For his father's fortress had lain barren and cold upon the summit of a mighty peak, deep within the Lands of Midnight. Within the abandoned hallways of his towering fortress, the Shadow had found no sign of his father, save the depressing and empty gloom that had hung about its cold and vacant chambers.

The Shadow had then sought his father's grave, which was said to lie deep underground. For many nights he searched beneath the fortress walls and cliffs, seeking a secret entrance, which was said to lead to a vast catacomb of the vampiric dead. Within those depths, he thought, would rest his father's colossal tomb.

But the Endless Night had finally lain himself, bloody and beaten, buried in a giant sarcophagus of stone, even deeper underground. Sorely wounded after years of war's countless defeats, he had finally succumbed to his injuries. But it was his broken heart which would take him in the end.

And so the Shadow and the Shade had both known of their father's death. But if the Shadow could find his father's tomb, then would he rip from him the mighty wings born of darkness eternal that hung from his corpse. And with these wings would he then have the power to slay Agapor, and at last be free.

As the Shadow flew past the iron gates of his father's fortress, he heard a whisper, faint at first, of an old woman, emanating from the corner of the wall. It was then he saw a tiny crack appear. Ripping away the stone, he found a narrow stair winding its way down into the darkness. Into the depths of his father's house he descended until, beneath a maze of dungeons, he entered a vast catacomb of the undead.

In its dusty depths were housed many tombs, wherein had slept the vast bat-like armies of the Endless Night. But like the demons of Oblivion, many of these pale armies had been destroyed in the wars with the Primordial Ones. Shattered bones and dust were all that remained in their crumbling caskets. In frustration, the Shadow ripped open the empty sarcophagi that lined the walls, one by one. But he saw only the sad remains of cobwebbed corpses, whose scaled armor and rusting swords crumbled to white powder at the touch.

But at the end of a long dark hallway the Shadow had come upon a massive black stone that blocked his path. The dark rock of its door had been welded together with great bands of iron to seal it from the outside. As the Shadow looked closer, he saw that in fact it was sealed from the inside, as if whatever hid within had desired its own undisturbed rest.

Carved upon the door he saw the image of a great tree, twisted and bent, beneath which lay a rocky pool of dark water. Beneath the well, he could barely see the carvings of dark roses, whose lithe and thorny stems drooped low with their shriveled and dying blooms. Upon the great bands of the door he saw etched runes of an unknown tongue he could not understand. As he touched the iron, from ages of rust and rot it fell away before him. The Shadow, seeing the door falling away, then tore at the last of its stones. And he watched as the image of the tree and well collapsed before him, turning to dust.

He looked into the darkness and saw only a strange table within. But upon its thick slab lay a dark and sensuous woman, clad in black and crimson capes, with long, dark, and tangled tresses covering her face. But as the Shadow pulled away her hair, he saw that her face was a sickly green color, sunken with great cracks upon it, born of timeless age. Her nose was long and crooked, and her eyes deep set and hollow, like a skull.

The Shadow bent down to touch her face. For it stirred a dark memory in his fractured mind of someone he had once known as a child. But just as quickly as that memory came, it was washed away. Suddenly her dark eyes opened. And he saw within them a swirling green cast, with cat-like centers black as obsidian. This was the witch called Anissa, a being of the underworld, who though beautiful in body, was most horrible in countenance and depraved in spirit. By the touch of a Child of Night alone could she awaken. And so by the hand of the Shadow was she now stirred from her eternal rest, as a newborn again reborn, her spirit returning to flesh from the nether worlds from which it had roamed.

But Anissa was an enchanted being, and not of this world. For she was a witch of the shadows. And she had been a queen of her sisters, the Cromwich, in a past life. In the youth of the world, the Endless Night had summoned her sleeping spirit up from the strange waters that had flowed beneath his fortress. By the black arts was she summoned forth to aid him. Pulled from the waters by him, she was then raised as a child by the Night, ruling the nighttime skies by his side. She ever after would do his bidding, using her coven and their black enchantments against his enemies, in the ancient wars that had befallen him and his kind.

Though she remained obedient to him, to another more malevolent being was she most devoted. For she had been spawned from a matriarchal spirit, which slept in the black waters of a pool that bubbled up from the bottom of the world. That well had hidden the broken spirit of her mother, a dark queen, whose existence and origin none had yet perceived.

The dark pool had belched forth many abominations from its malevolent waters. But most powerful of these were the witches, the Cromwich, which she had created from her own vile breath to curse the living, and do her bidding in this world. For she had made them to fulfill a malevolent purpose unknown to all, defying the larger destiny of the world through their deceit and duplicity. And so the Cromwich carried great hatred towards the Primordial Ones and their children who had sought to forge the world anew.

The Cromwich were the true children of the dark arts, conceived themselves from the ancient arts of witchcraft and wizardry. For the spirits of these sinister sisters had gathered together again to create a most treacherous coven. In time, fed by the lies of Anissa, the Endless Night had gathered their spirits to him, using them against his own brothers. But in his final defeat, they were all slain except for Anissa, whom the Endless Night had hidden away. For his cruel brothers had taken his children away in chains. And as a beloved child unto him, Anissa was all that remained of that which he had once loved and lost.

By the touch of the Shadow, Anissa's spirit was called forth from the land of the undead. Her arms crossed, Anissa rose up from her stony bed and looked upon the Shadow's face. Seeing the features of the Endless Night in the contours of the Shadow's rugged countenance, she knew who he was. But the Shadow, in frustration, threw her to the ground. For he sought only to find his father's enchanted wings. But as the witch crawled up from the floor, she saw that within him dwelt the will of the Nightmare Unending, a power whose manipulative and destructive evil she knew now had risen again. And she gazed at the fallen son with eyes that blazed with a sickly sap green light.

The Shadow then left her, seeking his father's tomb once more in the depths of the fortress. But not finding his father's crypt, he flew out of the keep in a rage. Overlooking the seas, he sat again upon the rocky crag where he had often perched, deep in thought.

But Anissa followed him. And seeing him there alone, she came to him, questioning him, "Tell me your thoughts, oh dark one. What tortures you so? Why have you returned here, to the empty house of your father and mother?"

The Shadow sat, unmoving, peering into the dark void that stretched above the tranquil seas. He then spoke in a somber voice, saying, "Be gone witch. You know nothing of me, or what has become of this cursed world since returning to it from your insipid rest. But I will tell you, if you wish. I am a slave of another, he who is named Agapor. But I seek my father's wings, the black wings he once wore in his dark victory over his brothers. For by the powers of the Wings of Night alone shall I find my freedom."

The Shadow walked to the edge of the cliff, looking down, saying under his breath, "Still, I am tortured, in pain, and bound to unending agony by my master's powerful geas and forceful will over me. He has sent me on an impossible errand which I cannot fulfill. And the black manacle upon his wrist shall bear down its full wrath upon my mind and spirit until this sacred vow to him is fulfilled."

Anissa then came to him, asking, "What mission is this?" The Shadow looked into the strange glowing eyes of the witch, saying, "I must find a Primordial One, he who is named the Twilight Mist. And in fulfillment of my master's mission am I now eternally bound." The witch smiled with knowing eyes.

The Shadow then turned away, and looked out from his rocky perch, searching again for a sign in the depths of the starless skies, as he brooded alone in the darkness, thinking upon the mystery of his father's lost tomb.

Hearing his plight, Anissa flew off on her broom of yew, returning to the ancient crypts that lay beneath Midnight's gloomy keep. With her dark enchantments, she then cast a spell of awakening, summoning forth her vile sister-spirits from the catacombs beneath the fortress. Then was heard a roaring within the labyrinth of the fortress, as of dry warm winds cast about its hallways.

The Cromwich took shape in their tombs, gathering the dust of their bones together, and rising forth as the Witches of Midnight. They then came before Anissa. For to her were they alone devoted. Anissa returned to the Shadow with her sisters, and gave unto him her powers to command them. The Shadow looked upon her with his cold and heartless eyes. But he now saw that within her lay a valued weapon, which he could use for his own benefit.

The Shadow, now pleased, spoke to the Cromwich that had gathered before him. And he sent them off on many errands, high into the Heavens, searching for the lands of the Twilight Mist. They could travel great distances, riding with wings of pitch upon brooms made of blackest yew. They alone could see, with their wide eyes of glowing green jade, the hidden ether, forbidden spaces, and secret planes which lay between this world and all others. And so, upon the currents of the nighttime skies, they flew, deep into the unknown realms that lay between the dreaming and the awakening world, searching for the Lands of Mist where the hidden twilit father had once dwelt.

The Shadow then turned to Anissa. He came upon her violently, grabbing her by the throat with his scaly black claws. He then demanded, "Tell me where the body of my father, the Endless Night, has been interred."

"I do not know of his tomb, Nor have I any knowledge of his death," she gasped. "For many untold eons have I slept, through countless brutal ages, as the spinning wheel of time creaked and groaned about my bedchamber. And so the fate of many has not been given to me." But in truth, Anissa had no knowledge of the Endless Night. For the memory of her forgotten lover had faded away forever from her cold heart, like last petals of a shriveled rose, whose rich color turns to ash with the passing of time. And so the Shadow released her.

The Shadow was thus denied the Wings of Night. But ever in his mind he pondered the whereabouts of his fallen father, and the powers denied him. For with those black wings could he slay his master and plunge this world into eternal night. And so had his sinister plot and passion remained. Yet, as he stared into the mysterious seas below, a new and even greater desire had grown within him. For he had begun to sense a more malicious power hidden beneath the waves.

The Shadow and Anissa flew off together, out across the far reaches of the Dreaming Seas, until something strange rose forth from the water before them.

THE FACELESS FORM

Agapor had sat brooding upon his throne alone in the darkness for many nights, awaiting word from his servant. Then was heard the beating of wings, and the rush of air. The Shadow had returned to Oblivion, riding upon the dark winds that continually roared down into the underworld from the Heavens above.

The Shadow swept down into his halls, landing before Agapor on the stairs. He came kneeling before his master, saying, "Master, I have seen something new and strange, hidden in the farthest corners of the world."

But Agapor looked upon the horrible face of the creature beside the Shadow, seeing in her eyes of jade a spirit of something odd and unnatural. He asked the Shadow, "Where have you found this creature of darkness?"

But the Shadow said, "She is Anissa, a witch and servant of my father. She has now awakened to guide us in our search for the Twilight Mist. For by her spectral vision and that of her witch-sisters, may we see beyond the gray veil of the fogs that wrap about the outer world, and discover the hidden enemy that dwells within it."

But as Anissa looked upon Agapor's hand, the dark ring glowed in the presence of the witch. And she was drawn to its strange light, desiring it greatly.

The Shadow then said to Agapor that high above the Dreaming Seas he had flown with Anissa, until they had come to the great falls of Wendalia, into which his master had fallen in ages past. But beyond that pit there had hung a thick fog, which the seas had made, dense and impenetrable to all eyes. With her dark magic, Anissa then commanded the mist to depart, removing the clouded veil that lay before them. They then saw dimly, between the clouds, a stretch of black cliffs, which had for many ages stood defiant, towering above the sea.

Here lay a savage land, mysterious and unknown, a realm apart, born of the rock and bathed in the dew cast up from the seas. Where the ocean and land met as one, black cliffs now stood, looking down defiantly upon them, casting their fearful reflections upon the water below. Upon those grim heights had grown ancient and hoary oaks, standing guard as one bastion, shoulder to shoulder, like impenetrable statues. Their wide rugged trunks had grown high into the skies, so that no light or darkness shone forth, into or out of the forest and fog that lay wrapped about the cliffs.

The Shadow told Agapor that for many nights he had stood upon the rocky cliffs that hung above the falls of the seas. But all he had seen were the impassable trees, which stood before him like an unending maze. For he could find no path beyond their trunks, nor mist, nor light, or any signs of life about them.

The Shadow, in frustration, had departed that cursed place. But Anissa had remained. For no pathway could escape her vision, nor doorway be hidden from her view. And the shining, cat-like eyes of the witch could see the dimmest light that might shine, and the faintest footsteps of the living.

She then saw the traces of a faint glow, which had shined out from the depths of that strange wood. Following its trail, she had found a hidden path through the wall of oaks, and the last glimmer of a guardian light that seemed to follow a track leading further into the forest. As she stood within its eerie radiance, she pondered its miraculous form and color. For the light seemed to shine with the essence of something she had once known. And she stood still for a moment, haunted by its memory.

She had flown off to find the Shadow, telling him of the hidden doorway she had found, opening into the woods. The Shadow had then returned, walking forth through the fog-enshrouded door, and past the monstrous black trees that had guarded it so well.

Travelling through an endless maze, he had followed a mysterious, misty light that lit up the trail before him. Suddenly he saw the faint fog of the Twilight Mist rising above the trees in the distance. Their strange curling clouds crept through the canopy, drifting down to the forest floor about his feet.

The Shadow then reached out to touch it. With his nose and tongue he tasted its wisps upon his black lips, as he had done many times before above the twilit seas. He knew its foul smell and taste. For it was of the Twilight Mist, his former master.

He cackled with delight. For now he had seen where the Twilight Mist had crept. But as he stood upon the heights of those cliffs, he saw something strange in the distance. Like a moth beguiled and baited by a fiendish flame, the Shadow was drawn towards it. It seemed to glow from the very heart of the woods, from some secret source he could not discern.

But the Shadow was fearful of it. For that lucid light burned his black skin with its radiant fire. It was not of this world, nor of the silver flames that dimly flickered upon the Mountains of Heaven. From the deepest interior had come this strange, living light. Its radiance soon blinded him, searing his eyes and face, so that in terror he fled from the forest. And so had he now returned forthright to his master's halls, to reveal to him this great and yet troubling discovery.

From his throne Agapor smiled, and said unto the Shadow, "At last, my father has been found. I shall now go forth and take him by force."

But the Shadow said to Agapor, "Thy father shall not be taken so easily, master. For his mists stretch back into eternity, into the hollows of the endless woods, whose depths no being can ever know or penetrate. Its earth is bound to the spirit of the Immortal Clay, whose form may not be sundered from it. Unknown forces dwell therein, derived from him, which may not easily be taken or harmed. Nor shall the earth or clay, or even the trees themselves, be consumed, except by the powers of the devourers that hide themselves in the Great Beyond. For the roots of its mysterious trees hold that firmament firmly within their grasp. And many ages would it take to destroy them. Their strange force sustains it still, against the violence of the frightful seas, which have long battered its stubborn shores."

But the Shadow now knew that the origin of its guardian spirit lay within the golden lights that beamed out from Phantaia's depths—a loving and giving spirit, whose burning lantern would remain hidden from all eyes.

The Shadow said, "Yet, by another route might you enter those woods and find your father. For the forest is sustained by its own sacred fire, which burns within its heart. With your powers, you alone might find its candle and extinguish it. And with the failing of the light the forest would perish. Your father would then be revealed to you."

But Agapor said, "I do not care whether this forest or its mysterious light lives or dies. For I know not its meaning or purpose, only that my father must be found. I shall wait an eternity if I must, to see him driven from that wilderness. For once he is found, then shall the seas falter and An be freed." The Shadow scowled at Agapor in the darkness of the chamber. For he did not understand the feeble and futile plots of his master.

But the Shadow told Agapor, "Master, I fear that the last powers of the Primordial Ones have gathered in that new land, joining as one in the forest depths to wage war upon the children of the Night and the Void. Within you lies the power and the will needed to destroy the living light that now sustains that wood. And so have Anissa and I plotted to discern the source of its life-giving glow, so that you might go forth and obliterate it."

The Shadow then looked down in thought. For he hated this new light, with a passion that burned to the core of who he was. But the Shadow in secret also feared it. He would not go near it again, nor could his servants find its source or face its blinding rays. For many nights alone the Shadow had sat, looking down from his dark abode upon the crags of Midnight, staring into the mysterious fringes of those twilit woods. And to him it remained a vast and terrible place, whose secret purpose, source, and design, like the seas, he could not yet comprehend.

But Agapor looked down upon the face of the Shadow in silence, and with a renewed determination. For he now resolved to find his father. He would destroy this new forest realm by force if he had to. Agapor then said to the Shadow, "Leave me to my thoughts."

As Agapor sat on his throne, thinking upon his father, a tiny ray of light beamed out from the black ring that lay upon his right hand. The spirit of the Limitless Void slowly issued forth from its dark crystal, his wisps of gray smoke rising forth before him, until the shadowy phantom of the Limitless Void stood before him.

The ghostly and wrinkled face of the Void looked upon Agapor with sadness, saying, "I have suffered horribly, my child, in the cruel confines of this ring. For within its crystal lies the collected evil of many worlds long past. That from which the ring has eternally fed—the angst and anger of perverted and poisonous love—is all that remains inside. For within it lives only corruption, and a deep and vengeful hatred for this world. My spirit has been wracked with suffering from its great malice bent against me. For I have no love or hate left in my heart to offer it."

Agapor stood up, and looked upon his uncle's woeful face. And he saw the sad plight of the Limitless Void, feeling great pity for him. But he thought upon the ruin of the world he had made, replying in anger, "It is *you* who have cursed this world with your own evils. And so have you and the ring now become one in purpose. But I am left with the ruin of this world, uncle, born of your hatred for it and your endless wars against it."

The Void looked with grim, but watery eyes upon Agapor again, saying, "I have come only to help you, my child. For I see, as I do in myself, your lingering hatred of your father." Agapor turned away, sitting back down in despair. For he saw clearly in his mind that he had become a creature like his uncle, the Limitless Void. But he told him, "My father alone now holds the key to An's freedom. I have no choice."

Agapor looked again upon the tortured face of the Limitless Void. And he saw that the ring, which he now held, had changed him. Agapor then told the Void he would shatter that evil relic, and release him from his agony if he desired.

But the Limitless Void in dismay told Agapor that he would prefer the torturous prison to annihilation at the hands of the

Nothingness. For should the ring be destroyed, his spirit would be free to roam the world. It would then be found by the Nothingness and devoured by him. So had he vowed to protect the cursed ring, even though he loathed it still.

The ghost of the Limitless Void then told Agapor that he had returned to assist him in his struggles. For he sought only to guide the boy, and help him in that troubled world. He would show him the twisting paths that led to the depths of the Great Beyond. For only the evil that dwelt in that decrepit space could help him find the Twilight Mist.

He should go to them now. By a pale blue light would he be shown the way. But he warned Agapor that he should hide the ring from the Nothingness, and place it about his neck where they might not see it. For they would seek to take it and destroy it. Yet are they fearful of it, knowing they cannot harm it. For it lives by a will beyond their own. And so had he hid in its crystal, far from harm.

The Limitless Void then disappeared into the dark crystal of the ring. And its strange blue light began to glow upon Agapor's hand.

Agapor rose from his throne, following the beam of the ring which cast a faint light upon the path before him. Travelling on a mission most secret, he followed the strange ghostly light down into the mysterious tunnels that led into the pits of Oblivion. Pursing the glow of the ring, he saw its pale light descend a black and slimy staircase, winding its way through secret tunnels, deep under the earth, until he stood before the yawning gray spaces that fell away into the limitless depths of the Great Beyond.

The spirit of the Limitless Void then spoke from within the opaline crystal of the ring, telling Agapor to call out to the powers that slept there. By the cryptic words given to him would those beings then come to him. Agapor quickly hid the ring under his shirt.

By the black words now bestowed to him, Agapor called forth the foul spirits that dwelt within those foggy depths. He then saw, rising from the milky clouds, terrible shapes begin to gather themselves in the distance. Great gray storms billowed and churned in the gloomy and infinite space, filling it in with their thunderous storms. Agapor watched with apprehension, as a frightening face took shape before him.

From out of the deepest pits of the abyss of the world had the sinister Nothingness now appeared. Looking down on the boy with its jet black eyes, it spoke to Agapor, saying, "Why have I been summoned forth, awakened from my timeless rest. The countless children in this world constantly come to me, calling for death. Their weeping spirits have stood before me many times, wrenched from their fallen bodies in unnumbered battles, seeking release from endless suffering. But on their spirits and flesh have my brother and I now become engorged. And by their consumption, I remain satiated."

Agapor stood before the bloated spirit, and with bold words, said, "Spirit, I come to you, seeking not death but desire. Share with me the secretive nature of the twilit forest, whose strange and shimmering woods yet live in a heavenly place apart from my own."

But the Nothingness looked down upon the brave child, and felt in the boy the presence of the spirit of the Limitless Void, though he could not see him. And he saw by the black manacles upon his wrists that the Children of the Night were his to command. The Nothingness then looked upon Agapor with a wary eye. For he did not trust the child. Yet in his matrix mind that being saw in Agapor one who might yet serve his will.

Agapor noticed that the spirit had seen the iron on his wrists. And he saw that the thoughts of that being might soon turn against him. And so he spoke boldly, saying, "Mighty Spirit of the Great Beyond, I have slain the Limitless Void and taken his powers for my own. And so have his lands been bestowed to me. For am I the lord and king over all of Oblivion. Its dark servants now serve only me. Soon shall I wage a new war upon this world. By your own will and assistance might I be victorious over it."

But the Nothingness in his cloud, twisting in ever-sickening shapes and coils, drew himself into a monstrous form in the gray depths—a beast most horrid with sharp horns and teeth, and with sunken cheeks and eyes, hollow and dark.

He then spoke in a thunderous voice, "Why have you come seeking my help, when within you hide the powers over the Limitless Void and the children of the Endless Night, who you alone now command?"

Agapor, frozen in fear of that monstrous being, said nothing. But the Nothingness looked down upon the boy again, and saw within his weak heart that which the boy had truly feared. For that creature was not of this world, and had in him the all-seeing eye that perceives the depths of the spirit of those that stand before it. He saw that within Agapor was hidden great anger and vengeance—born of his fear of the Dreaming Seas, for his father the Twilight Mist, and for his servant the Shadow. But seeing the pitiful truth of Agapor's mind and heart, the Nothingness only laughed.

The Nothingness then looked deep into the eyes of the child. His cloud slowly transformed itself, taking the form of a bearded man, dark-skinned and swarthy, with a crown upon his head. The Nothingness said to Agapor, "You have come for another reason. You seek your father, the Twilight Mist, who still hides in the depths of the Forest of Twilight, the wilderness they call Phantaia."

The Nothingness spoke again, saying, "Look upon my face, Agapor. It is one dear to you, thy beloved father. If you hate him so, go forth into Phantaia, find him yourself, and avenge your pain. For he now dwells beside the child of the river whom he dearly loves, the spirit of the sleeping spring that wells up its silver waters, and the golden child of the seed that shines forth within its heart. But he waits there for another, whose destiny in this world has yet to be revealed."

Agapor thought upon this mystery, for the Nothingness knew more than he had ever fathomed. But Agapor stood defiant, saying, "No eyes under Heaven can find my father in that savage wood, save by the destruction of the trees in which he now hides. I will speak the truth now. I need your help. For I seek to destroy

Phantaia so that I might find my father. If you will send a servant to help me, I will be a servant unto you ever after."

The Nothingness smiled at Agapor, saying, "If you desire to find your father, I will summon forth my brother's greatest servant to assist you, she who will be yours to command as you wish. And by her endless appetites shall Phantaia perish. But not until Phantaia's cherished one falls shall its demise be complete."

The Nothingness then smiled. He said to Agapor, "For I require an offering in return, a spirit born of the Primordial Ones."

Agapor asked. "What offering might that be?"

The Nothingness replied, "Your first child must be given unto me."

But Agapor said, "What child of mine do you seek? For I have no children."

But the Nothingness only smiled, saying, "If you shed a drop of your blood into the empty space below, then you shall be bound to our agreement. And the being you seek shall be your servant, ever after."

Agapor then stood upon the precipice, uncertain. Yet he thought upon An again. He would do it for An, for his sister, so that she might be free, and the world in turn, free of the seas' own nightmares.

But as he reached for his dagger, the ring upon his chest glowed with a warm light. For it lay close to his heart. And he had thought upon the mysterious child, yet unborn to him, whose life he was now sacrificing. He closed his dark eyes until it felt as though time itself had stood still. And without even knowing it, before he had opened his eyes, he had sliced his right finger.

As he looked down, a single drop of blood fell into the gray space below the precipice. And as it fell, he saw in its depths a horrible beast, the creature called the Emptiness, the consumer of flesh, stretch up its long black tongue through the mist to drink of Agapor's blood. And it was succored by it.

Then from the dark depths below, he saw a horrible blue cloud, billowing up from the abyss, rising slowly at first, a storm larger and more terrible than any he had yet seen. This was the cloud of the servant to the Emptiness, the Faceless Form who is named Yana, or Death.

She was a being most terrible to behold, the queen of her kind, and Oversoul of the Magra. But she had not come to battle the seas like her brothers. For fear of her powers, few would disturb her. She was a dreadful tempest, her form fashioned long ago from black and violent storms, whose vast cloud of many mouths had eaten away the last hollow rinds and remnants of past worlds. No being had ever escaped her. For she had consumed them all in the end.

She had no heart or mind. Neither the nightmare nor the dream, the darkness nor the light, the living force, nor the might of evil's worst violence pitted against her could ever destroy her. For she was born of the mind of the Emptiness, whose love for the taste of flesh, and death, lives on eternally through her.

To Agapor was that fearsome cloud of Death now eternally bound in servitude, until such time as his own death should finally free it, unleashing its angry rampage upon the world.

Agapor spoke to the sinister spirit, demanding Yana go forth to do his bidding. But as it rose up, Agapor saw that he could command its great form by just his thoughts and visions. For his violence and rage became her own.

He then commanded Yana to go forth and destroy the twilight forest that now held his father in its fastness. The storm boiled and seethed, straining to contain its innate fury, until it exploded out across the cliffs and peaks of Oblivion that hung above Agapor's head. Its sinister clouds rolled across those bleak lands, tearing away their jagged tops, and pouring over the Dreaming Seas, until its long billowing tendrils stretched towards the cliffs of misty Phantaia.

As Agapor watched the storm drift away, he thought he heard a faint whisper coming from the Great Beyond, the lips of the now-sleeping Nothingness as it returned to its gray depths. Only the word *Ana* did it speak.

* * *

Agapor had sent the great storms of Yana, the Magra Oversoul, down upon the cliffs by the falls of the Dreaming Seas. There the very fringes of Phantaia were most vulnerable. For beyond its falls the rocks were no longer protected by the seas. Below the misty waste of its lonesome cliffs there remained only a gray abyss, wherein nothing but a quiet space had dwelt since the birth of the world. Here the Dreaming Seas could not reach, nor guard its brother's lands from the evil that crept up from below. For Phantaia's wide cliffs of oaks stood exposed in that place, hanging precipitously above the emptiness of Wendalia, looking out across the ominous spaces that stretched away, back into the dark depths of that formless infinity.

Below the tranquil forests, the dark storms of Yana began to boil and seethe, drifting up from the empty waste below. For the Magra Oversoul had come to consume that virgin wood. Her vast vortex, with great wheels of clouds and fog, began to spin and churn angrily in the depths, until from out of her gaping mouth there blossomed forth a monstrous mass of clouds and storms, towering up and twisting forth in ominous shapes and tortured forms.

Above the heads of the wooded cliffs, a towering tempest soon formed, within whose walls flashed great bolts of blue lightning, crisscrossing in webs of chaotic light across the skies. From the shadowy gray depths, the colder clouds belched up a blast of violent winds, which bore their full fury upon the terrified trees above. The unbending oaks then began to creak and sway as the terrible tumult fast approached.

Her storm front soon encircled the trees, which had stood so bravely upon the rocky heights. Rain and hail, ice and sleet flew down from the swirling blue clouds, as a vicious gale beat upon the bent and wailing trees.

The ancient oaks, which had formed an impenetrable gateway upon the cliffs, were torn limb from limb in the violent storm, their trunks and roots yanked away from the rocky face. Slung up into the clouds, and shredded in the Heavens, their splintered remains were then thrown down into the mouth of the insane

Magra Mother, where they were consumed and devoured within the belly of the angry and churning sky.

All about the borders of Phantaia was heard the horrible roar of the savage destruction endlessly rent upon the woods. The ripping away of limbs and roots could be heard from far away, such that the insatiable hunger of Yana had caused the distant trees to shake and tremble in terror. For to them alone would be heard the screaming of the trees, their innocent brethren, crying out in horror in the depths of that terrible gale.

Yana's storms next turned their rage upon the stony face, tearing at the dark rocks of Phantaia. Monstrous boulders were ripped away by her ferocious winds, until great hunks of stone and earth were torn from the cliff face. The forces of the storm had penetrated the very firmament of Phantaia, clawing and tearing at its earth with relentless wind and rain, until wide swaths of the land succumbed at last to her violence. Yana sucked the rock and soil down into the gaping black orifice of her boiling tempest, which turned brown with the blood of the earth as it spun about in the endless waste of barren space below.

For many ages the fringes of Phantaia and the forces of Yana had fallen upon each other in unending war. Yet parts of the rock and forest had bravely resisted the devouring mouth of that evil. The storms had returned with even greater fury, pummeling the rocks and earth about the highest cliffs so that no trees would grow there, save the crooked husks of once-grandiose oaks who alone had somehow defied their wrath. Yana then wrapped her great arms around Phantaia's distant fringes, out into the infinite gulf. The wide storm front pushed deeper into the lands of Phantaia itself, tearing away at the new green growth that had sprouted there.

But like the Dreaming Seas, Phantaia had been created by the Primordial Ones. It had been forged within the fires of the Creative Flame that yet burned brightly within the Immortal Clay. And so, at its heart was it truly impenetrable and immutable like its father.

But so too was it sustained like the seas about its shores, by a mysterious enchantment that evil could not yet see or harm. And it had drawn to itself, by its own inherent wisdom, a vast and collective force, untamed and yet still unknown, born of water, earth, air, and light, and a will for life, self-sustained by the inner essence of its immeasurable spirit. What secrets Phantaia held within its depths, those storms could not know. For Yana soon found she could not penetrate its proud and hopeful heart, nor devour the lands that lay beyond its outermost woods and ranges.

Thus, after an age, the land and trees of Phantaia had persevered against the wrath of that terrible Magra. And so, like the seas, there remained a truce between the hand of good and the fist of evil. Though much was taken from that forest by the viciousness of Yana's hunger, much was replaced by the timeless growth of young trees, the pushing up of fresh earth, and the birth of new life in that magical realm, sustained by the spirit of the Immortal Clay and his son the Rock Eternal.

Yet it was the Sacred Seed that had fathered the forest, who would not allow Phantaia to be destroyed by Yana, nor its children to die in vain by her hateful hand. Its young trees had gathered in force upon the fringes of that wilderness, and by their limber saplings, newly born, bravely defied the winds and rain, and the dreadful carnage of the dead and dying that fell before them in the endless storm.

In time, they too would grow upon the splintered cliffs as seedlings, long ago shed from the boles of their dying parents, which had in ages past perished in the moldy ruin and wreckage of that storm-torn realm. And so had newer oaks risen, yet again, to grow valiantly upon the cliffs, defying the violent storms of Yana, and protecting Phantaia's inner children by their rugged vanguard.

But the endless battle with those storms and winds raged on, until in time there remained a perpetual no-man's land of weathered rocks and nightmarish trees, which yet clung to the faces of its blackened cliffs. It was a blasted landscape thrown into constant dread and terror—a battered middle-realm where the storms raged on through countless ages, to torture the living trees that had yet remained there. The mounds and mountains of rock and soil soon turned dark as pitch. The trees twisted into horrific shapes. Only a broken wasteland then remained, where nothing grew but the stern and defiant remnants of worn boulders and ancient plants, long ago bent and broken by the relentless winds of the Magra Overlord.

In time that land became distorted and unreal, molded by the unending tortures that Yana had wrought upon it. Within this treacherous realm of violence, the brighter spirits of that wood would not tread. For this undead place became a haunted space of forgotten dreams and forlorn dreamers who, lost within its blasted landscape of stumps and logs, were doomed to perish alone within its maddening mists. For all that came to dwell there were eventually cast into the oblivion of its tempests, or lost for all time, buried in its endless canyons and caverns of waste and rot.

Yet hidden within the ancient trees and dark soil of that black and cursed land dwelt many tortured spirits, which had come to possess it wholly. These demonic spirits had hid amongst the wreckage and the ruins of an earlier time, when those rocks had been a part of the Realms of Oblivion. So had the evil spirits of that brutal realm come to haunt Phantaia. For in the ancient days of the conflict of storm and sea, when the house of the Limitless Void had fallen, a part of his most distant domain was spared destruction by the seas, and cast up and onto the new lands that would become Phantaia.

Here, the last remnants of that evil kingdom, its many shattered keeps and castles, graves and tombs, yet survived as mossy monuments to its former glory. But so too had its sleeping monsters and hidden beasts come to haunt the silent wastes of Phantaia. For many demons of might, fallen in ancient wars waged in those lands, had remained buried under its vast piles of rubble and refuse.

These tragic armies of ancient conflicts would now possess the rocks and trees of Phantaia's farthest realms. Asleep in timeless nightmares, alone and undisturbed, these demon-spirits now returned to sleep, dreaming of past wars, and marred by the memory of the many evils they had inflicted upon the innocent in countless ages past.

These phantoms of the ignoble dead, the last fallen children of the Primordial Ones, would haunt the land until, summoned forth by their master, they would rise again to wage their insidious war once more. For they would soon turn their foul hatred upon Phantaia, creeping into its interior to extinguish the light of the living flame that had come into it, and seeking to slay the last of the children of the Primordial Ones.

This grim domain of demonic spirits was called Avaras, the land of the fading light. For this was the name given to Phantaia itself, long ago in its youthful days, before the coming of its trees and lights, when there had wrapped about its shores the eerie fog of the Twilight Mist. And so for him was it named the Forest of Twilight.

But in time, the Mist had fled to its interior, guarding the hidden powers that had gathered there with his lavender mists. The darkened half of that haunted forest had remained behind, sundered from its brighter living half that lay within its interior. For in Avaras never again would the faded lights of dreaming twilight, nor the spirit of hope borne by the shining lights of brighter days, nor even the lengthening shadows of the night's satin sheet, dare dwell in that cursed and evil wood. And so had the malicious trees of Avaras been separated from their nobler brethren that lived within its peaceful heart.

The cursed spirits that now crept within Avaras had long ago possessed its once-living trees with their demonic spirits. And so had Avaras became a haunted forest filled with ancient hazels and sinister oaks, whose pale eyes and bearded mouths peered up into the wicked skies, and scowled. Yet these dark trees would remain a bulwark against the never-ending destruction of Yana, whose fearful might still boiled about its phantom fringes.

So had the strange wilderness of Phantaia remained in this divided state until in time the evil that hid within Avaras would rise up again against its sibling trees, seeking to obliterate the source of the shining light that had long sustained them.

THE CHILD OF THE SEA

The Dreaming Seas had grown full and wide, gently rising and falling with the tide. Rocking back and forth in the deep, the waves to some rhythmic heart did beat. While that weary world, weighted by despair, waited for hopeful tidings the seas might bear.

In its depths had dwelt the lonely An, queen-of-the-seas, undisturbed in her timeless tomb. For in the gloom of her silent chamber, she fell once more into endless slumber, disturbed by dreams of things yet to be, strange visions of futures, fleeting and foreboding, yet vaguely seen. But within her mind there bloomed a visage, whose spirit blossomed forth a prescient image.

For in the darkness of her faded dreams appeared the unnumbered faces of her children. As they came to her, she saw a caravan of innumerable spirits walking through death's countless doors. But their lives acted out on the stage of time revealed to her the sad future that lay in store.

She saw them briefly flash before her, like a dim reflection upon a shining pool, until their faded shadows hovered there awhile, and were gone. Into her dreams returned the cold and empty night once more. For within her crept the constant sorrow she had before. She yearned with all her heart and spirit, within her omniscient mind, to weave their memory upon the empty Loom of Time, whose great wheel now about her turned.

Thus, in the heart of those seas, long ago was woven this tragic Tapestry of Woe, whose sorrowful tale all would know, and none might soon forget.

In the depths of the ocean was heard a mournful cry, as of a child alone and afraid. Distant at first, drowned by the roar of the crashing waves, its sound grew louder and louder until it echoed across the surface of the waters. As the song of the seas fell silent, the whispering winds of the woods also grew still, until under the gloomy skies only the pitiful cries of that child could be heard.

Birthed in those wild waters thus came the child named Ana, the heart-of-the-sea, lovely daughter of the dreaming mother An. In a warm and gentle embrace was she held by her mother, enjoined to her heart, and with her tender love entwined. She was the one and only child of that queen-of-the-seas. And of the timeless beauty of her mother's wondrous waters was she made.

Though of her mother's spirit was she filled, she was unlike her mother in many ways. Like the Sacred Seed, she was born of the living flesh, the Vatar. So was she, the silver-one, born into this world, separate from the ocean's sphere and forever sundered from the cursed prison of the seas.

But Ana had been given her mother's great heart and spirit. So, mother-like was she named. For the heart of An and Ana had come from the mother-seas, that which Agapor had broken. And so, by its rupture had the seas risen up against him, casting him away from the sea's beloved child. From that heart the waters of this world had then flowed, spilling into it their many blessings and curses.

This world would have been destroyed by those waters had the Dreaming Seas by their compassionate will not held them back. For that fractured heart, like a hollow cauldron, now held the last of her spirit. This heart-space was called the Luffa, the Sacred Heart, which she gave to her daughter An. She then gave it to Ana upon her birth. And Ana would come to treasure it above all other things in this world.

But within her heart had remained the last of the Sacred Waters. For they alone now held the life-giving force of the Essence Eternal within their enchanted dew. And so within Ana lay hidden the last of His great Hope for the world. She would covet those waters, holding them close to her breast, though she knew not their strange purpose. Thus was the Luffa, the heart that beat within her, a thing most sacred.

But her mother had not given her the vessel of her heart, only the vehicle to carry its precious waters into this world. For they could flow from no other. And so were those waters a gift to be given, yet never received. Both these treasures were given by An to Ana with deep love and care, and yet with the forethought and future desire that she would someday gift them with enduring love to another in their time of need.

But those mysterious waters would not be tamed, nor bound forever, by the heart of the sea. For they desired to flow wild and free, bold and boundless in this world. Fully unleashed upon it, only then could they bind the children of this world to their singular power and purpose, which few would ever comprehend.

Mother An had held her daughter Ana close to her, until the time when she could hold her no more. For it was not Ana's fate to remain in that watery grave, or to lay beside her mother in everlasting dreams. Storm clouds rose upon the horizon, until the threatening sound of thunder and the faraway flash of lightning drifted down upon the ocean floor. And the troubled skies seemed to grow dark again with the lengthening of an ominous shadow, cast down from the mantle of Heaven.

Yet the seas remained calm, silent and serene, until with gentle hands they reached down through the crystalline depths and gently pulled the crying child from her mother's arms. Out of that sea-tomb the child named Ana rose forth until she was thrown up from the ocean depths, wrapped in a red amaranth which blossomed forth upon the surface of the seas. Carried upon the dark waters, drifting in the arms of the ocean, the child lay quiet and sleeping once more, rocked gently back and forth by the loving waves.

Adrift alone, by currents swift and strong, the child asleep upon that wide-petalled bloom was carried far from harm in the silent gloom. On her mother's endless tears she floated, until her little form found its way to the shining shores of gloomy Phantaia.

Upon a lonely stretch of beach, the surf of the Dreaming Seas had now departed, depositing their tiny cargo upon the sands of that quiet shore. The petals wrapped about her melted into the sea. And the attentive tides retreated from the sands in which she lay, leaving her wrapped in the raiment of her mother's silver pall.

So was she was clothed, like the glistening waters that encircle this world, this tiny pale-faced shining girl.

But Ana could not awaken as she slept upon the warm sand, so that it seemed within a single moment a thousand ages passed again.

From out of the still ocean rose a gentle breeze. The breath of the seas now moved upon the surface of the waters and across the face of the child, blowing her dark hair from her cheeks. That whispering wind then moved beyond the shore, and through the trees of Phantaia. The leaves upon them softly stirred, until was heard from within some eerie voice of the forest calling out from some darker place, deeper within its haunted wood. And so was heard by the seas the woods' own returning cry.

Hearing that haunting sound, the daughter of the dreamer awoke, slowly opening her eyes. She stood upon the sand and looked about her. Before her stretched an endless shoreline whose bright beaches lay before a wild and wasteful sea. Its gray waters lay shrouded in clouds, bathed in sea foam, white and frothy.

Behind her stood the tall trees of Phantaia, whose wet limbs curled and twisted up into the Heavens, like the bent arms of towering black giants. The huge oaks stood before the dark woods like an ominous wall, thick, dark, and impenetrable. Ana wrapped her shroud about her, and walked upon the windy shore, stumbling through the cold sands which filled the gaps between her toes. The seas, whipped up by those winds, sent forth a cool spray of salt and sand across her face and arms. As she beheld the unimaginable space of that ominous shoreline, she began to feel scared and uncertain.

Deep within the forest of Phantaia there had arisen a mist. Its eerie tendrils sank down from the tops of the trees and crept out across the beaches. Its lavender lights seemed to cast strange shadows as it flowed past her. Her little form was soon entangled in its ghostly fingers which, whipped up by the winds, swirled about her as if to embrace her as its own. The strange fog then stretched its wide blanket out upon the waters, until it lay upon the surface of the sand and sea.

As she walked through the dense cloud, Ana found herself wandering upon the rocks by the edge of the sea. There she stopped to rest, looking down into the dark waters of a tide pool. She saw her reflection—her dark hair, thick and tangled, hanging down about her little face. Her violet eyes sparkled like crystals, as the tears that formed within them flowed forth, down her cheeks.

But as Ana looked deeper within the pool, she saw the solemn face of another being upon its surface. It was the soft face of her mother. She then heard the moaning of the sea upon the distant winds. And she knew it to be her mother's own voice, calling her from afar.

Ana crept down to the water's edge and knelt, trying to speak to the image she had seen. But the eerie mist grew thick about her, until the seas were hidden by its fog. Then there rose from the shadowy depths of the ocean a great fish, black and warty, covered with the weeds and slime of the sea. It bobbed upon the surface, staring at Ana with its great glassy eyes. Ana rose to her feet in fear, and began to back away from the water's edge.

With its thick broad lips, the fish-beast said, "Do not fear, child of the sea. For I am Lavanc, a servant of the Dreaming Seas. Your mother An has sent me to find you. For I am her messenger." Ana hesitated. She then turned to look curiously at the great fish.

The Lavanc then said, "Your mother, who dwells far away in the heart of the sea, wishes only that you know of her, and of her great love for you. For you shall forever be in her heart and mind."

Tears began to well up in her eyes, as she sat for a moment thinking of her mother. Ana then said to the Lavanc, "Great Lavanc, I have seen my mother's face upon the surface of the waters. She calls for me. And I desire to return to her in the depth of the seas. Will you take me to her?"

The Lavanc rose higher from the waters, drawing its monstrous form close to Ana, saying, "Never again may you journey to the land of your mother, or dwell in the gentle lands that sleep beneath the waves. For only those doomed to the eternal rest that is death, may travel to that realm. For them alone, her waters call. All others shall seek her in vain. Go forth into the woods and leave the sleeping seas forever. For great danger haunts this dreadful shore. And in the forests of Phantaia shall you now find your fate."

Ana wept at these words until she heard in the distance the sound of thunder. She looked into the skies and saw from afar dark rolling clouds, rising up from a swiftly-approaching storm. Violent rain and wind had begun to drift towards her from the heights above the seas, as an immense shadow stretched its ominous fingers towards her.

The Lavanc spoke one last time, "My child, do not fear for your future. Leave the realm of your mother's house behind and go deep into the woods, far away from this place. For it is your mother's desire that you find your way to the heart of Phantaia."

As the winds whipped up, the Lavanc began to disappear beneath the waves. But as it did, it called out to her, "Leave the seas, Ana. Run before the approaching storm. For it is conceived of an evil will that seeks to do you great harm."

Ana ran across the rocks, and up the dunes of the beach. But as she looked back towards the sea, she saw that the Lavanc had disappeared. All that remained was the turbulent waters of a rising tide. She gazed at the troubled skies and saw that the black and ominous clouds were now streaming overhead, drifting across the beaches, and were strangely quiet. Looking over the tops of the trees, she saw the sudden flash of lightning, and felt the rumbling of a distant thunder in the humid air. The ancient trees of Phantaia seemed to stand deadly still, as if in a state of horror from the sight of the approaching tempest.

Ana ran along the shore, seeking to find a way into the forest. But the black trees had formed an unending wall of trunks and limbs. The skies suddenly belched forth great blasts of cold wind and rain down upon her as she ran. Buffeted by violent gusts, she was tossed back and forth on the beach, until she was thrown down onto the sand. She then rose again, fleeing down the shoreline, past great piles of debris and timber. Dunes of shifting sand were thrown high into the air by the wild gusts of the storm, stinging her eyes, while her hair and dress were slung about in the gale.

Tossed about by the storm, she ran on, trying to reach the safety of the dark woods. But she saw no opening into them. For their colonnade of thick trunks stood side by side, impenetrable, their limbs closely intertwined.

Webs of lightning now snaked their way across the dark skies above her, when suddenly, from out of the misty Heavens, a great bolt of lightning struck down upon the heads of the tree line, felling a great oak. The ancient tree crashed into the swells of the dunes in one great heap of shattered limbs and bark. Split in two, its rotten trunk lay before her, black and wormy.

Ana screamed, as she fell back into the dunes. But as she climbed to her feet, she gazed upon the fallen tree. She saw that buried within its darker trunk lay a bright white woody core. But as she looked upon the place where the great tree had stood, a black opening had now appeared, leading deeper into the woods. She looked into its shadowy depths and she shook with fear. For hidden within that haunted forest, she sensed the presence of some unknown being—a peculiar presence whose penetrating eyes seemed to peer into the very depths of her spirit.

She could perish at the hands of the storm, or flee into the mysterious woods to face that strange presence. As she crawled across the beach towards the trees, the ragged eye of the storm above her had gathered into one great towering thunderhead. But as she gazed upon it, she froze in fear. For the storm had thrust its evil mouth down towards the beach to swallow her. In horror, she then turned back toward the seas, crying out for her mother, begging and pleading for her life.

Suddenly, out of the shadows of the monstrous trees, there appeared within its depths a ghostly figure. It began to take shape, gathering itself into a new form, until all at once it erupted out of the forest in one mighty leap, falling into the swales before the tree line. Seeing it running at full speed towards her, Ana fell back into the sand in shock, screaming in terror.

The large, white, four-legged beast then came upon her, encircling her in a violent fashion. But this was no monster, but a mighty horse, tall and proud. The strong stallion had a coat, white as sea foam. Its thick mane, wild and tangled, flowed out from its long neck, cast about by the storm's winds. And a short but shining horn grew upon its head.

The clouds and rain above had suddenly ceased, as if in fear, uncertain and confused. The great horse stopped and looked down at the small girl. But Ana had risen to her feet, seeking to flee from the strange creature. As she turned to run, she heard its powerful hooves beating upon the sands, and the snorting of its large nostrils. The seas and mists about them then grew still. But the evil eye of the storm had now turned its curious gaze upon that powerful beast of the woods.

Ana looked into the warm face of that creature, and sensed the presence of a kind and gentle spirit. The great horse beat its hoof upon the sands again, as if to signal her to come to it. She hesitated. But seeing the great stallion unmoving, she grabbed its wide, white mane in her tiny hands and pulled her body onto its broad back.

Ana and the horse fled down the beach and across the dunes, winding their way up a narrow swale, until they stood before the tall cathedral-like opening of the black woods of Phantaia. Above their heads, the storm had gathered its forces once again. But Ana, with all her strength, had pulled back upon the horse's mane to stop him at the gloomy doorway. The beast stood still and quiet, almost frozen, as in a trance. Ana then peered into the black opening. And a terrible fear filled her spirit again. For the haunted trees within seemed possessed of some ancient spirit.

The storm erupted over their heads, bursting forth with great cracks of lightning and thunder, which lit up the tops of the trees, reflecting off their wet limbs in flashes of bright silver. A swirling tempest of rain and wind poured down around them, so that the seas almost disappeared behind a veil. Ana then looked up and saw, in the dark swirling clouds, a gigantic pair of claw-like hands, descending down from the dark skies to grab her. She screamed, tugging upon the mane of the pale horse until he lunged forward, diving head first through the gloomy doorway, and into the dark woods of Phantaia.

* * *

Far away from Phantaia, in another realm beyond the storms and seas, there had sat brooding in the gloom another forlorn being. Deep within the bowels of Oblivion Agapor had sat, unmoving upon his ghoulish throne, dreaming alone in the quiet of the ephemeral night, whose foul miasma of death and decay hung upon his silent chamber like a funerary pall. In his silent and shadowy chamber he was want to roam, thinking upon the utter futility of his long-held desire to find his father.

He had sent forth his servants, the Shadow and the Shade, to find the Twilight Mist, and bring word of him. And Yana, the terrible Magra, he had sent to destroy Phantaia, so that his father might be driven from its depths. But after an age, no word came to him of his father, or his fate. For the Twilight Mist now dwelt in a secret inner realm, deep within the woods, beyond the reach and knowledge of Agapor's greatest servants, who had been sent to drive him out.

As Agapor sat alone, he stared at the sinister phantoms that played their eerie forms upon his candlelit chamber walls. His hope of seeing his sister An had now faded from him, like the fading flame of a dying taper that flees before the slithering shadows.

But in secret Agapor had toiled away, drawing to himself ever-increasing power and knowledge. His inner rage, born of his past injuries, seemed to have no bounds, fueling itself into ever greater desire for revenge. For in his heart had grown a relentless craving to obliterate this tragic world, which he had long hated.

Embittered, he had embraced at last the morbid mind and will of the Limitless Void, his uncle, whose sleeping spirit within the crystal ring had ever crept into him, whispering in dreams its own desires to him, and driving its sinister will down onto his own. Like that tortured being, Agapor soon determined that his destiny lay in the conquering of the remnant states and forgotten domains of that embattled world. And so he began to resurrect even darker powers, much maligned in earlier times, aligning them once more against his remaining enemies, plotting war with the last domains of sea, mist, and land. For these still lay before his realm, like tempting treasures, waiting to be taken.

Agapor had begun to collect the Void's remnant armies from distant parts of his world, making them his own, commanding the countless gruesome beings of that depraved underworld, to come before his throne in throngs. These beings came from far and away to serve him. For the droning of his brassy horns upon his tower gates ever groaned, like a siren calling deep into the night, drawing forth the amber-eyed demonic black masses, which had long hid in the depths and holds of Oblivion.

By the strange lights of the ring did he command the terrible servants of his mother's house to flock to his own caverns, until the last that had survived the horror of the seas—giant black behemoths, ghoulish beasts, dark messengers, and the phantoms of demons that yet resided within the caverns under Oblivion's icy peaks—had all awakened and returned to him.

He summoned forth the slithering and slimy monsters that were spawned long ago, and which now hid in the depths of the underworld seas. Those beings arose from the foul waters and waste of the earth, and walked again, defying death itself, driven only by their desire for bloodshed and violence.

In a great procession did their black forms flow into his towering halls, until beneath its great walls, bowing before him, they vowed to serve only him, until his will had been done. For as long as that ring, which yet held the spirit of their master, hung upon Agapor's hand, they were enslaved by its enchantment over them. And so Agapor came to see the strange ring as his salvation in his war against the world.

These forces of power he had gathered in preparation for the final days, when he would destroy the sea and forest utterly, and take what remained of its corpse as his own. So like his mother had he become a master over the sad denizens of that realm.

In time, Agapor had prepared the seething multitudes, sending them forth to colonize parts of the vast cities of ancient Oblivion. They set about rebuilding its walls and keeps. For with the cracking of dark whips, did their demonic captains drive the endless throngs to carve great blocks of stone from the mountains, fashioning the thick walls of its fortresses anew.

They set about rebuilding the Limitless Void's terrible war machines and catapults of iron, creating vast armaments and armories within their many foundries, whose flaming tongues lapped the walls of his vast underground holds, burning blood-red again. And so there returned into this world many terrors thought destroyed in the ancient wars with the Primordial Ones.

Yet had the horror of war, and the nightmares it would spawn, not yet been fully rekindled by the will of Agapor and his dark ring. Nor had his drive for violence been fully fueled by the vengeance his hateful heart had long borne.

For none of these endeavors seemed to fulfill his deepest desires, that which had lain hidden within his restless heart. Agapor had remained trapped in his lonely chamber, fearful of the future and of fate, imprisoned within his weakened mind, and haunted by nightmares of his own making. Many nights he had arisen from his cold bed and thought again upon his sister. But he had given up all hope of ever saving her, as she was now eternally bound to a cursed sleep, which still held her firmly within the grip of the Dreaming Seas.

Yet had he awakened, hearing the strange cry of a child in the night, one he could neither see nor find. Was it his sister? Then returned his feelings of deep regret and his anger against the one who had abandoned them. For his desire for vengeance against him burned ever brighter within his heart. But his father had fled far away into a distant land, alien to him. And in the fastness of Phantaia would he remain, far from the eyes of Agapor's many spies and servants who had sought to find him. Thus had the twin powers of land and sea, like mighty fortresses, stood firmly between him and his great desire.

Agapor fell into a deep despair. Sundered from that which he loved, he now saw he was truly alone in the world. And in his solitude, tortured and torn by anger and regret, he eventually succumbed to his own self-imposed imprisonment, embracing it wholly, and condemning himself to an isolated fate. In his cavernous hallways, he slunk about his underworld cities, deep in thought, wrapped in his enchanted cloak.

He often abandoned his servants, walking alone, roaming through towering corridors with their twisting stairs, over narrow bridges spanning cold chasms, down subterranean tunnels that twisted maddeningly through the rock, under carved archways of colossal height, and out across windy wide balconies carved from the jagged and treacherous stone, which looked down from their haughty heights upon the dark and dismal depths of Oblivion's vast underground seas.

In those depths, Agapor could see the frothing waves of that vast ocean upon whose surface a phantasmal fog had crept. With the saddened glow of a sick and putrid light, its mists shined forth their strange reflections upon the surface of the seas and the cavernous walls. At times he thought he could see something strange, writhing within the depths of its dark waters—a being or spirit of something unknowable yet vaguely felt, whose monstrous cries he had heard echoing out of the depths. But always, as he looked more closely at the surface of those seas, it seemed the mist upon its greasy surface had created a mirage to play upon his imagination.

Agapor thought again upon the cries of the child he had heard in the night. Then he would walk again, clothed in the darkness of his hooded robe, until after many nights he wound his way through the farthest fringes of his empire. There he stood before the window of a long-abandoned tower, which hung upon the forgotten cliff of some dizzying height. Here the last ordered and ancient architecture of Oblivion looked down upon the entropic depths of the Great Beyond.

There he sat alone, hollow-faced and gloomy, listening to the endless roar of the icy black rivers as they poured forth from the great caverns of the Realms of Oblivion, down into the silent gray of the void. He knew all things would eventually pour into that bottomless pit of death. For all things would come to die there, never to return in flesh or spirit again. It was just a matter of time.

He pondered the unending emptiness of that cold space, and the frightful beings that dwelt in its gulf, waiting to rise up yet again, when their time would finally come to annihilate the world and the last of its fallen children. As he climbed upon the edge of the window, he thought upon the meaning of his own sad life. Had any of it mattered? Too many questions remained unanswered. It was then he saw again the strange glow of the ring. And he thought about the Limitless Void. He then returned in haste to his halls.

With a new purpose, Agapor began to roam through the cities of the dead and dying, which lay in the lands above his own. In that eerie place stretched unending cityscapes of vast graveyards, the high walls of abandoned crypts, and massive mausoleums of thick stone and ice, upon whose rotting rock walls had been carved the many names of demonic heroes and their celebrated victories in war and death. For they had fought bravely against the children of the Primordial Ones.

Agapor often climbed those great crypts to read the crumbling words carved upon their colossal tombs. Fallen in war, these ancient battle-lords had perished with honor in the fight. And in some gruesome celebration of the dead, their terrible deeds and names had been engraved upon great slabs of stone in cryptic symbols unknown to Agapor.

Past those halls of the dead, Agapor was want to roam, through the towering hallways that connected their many underground arteries, entering shattered doorways to abandoned chambers, where once the demonic legions of the Limitless Void had dwelt, before the terrible wars had all but consumed the last of their kind.

It is then that Agapor stumbled upon a vast treasure, which in time would be of great value to him. For he had come upon a rusting portcullis beneath the city, which had stood unnoticed for eons within the shadows of a great triumphant arch. Breaking through the iron of the gate, he saw that there stretched beyond it a vast network of long-abandoned archives and libraries, a limitless source of knowledge once coveted by the Limitless Void.

Here were housed many lost codices of forgotten enchantments and black magic, countless dusty and disintegrating tomes of terror, arcane scrolls of ancient origin, parchments of demonic summonings, and thick volumes of trailing histories stretching back in time. In many of these manuscripts had been hidden a wealth of forbidden enlightenment and learning, which the Limitless Void had used in his wars against his kind. These his servants had collected and long coveted. And so came to Agapor a vast fount of wisdom and knowledge, which he had long sought.

In the lonely alcoves of those dark and dusty libraries Agapor often sat alone, poring over piles of books, deep in thought beside the pasty demonic scribes who, bent and trembling, endlessly scribbled ancient enchantments, bleak histories, and the cryptic words of dark and dismal discoveries upon rotting scrolls and faded parchment. Under Agapor's guidance, these knowledge-keepers of the underworld had begun to record new secrets, brought to them by his winged servants. For Agapor had sent many of his own messengers to travel the distant fringes of that forbidding world, seeking hidden treasures, powerful relics, cryptic scribblings, mysterious books, and strange objects of enchantment, all of which had been thrown into this world from others long ago destroyed and forgotten.

Of the knowledge he gathered, Agapor had cherished most the ancient histories and texts concerning the Primordial Ones. Long into the night, he pondered the strange words written in various books and tomes, struggling to understand the twisted and distorted lives and destinies of his uncles and their brutal conflicts of old.

Over time he began to collect the secretive knowledge and wisdom of the Primordial Ones, as given to them by the Great Father, much of which had been lost. Their fragmented history fascinated Agapor, tempting his imagination with its seductive tale of unending woe and heartache. Yet the more he read, the more he saw the scale and scope of their horrific crimes. And these began to haunt him.

Agapor then came upon the Mystical Narratives, which recounted the sacred gifts granted unto the Primordial Ones at birth by the Essence Eternal, their father. He learned of the power of the Creative Flame, whose spiritual fire lived in them. And he learned of the Sacred Light, which had been lost. And he read of the hanging of the Veils of Night, and of the forging of the Arch of Heaven by the Essence Eternal, where the stars that had yet been created would someday reside. These wonders the Essence Eternal had left for his sons, so they might remake the world in their own image.

Agapor then learned that the Essence Eternal had commanded his first-born son, the Endless Night, to construct the nighttime sky, so that the stars of the Heavens soon to come could be hung upon its black cloak. For this one purpose he had given his son the Wings of Night, so that he might rebuild its mantle. But the Endless Night had used them instead to suffocate the failing light of this world. It had then been drowned in his terrible shadow, until his brothers had risen up to defeat him.

But Agapor learned that the last light of this world had yet lived. And this shining presence even the sinister twins that dwelt in the Great Beyond could not face. For it ever burned them from a distance. And so Agapor knew why they had remained in their prison, bound to it through their own desires, until the last light of the world had been extinguished. Yet the true light lay not in the stars, but in the children of the world. As their spirits yet shined had a hope remained that the Sacred Light would live again in the lanterns of their hearts, blessing the world with its love through them.

By the corrupted Wings of Night alone could this last divine candle of the world be hidden from both their eyes and hearts. So had the Endless Night secreted those wings far away from the world, and from its evil, which had long sought to find them and pervert their powers again.

But most mysterious to Agapor was the story of the Sacred Waters, which had been handed down to the sons of the Essence Eternal as a gift most treasured. Little was written of them, save that the waters had been placed into the hands of a chosen child. In him the Essence Eternal had placed his last hope for the world, that by his son's children those waters would be reborn into it someday, to birth a new world, and grant to all a lasting peace eternally bound to its strange essence.

But Agapor read that those waters contained something else—a darker and more devious will. And he sat in silence for many nights, bewildered by the enigma of those faded words. And he thought upon the brutal seas whose terrible violence had nearly destroyed him.

He had also stumbled upon a small crumbling tome, whose pages fell to dust with every turn. He studied it long into the night. From its sad tale there began to unfold in Agapor's mind the meaning and purpose of the Limitless Void's long toils and troubles in the world. Yet, strangely from the Limitless Void, no word was ever spoken of his own children, nor his love and care for them, except their slavery to him and the sinister powers he himself was bound to.

Agapor then saw the futility of their service to their grim father, and the long toils toward a dimly-seen victory which had never come. For that blinded father's love was cruelly tied to their success in the world. Agapor read the sad tale of their torturous end, most cruel and savage, at the hand of their own father. For in the end, by the will for total power over this world, the Limitless Void had sacrificed his own children to the beings that dwelt in the Great Beyond. And the full horror of that act weighed upon the heart and mind of Agapor. For he too had made the same vow.

These sad truths Agapor pondered over many nights. Yet he could not see the true cause for the strange bent towards self-destruction, which the Primordial Ones had taken. He saw in their dire fates a mysterious yet tragic play, one in which their children's parts had been reflected and reborn yet again. But to what end their lives were sacrificed Agapor could not fathom or foresee. To what purpose was his life and that of his sister's?

Beneath these libraries lay an immense underworld of dungeons and vaults. These were filled with strange objects of devious magic, cursed relics, and infernal weapons of unnumbered wars, all forged in the spirit of the dark arts. These malicious objects of power the Void had collected for himself over the many wars he had waged against his brethren. And these Agapor dug through, searching for that which would bring him some message or truth concerning his father.

In time he found such an object buried deep in the corner of an underground cavern, which had lain hidden beneath his cities for untold ages. In his hands he now held a small globe, within whose mysterious crystal hung the strange fogs and phantom visions of his family's past and future fates. Like a firefly, its eerie lights seemed to bob and weave new images upon his chamber walls, hypnotizing Agapor by the eerie ghosts of those he had known, and others he had not.

* * *

Far from the Realms of Oblivion, beyond Agapor's gloomy halls, a nightmarish being created from evil's own twisted mind had raged on, uncontrolled and with never-ending fury. For upon the fringes of Phantaia the endless savagery of the Yana, the Magra Oversoul, had long endured to terrorize those woods. Its dark storm clouds rolled about in the Heavens with unrelenting winds, rains, and lightning, hurling itself down upon the fringes of Phantaia. For the slaughter of its mighty trees, born of its ravishing and all-consuming hunger, had continued unabated. The unending maze of oaks, which had for ages guarded it, had at last upon its cliffs and boundaries fallen like sheaves before the cutting winds of its furious tempest.

Yet for all of the carnage that Yana had unleashed, she could not penetrate the heart of Phantaia. For it had hid within its very depths a seductive light, and the wondrous source of its immense power. It alone had chased away the evil which had tried to enter its borders. The great mass of trees within its interior had thus endured, renewed by youthful growth, and fed by its miraculous light.

No force in that world could now extinguish its mysterious candle, which burned ever more brightly at its center. So was it the source of life and the hope of the world that yet lived on by its seminal flame. Thus had Phantaia and its many hidden wonders remained a mystery to Agapor and his servants.

Yet had the Shadow seen its lights with his own eyes. And so the knowledge of its true essence was partially revealed to him, though its strange source still remained unknown. But Agapor, like the Shadow, now knew that the Magra would never penetrate Phantaia, nor chase his father from those woods. For something yet remained there that had to perish. This hidden truth even the Nothingness had revealed.

The Shadow had told Agapor that the last of the children of the Primordial Ones had fled into Phantaia's depths. And in its heart, their spirits and powers would remain, defiant and united as one to defy him, the new Lord of Destruction and Darkness, until he should find the shining source that now sustained them. And so had the beguiling tongue of the Shadow slowly turned Agapor's prideful spirit towards the destruction of its secret light.

Agapor sat in his hidden chambers, deep in the farthest corners of Oblivion, and peered into his magical crystal. Within its inner clouds he had hoped by chance alone to see some glimpse of his father's mist in that faraway forested realm. But those globes had been forged by the Limitless Void for another purpose. For they were most treacherous, and had been designed to curse his brothers with shattered memories of their troubled past, filling their minds with endless lies, revealing the cold truth of their failed lives, and hiding the uncertain future from their eyes, until they would become a slave to the will of their deceitful spheres, and thus to him.

Tortured by his own visions, Agapor would look into that glass each night, seeing only the contorted and twisted face of his evil mother, and hearing the tortured cries of his sister's spirit. And so he turned away from them. Yet slowly he began to see, in the shifting lights, the faint images of the true future that would befall that sad world and all its children. In an epiphany, he began to understand his own destiny, though partially revealed, and embrace the strange fate into which he was thrown.

In his gloomy chambers, weak with exhaustion, Agapor lay down once more to sleep, drifting back down into nightmares, where he tossed and turned, trapped and tortured by the horrible visions that wracked his mind. But the dutiful Shade heard his cries in the night. And she rose forth from the shadows of her own dark bed. She found Agapor in his chamber, where he long had suffered alone, night after night, crying out from the shadows of his room. Her long dark hair and sensuous form now lay beside him, tempting him to her seductive passions. And so for a time Agapor was comforted by her.

But each night, as he looked into her blackened eyes, they appeared to him sterile and cold, devoid of the light he once saw in the shining eyes of An. He turned away from her in disgust. But the Shade would not leave him. For she desired to be near him, and would not abandon him in his time of need.

Agapor then heard the thundering footsteps of the terrible Shadow, echoing forth from deep within his halls. His greatest servant had returned to him from the dark errands he had been sent to fulfill. For he had been told not to return unless he brought news of his father.

The Shadow now called for his master from the darkness of his hallways. Agapor rose wearily from the secret bed he had shared with the Shade. But the Shadow had watched from the dark corners of an antechamber, and had seen them together many times. And so he had long known of their tryst. He walked forth from the corners of that room and laughed as they rose from their carnal bed.

Seeing her brother, in terror the Shade fled from the room. But the Shadow caught her by her arm, saying, "You should not be fearful of me, your loving and loyal brother. Nor should you hide in shame. Relish in the desires you have for Agapor, and which you for so long have fought hard in your heart to deny." The Shade then fled away in shame.

Agapor looked in fear at the Shadow's towering dark form as it stood before him. For he had seen a glimpse of some tragic future in the crystal, in which that creature strangely played a central part. And so he distrusted the Shadow, and feared he would soon turn against him in vengeance.

But the Shadow saw once more the black manacles upon Agapor's wrists. And he looked away from his master, hiding his own face in fear. For he could no longer feign his own denial of the painful shame of his own cruel enslavement.

The Shadow then knelt before Agapor in subjugation, saying, "Master, I bear strange news. For many nights I stood upon the crags, looking down upon the seas and the shattered shores of the forest, thinking upon the source of its secretive illumination. It was then I heard the cries of a baby, coming up from the ocean depths. Cast up from the waves of the seas, a strange girl-child appeared before my eyes, floating upon its surface. For many nights she drifted upon the ocean waves, until I saw her flung upon the beach beside the woods." Agapor stared at the Shadow, unsure of the meaning of this vision.

"Shadow, what more did you see?" Agapor asked. For Agapor thought her dead. He had sent the Magra Lord to wrap her destructive storms about Phantaia, such that no creature could enter or leave its woods. And he feared that Yana, the Oversoul of the Gray Ones, had by her vast powers drawn the child into her monstrous mouth and consumed her.

But the Shadow said, "By the hand of some unseen force I saw a doorway made for her, which lead into the forest. A strange white beast then appeared, capturing the girl, and ripping her away from the claws of the Magra." Agapor stared at the Shadow in wonder.

"What do you know of this white beast?" Agapor asked.

The dark servant said, "Master, I know nothing of this monster only that it seemed to be a spirit born of the forest itself. And that the child fled into the woods, riding upon the back of that creature, never to be seen again."

Agapor then asked, "Did you see the violet mists of my father?"

"I saw only the hands of the Twilight Mist, stretching forth across the seas from the fringes of the wood. But it drew itself back into the forest to pursue the girl," the Shadow said. Agapor then turned away from the Shadow, whispering to himself, "Could the child still be alive?"

But hearing his words, the Shadow said to Agapor, "The girl has likely perished in the depths of the ancient wood. For it is a wicked place in which many horrors now hide—a decrepit world where even the servants of darkness now fear to dwell. For the dark earth there has swallowed many of my own brethren within its murky hollows, never to be seen again, while in the skies above, the forest's colossal lights singe and sear away the very air, such that even the storms of the Magra flee before it. Nothing that enters those woods ever returns, Master. Therefore, the child has truly perished within its depths."

With these words the Shadow looked upon the troubled face of Agapor. And he smiled with a perverse joy at the pain wrought upon his master's heart. For he sensed that Agapor in private cared for the child.

Agapor sat down upon his great throne in the darkness, thinking again upon the wonder of this strange new sight. For in his heart he knew this child of the sea to be his daughter. And he felt that she had in truth not perished, but was alive in Phantaia.

Agapor also knew that his father would not harm her, though he now had hidden her far from him. Yet Agapor knew he could not easily find her in that forest. For he had known that the vast realms of that wilderness would not easily be penetrated or destroyed. He had used the Magra to try and drive his father from those woods, but with no success. His daughter would now remain hidden from him, in a place nearly impenetrable, just as An had been secreted away from him by the Dreaming Seas.

Agapor rose from his seat enraged, saying to the Shadow that his own father, the Twilight Mist, must have planned this wicked deed. The child of the sea, therefore, had not perished, but had been summoned forth into the twilight forest of Phantaia by his father's own pernicious powers. For he had vaguely seen within the Limitless Void's crystal mists that his father would use such a presence against him. And so the Dreaming Seas had sent that child to assist the Mist in a dire plot against him.

But Agapor looked down with weariness upon his face, telling the Shadow that the girl would likely remain hidden forever from the world's eyes, dwelling within the impenetrable wilderness of Phantaia, until such time as his father's evil plans would be revealed. Soon would the powers of sea and land unite against them, and his ancient father's war against the realms of Night and Void would be resumed.

The Shadow now stood sternly before Agapor, saying that he himself would go into Phantaia and find the child. If she lived, he would take her and bring her to him. But he required something special to protect him from its light. The Shadow then stood quiet and unmoving, staring into the pale face of Agapor, his plotting mind turning over and over.

But Agapor did not trust the Shadow. And so he hid his true fears for his daughter's fate from the prying mind of that vile creature. He knew the Shadow would go forth to find the child and harm her, as the Shadow cared not for the life of any living thing. And Agapor knew through the Shadow's own evil designs against him, he would seek to slay her.

Yet Agapor was haunted by another more terrible truth. For unknown to the Shadow, he had made a vow to surrender his first child to the evil twins. By the powers of Yana that had been given to him to wield, was he to give his only child to the Nothingness. And Agapor fell back onto his throne, aghast with the horror of this grim truth.

But he would not abandon his daughter to the same cruel fate the Limitless Void had inflicted upon his own. He would not condemn her to the same suffering he had endured, nor lead her to her death.

Yet he had seen that, like a web of doom, this evil world had entangled them all in some foul maze of treacherous traps they and their children could not escape. Tempted by fortune's honeyed dew, their hallowed lives were now but an empty corpse to be fed upon by the evil horrors that dangled at the end of the strand of time.

But though Agapor's feelings for the child remained within the confines of his heart, the Shadow had the powers of the Nightmare Unending, and could see deep into him. The Shadow saw that a new temptation had arisen within his master yet again, to ensnare him in its net. And the Shadow saw that Agapor's mind and heart were weak, and that he would sacrifice everything to save and protect this child.

But in his plotting mind the Shadow had felt great apprehension and uncertainty about that child, which he withheld from his master purposefully. Upon seeing the child rise forth from the sea, a new perception had come into him. He felt fear for the first time, not knowing yet what secrets lay within her. For the mysterious forces he had seen within the seas, he now saw hidden within the girl. That enigma troubled him. And the Shadow realized that the strange fate of the world, like the hub of a wheel, would now turn about her.

Agapor stood before the Shadow, speaking with bold words, saying, "I will go into Phantaia and find the child, and confront the Twilight Mist who yet guards her. By my hand alone will she be taken from him."

But the Shadow said to Agapor, "This is a doomed mission. For neither you nor I may enter Phantaia. As long as the enchanted lights of that forest still shine, shall the Children of Night and Void be burned and blinded by the golden beams of its relentless flame, which ever emanates from its heart."

"Do you not remember your own defeat at the hands of the savage seas?" the Shadow said, his eyes glowing with contempt. "Like that mother-ocean, within those woods now dwells a preternatural force you cannot face, nor force, nor ever break. This you know now to be true." Agapor thought upon the truth of the Shadow's words.

But the Shadow stared coldly into Agapor's eyes, saying, "The true destiny of the child lies within the heart of Phantaia itself. For this is where she is now being taken by the white beast of the woods. Therefore must the source of the light of Phantaia be found and destroyed. Should its light fail, then shall the forest fall. With Phantaia withered and dying, then shall those who they hide be yours. For in that light lives not only the fate of the child, but the destiny of the world, master."

But the Shade, daughter of the Night, had returned. She saw the secret desire of Agapor to save the girl. And she felt her brother's hatred for the forest and its magical light. She then said to them, "There is one thing left in this world that yet may guide you both. Only the Wings of Night have the power to shield the lights of Phantaia. Only then might you enter those woods and find the child. Though my father has perished, these last powers of his yet remain with him, hidden within his sepulcher. With those dark wings one could summon the last winged servants of the Lands of Midnight, which still dwell in its deepest catacombs. Then could you clothe Phantaia in unending darkness, dimming its golden glow, and hiding the pale lights of the Twilight Mist, which yet shine there to protect the child. Under the cover of midnight's mantle might you then enter Phantaia, unharmed and unseen."

Hearing his sister's words, the Shadow's eyes glowed with a vile and vengeful light. For in secret he had desired the Wings of Night, having sought them beneath his father's keep for many nights. Yet his father's crypt had remained a mystery to him. The Shadow then looked upon his sister with great derision, saying, "Our father is now gone. And the Wings of Night are lost for all time."

The Shadow gazed upon Agapor with his penetrating eyes, saying, "But Master, if you truly know where the Wings of Night lie hidden, you should not hesitate to take them. With those wings, we could seek out the living source of Phantaia, and not just shield it, but destroy it utterly. With the last light of the wood now extinguished, the twilit forest would perish. And Yana would be free to penetrate its heart, and devour the evil which hides there. She would devour them all. The ruinous remains of that blasted earth would then be yours to rule over for all eternity, Master." The Shadow laughed at the thought.

Agapor looked with uncertain eyes at the Shadow. For he now saw the true madness of his plot. But Agapor had concealed from him his own knowledge of the Wings of Night, and the truth of their existence, which he had learned in the bowels of Oblivion's libraries. And he had seen that with those wings the Shadow could gather the powers he needed to free himself from his long bondage. Then would a new Prince of Darkness rise again, to devour the world in its eternal night.

Yet Agapor realized that with the last powers of the Endless Night lay his only hope of saving his daughter. For with those wings could he cloak himself from Phantaia's burning beams. And with the winged armies of darkness he commanded could he enter its forest unseen by his father. He could then escape the fallen world with his beloved daughter, taking flight upon the dark winds that blow beyond the Heavens, carrying his innocent child far away to a distant place, hiding her forever from the doom of that world's abiding evil, and cloaking his child in the safety of its shadows.

Agapor now looked upon the sad face of the pitiful Shade, whose knowing eyes spoke to him. For she knew what he must do.

Agapor raised his dark manacles above his head. And they glowed with an eerie light that lit the darkest corners of his chamber. He now commanded the Shade to go forth into the lands beyond the Veils of Night, and find the crypt of her father, the Endless Night. His corpse had lain in a hidden crypt within his own city-tomb, which lay deep within the Corridors of Darkness beneath the Lands of Midnight. This knowledge he alone had gained. And to the Shade, his lover, had it alone been imparted.

Agapor then told the Shade she must take the wings from his form, and bring them to him. Agapor turned to the Shadow, commanding him to go forth to the dark shores of Phantaia where he had seen the girl and wait for him there. They would then travel together into the forest and find the child.

Agapor said to the Shade and Shadow that he himself would now go forth to the precipice that hung before the Great Beyond, and speak to the gray powers within its depths. For they were all-knowing. They alone would reveal the secret paths within Phantaia's vast reaches that would lead them to the child.

But Agapor looked upon the troubled face of the Shadow. And to him he made a vow most sacred, saying, "Servant, if you will find the child and bring her to me, I shall free you from your bondage. Vengeance against the magical lights of Phantaia will then be yours." The black manacles upon Agapor's wrists then began to glow with a faint lavender light.

Hearing this vow, the Shadow bellowed forth with great laughter, saying to his master, "Thy will shall soon be done." Agapor now knew his daughter would be found, and safely given unto him. For nothing would stop the Shadow from fulfilling that vow. But Agapor did not surmise the vengeful plans and secret plots of the Shadow. Despite his vow, the Shadow would never allow Agapor, a Child of Mist, to wear the wings of his father. By birthright they were his alone.

But the mystery of the girl-child still haunted the Shadow. He had vowed to himself he alone would learn of the terrible secrets which lay within the child of the sea. He would find her. And by his hand would she soon perish.

The Shadow rose up before Agapor, drawing out his wide black wings, and flying forth into the emptiness of Oblivion. He disappeared into the gray fog that hung about the chamber ceiling. And with every beat of his wide wings did the halls of that underground city tremble and shake.

The Shade drew forth her own lithe wings, the black satin of her oily feathers shining in the somber glow of the chamber. She then walked to Agapor. And they kissed passionately. In her eyes were tears, shed only for him. She said, "Do not go, my love. Do not do this terrible deed. For I fear great harm will come of it. And

I see that in that forest a dark and terrible fate awaits you...awaits all of us."

Agapor looked down into her dark and tearful eyes, saying only, "You know now what you must do." For in secret he had shared with her a strange truth about her own father, which the Shadow had not known.

For the love of Agapor she would now obey, flying forth from his warm embrace out into the cold skies above. Beyond the heights of Oblivion she flew, out beyond the Veils of Night to find the form of her fallen father hither in the darker lands. She would find his Wings of Night, and bring them to her love. For her loyalty to Agapor was unwavering.

Agapor fled his dusty caverns, travelling through countless lost hallways, and over the lonely bridges that spanned the icy underworld seas. Travelling secret catacombs and winding stairs, he finally arrived at a vast opening in the mountains, which looked out upon a wide precipice of rock. Beside it, the icy rivers of the underworld ocean fell away, past the last of Wendalia's foggy and bottomless pits, and down into the pitiless gulf that lay beyond.

He stood once more, trembling, before the vast spaces of the Great Beyond. He then called forth the spirits of the Nothingness and Emptiness. From out of the great gray waste a monstrous form took shape, slowly rising up from the depths. And the full terror of its great face swirled up from the rippling mists, looking down on the tiny form of Agapor as he stood uncertain, yet determined, upon the edge of the cliffs.

Agapor appeared again before the swirling presence of the Nothingness, saying, "Where lies the hidden path that leads into Phantaia? For I seek to find the heart of that wood, where my father now dwells. Yana has failed to destroy Phantaia, as you promised." Agapor looked with anger upon the storm, as he spoke. But the billowing storm of the Nothingness did not speak.

Agapor said to the Nothingness, "Spirit, I go to Phantaia for a greater purpose. For I seek to discover the source of Phantaia's living lights so I might obliterate them. I sense that the Sacred Light, lost long ago, now dwells there—a secret source of light, whose beams burn forth like the spiritual fires of legend, and which once lay upon the Mountains of Heaven. Toward its willful destruction is my mind now set. With the demise of the living light shall the life of the forest be extinguished. And with the death of the Sacred Lights of Heaven shall you and your brother then be free to consume the dying world as you please. So I come again before you, asking for your help."

But as Agapor stood before the Great Beyond, a cold chill came upon him. For the Nothingness turned dark, billowing forth into a mighty boiling cloud of wind and dust. Its blast threw back Agapor. A great face then formed within its cloud, with twisted and horned peaks of anger upon his head. And a terrible voice boomed like the thunder of a thousand tempests.

The Nothingness then bellowed, "Do not lie to me, Agapor. You know of the child that hides within Phantaia. It is your daughter you now seek, your first, last, and only child."

The Nothingness then said to Agapor in anger, "Whether you destroy Phantaia, or slay your father, it matters not to me. You must go to Phantaia and bring your daughter to me, so that her flesh may be consumed by my brother, the Emptiness, and the life force within her devoured by me. Her tiny spirit shall then be obliterated forever from this world. With the child's death shall the forest fall, the sea's heart break, and the last of the Primordial Ones perish."

But the Nothingness laughed, saying, "With the death of this child, then shall Yana be free to devour Phantaia completely in her jaws, and the last rays of hope that yet had arisen within its wood, be extinguished forever. Utter ruin, death, and darkness shall then be this hopeless world's fate. Only then shall I grant you freedom from bondage to me, Agapor, and the debt owed to me by the summoning of Yana."

But the Nothingness came down upon the head of Agapor, with a terrible blast of winds and gales, saying, "Though you have failed to sunder the seas like the Limitless Void, my servant, you shall not fail to bring the child to me! For should you fail, my brother and I will seek you and your child in the farthest corners of the world, devouring your flesh and obliterating your spirits. You cannot hide, nor shall your vow be broken. To this promise, long ago, were you bound to me."

Hearing these terrible words, Agapor looked in horror at the distorted face of the Nothingness, and fell to his knees. He could not speak. And so, he cowered before the evil spirit, saying only, "I shall obey." But though he was fearful, yet was his heart torn.

But as he held his hands before his face, the Nothingness saw the strange ring upon his hand. And the Nothingness in a booming voice, shouted, "Where did you find this ring? For it is a thing most foul. And its black purpose is beyond the will of any spirit in this world to control."

As Agapor held out his hand the colossal clouds of the Nothingness writhed before him as if in fear. The terrible face of the Nothingness then turned black with rage, saying, "Cast it away, back into the dark waters in which it has slept for all eternity. For it is a curse and a blight upon us, and bends time and space, hearts and minds, and all things to its poisonous will and darker end, which none might fathom."

Agapor then saw the strange power the ring had over that being. And he held it before the Nothingness, saying, "I demand to know the way into Phantaia!"

The Nothingness drew his great cloud back into the depths of space. And there it hung for a moment. He then opened his huge black eyes and saw the hidden spirit of the Limitless Void, shining from within its crystal.

The Nothingness said to Agapor, "If the spirit of the Limitless Void yet lives inside the ring, then within it hides your answer. For the demonic servants of the Limitless Void, which dwell in the trees of Phantaia, know of her many secrets. The spirit within that ring still controls them, as the spirits of those trees are still bound to him. And so may the spirit of the Limitless Void alone command the demonic armies that yet possess the darker lands of Avaras."

The Nothingness then said, "Go to Phantaia and use the ring to speak with the tree-spirits that dwell there. For in their trunks sleep the wicked demon-lords, which yet reign over the darker forests. Only the twelve haunted hazels, which rule the vast wilderness of Avaras, know of the hidden paths into the heart of Phantaia. They shall reveal to you the woods' many secrets, which they alone now keep. From their knowledge shall you learn of the winding paths into Phantaia's deepest heartland. For the blinding light of truth, which blazes forth from its middle-realms, hides the knowledge of its secret source even from me."

The great cloud of the Nothingness then spoke from within the depths of his hidden cloud, saying, "This knowledge I give to you, so you might fulfill your vow to me. You must bring the child hither, Agapor, and then cast the ring back into the waters from which it was made. Only I can free you from it. For that ring desires to undo all that was, is and shall be." Agapor then stared at the dark ring, as it glowed eerily upon his boney hand. The Nothingness faded away into the darkness, leaving Agapor alone and confused upon that solemn shore of death.

But Agapor was in fact not alone. For upon a distant precipice, high above him had hid his deceptive servant, the Shadow. He too had heard the words of the Nothingness, and of the secret vow of Agapor to give his only child to that vile spirit. The Shadow thought upon this new knowledge, and about his own freedom. Soon would he have his justice, be freed of his master, and destroy the hateful lights of Phantaia.

But first he must seek the child. He would then slay her himself. And by her death would Agapor's fate be sealed, and the world itself doomed, by the breaking of that vow. For he hated this world even more than the powers that slept in the Great Beyond. But more than this, vengeance upon Agapor would soon be his.

THE FALL OF NIGHT

As Ana and the horse entered the woods, before them a realm of darkness stood. All light and sound seemed to fade away, as sky and sea changed to woods and clay. From the darkened soil grew towering trees, whose bent black boughs bore bountiful leaves. Thick roots underground, hidden deep in the earth, thrust up from their mounds huge trunks of great girth.

In this dark forest, shifting shadows held sway. For long ago, the pale lights of Heaven had faded away. The phantom trees, twisted and distorted, stood bent, broken, battered, and contorted. Yet from worthy seeds had they been sown, growing defiant and by their pride, survived alone. But the tortured trees revealed a splintered past, the merciless cruelty of the storm's ruthless and relentless wrath.

Ana and the strange horse fled into the safety of the woods, leaving the troubled shore of Phantaia behind them. As she looked back, she saw the dark doorway had closed behind them. The scent of the humid air and rotting leaves of the forest had now worked upon her senses. And she could smell the ancient forest's almost timeless nature.

As they travelled down a dim path through the woods, the forest's deepening darkness had enveloped her and the horse in its gloom, strangling her sense of vision. The wide shadows of its towering trees rose up on either side of the trail, until only a faint violet glow from the trees above shined upon their path.

But that dim light was odd, almost out of place. Ana looked up to find its source. But she saw only a ghostly purple mist writhing about the tops of the trees. She realized it was the same mist she had seen earlier upon the beach. As it descended about them, it seemed to float, ghost-like, just above their heads, twisting and distorting its horrid and phantom-like form above them. The mist was an unnatural thing, born of some alien world, stretching its eerie tendrils into the black woods, drifting down and around them, and then back up again, rising and falling like the waters of a great sea. Oddly, the pale horse did not seem frightened by it, and so pushed on.

The horse was also unaffected by the ghostly shadows that surrounded them. For it seemed to follow some unseen path through the darkness, winding its way between the dense trunks and black foliage that rose up on all sides to consume them.

With an almost galloping gait, the horse rode past great mounds of logs and broken stumps, over masses of tangled roots and hollow husks of dead trees that lay around them in large piles of rot and wreckage. On they went, riding through the wooded hills, and then up a rocky ridge. Across bridges of timber and stone they travelled, riding over vast pits from which rose up deep piles of shattered limbs and logs that stood up like sharpened knives in the depths below. These fallen trees seemed to be remnants of the unending and violent struggle between earth and sky, which for ages had devastated this part of the forest.

They had ridden up many steep hills, and crossed many lonesome valleys, until they had come to a narrow canyon blocking their path. A massive log had fallen over its deep chasm. This dark pit seemed filled with many morbid spirits, which Ana could not see, only sense. As the horse rode over the chasm, it seemed wary of the eerie forms that now drifted about in the shifting and shadowy depths.

As Ana looked down, she saw blurred glimpses of strange forms, crawling and twisting about in the dimly lit hollows of the pit. They appeared like mounds of writhing bodies, piled together in some perverted embrace, deep in the blackness of the earth. These were the tortured spirits of Avaras, which had long ago come into Phantaia to possess this part of the woods. She shuddered at the sight, closing her eyes, until the white horse had crossed the forbidding canyon. Yet she could still hear their strange erotic moans and groans in the lecherous depths.

They now climbed a short hill that rose up into the darker parts of the woods before them, until they came to a vast and boundless plain of trees. But the white horse did not stop to rest, weaving his way among the huge black logs and rotting limbs that lay strewn about them in broken and tumbled piles. As they travelled deeper into the haunted wood, she saw around them the rotting remnants of once-monumental trees, which had fallen in some violent age. They were so large and hollow that many had formed great cavernous tunnels and mossy openings through which small streams now flowed.

Ana could barely hear the howling storm in the distance. Yet the savagery of its rage could still be felt in the distant rumbling of thunder that shook the earth beneath them. But Ana could still hear the shredding of limbs, the ripping away of roots, and the crashing of trunks as they were slung about in the farthest fringes of the forest. Such was the violent struggle of the storm in its futile search to find her.

As they travelled deeper into the woods, the trees had grown larger and more threatening. Ana felt a strange presence in this part of the forest. For it lay still, as if in fear of something unseen in their midst. The white horse paused for a brief moment, his head turning back and forth, as if looking for something. He then continued on, following a new path through an open corridor formed by a vast colonnade of massive hazel trees. Like a dark blue shadowy sea the misty gloom of Phantaia now seemed, its ghoulish gloom punctuated by the massive trunks of crooked trees, whose bent and black shapes stood partially hidden behind the silent fog that flowed between them.

As Ana's eyes adjusted to the gloom, she could see about her the distant and faded incandescent glow of multicolored mushrooms, poisonous toadstools, phosphorescent fungi, and carpets of illuminated spores, whose curling tendrils and bulbous heads poked up through the black mulch. The luminous growth of that enchanted realm stretched away into depths of the foggy forest. And their sickly orange, green, scarlet, and purple shapes shined like distant stars above a moldy sea of rotting logs and leaves.

As they rode on, the phantom mist seemed to flee before them, up into the canopy of the forest, until it finally disappeared above the tree tops. Something must have driven it away, thought Ana. A strange, ephemeral night had now descended upon the woods, enveloping them in its grim and lightless shade. Only the dark and distorted figures of the ancient trees remained, their creeping shadows rising up monstrous and mighty before them.

But in the midst of that eerie landscape, Ana thought she saw the unblinking eyes of beings much more sinister, staring back at her from the hollows of the trees. And she began to tremble with fear, not knowing what lay waiting there in the darker depths of those woods.

Yet beyond the quiet gloom of the haunted forest, Ana thought she could barely hear the crashing of waves on a faraway shoreline. She longed to return to her mother's seas and the gentle flow of her tides. They had held and protected her. If she closed her eyes, she could almost picture herself floating upon her mother's waves. For the motion of the great horse made her feel she was drifting upon the ocean.

But when she opened her eyes, she saw that she still lay trapped in the suffocating shade of the woods. The pale horse was all that lay between her and that which crept about in the darkness. She clung to its back, closing her eyes again, only opening them when she heard the sound of the wind in the trees or the rustle of branches, which now hung low about them. But it was the icy breath of the shadows as they drifted across her neck, which caused her to grip the horse's mane even tighter.

Ana and the horse rode on for what seemed an eternity, weaving along a crooked trail, which carried them beyond the dreamy mire of phosphorescent growth, and deeper into an even ghastlier wood. She sensed she was now passing through a more ancient part of the forest. Like relics of some other world, the haunted trees here had withstood endless eons of ferocity and violence wrought upon them by the storm. Her brutal winds had beaten their great trunks into monstrous and distorted shapes. Their twisted roots bulged up from the rotting corpses of their fallen brethren, while their bloated, black, and knotted limbs bent low to the ground, as if to strike it with their fists.

All of a sudden, Ana felt a sharp point in her back. She winced, screaming out so that the horse paused to look back at her. But as she looked up, she saw it was just a tree limb that had scraped across her back. She then saw it was part of a vast row of knotted witch-hazels, whose giant stand of trees stretched into the darkness about her. Spaced evenly, with arms outstretched, the crooked limbs of these black giants seemed almost animated. And Ana cringed, as they passed between them.

Ana saw that the trees appeared to have many strange faces wrapped about their trunks, like that of ancient seers tortured by some unending madness. Bearded and black, with crooked noses and hollow cheeks, the largest trees seemed to bear upon their trunks the grimaced and distorted faces of possessed and hoary wizards, born of some lost arcane and evil world. Wrinkled and worn, their countenances bore the struggles of an endless and apocalyptic war, in which the horrors of some uncontrollable black magic had been unleashed upon them, lashing its full fury back upon their masters.

With the sound of the horse's hooves, the faces of the trees now awakened. The glowing orbs of their cold and expressionless eyes poked through their crumbling and ragged bark to stare at the small girl as she passed between them. Their eyes shined forth with a ghoulish glow, their numerous orbs hovering in the hollows of the distant woods as they passed. Some burned from deep down with a devilish fire, like that of red-hot coals, while others shined out with a pale green or aqua glow. Most just simmered with strange and bewitching, smoke-filled globes, hypnotizing her with their enchanting lights.

For the spirits that dwelt within these demonic trees could use their seductive gaze to tempt the living. The wary traveler so entranced would then fall into a cursed sleep. They would then be dragged to their death in the cold mud beneath their roots, their flesh consumed by the devilish trees that had reached up to grab them and pull them down.

But the pale horse seemed to know of the tricks of the witch-hazel, and would not tarry long. The spells placed upon Ana were soon broken by his brisk and determined gait.

But as Ana passed close to their trunks, the vile trees began to whisper into her ear, strange half-heard words of ominous forebodings, mutterings, mumblings, and meaningless babblings of an ancient and forgotten tongue. Some shouted out in rage, unintelligible incantations and lost enchantments left from some cryptic age of dark sorcery. But nothing came of their archaic words. For the demonic spirits of the trees had been sundered from their ancient homeland long ago. And so their black magic could hold no power over the living in Phantaia.

But the evil trees began to change, bending their great trunks towards the strange travelers passing through their lands. Crooked limbs bent slowly towards their path, their dark boughs oozing an evil sap from their bark, which dripped down like black stalactites. The trees stretched their knotted limbs across their path to block them. But the horse galloped past, going under and around their boughs. For it was swift of foot and determined to avoid their grasp.

Ana hung on to the horse's mane. But she could not see the increasing numbers of nightmarish forms that moved about her in the darkness. She held on tight as the white horse galloped even faster, racing past the towering witch-hazels, which lumbered through the woods on their writhing, snakelike roots, as they strove to close off the path in front of them.

But the horse would not be caught, and galloped on with great haste. As Ana looked back, she saw the sinister trees had continued to pursue them along the shadows of the path, until their dark masses faded from view behind them.

Ana clung again to the horse's neck, and closed her eyes at that horror-filled sight. She trusted the white horse more than ever. Warmed by its wide back, and rocked by the gentle rhythm of its four-footed gait, she soon felt sleep return to her. As she did, she could hear in the distance the last sounds of the whistling winds of the storms as they drifted away. For a time it drowned out the endless babbling of the trees that still drifted up from the depths of the demonic woods about them.

But as she drifted into dreams, she saw that they were once again enveloped in that odd lavender mist. It had descended upon them, wrapping its cool blanket about their bodies. Its faded lights cast back the shadows of the trees, illuminating the dim path that wound its way before them. The strange fog seemed to protect them, hiding them from the eyes of the evil trees that still crept about in the farthest hollows of the woods. Like a cocoon, that lavender cloud surrounded and encased them, so that she and the horse could only see the path lying directly in front of them. And Ana felt protected and embraced by the eerie arms of that fog.

Yet when it fell, it seemed to signal some strange change from the day to night. For in that twilight forest only half-light could exist, so that neither the faded light of day, cast from above, nor the darkness of the forest's night below could penetrate its somber glow. As it curled about them, the mist seemed to draw from within her the feeling of relaxation and sleep, so that soon she returned to the land of dreams.

A strange vision had come bubbling up into Ana's mind from some hidden place, deep inside her. She saw herself sleeping beneath the waters of a serene sea, whose surface was like a pool's—cool, calm, and bright. When she looked above the water, she saw a glorious garden around her, bathed in the light of youthful green grass and flowering plants. Their many hues and tints seemed to cast away the shadows that had descended from the gloomier forest about it.

A blinding light shone down from some living source she could not discern. And she saw the smiling faces of many creatures of wondrous beauty and form gathering about it. Upon a hill, stood two that had been wed together as one. About them a wondrous host of birds and beasts had gathered. And the loving couple's hopeful and happy eyes, in the flowering of their youth, shined and sparkled like jewels in the midst of their joyful union.

Suddenly a horrible pain filled her body. She looked again and the pool was no more. The creatures were gone. And the lights of the garden had dimmed and turned ashen. The beautiful growth now lay dry and dead at her feet. She looked with sadness upon the wreckage the shadows had wrought upon the woods, and she wept. Yet she shivered with the evil that now clearly possessed it.

But as she looked at the middle of her body, she saw she was bloody. And she screamed in terror, falling back again beneath the waves, drifting down into the dark pool of her nightmares. As she held onto the warm neck of the horse, its gentle spirit seemed to speak to her, telling her not to fear. And in her half-awake state she could feel, by that beast's presence alone, her fears drifting away. Holding onto his neck, she then returned to peaceful sleep, as the mist enveloped her in the safety of its arms.

* * *

Far away, in the shattered Realms of Oblivion, the Shade had flown alone, out across the barren fields of dark ice that bordered the bleak Lands of Midnight. On she flew through the foggy skies until she had come before a tall opening in the side of the mountains.

Here lay the Corridors of Darkness whose decadent hallways descended into the depths beneath the Lands of Midnight. These had for many ages connected the lightless lands above with her father's secretive realms below.

A towering concourse stood before her, rising up from a vast gorge that lay beneath the barren cliffs. Its great vaulted ceiling lay cracked and open to the skies. For its massive stone roof had long ago been shattered by an ancient struggle. The last of the grim Angels of Night—those who had guarded the dark halls with their shining shields and spears of jet—had long ago fled away through its broken ceiling, never to return.

As the Shade flew into the great hallway, she saw upon the vertiginous heights at every level countless dark doorways, which opened up into a nightmarish maze of endless balconies, chambers, bridges, and gateways. Beyond these lay even more doors leading into yet wider corridors, which penetrated even deeper into the rock of the mountain.

Travelling down the massive corridor the Shade saw that the towering hall was now intersected at intervals with ever-widening highways and tunnels. These grim underworld corridors trailed off into the dreary depths in either direction, eventually merging with the misty Halls of Time into which many a lonely traveler had been lost. These eerie blue spaces stretched into the pitiless gloom of the forbidding underworld. The beating of the Shade's wings could be heard echoing through their yawning spaces.

Once bustling with the denizens of the Midnight realms, these great catacombs were now wrapped in a pitiless silence, abandoned, long forgotten, and empty of any spirit living or dead that might have crept there.

On her feathery wings the Shade quietly drifted down the long gloomy corridors, descending ever deeper into the cold hollows of the mountain. The hall's curved roof of stonework, supported by monumental buttresses of rock, had collapsed into the depths below. This had allowed the roof above to shatter in places, and the last of the feeble lights of Heaven to drift down through the rock, dropping their sad shadows in long shapes across the mottled walls and into the exposed depths below.

Below her on either side stood ornate iron gateways, rising up in the shadows as wide cavernous openings in the rock. These had once led into her father's secluded cities. Now broken by long-forgotten battles, these gloomy gates stood rusty and bent, their iron grating torn from their hinges by some horrific force.

The remnant army of the Endless Night had once dwelt behind these latticed archways, standing guard before the many entrances to his underworld cities. Beyond these great entrances now lay the bones of giant sentinels long dead, rotting away in their sealed tombs. These great beings would never rise again, their heroic spirits long ago having fled their dried corpses, and disappearing into the haunted wasteland of Oblivion. For the heroic yet tragic age of night had come and gone.

Yet hidden within the catacombs behind secret doors and walls, a few of the Endless Night's surviving undead servants still crept about in the shadows. These sleepy and sad vampiric beings watched the lonesome traveler from afar. For they alone had remained to guard his realms and prey upon the wary. But they did not know if their lord would ever awaken again, to summon them to defend their lonely posts against some invading army.

As the Shade drifted down the hallway, she looked up in awe and wonder at that which rose up before her. At the end the corridor stood a towering gate of iron and stone, monumental in height and width. This was one of the great Gates of Midnight that had guarded its many underworld realms.

The Shade knew that no spell could open that door, nor giant's hand break its bands. But high above in the darkness of an upper balcony, she saw a small opening whose shattered grate of iron would allow her to pass beyond its great door.

The Shade quietly drifted on silent wings through the opening. But as she passed through the window she saw that she was but a tiny speck compared to the dizzying depths that opened up before her in the gloomy beyond.

Stretching away in front of her lay a vast domed cavern, whose supporting walls disappeared into the unseen spaces below her. Giant carved buttresses of stone lay around the periphery of the vast chasm, rising up out of the empty gulf below to support the shadowed ceiling above. Countless colossal hallways opened up at intervals around its circumference. Their farthest walls were hidden by ghostly clouds, which poured around them from some unknown source in vast rivers of fog and steam.

These were the lost entrances to the boundless Halls of Time, whose treacherous pathways stretched from this nexus of dire shadows, through the vaulted Corridors of Darkness, and into the ethereal infinity that lay past the Great Beyond. But their misty halls had also stretched into the frontiers of Phantaia, the inner realms, so that their secretive doorways could yet be found in the forbidden depths of that wood. And so could those children, who sought the dark lands by these mystical corridors, make their way eventually to the Lands of Midnight and the timeless spaces that lay beyond them.

As the Shade floated out across the underground chamber, she saw that she was in some great cavernous city of the dead, whose teetering black walls and bridges stood above the fogs that flowed below her. Ghoulish buildings and maddening streets of the undead stretched away into the darkness, as huge iron chains and tangled ropes draped down, torn and battered, from the ceiling of the great chamber into the haunted cityscape below. What was this macabre metropolis, thought the Shade? For by its gigantic machinations and structures, it appeared to have been built for the confinement and torture of giants in a dreadful and horrific age of titanic struggle long past.

The Shade then heard a piercing cry. As she looked far below, she saw the winged forms of vile succubi and their many vampiric lovers fleeing away into the fog, like specters fleeing before the rising dawn. For they were frightened by the sudden appearance of the Child of Night that had come into their midst. Here the last vampires from the Lands of Midnight had hid from the many mouths of the Emptiness, who had sought their blue veiny flesh in the last age of the Primordial wars.

Down she flew, into the heart of that underworld chasm. Here she knew she would find her father's tomb—the fallen form of the Endless Night who had been hidden from the eyes of all others. For Agapor had shared with her the knowledge of her father's secret crypt.

The Shade could feel her father's presence near her. As she descended into the impenetrable darkness, she saw in the rubble-strewn depths a monumental platform of rock rising up from the darkness. It appeared as a great pyramid, standing proudly above the tangled underworld city that had wrapped itself about the mountain of stone. There upon its summit stood a massive head of jet black rock thrusting up its blocky head into the heights of the cavern. Within its side was carved a great doorway leading into its interior. The Shade now sensed the dim shadow of her father's spirit emanating from its opening.

But unseen by the Shade, the servant of the Shadow, Anissa, had followed her deep into the Lands of Midnight. With her cat-like eyes aglow, she stood upon the crumbling heights of the tomb, looking down upon the tiny form of the Shade, as she descended. Anissa then looked up and smiled with an evil grin, as an ominous shape suddenly appeared from the shadows of the domed ceiling high above her.

The Shade alighted upon the base of the steps, folding her long wings behind her. As she stood upon the stairs leading up to the opening, a cold waft of air drifted out from it. She thought she could faintly smell fresh blood. She then looked down at her feet and saw a wide pool of black blood had slowly dripped from the doorway down the dark steps below her.

Reaching the summit, she walked through the strange opening in the rock. Its door was carved in bas-relief, revealing unusual runic scripts and strange imagery. There in its innermost chamber she saw a short rise of steps, upon whose wide pedestal sat a thick stone sarcophagus made of blackest basalt. But beside the crypt stood a majestic throne made of strange dark crystal. The Shade knelt before it, knowing it to be her father's chair.

The Shade then saw a black pool of blood beneath the seat of the throne. The Endless Night had bled there for many ages. For his brothers wielding cursed blades had inflicted many war-wounds upon his flesh, cuts that could not heal and which slowly drained his life from him. His living essence had gradually poured down and around the chair, and out of the tomb in great rivers. The Shade then paused, with tears in her eyes.

As she climbed the last rise she saw that the lid of the tomb was shattered. Hesitant to face her father, she cautiously removed the broken lid. She then looked upon the aged and shriveled face of her father, the Endless Night, and wept. Many battle scars did he wear. Yet his dark eyes looked peaceful. Clad in his gothic armor, bloody and gored by endless wars, he had lain there alone for many ages. But it was the old wound, the hidden one she could not see that had hurt him most. For his mighty heart had remained shattered by the loss of those he loved.

The Shade bent down to touch the wrinkled and bearded face of her father. For she only vaguely remembered it as a child. But by her cruel bondage to the black manacles had she been forbidden to return to him. Only the sad memory of their long separation had she known. And it weighed heavily upon her, feeding her own deep regret. Yet she felt no bitterness, only sorrow.

As she touched his wrinkled face beneath his mighty helm, she heard behind her the thunderous sound of feet, shaking the very rock about her. As she turned, she saw her brother, the Shadow, standing in the doorway, his evil eyes looking down upon her with great hatred, and sinister delight.

But before she could flee from him, he strode across the room, placing his long hands about her throat. As he began to strangle her, he looked down upon her pitiful form, saying, "You betrayed me, my sister, to the Child of Mist, our master and most-hated of enemies. And for this you must die." The Shade gasped for air, as she looked upon the black face of her brother, grabbing at his long arms, trying desperately to free herself.

But up from the crypt rose the body of the Endless Night. For he had not perished, but had remained in a dark sleep, awaiting his children whom he had somehow known would return to him. Seeing his daughter in the grips of death, he called out to his son, "Release her."

The Shadow looked in shock upon the strange form of his father, releasing his sister, who then fell to the floor. Seeing her father alive, the Shade cried out to him, "Father!" The Endless Night looked upon his precious daughter. And a single black tear fell from his eyes.

The Endless Night climbed forth from his crypt. He looked down at his lost son, who now stood proudly before him. He walked with a weary gait, down the stairs, and gazed upon his beloved daughter's face. And he smiled. The Endless Night then returned to his son, staring deep into his eyes. But the Shadow stood still and unmoving. The Endless Night then felt within his son a strange presence, the emptiness of something corrupted and evil he too had once known.

But the Shadow glared at his father with hate in his eyes, saying, "Father, I do not know you. Nor do I care to know of you. For you abandoned me long ago, when I was but a young child."

The Endless Night then said, "My son, I sought you in the depths of the world for many weary ages. The Twilight Mist took you from me long ago, in the last of the ancient wars. Your own uncle did this cruel deed, so that I would suffer from the loss of my own children. Not knowing if you still lived or died, I roamed the farthest corners of that world seeking you, until I had given up all hope of ever seeing you alive again. Never had I stopped, my son, until by the cursed light of another my heart had finally broken. I then turned away from the world, returning here, uncertain if I would ever see your face or that of your daughter's again. Yet had a vision come to me in my sleep that I would see you again at a chosen time. And so has that time come at last." The Endless Night then smiled, reaching out to embrace his son. But the Shadow turned away.

The Endless Night reached out his hand to his daughter, who ran to him and embraced her father, shedding many tears. The Endless Night then said, "At long last. We shall now be joined as father, son, and daughter once more, remaking the nighttime skies together as one, as it had been destined we should do by our Great Father. For this is now my one desire, which my troubled mind had not known until I saw your faces again. By your presence—given unto me by the grace and mercy of the Great Father—I now see our truer purpose."

The Endless Night then looked down at his daughter with joyous and peaceful eyes. Content and blissful he seemed to her. And she saw the true majesty and strength of her proud and fearless father.

But the Shadow had turned away from him, walking out of the dark temple, and looking down upon the wreckage of his father's city in the darkness below. He grimaced, seeing all that had been abandoned or destroyed, witnessing with a single glance the full decadence of the ruin, waste, and decay of his father's once great city. And he thought about all that had been lost.

He then returned to his father, saying, "All that you have fostered and fathered has failed. Can you not face this truth, even now, in your final triumphant revelations? Eons ago you failed to bind the minds of your brothers to your own shadow. From their final siege upon your cities was the dominion of darkness destroyed, and your own children ripped away from you and imprisoned."

"You ceded the powers of the night to your brothers. And your own children you willingly surrendered to the merciless hands of those same sadistic siblings. Even now, my sister and I remain tortured and enslaved to the magic iron that your brother hath made, bound to the weak will of his own bastard child. Your own daughter whores the last of herself to that vile enemy through her own self-loathing and pity for him. Is your own fallen daughter—long forgotten and yet most precious to you—not deserving of thy great and noble house? Has her own father forgotten his abandoned daughter and her plight so easily?" said the Shadow, grimacing at his father.

The Endless Night looked down in shame. But before he could speak, his son came at him with great anger, saying, "Father, the length of your own shadow now shortens. It is fading quickly now. Yet you are brazen. For you have so easily forgiven yourself now, before your passing, releasing yourself from a lifetime of evil you have spawned, while your own children still live, only to suffer as a result of your sins, bent and bearing proudly upon their backs your burdens. You dare to dream of a better world, an idyllic world for yourself and that of your enemies' children, while your own flesh and blood remain enslaved, bowing down in servitude to them."

The Shadow defiantly said, "But my sister and I will not suffer in vain for your sins, Father. For we have come here to defy you, we who are the ghosts of your troubled and failed past. It is our time now. And so we shall defy you and your will, and like our blessed father of ages past, defy the will of the world."

The Endless Night could only look upon his fallen son with weak and sorrowful eyes. But the Shadow turned to his father, his eyes ablaze with an angry red fire, saying, "Look at me, Father.

Face me now. Surrender to me what gifts and powers of yours that yet remain. Grant to me, your only son, the right to the justice I deserve...we deserve. I am the Prince of Darkness now by my birthright, the Lord of thy Midnight Lands. I alone shall reclaim the shadows of this world for us, bathing it in my own, so that nevermore shall the living know the lights of Heaven, serving only darkness. Father, I alone shall take back from the Primordial Ones what was promised to us. The Limitless Void has already fallen, as shall the Twilight Mist who has imprisoned me. The time has come for you to relinquish your powers to me so that your remaining brothers may perish by my hand."

The Endless Night then looked in horror at his son. The Shadow then held his great black fist before him, saying, "Father, give me the Wings of Night! Give them to me now. For only they may shade the world from the scarring flame of the Sacred Light that has arisen in the farthest woods of the world to punish us. It has arisen, father, yet again, because *you* failed to extinguish it."

The Endless Night now saw the true terror of that which hid within his son. And he realized that the Nightmare Unending, which he himself had made, had filled his son's corrupted heart with its lies. He saw that his son possessed within him the full wrath of that dire spirit, which had before dwelt as but a blight upon him. His son would soon seek to enslave the children of this world, as he was so enslaved. By those evil bonds would a fate worse than death be born within their spirits. With its powers would the Shadow now curse the living, planting not only terror within their weakened minds, but despair and hopelessness in their hearts, so that they would turn to evil, hate, and murder. And that cruel destiny was unconscionable to him.

The Endless Night then said to his troubled son, "I shall never give that power to you, my son. For it was not made for evil purposes. It was created so that the lights of Heaven's stars might shine forth from their dark celestial wings, and their music sing out in great harmony."

But the Shadow grabbed his frail father, throwing him to the ground. Then with his horrid strength, he reached down to rip the dark wings from his father's back. But the Endless Night rose to his feet to face his son. He then drew his great jagged sword of jet, and swung its smoking blade to strike down his son.

But his father was weak. For the Shadow caught the dark misty blade in his iron hand. And with his might, he wrested it from him. The Shadow cried out, "Then I shall cut them from you, Father, if I must."

He took the savage blade and slew his father with it so that the last of his dark blood poured from him. With the sinister sword the Shadow then chopped the black wings from his father's back. These dark wings he placed into his own flesh, so that their black roots grew into his shoulders and back. He stretched forth their leathery sails, full and wide across the room. And they shimmered like dark satin sheets, casting strange shadows about the chamber walls.

With those powers the Shadow grew in might and strength, so that he towered over his fallen father. And so that which his father once held was now his. The Shadow then looked upon his fallen father. And an evil grin grew upon his face.

With a booming voice, the Shadow spoke to the Shade, "Rise up, my sister, and leave us. Go to Agapor and tell him the Wings of Night are now mine. I shall go to Phantaia and do all that I had vowed, and more."

The Shade then cried for her father, seeing his sad figure upon the floor. But she fled away in terror from her brother, out of the temple, flying in desperation to reach Agapor. For she knew what her vengeful brother would do.

The Endless Night lay upon death's doorway, sprawled upon the ground before his son. With burning red eyes of hate, the Shadow looked upon his father's weakened form with great contempt.

Hovering over his dying father, he said to him, "Father, in truth, I no longer care for this broken world. For it was destroyed long ago by the Primordial Ones, and doomed by their flawed designs upon it. With the Wings of Night, I shall now consume the world in darkness, then go before the evil that dwells in the

Great Beyond and help them obliterate it back into dust. Its remains shall be blown away into the many mouths of the Emptiness. And the spirit of the dust consumed by the Nothingness. Then shall I alone dwell in the unending and black despair that remains. That is my only desire now. For in my mind and heart I hear their voices. I now know it was their servant who came into me as a boy, filling my heart with their whispers. And so, like the seductive servant that haunts my heart, shall their secret will and desire be completed through me." And the Shadow looked down at the figure of his dying father with grim and resolute eyes.

The Endless Night then looked with sadness upon his son, as his life force faded from him. The Shadow picked up his father's limp body, and carried him to the edge of the stairs. He cast him into the darkness, down into an underground stream that flowed through the slimy sewers of the city. And he watched with fascination as the dark form of his father disappeared beneath the waves. But a pair of green eyes from high above had also watched that scene with malevolent interest.

The Shadow climbed to the top of his father's tomb, stretching his great black wings out over its apex. He then commanded the last of the servants of Midnight to come to him. From out of the deep holds and labyrinths beneath the Lands of Midnight they billowed forth, climbing up from the foggy depths, and circling about the great dome of the cavern. These were the last of the bat-winged creatures that had once darkened the world in its youth.

The Shadow now gathered them together in a great host, commanding them to fly to Phantaia. Screeching and wailing with excitement, the winged beasts of Midnight flew out of the cavern through a huge hole in the ceiling, up into the misty skies, and over the black peaks of Midnight. They flowed forth in an endless stream, across the seas and through the Heavens, flying towards the misty shores of Phantaia. The Shadow then departed his father's tomb, never to return. And so, with the wings of his father the Shadow had finally gained the power he had long sought.

* * *

Meanwhile, far away in the silent splendor of Phantaia's vast wilderness, Ana awoke to the sound of hooves, and the rhythmic beat of the hardened path beneath her. Once more she found herself travelling upon the back of the mysterious horse. As she opened her eyes, she saw that the horse seemed to be following a well-worn trail into a wood she did not recognize.

As she rested upon his warm back, she thought of the horrors of the previous night. Its memory, though evanescent, yet lingered. For with each new shadowed glade they passed through, her fear of the haunted trees had returned. Yet strangely, the horse had removed that fear. The confidence and trust she had in it had not diminished but had grown, and was a part of her spirit now. The creature seemed ghostlike, almost from a dream, yet connected to the forest itself somehow. Ana held onto its neck, trusting it fully, and letting it carry her on their mysterious journey. But where were they going?

The white horse had travelled a great distance while she slept, going deeper into the endless forest, climbing higher and higher into its farthest reaches. Only the dim flash of blue lightning in the distance remained to light the winding trail. And the gentle sound of a dewy rain had begun to drip down from the wet boughs above.

As they travelled beyond the murkier wilderness, the trees had changed, almost imperceptibly at first. She saw that the forest was lit by a faint inner light glowing forth from every rock, tree, root, and leaf. The evil trees of the dimmer wood had faded back into the shadows, giving way to loftier timber whose imposing gray trunks had risen up from the umber soil to challenge them, casting back with their humble shade the malicious shadows of their evil brethren.

With each bend of the trail, Ana felt a new sense of anticipation. They had begun to climb a massive hill, passing through wide glades, which lay open to the skies about the hillsides. Deep cliffs fell away beyond the trail, spanned by precarious bridges of mossy rocks, which they now crossed at intervals. She saw wide mountains above her, shining with dark green woods about their slopes. Far below her in the curving canyons, she looked down at the meandering waves of misty tree lines, as they stretched away into the sleepy depths of foggy valleys.

In the rocky depths she heard the sound of rushing water—small silver streams flowing clear and bright—descending from a place high above her, falling away as cascading white waterfalls down into the dewy chasms below. About the cliffs clung a rich verdure of tangled vines, drooping ferns, and rich moss, which hung down in masses about the path.

As they reached the summit of the hill, the glowing mist that had hovered about the forest seemed to have departed again. And she saw in the valley that fell away before her, a brighter and more hopeful landscape.

As they descended into this wide valley, she noticed the forest was filled with even larger trees, monstrous in size, with trunks of even greater width. This sea of trees, dark and dreary in the deepening shade of the canyon, stretched their pearly trunks up from the purple depths into the starless Heavens above them. These ancient behemoths had grown apart at wide intervals, so that in the dim light they appeared like aged warriors returning from some grim battlefield from which they alone had survived. Beside the many bubbling brooks, the trees' giant roots had draped beneath them like cobwebs, weaving their way across the green mossy earth until they entangled themselves in their neighbors' feet.

Although this wilderness of giants felt threatening, the trees here felt more alive, rich with new growth, and filled with a happier spirit that Ana could but faintly sense. For the opaque ebony of the earlier woods had been replaced with an emerald opalescence. Below the trees' deeply shaded verdure had grown a dense carpet of dark green ferns, silver streams, and moss-covered boulders, who untouched by time appeared almost pristine, yet a relic of an ancient paradise tragically fallen and faded. The undulating wood, perpetually renewed by its lush green growth and bathed by the spray of its tumbling waters, appeared to resonate with the living spirit of its magnificent trees. But few would ever know that its true essence lay hidden in the treasure of the black earth beneath it.

Large plants, cast in various shades of faded viridian, had grown up from the forest floor, thick and bulbous in the shadowy soil. Erupting up from the dense piles of leaves and logs, they grasped at the air with their thick vines and wide wet leaves, until they stretched their tendrils into the air about Ana. Many of the thickest vines, wide as her body, had curled themselves around the great trunks of the trees in one mass, until bursting forth from their tops, they hung down from mossy limbs in wide drapes of thick growth.

Many odd blooms and translucent flowers seemed to burst forth from the soil below their feet, like pale ghosts rising up from some mossy graveyard of the dead. Blanched orchids and purple foxglove crept up from below and lay in thick blankets beneath the feet of the trees. Black pansies with centers of faded gold stared up at her from along the trail. And endless meadows of ghostly asphodel, springing forth from the rich soil, now bent their sad starry faces to peer up at the forlorn girl as she passed by.

As they rode through the peaceful valley, they had begun to climb a small misty rise again. Upon this small hillock grew yet another shining wood whose trees were cast aglow with an even stranger light. For many ages, the soft dews of the purple mists had dripped down upon the trees here, soaking their solemn glades with their rains, so that in the faded light every bud and leaf seemed bathed in a grim yet glistening glow.

Ana saw that the dense violet mist had encircled these woods, filling them with its cloud as if to hide them. It had risen up from the piles of leaves and roots below her, casting its shimmering and shadowy light about the trunks of the trees and plants which remained almost trapped in its haunting color. And as the pair passed through the mist, its motionless sheets swirled about them, as if welcoming them with its eerie dance to its true home.

In this part of the forest, the powers of the Twilight Mist had long held sway, guarding the middle realms of Phantaia with his great clouds, unchallenged. His twilight had enveloped and colored the land, so that the trees and rocks were bathed and imbibed in his violet dew. They could not escape it. For by the ever-present mist Phantaia had in time become stained, so that all living things that had entered it were now cast aglow with a soft lavender shade.

But Ana knew she had been followed by that creeping fog. It seemed to stare down at her, to peek behind trees, pause awhile and then disappear. Hidden behind trees and rocks, the mist had climbed up and over the treetops, weaving its violet fog through the boughs, until it dissolved itself in the inky depths of Heaven. Then it would rise again from the leafy floor below their feet, snaking its way through the forest's darkest, most cavernous depths, until but a pale shade of its strange hue had remained.

But all who had come to Phantaia seeking to penetrate its many mysteries would find great peril within that mist. For no guiding star yet shined through its faded fog to show them a path. Nor could the darkness that still crawled about the rocks and trees yet devour its native light. Nothing could despoil the many secretive works and labors of the Twilight Mist in Phantaia. For this was his princely home. And his spirit would remain in those woods ever after, having long ago chased the light of day and the dark of night from its midst.

And so was this gloomy land named Avra, the twilit realm, where the haunted mists, torn between day and night, perpetually flowed.

But the two worlds of light and dark had waged a brutal war in this part of Phantaia for many eons. And the Twilight Mist alone had witnessed the savagery of the Battle of the Trees that had long plagued it. But the victors in those conflicts were given a mysterious gift by him. For the Twilight Mist had cast his somber glow down onto the last of the monstrous trunks that had stood so proudly upon the heights, until their gray bark shone forth with his light. And so had his mists wound their way among the warring trunks until his dew, born of sorrow for the many fallen forest children, clung to the trees and the rocks that hung upon the hilly heights, dripping his tears down into the earth that lay about their feet.

His rains formed rivulets and small streams, which disappeared into an underworld of roots and rot beneath them. Those streams then formed rushing rivers, which flowed endlessly over moss-covered walls of rocks and logs, carving great arteries across the land. Cascading down into the wider valleys below, they merged with the mighty river called Avalyr, where they had gathered as one to flow to the sea.

But in Avalyr, the Twilight Mist's own daughter had hidden, dwelling in peace far from her father's fogs of war. Although she was a child of that river, was she ever nourished by her father's tears, which had for untold ages poured down from the mountains and hills high above her. The Twilight Mist had thus sustained the river, his daughter, and the land of Phantaia with his own loving waters. And his mists would ever after hold dominion there, gripping the forest in its phantom fog, until long after the time of his own passing.

Ana and the horse rode through this twilit arcadia, between the solemn groves of lavender trees that stretched high above them. Their dense canopy of dark umbrage scattered mottled shadows down upon the narrow path. Here the ancient elm and ash trees had grown, thrusting up from the dark soil with their erect trunks, whose shining bark glistened and sparkled with the dew of fresh rain.

As they rode past, Ana gazed with wonder at the majesty of this silent gallery of trees. Their meandering limbs and trunks stretched upwards, thrusting their powerful boughs out into timeless space, and spreading their silver leaves through the Heavens. They seemed almost to be seeking some unseen light, thought Ana. But as she looked up, she imagined she glimpsed a small golden beam, reflecting its light off their uppermost limbs. But from what source had it shone?

Standing tall, proud, and defiant, no storm nor wind, time, age, or force of evil could fell these giants. For these trees were guardians. Hidden by the Twilight Mist, they were the last of the great armies of Phantaia that had protected its inner realms from the demonic trees of Avaras. For its possessed witch-hazels had waged war against the elms, seeking to tear them down and breach the brighter lands of living green growth that had, for almost an eternity, dwelt peacefully beyond their reach.

As they plodded on, Ana saw they were heading towards an even brighter place that lay just beyond the trees. At the summit of a large round hill, they came to a last stand of trees. There she saw before her an unending line of rowan trees, soaring up from the hilltop. Standing side by side, they formed an almost perfect wall of trunks, whose solid row of trees crowned the hill in either direction.

These were the Avalumlea, the rowans of light, whose silver limbs and trunks stood like an endless castle wall between the two realms of Phantaia –the domain of the darker woods behind them and the brighter lands beyond. Ana had passed through the storm-wracked, spookier realms of Avaras. But beyond this wall of trees lay another world yet unmarred by any living thing. And so had the rowans carefully guarded all entrance to that shining land with their impenetrable trunks. But these ancient trees seemed much grander than all the others Ana had seen. With their heavy roots and straight trunks trailing down the hill to either side, these trees now blocked all travelers by both land and air. For their trunks grew so high they disappeared beyond the mists that rolled high above their heads.

As they neared the trees, the horse seemed to know of a hidden place along its walls—perhaps some unseen door that would allow them to pass through. For much like the trees upon the beaches of Phantaia, this strange beast had known the forest's many hidden paths and unguarded gates. Ana knew by his determined look that soon they would travel beyond them.

As they neared the wall, from out of the dense foliage there appeared a massive giant of a tree, whose dark serpentine limbs curled up and around each other, spiraling up into the sky. It was like no other tree she had encountered. For it seemed to be of great age. Its wide knotted trunk had great cavernous cracks about its base. And she noticed that its bark was covered in thick ferns and wild moss, which had embraced the tops of its many black boughs.

Yet its bark bore the scars of many battles. It looked forlorn and out of place beside the others. For it had once lain at the heart of some ancient forest, now destroyed and forgotten. Its appearance was strange and otherworldly. As its trunk bent back and forth in the breeze, she thought perhaps it was possessed of some unusual spirit.

But this was the fatherly yew called Iwu, one of the many chieftain trees of Phantaia. He appeared to be sleeping. But as they approached, he came to life, slowly unravelling his entwined arms and bending his long limbs down to the ground before them.

The white horse now stood before the great tree and bent his head down. He scratched his hoof upon the ground, while shaking his head, as if communicating to it in an unknown language. The trunk's bloated bark started to move slowly, until Ana saw his dark eyes and warty lips begin to open. Nearly expressionless, Iwu stared down at them with his great amber orbs. But seeing the small child, his wide mouth smiled. Then a strange melancholy fell upon him. And he returned to deep thought again, ever-enlightened by the mystical knowledge of lost ages, which he had gathered into himself.

For the yew had seen many unusual things in this fallen and violent world. And he had faced the agony of endless war, and the constant threat of dark spirits and forces aligned against his many children. He had fought so bravely against the vile children of Avaras. And yet he had sadly seen many of his own brothers and sisters fall. And so he was weary of war in his old age, ready to leave this world. Yet had Iwu stood defiant and strong. For long had he guarded the secret gate leading to Phantaia's interior.

Iwu turned to the horse. And with his great arms, pointed to a small corner of the rowan trees behind him. For he was the sole guardian of the gateway that yet remained within the trees of Avalumlea. Beyond this door lay glorious Phantavra, the shining lands of Phantaia. And so, for countless ages had the ancient yew barred the evil trees of darker Avaras from entering that land.

Ana looked where the yew had pointed, when suddenly a glowing door appeared. The entrance to a secretive new world now lay open before her. Beyond it she saw a greener and grander landscape, glowing with a warm and vibrant light from an unknown and unseen source. An eerie silence then fell upon them. For the winds had died. And the skies grew grim and dark, though Ana could not see any clouds besides the pale mist that had followed them.

Then was heard the beating of leathery wings rising up from the depths of the woods. From out of the trees erupted a hoard of flying beasts. Their ebony wings beat upon the air with thunderous force, as their dark streams shaded the woods about them. They swooped down upon the rowans, which shuddered in fear before the black bat-winged host.

The ancient yew then turned to Ana and the horse, and pointed his knotted limb towards the opening again. Soon it would close.

As Ana and the horse looked up, they saw the terrible creatures of the night descending upon the tops of the trees, rending their leaves from them. And with the force of their wings, they sent their boughs flying to the ground. They bit into their trunks with sharp teeth, until blood-like sap dripped forth. Ana looked in horror as the trees began to turn dark and shrivel with age.

Iwu, the giant yew, spread his monstrous limbs high into the Heavens, striking the beasts from the air with wide sweeps of his arms. Many of the creatures were then thrown back into the woods before him. But soon there appeared even greater streams of bat-like beings, their burning eyes set aglow and enraged. As they streamed across the tops of the trees the sound of their screaming and screeching echoed through the woods. Ana saw that soon their great masses would completely blacken the skies and consume them in their suffocating shadows.

Ana and the horse galloped quickly towards the doorway. But as she turned to look back, she saw in the depths of the woods a monstrous form, rising above the forest in the distance. Its great claws gripped the tops of the trees. And they swayed with every beat of its black satin wings. As Ana gazed upon its crooked face, its red, fiery eyes peered down into hers, penetrating her very heart with its evil stare.

As Ana screamed, the white horse jumped through the doorway. Bursting through the opening, the shining door just as quickly closed behind them. And the terror of that scene seemed to fade instantly from view. All was quiet now. For the Avalumlea had completely sealed the inner lands of Phantaia from the darker realms beyond. The living trees were all that now stood between them and the battle that raged on the other side.

Only an eerie quiet remained, as Ana and the white horse raced ahead into the depths of a bright new land. As they galloped down the path, Ana contemplated the fate of the poor yew and shuddered. But the horrible vision of that black being remained. For it was clearly her it had come for.

THE JOURNEY'S END

Ana had escaped evil's grisly hand, carried by the horse from a shadowed to a shining land. She held onto his mane with all her might, as it raced on towards a distant light. As they galloped past the swaying trees, she felt the touch of a warmer breeze. For within the canopy of those brighter woods, the dusky leaves sparkled where a golden light now stood. Yet no lustrous lantern in those woods had shined, and no blazing star or shimmering sun could she find.

As they rode on down the bright white paths of the forest, the haughty dense umbrage of Avaras was now replaced with green glades of younger trees. This was the youthful forest of Avalumlea, that which had bordered Avaras, its darker brother. Yet was it strangely a part of Phantavra. For here grew the rowans' many children, who in time would replace their fallen parents. Seeing this vast nursery of younger trees so closely guarded, Ana now knew the truer purpose of Avalumlea's mighty wall.

A white fog had wound itself among the limbs of this youthful forest. For pale clouds had replaced the darker mists that had snaked their way through the blacker boughs of Avaras. But through the slow breaking of the clouded veil by winds aloft, Ana was able to see clearly the full scale of this much brighter wood. The young trees here had thrived, no longer half-dead, but fuller and more alive. And every living blade of grass and leaf here seemed imbibed with a kinder spirit and more loving nature.

For this was an enlightened wilderness, free of the darker spirits, where the brighter and lighter trees had grown unhindered by the weight of evil's lifeless insipid earth. For here the new trees seemed drawn together by a shared joy and bliss, blessed by a timeless peace granted to each and every living thing. A thriving forest, the trees here seemed to speak to Ana in a softer tongue, their breath mingling with the windswept tops of their sister trees.

For swift currents now cast their limbs aloft, dancing in the breeze, swaying back and forth with thick heads of whispering leaves.

Below her appeared the buds of small gold and silver flowers, which for the first time shined forth with their own inner illumination. And the young green and yellow leaves of spring's first buds opened up on the trees around her, as they passed. The limbs of the trees reached out to touch Ana's face, as if clamoring to feel her presence. And she felt their loving leaves upon her face, welcoming her as one among their own.

Crystalline dew had gathered on the larger limbs as before, dripping a constant rain down upon them. And their moist leaves sparkled like diamonds overhead, shining with a strange prism set aglow by the mysterious unseen light that beamed down from the distant Heavens. But the silver-colored bark and bright leaves of the forest seemed to cast their own loving light. For a brilliant emerald sheen was thrown down upon the land from the thick leaf-laden boughs above, as the soft chartreuse of young grasses shined up from the moist earth below.

The smiling forest of youthful Phantavra had directed its sunny beams upon Ana and the horse, with little fingers of light, silver and bejeweled, cascading down across their faces. She felt the warm breath of the trees, hearing their voices aloft, soft and sweet in her ears as they passed by. Ana was so comforted by the woods that the former terrors filling her mind now drifted away, replaced with the peace and beauty of this new joyous new landscape. Still she failed to find the source of the warm glow that filled it.

Ana and the horse rode on through Phantavra's many shining glades and valleys, until they began to slowly climb again. The winds had increased as they rode on. The horse had begun to stray from the path, climbing past vast groves of grand old alder trees, which grew along the misty margins of a tumbling stream. These tall trees lined up in almost perfect columns in the depths of the primordial wood. Their leafy heads bowed to the happy winds that blew past them, their white limbs creaking and groaning in the sway.

As they neared the top of the breezy hill, Ana saw that they had come to a high cliff, which overlooked a glorious vista. She gazed with wonder upon the breathtaking scene. Before her stretched a wide wooded valley in which a deep green river flowed, gleaming in the lustrous light as it wound its way through the peaceful landscape.

About the shining river, in either direction, lay the secluded wilderness of innermost Phantaia, whose dense woods stretched off into the distance. Its tangle of growth, wild and forbidding, filled this shining valley. The leafy heads of dense umbrage were bathed in the warmth of a far-off light, while its dark roots and vines crowded upon the edge of the high-banked river.

To her left Ana could see the waterway, curling like a shining serpent as it wound its way through the forest. But its hidden wellspring she could not discern. As the river twisted its way through the bountiful hills of the endless forest, Ana noticed the most distant trees seemed to have grown even taller. As she gazed into the haze of the horizon, Ana observed an unusual aurora of golden light beaming through the tangled boughs. And beyond those trees, a strange land where the warm glow of some secret sun emanated from a faraway, mist enshrouded hilltop.

Looking to her right, she could see the river disappear far away into the gloom of a more shaded land, until it poured over a rocky precipice in the far distance. White fog and spray climbed up from the roaring cataract, rising up from the darkness beyond, and casting a billowing mist that drifted far and wide above the tops of the trees. Beyond the falls lay an open sky that flashed with great bolts of lightning, and roared with the crashing surf of the seas. Above these waters spread a dark and somber sky, writhing with dark clouds, borne up by some distant storm, which boiled and brewed on the gloomy horizon.

But as she stared at its distant fury, something seemed to pull her back towards it, calling her from the great abyss that lay beyond the falls. Ana remained curious, standing and staring for a time into that dismal gulf. She turned to her left again, looking up the river to feel the warm light once more upon her face. That strange light had also summoned her to its source. And she felt torn by those two natural spirits.

The white horse turned its great head and nudged her. It was time to descend into the valley.

Ana and the horse climbed down the hill, following a narrow wooded glen, until they came to the rolling grassy hills that lay before the tree-lined river. There the horse stopped, lying exhausted in the warm rich grass. Below them stood a grove of huge ash trees, thick with new green growth, standing in the midst of a dense thicket that lined the banks of the river.

As Ana looked past the trees, she saw the true power and expanse of the wide rolling water as it flowed past them. But the horse did not seem anxious to cross it. With a nod of its head, it signaled for Ana to lie down and sleep beside it. She then sat alongside the great stallion. But she could not sleep. She was still curious about the unusual river and the peculiar music its waves and whirlpools now made. It was then she thought she heard the haunting voice of a child, a young girl, arising from its depths. She lay down, uncertain of it, curling up closer to the horse as it slept.

Through most of the night Ana tossed and turned in a troubled sleep, half awake and stirred by unusual noises. For the eerie sounds of the river haunted her. But soon she could no longer resist their incessant calls. She then awoke as in a fever. But seeing the peaceful form of the sleeping horse beside her, she felt calmed. She brushed its gentle face as it slept and then climbed to her feet to walk down the hill to the river below.

Traversing the grassy slope, she came to the thicket of giant ash trees that lined the fern-covered bank of the river in unending rows. As she walked into that bracken of fernal delight, the limbs of the trees seemed to toss about to some steady and measured wind. Their trunks and bent boughs had stretched themselves high above the rushing river, as if drawn to it.

As Ana climbed down to the river, she saw that the trees' massive roots, tattered and torn, had clung to the muddy riverbank, sending their thick shoots down into the depths of the river's swirling waters to draw forth its sustenance. Ana now stood upon a great root at the water's edge, peering into the depths of the mysterious river.

This was the ancient river of Avalyr, whose many twisting arteries flowed with great force through Phantaia. For many ages it had carried the collected waters of that land to the widening and beckoning gulf of the seas. It was a river ever young and alive, with the spirit of hope and the power to cleanse, so that many living things would seek the succor of its cool waters and be revived by its sweet refreshment. Yet many other strange gifts would it give to those who drank of its rare essence.

Far upstream, Avalyr had first gathered upon a mighty hill, which rose up from within Phantaia's forgotten heartland. In its center had slept the twin spirits of the Secret Spring and the Rock Eternal who, as brother and sister, had been enjoined as one to the land with a purpose most sacrosanct.

Deep within their hidden realm, the bubbling brook of the sister-spring had first fed this youthful river of Phantaia, its crystalline waters spilling out from silver pools that lay hidden within her brother's mound. For within the hill of the Rock Eternal the river was most alive, filled with the hopeful spirit of life that would long sustain it. But it was his sister, the Secret Spring, who had poured the wondrous Sands of Time into its stream. Those sands had slept beneath the river's currents, and imbibed its waters with the primal power of eternal youth so that all who drank of those wondrous waters would be free of the curse of Time, and yet married in spirit to Phantaia and its strange destiny.

Through their twin spirits had the blissful waters of Avalyr and the blessed earth of Phantaia thus remained enjoined, their fates entwined in the endless dance of youthful splendor. So would those siblings remain together, hidden in the earth, their two hearts beating in unison within Phantaia's dark bosom. Never would either spirit part from the other, until one among them should perish. For they were bound to a solemn vow they had made to the Immortal Clay, their father, to sustain Phantaia with their merciful gifts until their dying days.

But the river served a more vital purpose. For her waters yet encircled Phantaia in a protective embrace, such that none might enter its heart unless they dared to cross its perilous waters. For they alone sustained and jealously guarded the last of the secret paths to its innermost paradise. Beyond them would remain apart the outer lands of Avaras, where the misty realms between fantasy and reality, and the forces of darkness and evil yet roamed at will, unchecked. Yet, all who sought its tranquil inner nature were permitted to cross her powerful stream, and dream there without fear or danger from the marauding evil that ever crept beyond its boundary.

In time, a lonely spirit had come to dwell in Avalyr. A strange child had come into it, bubbling forth from the mother-spring that lay within the great hill. That lonely child had then been thrown into the depths of the river to dwell there alone. This was the solitary child called Atar, whose twin sister had perished beside her mother within her well. But though the spirit of her sister was bound to her grave, Atar's had remained free to roam the land, flowing from her mother's hill, down into Phantaia, alive, wild, and untamed.

Upon Atar's birth, her father the Twilight Mist had come to that land from the faraway seas. Enamored of the Secret Spring, her mother, he had bound his rains and dews to the waters of her sad well, so that they were joined in an unbreakable union of form and spirit most sacred. For their love long sustained the river, which then held within its gentle arms the mysterious river-child. So was Atar reared by her parents' nurturing fount.

In time, her father had returned to Avalyr, seeking his abandoned child. For he had sought to rescue the lonesome girl and take her away from Phantaia, so she might be hidden from the eyes of evil. The Twilight Mist had found his daughter hidden in a tiny pool. But as he reached down to hold her, in fear of him Atar turned into a silver fish, slipping away through his fingers. For her life was the river now. And her spirit would remain enjoined to it. Nothing would ever take her from the river, or Phantaia, until for another she would leave upon the Altar of Love its grave sacrifice.

Atar now dwelt alone within the depths of Avalyr, far from the eyes of all others. She sustained the river's essence, holding close to her the secrets of Time's turning wheels, which now churned within Avalyr, spinning endlessly in its cold depths. Through those wheels the river-daughter could see many things, though she could not spin the fates of the children of the world as could the daughter of the seas, her sister. But in waking from dreams, still remembered, she could read them. So to her was known the future of many worlds. Long ago were the destinies of their many children, yet unborn, revealed to her. And the melancholy truth of those visions would ever haunt her.

Atar's visions would also be clouded by another, whose strange waters would come into her own, dripping down into her mind from the heart of that wilderness. Those sad waters would forever bathe her tortured mind with the joys and suffering of the living, whose lives would be sustained, yet stained, by that mysterious pool.

Ana climbed down the roots of the ash trees and stared into the depths of the cool river as it flowed past her. She pondered its beauty and majesty. For the swirling current appeared to soothe her, calming her mind, and bringing a quiet peace to her heart. Its emerald waters shimmered and shined with soft lights and strange hues that reflected up from the mossy rocks and pebbles below.

The violet fog Ana had seen in the forest above had now flowed down the valley, laying itself across the river like a thick blanket. For Ana had sensed a living spirit dwelling in the river, one the fog had sought to hide. She searched the river for a sign of life. Yet all she saw beneath the mist was a cold and swift current flowing briskly by.

She then reached down to drink from the river's sweet waters. But as she did, she saw upon the surface the face of a young woman with hair as white as the crest of the waves. It was a face not unlike her own, staring back at her in curiosity. Strange, silent words came from the apparition's mouth, as if it was calling to her, the voice echoing out from some faraway place hidden deep within the river.

It was a voice that seemed oddly familiar, as many things had been in this world. And its shadowy sound stilled her heart's own waters, allowing her mind to reflect upon her past, her present, and her future. But in that vision all she saw was the sea, the river, and a strange pool she did not recognize. Ana reached out to touch the visage, as she had her mother's face upon the shore. But it was gone.

Ana then stood upon the roots of the tree, bewildered by the image. She climbed to the riverbank above, wandering as in a dream back to her grassy hillside bed beside the white horse. There she fell into a sleep much deeper than any she had yet experienced.

The booming sound of distant thunder woke Ana in the night. As she opened her eyes, she saw that the golden dawn of the distant light had faded into amber. The brighter green of the grass that grew about the hills had also grayed. And the rich jade of the trees had turned ashen. Only a pallid shade lay draped across the valley where the purples of the deeper shadows had once stood.

Everything around her seemed different and out of place. For the warm glow in the horizon had oddly dimmed behind a gray veil. She felt a strange stillness in the air, as if time had stopped. Was she awake or in a dream? A strange pull then overtook her mind and heart. For a haunting desire to leave the forest, the river, and even the horse now possessed her spirit. She would rise and go forth to a place high above in the mountains, where the great waterfall poured into the sea. For she longed to see it.

Leaving the sleeping horse behind, she rose to her feet and began walking along the quiet riverbank. The warm lights that had reflected upon the river's silver surface had died. And the fogs that drifted about its shores had all but disappeared. Only the shadows of the distant trees upon the farthest bank now remained. They cascaded their faded shapes and shadows down onto the river's glassy surface so that their own reflections seemed trapped in its watery mirror.

Ana then heard again the sound of a distant waterfall. The great roar of its wide cataract echoed up from the river, far away to her right. Was it the sound of her mother's spirit calling her from the seas? As she walked through the forest that lay beside the river, the strange sound of the falls drew her away from their shore. She then began travelling up into the grassy hills above.

The sound of the mysterious river pouring into the seas possessed her. She was determined to climb above the cliffs so she might see it with her own eyes. For she desired to gaze upon the spirit that dwelt within the falls, to look again upon her mother's ocean, and peer out across the cold abyss that lay beyond it.

As she climbed higher into the hills, she noticed a strange shade following close behind her, mimicking her every move. But as she stopped to look more closely at it, she saw only her shadow in the grass. Since she had left the horse, it had grown and lengthened, however. As it followed her up the hill, the shade seemed to move independently of her. She was unsure of its nature or purpose, and rushed ahead to try and escape it.

She ran on, climbing up the slopes and onto the high grassy hills that rolled on before her like endless waves. It seemed as if she had run for several nights, up and down the hills, caught in a nightmare she could not escape. For the evil shade that followed close behind, and the calling of the falls beyond the hills, haunted her exhausted mind with their constant presence.

The twilight gloom and the humid, thick air made her doubt whether she was awake. For the distorted shadows of the trees in the valley below her and the black sky above seemed grim and unnatural, almost dead. It felt as though some scheming spirit now held her mind within the firm grip of its own.

As she topped a grassy vista, she saw before her an imposing mountain, upon whose shadowy heights lay great rocky cliffs of jagged rock. Just beyond them rose up the white and curling spray of the falls. She was getting closer.

Through tangled thickets and broken limbs, over boulders and cold mountain streams, Ana climbed, up into the towering heights of the cliffs. Yet, with her fragile hands she had struggled to pull herself up past the towering walls of stone that stood teetering before her. As if in a dream, she climbed up and over the last precipice of rock, until she walked out onto a windy ledge that overlooked a deep blue gulf of emptiness.

Peering into the depths, she saw the white waterfall at last, as it poured down its raging torrents into the dark blue seas below. Here the wide river of Avalyr, cold and deep, flew with great fury over the last of the black cliffs of Phantaia, down into the depths of the grim seascape below. Its great clouds of frothing sea spray and fog billowed up like storm clouds about her.

Ana stood in awe of its grandeur and beauty, calmed by the sound of the roar, and cooled by the ghostly mist cast up from it. She looked down into the Dreaming Seas far below, and felt the presence of her mother again. She then walked to the edge of the cliff. For a moment she thought of diving down into the wasteful sea. Lost in a strange trance, she would jump into the falls. For she desired to return to her mother. And by her death, she thought, her troubled spirit might rest beside her in peace. She knew if she could summon the courage, she could make the final leap.

As she neared the edge, pondering her sad destiny, she suddenly felt the cold presence of the strange darkness that had followed her. But turning around, she saw that her own shadow had departed. She then watched the seas darken and an even larger shade slowly envelope the land. As she looked out into the Heavens, a strange black cloud approached, rising up from the mountains in the distance. From out of the depths of Avara's black woods it came, growing slowly, swirling and boiling with malicious intent. As Ana looked below the cliff, she saw that it had encircled the seas beneath her. It then wrapped its sinister coils, like a long black snake, about the shore and the slopes of the mountains, so that all was hidden within its cloud.

Ana then realized it was not a storm, nor made of the wisps of clouds. It was an amorphous shape, bearing within its streaming mass, millions of bat-winged creatures, the same ones she had seen before the rowans. The black host now spun about the cliffs, drowning out the last lights of Phantaia with the sheer beating of their wings. Ana then turned to flee.

But from out of the rocky face of the mountain behind her grew the filaments of an ever-lengthening shadow. Ana saw its murky form, slowly rising up from the black face of the cliffs behind her. It stretched its ominous shape above the shadows of the rocks until it towered over her head. Then she saw with horror that it was the same monstrous form she had seen before at the door of the rowans. For within the crevices of the cliffs that ominous shade had opened its sinister eyes, which glowed forth with a red fire that burned away the very surface of her heart. They were searching, penetrating eyes.

Then from within the rocks, there boomed a voice, deep and dark, so that the very cliffs trembled as it spoke, "*...Ana...Ana...*"

But with each word, the dark form took within itself deep breaths of the moist mountain air, exhaling them out in frosty plumes, until an icy fog billowed forth from its ragged mouth. Its foul breath formed clouds that wrapped about Ana, like phantom hands, long and sinewy, reaching out to grab her. But she could not run from this black specter. For something in its seductive eyes drew her to it.

Ana walked through the eerie fog and stood before the dark spirit that hid in the shadows of the rocks. The great being then looked down on her small form, its large reflective eyes glowing with a vengeful, yet sensuous light. But Ana stood bravely before the dark form, saying to it, "What spirit of the night comes before me? Who dares to hide in the shadows of the rocks? For I saw such a spirit rise from the forest below the doorway of the trees."

The black spirit then spoke, "You do not know me. But I know you. For I have looked into your heart, Ana. And the darkness that yet dwells within you has revealed itself to me. I am the Shadow, sent by your father Agapor, who now dwells in the Realms of Oblivion. He is the last lord of that grim land, whose storms you see boiling about you. And he it is that has raped the seas, and whose storms now slaughter the rocks and trees of this land with his iron hand."

Ana looked up in horror, hearing those words. She then told the spirit, "I know not who my father is. Nor have I known of any other but my mother. She dwells in the depths of the Dreaming Seas, where only the spirits of the dead may go."

Ana held back tears, saying to the Shadow, "But I desire to return to her. For I know not where I am, nor why I have been taken into this strange land."

The Shadow then smiled, with his long ebony teeth exposed, saying to Ana, "No spirit, living or dead, may ever return to the sea, child. It is only a gateway to the Other World. For beneath it lies the Land of the Dead, where all that perish in this world shall go to dwell, trapped in endless misery and suffering for all eternity. The cold seas do not forget the dead that dwell under them, yet give their love and care to no one, not even the living. For your own mother is enslaved to them, cursed to weave upon a loathsome loom the doom of the children born into this world. And so like them are you wrapped by your mother's pall, to walk the earth as the dead, clothed in the same tattered fate she hath sown for us all."

"Forsake thy mother and thy father," the Shadow proclaimed. "All filial affection is but a false love, and the source of our downfall. Your own parents care not for you, as they care not for each other. For long ago, they were torn apart by strife, born of your father's desire to destroy your mother. She was but a victim of his perverse desires. But his violation of her in turn spawned her violence against him. And so was he sundered from the seas long ago. Divorced of all love, they now dwell far apart from each other in their own sad domains. Yet engaged in perpetual struggle, as mortal enemies they shall remain, waging continuous battles born of their unending hatred for each other."

The Shadow then spoke again, solemnly saying, "Look for yourself, Ana, out across the seas and skies. Do you not see the spirits of your parents dwelling far apart in their own miserable realms? Do you not see the storms in Heaven and the seas below still fighting upon their fringes?"

Ana walked to the edge of the precipice, and looked out into the gloom. She then saw the flash of lightning in the distance and the frothing of the sea below. And she gazed upon the residual turmoil of the savage broil between her parents about the shore. Ana saw that a wide and wasteful gulf lay between them. Ana looked down in despair, realizing her family was truly shattered just as the Shadow had said. Her parents cared not for her, nor for each other. They had abandoned her, as they had abandoned each other and all love. And they had left her to struggle in the depths of that gloomy world alone.

Saddened and confused, Ana began to feel cold and alone. The Shadow then looked down at the small girl with his eyes ablaze. For the evil seeds of doubt had been planted within her mind and would soon take root.

"The destiny of your parents no longer matters." The Shadow said, grinning as he spoke. "From their failed love are they now doomed to dwell apart, forever after. By their division shall your father's storms soon fail, and your mother's seas fade away. Then shall the terrible twins that dwell in the abyss, like ravenous beasts, rise from the dark pits of the world to chew upon their carcasses. For it was destined to be so at the end of days."

The Shadow grimaced at Ana, saying, "But you are doomed to follow the same ill-fated path as they, Ana. For a long and languorous road lies before you in the depths of these cursed woods. If you remain upon this path, you shall find a sad terminus in the dark depths of the forest, dwelling there in total isolation, and begging for death in the misery of your own isolation and loneliness."

"But you may leave this place for a happier world, which I alone have seen," said the Shadow, his eyes aglow. "Leave with me now Ana, before your father comes seeking you. For he shall soon enter Phantaia, not for love of you but to use you to draw forth his own father, the Twilight Mist, out of the woods. For he has vengeance in his heart against that vile being who hides, even now, in the trees and rocks, as a criminal and coward hides from the judgement of his accusers and crimes." The Shadow then looked about the woods below the cliffs, sniffing the air, as if sensing a presence.

But Ana stood unflinching before the beast, saying boldly, "Shadow, I can no longer face my father. Whatever he was or is I care not. He never loved me or my mother. But I fear I will never see my mother's face again. For I see that she lies forever trapped in a trance, bound to endless visions and dreams tied to this world and its fate. This, I feel, shall also be my fate in the forest. And so I cannot go with you. But this prison shall not be a bane, but a blessing to me. I accept my lonely fate in Phantaia." Ana then placed her hands on her face, and began to cry.

The Shadow, seeing her vulnerability, cautiously rose up from the rocks, stretching forth his tall form, and casting his full shadow down upon her. As his great figure stood over her, the black clouds above him grew still, and the dark winds of the wings of that storm abated.

Ana then saw the true form of the Shadow. He appeared as a tall, gaunt creature, bathed in eternal darkness. His ebony skin seemed to draw within itself all light. She looked into the deep, blackened eyes that sat upon his long and sinister-looking face. And she cringed as she saw his curled, foul mouth open, revealing its numerous shiny, ebony teeth.

"Ana, you and I are more alike than you know," the Shadow said, with a beguiling smile. "We are kindred spirits. For I too have been betrayed by my father, and turned away from the sad fate in which I lay imprisoned. So are we both destined to defy our families, be free, and rebel against the world."

The Shadow's long black arms stretched forth from the darkness, like the black limbs of a tree. He reached out with his spidery hands and held up the sad girl's tiny chin, touching the tears upon her face. He then looked deep into her eyes, as his own eyes flickered with an ambient light, shining forth like prisms. For his great orbs reflected out all light that came into them. Ana then gazed upon the bewitching eyes of the Shadow, and felt the utter emptiness of his own cold and pitiless heart. She turned away.

But the Shadow said, "You must not fear me, child. For I have come to rescue you from this nightmare world our parents hath made. You must leave with me now and flee this wood. In my own lands you shall dwell in peace under the cloak of Midnight, far from Phantaia. There I will protect you from the horrors of the world, and from your own cursed family, which have wrought so much pain upon you."

But the Shadow had plotted in secret to carry her away, taking her into the merciless underground realms of Midnight to suffer there alone. By his own villainous plot, he would then cast that child of the sea into its black and oily waters to drown, and to die there alone. By her death would vengeance be his, and the world free of its last living hope.

But as the Shadow stretched forth his great wings to wrap about her, he felt within her a strange presence. It was something he had earlier sensed—an unknown power within the girl that he could not fully comprehend. He had seen a strange glint of its lurid visions when his heart had first penetrated hers from afar. His eyes now looked deep into hers, searching, exploring, casting lights and strange reflections upon her face and eyes, so that she stood hypnotized.

He had known of a secret hidden deep within her heart. But he could not divine its meaning. He strove with all his power to see inside her, to discover her true purpose. Her heart now pounded within the cockles of his own, like two that are bound together as one. And the insanity of its chaotic beat echoed in the dark hallways of his spirit. The Shadow hesitated. For he now sensed some terrible part of her that he had not foreseen.

The Shadow grabbed Ana with his claws, striving with all his might to look into her heart's depths, until he saw from afar bejeweled reflections cast up from a distant fountain. He then glimpsed at last the shimmering surface of the Sacred Waters, which had lain hidden within the deepest chambers of her heart.

As the Shadow's spirit entered her inner alcove, he found himself standing before a shining pool of silver waters. In his mind, it bore upon its surface strange and smoky visions of unknown events, clouded and strange, fractured and surreal. But as he looked upon the waters again, he saw a vision fully revealed unto him, clear and crisp, as a shining sun that throws its brilliant light through a cloud, burning away its lining, and revealing to the viewer the magnificent sight that lies beyond.

The Shadow saw himself standing beneath a golden hill, upon whose peak stood a towering tree of great strength and majesty. Its light seemed dimmed, yet it burned his eyes. But by some force within was he immune from its powers to harm him. As he turned away from the light, he looked below him and saw that he now stood over the body of a young woman of great beauty. Through her breast was a shining spear of silver, splattered with blood that covered her green and white gown. Beside her knelt a young man, weeping over her. But as the Shadow looked down, he saw in horror that the woman's blood was dripping from his own hands.

Then there appeared an angelic woman, tall and serene, with broad wings of silver. Her pale form was armor-clad. And her bluish skin cast forth a white light that shined out like a radiant star as she approached. She looked in horror at the death of the girl and knelt beside her to grasp her hand. She then withdrew the silver spear from her chest. She backed away from the Shadow, as if in fear of him and his murderous deed.

The Shadow remained frozen. For he felt a strange anguish for the girl that had died, though he knew not what it meant. Then as fast as that vision had come, it was gone, whilst a strange feeling of dread had remained. Through that image the Shadow had foreseen the sad and final act of a drama yet to unfold, one he could not understand but in which he had played a tragic part.

Ana broke free from the Shadow's gaze, crying from the pain and horror of that vision. The Shadow then stumbled backwards, waking from his own nightmare. A terrible panic came over him as he looked with suffering eyes upon the child. For he now saw the truth of what she carried inside her. But Ana had begun to back away from him, uncertain of whom or what he was.

"*He* has brought you here, to curse us all with this horrific power that shall soon bring about our doom," the Shadow shouted, his face sweating and hands trembling. "For your own father revealed to me that you would fulfill some terrible purpose."

The Shadow then slowly backed away from her, his eyes glowing with a dim ember.

"Be fearful of it child," he told her. "For it will soon bring great pain and heartache upon you, and an unending agony that even death itself shall not ablate. A fate much worse than all the power of the Dreaming Seas shall soon be unleashed upon us. For I have seen a piece of it. The cursed destiny of a vast and unending play of suffering shall be our fate. And all who play a part may never escape it." The Shadow then stood in the darkness, his quick breaths billowing out in great heaps of smoke.

Ana looked with horror upon the dark creature as he spoke. For in her own confusion and fear, she knew not what his words meant.

But below the cliffs there grew a mist, unseen by all eyes, rising up from the forest depths, then wandering its way over the roaring river. Slowly it climbed through the jagged rocks, streaming up into the skies, until its strange lavender light had cast away the grim grays of the clouds that wrapped about its peaks and valleys. Its great cloud then drew itself about the mountain ledge, encircling Ana and the Shadow in its violet mist.

The Shadow grabbed Ana with his long black fingers, yelling out into the thick night air, "Begone vile mist! I will now take the child away with me, far from the terrible doom that awaits her here."

But the violet mist curled around them until, like a net, it caught them in its thick sheath. And they became blinded and lost within its cloud. Encircled by its strange violet dew, Ana and the Shadow could see no further than their own faces. In the swirling confusion, Ana then broke free of the Shadow, standing alone in the midst of the lavender cloud, scared and unsure.

From out of the violet fog there appeared a tall figure, the Twilight Mist. For he had gathered his wisps about him, taking form as the mist incarnate. He appeared to Ana as an aged king, with a wide, flowing beard. Upon his brow lay a mighty crown, which shined forth with strange lights of a purple and greenish hue. His skin was dark and lavender, like that of his cloud. And his wide and bejeweled robe glistened with shining dew, flying about him in the winds that blew around his form.

The Twilight Mist held out his hand to Ana. "Come," he said. "Leave him. For he is a dire servant of your father, and a being impelled by great evil. He is filled with treachery, feigning truth with his lies. For he would carry you away from here, not to save you but to condemn you to certain death."

Ana looked upon the Shadow, and then the Twilight Mist. She felt confusion, and great fear of them both. She then looked into the face of the Mist and felt some goodness in his spirit that connected her to him. His eyes appeared sad and weary, yet burned with the enduring light of hope. She then ran to his arms, turning her fearful gaze upon the cowering Shadow, who now looked up from the fog with amber eyes that felt betrayed.

The Shadow looked warily at them both, and then gazed upon the aged face of the Twilight Mist with great loathing. For the Mist was his most ancient enemy. Long ago the Twilight Mist had taken him from his own father, the Endless Night, cruelly imprisoning him and his sister in the black manacles Agapor now possessed. And so, there still raged within the Shadow's heart an unrelenting hatred and desire for revenge.

The Shadow stood proudly before the defiant figure of the Twilight Mist, saying, "I now know of the secret hidden within the child. It cannot be shielded from my eyes any longer. You are the one who has corrupted her, perverting the will of the Essence Eternal for your own purposes. It is you who placed those cursed waters within her breast. Like the seas that nearly destroyed your own son, you would use his child of the oceans to bind this world in a new curse, tied to those evil waters, such that none might leave it unscathed." The Shadow laughed quietly at the irony of it all. For he now knew that what the Twilight Mist had done was even more sinister than his own plans for the world.

"But I have come to stop you. For the girl must die," the Shadow cried, his voice echoing through the mountains.

The Twilight Mist spoke to Ana in a gentle tone. "Child, go hide behind the rocks." To Ana his sad face seemed filled with a faded spirit which, though dimmed, still contained some hidden strength. Ana then fled away to the rocks that stood upon the edge of the cliffs.

The Shadow stretched his dark form above the mist, his great wings growing larger, expanding outward, until his immense shadow cast its shade down upon the Twilight Mist, drowning out his feeble glow. With his father's black wings and the spirit of the Glourun they contained, the Shadow transformed himself, taking the shape of a mighty black dragon born of the night. He had a black and horned head upon his serpentine body, with great feet and claws of dark ivory. And his iron jaws dripped with drool, as he belched forth black pitch and smoke from his nostrils. He was a formidable beast to behold, such that even the Twilight Mist stepped back in awe of the monstrous serpent as it stood before him.

In the Heavens above stirred the many wings of the minions of the Lands of Midnight, so that the lavender fog was blown about in their winds, fleeing down the mountainside. But the Twilight Mist stood unmoving before the massive monster, his wide cape blowing in the shadowy winds now cast about by its heavy breath. Ana cringed at the sight of the frightful beast. And she watched in horror as it slowly drew its long scaly tail in wide sweeps before the figure of the Mist.

The Twilight Mist then looked sternly upon the towering creature, telling the serpent, "The girl shall not be harmed. She must remain with me. Leave us now, oh Child of Night. Depart this realm and never return."

But the serpent hissed with indignity, as he looked upon the frail form of the Twilight Mist. "The child shall soon perish," the serpent said to the Mist with his deep slithering tongue. "And with her death shall the evil waters she now carries also die." But the Twilight Mist now stood between the great serpent and the rocks where Ana lay hidden.

The serpent stretched forth his long ebony body, saying, "Your powers have faded. And your time in this world has passed. The vanity and greed of the Primordial Ones have destroyed this world.

But two of your brother's have died, my lord. Like them, you too must perish, so that the children of this world can finish the destruction you started. The powers of darkness will then be free to take from this world what is rightfully ours."

The great serpent then strode before the Twilight Mist, standing over him with his great jaws agape. "You cannot quite see what I have become, can you?" the black serpent said. "It is I who hath slain the Limitless Void, thy benevolent brother. And it is I who hath slain the Endless Night, my father, he who hath failed so miserably to stop you. But you shall be my next victim. For by the words of the sinister twins, who have known the future, was it granted to me that the Primordial Ones should all perish by my hand."

The Shadow then lashed out with his great serpentine tail, striking down the Twilight Mist. As the Mist rose to his feet, the Shadow struck him with his great fist, so that he fell to the ground, broken from his mighty blow. Great bolts of blue lightning and thunder crashed about them, as the fractured spirit of the Twilight Mist lay upon the rocks.

With thundering feet, the Shadow came upon the fallen figure of the Mist, looking down on him with his wicked black orbs. He picked up the beaten body of the Lord of the Mist in his claws and carried him to the edge of the precipice. He then cast the Twilight Mist down the mountainside and into the waterfall below. The rocks and trees of the mountain shook, as the black wyrm roared with laughter.

Ana screamed, as she watched his body plunge into the waves of the roaring falls below. Hearing her pitiful cry, the beast then turned his great horned head, and gazed upon the rocks where she lay hidden. As he slithered over to the rocks to find her, Ana fled, climbing down the treacherous cliffs of the mountain that lay below her. But the serpent reached down with his long claws and grabbed her by the waist, holding her helpless before him. He would no longer carry her away. He would rip her heart from her chest, there in the shadow of the mountain, and take the cursed waters from her.

But as he curled his long black claws towards her breast, Ana saw behind him the strange mist again, rising up from the depths of the river below. The fog of the Twilight Mist had risen once more. For Atar, the child of the rushing river, would not let her father perish in its currents. She had carried her father's fallen form up from their depths, and out of the violent waters. And so, by her love had the river-child given her father new life.

The Twilight Mist stood again upon the mountainside. He then drew his purple clouds about him, gathering from the forests and rocks below a vast shroud, which swirled like a mighty cyclone, slinging the dark denizens of Midnight from the skies. Their battered bodies were heard screeching, far and away, as the last remnants of the dark host were chased from the skies.

The Twilight Mist then drew his twisting and turning clouds away from the precipice, revealing the golden beams of the Sacred Light that had burned bright again on the horizon. For with the fleeing of the hosts of Midnight, the bright radiance of that burning sun was set free again, to shine its forceful flame upon the mountain face.

The bright beams broke through the remnant fog, falling upon the serpentine figure of the Shadow, so that he was blown back, burned and blinded by its rays. Ana then saw the dragon-like form of the Shadow melt away. And he stood again as the creature he was before, his shredded wings pitted with holes from the searing light.

Ana then fell from his grasp. For the Shadow had held his ebony hands before his face, shielding his eyes before the golden gleam of that sun. He then looked up and saw the Twilight Mist peering down upon him with a countenance most terrible to behold, like that which he had seen when he was but a small child ripped away from his dark father.

As the warm winds of Phantaia swirled around them, the Twilight Mist stood before the cowering Shadow. He draped his merciful mists over him, covering the light from his eyes, saying, "You may not harm this child of the seas, oh dark one. For there is much yet to be done. And great goodness yet dwells in her which you, who are blind to the will of the Spirit Divine, can never see." The Mist then raised his mighty arms. And great bolts of purple lightning, like cobwebs, crackled in the air before him.

The Mist then uttered strange incantations, such that the Shadow returned to his ancient form—the shape of a small pale boy. The skin of the Shadow had turned from ebony to gray, his eyes hollow and ghostly. For the Glourun had been stripped from him. The Twilight Mist then drew his strong hands into the air above his body, as the Shadow floated over the earth before him. The sad figure of the Shadow then lay curled in the air, shaking with fear.

"Your time has not yet come, my child," said the Twilight Mist, speaking in soft words. "For the light of Phantaia still burns your flesh. The children of the night may not dwell here in these woods as long as it yet beams out from its heart with the Sacred Light of the Great Father. But I will not allow these woods, or their loving light, to be harmed by you, as long as I am alive in this world." The Shadow lay still, his white eyes staring into the emptiness of the Heavens.

"But I know why you have come here. Know that it is the design of the Essence Eternal that Ana should dwell in Phantaia. For the mystery that lies within her shall soon enter the heart of this land, and become one with it. Only then shall *His* will be done," the Twilight Mist said, as he looked down in rigid defiance.

The Twilight Mist then looked upon the frozen and ghostly form of the Shadow as he lay powerless before him, floating in the air. As the Mist stared at the helpless boy, with compassionate eyes, he spoke again. "By the dark magic which lies within the manacles are you still imprisoned, my child. And by their powers, you shall remain bound in servitude to those who possess them. Long ago, I was forced to imprison your spirit within that which the Immortal Clay, my brother, had forged, using enchanted metals given to him by the Great Father for that purpose. For it was your own nightmarish power—the evil within you that had polluted your heart—that we needed in order to imprison the Limitless Void, our brother. Our many children were slain by him, and his violence nearly destroyed this world. Only that which dwelt in you could stop him, as it had stopped your father. I had no choice, my child. I am sorry." The Twilight Mist then looked down in sadness and shame.

The Twilight Mist then touched the chest of the Shadow. And he knew by that which lay within him that the magical bracers were upon his own son's wrists. For he felt the beat of his son's troubled heart through him.

He then said to the Shadow, "As long as those irons remain with my son, shall you be a servant to him and my house. But should Agapor be separated from them, only then shall you be set free." The Twilight Mist then touched the face of the Shadow, as a father to a son. Ana saw him look with grieving eyes upon the hateful monster he had made, and she was moved.

But hearing Ana stir in the rocks behind him, the Twilight Mist turned away from the Shadow, for a moment peering into the gray rocks to find her. Seeing her unharmed, with great joy he then held out his hand for her to come to him. But as he did, the spell placed upon the Shadow strangely waned for a moment. The Shadow then resumed his shape and color, turning black as night. For within his father's battered wings still flowed the power of the Glourun to resist the enchantments of its spiritual twin, the twilit essence of the Avara.

The air about him turned gloomy again. And the light of that distant sun faded from view once more. The Shadow then rose up from his cursed bed. And with his long black teeth, he bit the shoulder of the Twilight Mist, from whose body flowed great gushes of violet blood, spilling out upon the rocks. The Shadow fell back to the ground in pain. For he still suffered from the burns and blisters inflicted upon him by that enchanted light.

The Twilight Mist, stumbling in agony, slumped to the ground, wounded and holding his shoulder. As he did, the Shadow slowly climbed to his feet, and looked upon his bleeding master. But seeing the terrible wound upon his right shoulder, there came into the Shadow's mind a dark epiphany. And he stood deep in thought, pondering his long enslavement to Agapor.

As Ana ran to the Twilight Mist, the weakened Shadow slowly crawled away, back into the shadows of the cliff. For the warm lights of Phantaia had returned, casting a ruddy glow upon the rocks about them.

The Twilight Mist stumbled again to his feet, as great rivers of purple blood gushed from his shoulder and down his leg, covering Ana's arms and hands in its flow. Though sorely wounded, by Ana's healing touch was the Mist mysteriously renewed. Holding his shoulder, he called out into the darkness of the rocks, "Leave the woods of Phantaia and never return. For your mission here is now fulfilled...I shall soon perish. It is done." The dying form of the Twilight Mist then lay back in Ana's arms.

But from the darkness of the cliffs, the Shadow looked upon the wrinkled face of the Twilight Mist. And he saw that the last of his essence was now quickly draining away. His face seemed flushed and ghostly. But the Shadow, weak and injured, was still smoking from his own searing wounds. He would return to the Lands of Midnight before the last of his dark essence drained away. He then slowly crawled out of the shadows and stretched forth his gray, ragged wings, once more.

The Shadow turned to face the Twilight Mist, saying, "You are dying, Uncle. Soon, your spirit shall leave this world. Your own lights will then falter in Phantaia, passing away forever. Your powers over it shall then dwindle and die." The Shadow stared down at him, emotionless.

"But I shall soon return to Phantaia, and be free to destroy it and its noble light. With its beams extinguished, shall the woods then fall before the Magra. But Uncle, I need not slay the child. For Agapor, your own son, shall soon claim her, taking his daughter away, and sacrificing her to the monstrous beings that dwell in the merciless pits of the Great Beyond. For I have heard him speak of it myself," said the Shadow, grinning with delight, seeing the sadness on the Twilight Mist's face. Ana then shook with fear in the arms of the Twilight Mist who looked into her eyes, saying nothing. But his eyes revealed his own secret fears.

The Twilight Mist, growing weaker, whispered to the Shadow, "Tell my son, his father desires that he come to Phantaia and sit beside him in peace. For I wish to see him and to know of him...to know of my forgotten son." The Twilight Mist then fell back, suffering with terrible pain from his wound.

The Shadow looked at the Twilight Mist in disgust. But before he could speak, he saw that the golden luster of the living lights had begun to shine boldly again on the distant horizon. With an evil grin, the Shadow then looked upon the frightened face of Ana. He then flew away into the fading mists that lay beyond the cliffs, disappearing from view in the midst of the gray skies that now slowly faded away above them.

Ana now lay exhausted in the arms of the Twilight Mist. He comforted her for a time, until about them a great gale began to blow across the peaks, and dark clouds gather again beyond the seas. A storm was coming. The Twilight Mist then told Ana they must leave the mountain's cliffs. For the storms of Yana would soon come to take them away. The Twilight Mist climbed to his feet and onto a great rock. There he raised his frail arms and cast one last enchantment, emitting strange words, which caused his purple mists to swirl and dance around them. He then called Ana to him, wrapping his great cloak about them, until they were consumed in a swirling fog, and were gone.

Ana found herself floating beside the Twilight Mist, her hand in his, as their spirits drifted beyond the cliffs. Bathed in that odd dew, they floated above the trees and rocks, hovering over the dense woods of Phantaia. She saw the Mist standing beside her as they travelled through secret groves and misty valleys, past tangled gates of wild growth, and into dim hallways of rock under the shade of the peaks. They drifted through a mountain pass and across unseen ethereal spaces, until they crossed a wide and bottomless gulf, black and terrifying. But always a quiet cloud of mist and rain swirled about their heads, pouring into the wide expanse of space that lay before them.

As they floated over the dark land, Ana held onto the arm of the Twilight Mist, until they came to a dim valley at the base of a wide row of gray mountains in the distance. These were the spectral mountains of the Great Father that had stood beyond the Arch of Heaven since the birth of Time. A dimly glowing gateway led through them, into a secret grotto of fog and rock, which cast up a strange blue-white light before them.

The mist suddenly parted. And before her shined forth a radiant valley whose silver forests of crystal stretched back into the black shadows of infinity. A bright lavender light glowed within its center. It appeared to emanate from a shining grove of purple and white trees that lay deep within the sparkling forest.

The trees appeared like glass, tall and almost translucent, with wicked thorns, long and sharp, preventing all entrance into their wood. These were the magical and ancient blackthorn trees of Nemedd, the Lands of Mist. To Ana it felt as though no darkness, nor light, nor water, nor wind, nor living creature might penetrate its sharpened brambles. For these strange jewel-like trees guarded a lustrous grove of taller ones within its center.

The Twilight Mist stood still before the opening, as he spoke to the trees. Ana then saw the glass boughs parting slowly before them, so that a brighter light seemed to shine forth from its opening. As they entered, they walked past the glassy trunks, whose icy limbs and leaves rang like musical chimes within an eerie symphony of crystal. For they bore upon every limb a wondrous music of bright notes, played by the gentle fingers of heavenly winds that stirred within them.

They followed a short winding passage until they came to an even larger gateway. There the glass trees opened out into a small clearing, encircled by a ring of huge, impenetrable quartz-like trees. These in turn were ringed by an inner circle of blooming eucalyptus trees of most ancient age, whose sad pink and white flowers hung low from their bent limbs. Everything seemed half-alive, completely still and frozen, as if trapped in some eternally twilit world of ice whose peace no creature or presence beyond the cosmic winds had or could ever disturb.

Ana then looked upon the center of this circular hollow and saw a small mound rising before them. Upon its summit grew a gnarled and bent fruiting tree, whose crooked branches held many shining apples of purest white in color. This knotted apple tree had, upon its wide leafy head, a bountiful growth of violet-colored leaves and limbs. Its fruit-laden boughs hung low to the ground. Beneath it grew a delicate blue grass, whose odd color was mingled with that of the lavender bark of the tree. Ana then saw the fog fade away from the strange scene, drifting up into the skies. There appeared above her a great hole filled with a black heaven, whose unseen heights felt vast beyond reason.

This was the twilight tree named Kurtavla, a hoar apple born in the youth of another time and place, when the Lands of Mist were first made by the Essence Eternal. It remained hidden beyond the mystical Mountains of Heaven, through eons of time, living on through the destruction of many prior worlds. This magical tree would stay concealed to all but those born of mist. Only they could eat of its timeless fruit. For its sustenance was meant for their children alone.

The Twilight Mist pointed to the trees with his aging hands. And with soft words, he spoke. "Here is my true home, the hidden heart of my lands, Ana. In ages past, this place had been filled with the sound of many children playing, forests ringing with laughter, and many shining wonders now lost. This remnant Forest of Nemedd is now all that remains of my forested lands. For in ancient times, the endless wars of my brothers had destroyed all others. The Sons of Night had then come and shadowed what remained, strangling them of the last of my lights, so that those fallen forests fell into darkness and decay, beyond my power to save them. The Limitless Void had then come with great violence, shattering the last of the sacred groves that lay in our realms, consuming the shards of what remained, until only this forest and its single life-giving tree had survived. The ghostly spirits of the last of my kind still live here, trapped in these trees, yet guarded by the icy mists that surround them. And so you hear their mournful music upon the cold winds. For they cry for their lost brothers and sisters which are no more."

Ana then knew why the Twilight Mist had come to Phantaia. For in that wilderness, his heart had yet lived again, its beauty magnified by the loss of his own. He had tried to save the woods and protect them with the last of his great powers so they might not perish as his forests had done.

She walked towards the old tree that grew upon the hill, standing beneath its giant limbs, touching its wrinkled bark. This tree seemed comforting to her, yet sad. The Twilight Mist then walked forward and looked upon Ana with gentle eyes, saying, "You may eat of its fruit. It will be a form of sustenance to you. For you are a Child of Mist. You are my grandchild." Ana then looked upon her grandfather's face with happy yet knowing eyes. She reached up and took a bite from the sweet white apple. She slowly became aware of a change within her body. She could almost see through her hands.

"This last realm of mist has remained hidden and ever-renewed by the breath of an enchanted dragon of twilight which I summoned forth to guard it in ages past. He shall now sleep in its woods for all eternity, long after I am gone. The tree of Kurtavla is of his transforming spirit. And so its fruit will soon change you into a mist, the fog of the heavenly mountains that fills this great valley," the Twilight Mist told her. "Like me, you were born of the mists that fill this valley of Nemedd. And so may the apples of the dragon's breath carry you home."

The Twilight Mist hobbled over to the great tree where Ana stood, and lay his broken body beneath its trunk. Seeing him in pain, Ana helped him down, kneeling beside him to comfort him. The Twilight Mist reached up to touch her soft face and brow. And he smiled.

"Grandfather, who am I? Why have I been brought here?" Ana asked, holding his hands close to her.

"You have been thrown into a torn and tortured world, my child, one in which has always dwelt great evil. Much of it was created by the Primordial Ones, my brothers and I. We committed great crimes against each other. For our violence nearly shattered the works of our heavenly father, He who had made them for us to treasure. We had nearly destroyed each other by our selfishness, our jealousy, and our pride. I was tempted by my desires many times, falling to evil acts which brought great ruin upon me and my children. Many perished through that which I had done, Ana." Tears then started to well up in the eyes of the Twilight Mist.

"Agapor, your father, is my child, as is Atar of the river, and An your mother, my precious child of the Dreaming Seas which I had made from the Sacred Waters given to me. And so are you, my beloved grandchild, both a child of mist and sea. You have more of me than they, Ana," said the Twilight Mist, smiling up at her.

The Twilight Mist then turned morose, as he continued, "But, so too are you born of the Void. The dark spirit that dwells in your father yet dwells in you. Your father is a fallen spirit. For he now strives to gather to himself the last of the powers of destruction and darkness, so he might destroy me and the remaining children of this world. Agapor now possesses the relentless powers of the all-consuming Void, who his servant has slain. And the manacles upon his wrists that I had made are now his, and used against me. And so the sins of the father haunt me still, as it should be. Your father, my fallen son, has chosen a dark path, Ana. And his intentions are not to be trusted."

The Twilight Mist paused, as he groaned in pain, feeling his life force now quickly fading. "It has now come to pass, as all things in this world are cursed to do, that my own child would rise up to destroy me. So has he sent his greatest servant to slay me. For it was revealed long ago—in mysterious visions from the enchanted waters given to me—that he and his dark servant would come for me." The Twilight Mist then lay back, feeling weaker.

The Twilight Mist then continued, "But Agapor has aligned himself with the Nothingness and Emptiness, the terrible twins which sleep in the deepest abyss of the cosmos. They shall soon destroy the last of this world. For they had long ago sought to sunder the Primordial Ones from each other by their dire plots. Through my fallen brothers, the Limitless Void and the Endless Night, they had nearly succeeded. But they rise yet again to pollute the minds of the last of our innocent children. Few remain to challenge them now, Ana. Very few." And he looked upon her with great sadness. Ana felt as if the weight of the world had been placed upon her shoulders.

"Soon my own spirit shall leave this world, my child. In the end, Agapor was victorious in his plans against me. You must now face your father alone. My work in this world is done," the Twilight Mist said. But he assured her, "Know that with my own passing, my violet mists shall remain behind in this world to protect you, and all of Phantaia's children, until in time the last of my fogs have all but faded, never again to haunt those twilight woods again. Then shall you know our time in this world has passed away. You shall never see my face again, nor shall I see yours. But do not fear for the future, Ana. For I have planted a part of my spirit in you, as I have left a part of myself in all my children so they might carry forward the works and plans of the Great Father who hath made them. The destiny of this world now rests with you." And the Twilight Mist held his head down, as if the last of his energy was nearly spent.

The Twilight Mist then looked up, as if discovering some last fount of life hidden within himself. "Hold my hand, Ana," he said. The Twilight Mist had almost taken his last breath. For he was growing weak. He sat at the base of the tree, peering up into the Heavens as if deep in thought. He then looked up at the wondrous fruits of the twilit tree. But his terrible wound now held the Shadow's dark poison. And it coursed its way through him, as his own blood dripped down about his chest and arms, and into the blue grass.

"My time to depart this world draws near," he told her.

The Twilight Mist spoke in fading whispers, grasping her hand firmly. "Ana, I must tell you something more. Long ago, I was given a great gift by my own father, the Essence Eternal. He had given me the last of the Sacred Waters, which had held many mysteries that I could not fathom, but had tried so hard to understand. I discovered that they had been sent to us from an earlier world, to heal this one. And so was I destined to create the Dreaming Seas. But I saw too that they had been created to give life and bless the living. Yet within their darkened essence lay something more malevolent that could take life away. I then knew that they were both a blessing and a curse upon this world.

"Your mother An was given those waters by the seas," said the Twilight Mist. "Defying the evil that had sought to take them, her own heart held them dear to her. But your father's violence against your mother had shattered her heart. And much of their wrath was unleashed upon this battered world, their violence nearly consuming it. And so were they and this world nearly lost. But your mother had kept the last of their essence, which remained within her, unmarred and pure. Inside her own heart they flowed, those waters of hope, so that evil might not find them and destroy them, nor they destroy the world. So were you, her only child, given those waters. You were then cast away from her, hidden from your father, and taken deep into the gloomy woods of Phantaia. Many dark forces now rise up again seeking to find you. So have I sought to protect you and that which you now carry."

The Twilight Mist then looked up at her with a solemn face. "For it is the will of the Great Father that it be so."

"You see, Ana, the Sacred Waters must flow again so that a new and brighter world can be born. For the welfare of the innocent children yet to come must it be so. Within those waters now dwell the unfulfilled promise that our world might be united again in an eternal and unbroken peace, and its light shine forth against the darker will that yet returns to destroy it. To you has been given the last hope of saving this world," said the Twilight Mist. He then looked into the fearful face of his grandchild.

Shedding a tear, Ana then said, "I understand now, why I have been brought here, Grandfather."

The Twilight Mist placed his hand on her heart. But as he did, his happy eyes suddenly turned dark and gloomy. He then stared up at her with a cold expression, saying, "You must know one last truth, Ana. All things in this world must follow the path of those waters. Through them shall this world be saved and reborn. But those who resist their will shall fall under a terrible curse from which they shall never escape. So must you, Ana, also follow their will, else this world fall like all others before it, to its final doom."

"I'm scared, Grandfather," she said, holding him. "For I have seen many portentous visions in the waters that lie within me—horrors which, even now, reflect upon my mind. These nightmares speak of a troubled future, one whose struggles I cannot fully grasp. I too heard the fearful Shadow's words. And I am frightened of the future that he has revealed."

But the Mist held her hands close to him, as his spirit started to fade, telling her, "Do not live by fear alone, Ana. For a new and hopeful future awaits you. A brighter destiny, with many more to come, is given freely to those who have courage. But you must do what is not always best for you, but what is best for the world and those you love," he said. "Follow the goodness in your heart, turning away from temptation and evil. Let the voices of your heart and the visions of the waters guide you. You will find your way. Know always that a piece of my spirit and that of the Great Father shall always remain with you. Have faith, child." The Twilight Mist smiled. But Ana felt the grasp of his hands in hers grow weak.

"Eat of the fruit of the tree, my child. You shall then take the form of the mist and return to Phantaia. For the Doors of Evening that lead to Phantaia still remain open to you, as they have to me," the Twilight Mist whispered, as he closed his eyes.

The Twilight Mist embraced his grandchild, one last time. She then looked in sadness upon his fading image, as he disappeared from view. His lavender mist then drifted up into the skies above, melting away into the darkness.

She felt alone, more than she had ever felt. She longed for a friend, for the white horse who had so lovingly carried her into the Phantaia. She would return to him. Ana then ate the rest of the pale apple she still held, and soon fell into a deep and troubled sleep beneath the old tree. Her body drew forth its last breath, as she was transformed into a dense white mist. A wide door then opened up within the trunk of the old apple tree. Her mist then flowed into it and disappeared.

When Ana awoke, she lay once more beside the great stallion. The horse's warm face looked down at hers, as she lay beside him in the cool grass. She had returned to him somehow. As she looked around her, she felt comforted by the green woods of Phantaia. She was drawn, more than ever, to the enduring promise of its eternal paradise and its living spirit. But she was happier seeing the beautiful white stallion again. She would not abandon him nor question the purpose of their journey again. She now trusted in it fully, though many mysteries yet remained.

But as she looked at the horse's face, she saw that it had looked into hers as well, as if reading her mind. A small tear appeared on his cheek, which seemed strange. The horse had seemed possessed of an amiable spirit until now, one she had grown to love and accept. But now they had shared a mutual sadness for the passing of the Twilight Mist, which strangely it had sensed. She curled up closer to him, holding his muzzle close to her, and sleeping for a moment more beside him.

When she awoke again, Ana felt renewed, wrapped in the purple mist of her grandfather, which had returned again to fill the river valley. Like he had told her, his spirit had yet remained behind to guide and protect her. She felt comforted by it, as if some new courage and hope was reborn within her by its presence. But that mist contained many mysteries it had yet revealed.

Though the events of the previous night now weighed upon her, her mind was less clouded and confused. For that sleep had seemed to fill an endless moment in time wherein was washed away many memories. For the thoughts of the sea and the longing for her mother had begun to fade away. Yet she was still adrift in her mind, as far as her future. And though many questions had been answered by her grandfather, she was still unsure of what lay ahead. But the long journey through the strange wilderness of Phantaia had at last set its roots deep into her imagination, entangling her mind with the uncertainty of what still lay ahead.

As she looked up from the grass, she saw the white horse standing over her, his muzzle nudging her face. The horse then looked curiously at the river. It seemed to be signaling to her that it was time to go. It nudged her shoulder and head in play, licking the warm sweat from her face and hair until she at last shook the sleep from her eyes.

They walked together in the wet grass, as the horse led her to the river's edge. There the wise old ash trees of the river had turned their smooth limbs in the night, their lower branches all pointing to an unseen path upstream. They alone seemed possessed of the knowledge of the secret trails into the interior of mysterious Phantaia. She and the horse walked side by side along the high wooded banks of the lonely river for a long stretch of time until the trees began to tower higher into the sky, the river grow narrower and smaller, and its waters clearer and more pristine.

Ana looked across the emerald river, beyond the swiftly flowing water, until she saw rising from the middle of the misty waves a majestic island, mysterious and serene. About it swirled pale blue clouds floating up from its banks, so that its summit lay hidden from view. Then a brightly lit visage of its wooded head suddenly broke free from the clouds, shining out bold and bright above the river. As an unseen sun shined its warm lights upon its high rocky crest, Ana gasped at its beauty.

It wasn't a large island, but a tiny secluded and secretive isle. Upon its lower slopes grew delicate trees of whitest bark above a golden beach, whose large rocks of dark brown hue stood within the waves that crashed about its tiny shore. A small hill stood upon one end of the isle, so that she could see the beauty of the bright sandstone cliffs that lay exposed about its slopes. Upon its summit stood a dense grove of flowering trees, whose blossoms caught the reddish glow of the radiant light. Their blooms and dark bark glowed as one with a ruddy color set aflame by the sunny beams, such that they shined with bright corals, peaches, and pinks from the top of the island, reflecting their hot hues in coruscating color down into the deep green of the flowing waters below.

Ana then felt a strange sense of timelessness, as if she had seen those trees in a dream. The horse turned to look at Ana, and then turned towards the light as if to indicate that here they would ford the river.

The powerful stream of Avalyr flowed before them with great force and fury, deep and green, yet crystal clear in its depths. Ana could see jeweled pebbles of many colors, their translucent stones shimmering beneath the waves. The white stallion stood still, looking far across the great girth of the river at something Ana could not yet grasp. As she gazed at the distant shore, she saw only a line of towering trees beyond the island. Through their branches sparkled a warm light that glittered with a golden hue. But she could not see what lay behind those trees. For a white fog lay draped about the heights of the wild and tangled realms that grew beyond them.

The horse turned to Ana again. It then looked back at the river as if signaling to her that it was time to cross. But seeing the raging river, Ana was hesitant. The white horse then rose up with his front hooves and struck the ground with a thunderous sound. He then gave out a great snort of his nostrils. From above them appeared the purple fogs of the Twilight Mist once more, sinking down from the tops of the trees. Thin wisps of mist curled around the trees from above and drifted out across the skies about their heads. It sank down and hovered at their feet awhile, then swirled out across the river before them like a sheet of clouds. Oddly, the river had now ceased its flow. The lights that shined from beyond the trees had dimmed before the lavender mist. Ana then felt the presence of her grandfather, the Twilight Mist, telling her it was time to cross.

The river of Avalyr lay still beneath the mist, appearing like a serene pool, shimmering like glass in the pale light of the ghostly fog. The horse signaled for Ana to climb upon his back. Ana and the horse then walked forth through the waters, as if they were walking on clouds within the sky. Yet she felt the water upon her body. It was cold and pure, as if poured down from some divine fountain hidden within the Heavens.

As they crossed, Ana felt a strange pull within her, one that seemed to divide her spirit in two. Into her came those strange longings again. Something called her from far away downstream. She could drift off into the water, floating away downriver, and falling into the arms of that which called her. But as she looked upon the shining lands that lay beyond the river a feeling of hopeful anticipation welled up inside her. She knew now she must rendezvous with whatever lay waiting for her just beyond the farthest shore.

As they reached the midpoint of the great river, Ana suddenly saw the island rising up from the mist in front of her. This was the Isle of Adda that had survived great destruction in ages past. Alone of its kind, it had somehow remained. For Adda was once a beautiful flowering hill filled with lovely gardens that stood high above an ancient, much earlier forest. Here had once flowed an argent spring that had poured forth from its heights, until some sinister power had finally found it and destroyed it.

But in this age the waters of Avalyr had flowed forth and discovered the lonely hill of Adda shrouded in the darkness of its destroyed past. The river then reclaimed it for its own, wrapping its loving waters about it, and hiding it away far from the penetrating eyes of an even more dangerous world.

Upon its summit still grew the remnants of a flowering orchard of ancient apple trees, which like Kurtavla, stood aged, shriveled, and dying. Yet were its trees born of a seed that had been planted upon its soil long before the birth of this world, when another age of conflict, conceived of evil's malicious designs, had returned to wage war upon it. And so the fading glory of these island trees was all that had remained of the isle's tragic past.

To this lonely isle was drawn the river-child called Atar, who had come up from the depths of Avalyr to sleep alone upon its rocks. She it was who now tended the apple trees that grew upon the crest of the golden hill called Anadelling. For many ghosts of the earth and rock dwelt there still within that river-mound. And so, much mystery remained attached to this solitary place.

As Ana clung to the horse's neck, they drew close to the island. The mighty stallion felt no fear, and seemed almost drawn to it. Yet to Ana that lonesome isle seemed haunted by a spirit. As the mists that swirled about it fell away, she could make out the lines of the ominous dark rocks and waves that crashed about its beaches. Above the rocks, its solemn banks of golden sands blended there beneath the shadows of the phantom trees that ringed about its solitary hill.

As they neared its rocks, upon the isle's summit she saw the dark flowering umbrage of its twisted fruit trees, as they thrust upward above the mist. Their blossoms cascaded down across the water and about her face as they passed by. Their tiny pink and white petals lay upon the tranquil waters about them. And Ana felt a strange sadness—of the passing away of time—as she watched them float away upon the dark water.

Ana then saw an unusual figure sitting upon the rocks. A young woman clad in light blue garb sat alone on a wide rock, her long ghostly white hair lying across her pale alabaster shoulders. As the fog drifted about them, the strange girl seemed to go in and out of view until the horse drew closer to the rocks. She then suddenly appeared before Ana, her strange lavender eyes staring deeply into hers. Her face looked so much like her own. She then knew it to be Atar.

Ana reached for the strange girl through the mist, drawn by some desire she could not resist. Atar also stretched her pale arms towards Ana. Atar then placed her hand on Ana's heart for a brief moment, listening to it with her eyes closed. She then placed her other hand on the face of the horse, as if joining Ana and the horse as one.

Atar then opened her violet eyes, looking into the eyes of Ana. Ana then saw that her eyes were mournful, as if her inner thoughts were torn by some foreboding knowledge. She then saw tiny tears upon Atar's cheeks. Atar then removed her hand from the horse, holding her chest as if in pain. She then reached out one last time, slowly touching Ana's hands with her own. But just as quickly, Atar disappeared into the mist that now enveloped them. Ana reached into the fog to find her. But she was gone.

All of a sudden Ana and the horse seemed caught within the wild currents of the river. For the river's flow had suddenly returned without warning. They struggled to find their way through the mist and waves that began to throw them about. Ana held on to the neck of the stallion, clinging desperately to his mane as the waters rushed over them.

But the clouded air at last had begun to clear in front of them. And Ana saw near the shore a miraculous sight. For through the clouds she glimpsed the shining shoreline that lay before them. It danced with the happy lights of a distant beacon that beamed and sparkled through the swaying limbs of the trees. The waters then seemed to push them towards the muddy bank of the shoreline.

Before them now stood the sacred shore of Olybana. Upon its sandy banks lay many brightly colored stones containing strange and mysterious powers. For here had fallen the ancient tears of the trees over many eons which, mixing with the river's golden sands, shone like shining amber set aflame with the strange lights of that land.

These were made of the enchanted Glessa of Phantaia, which many would covet though few would find. For the secretive ones had shed forth their sap down into the streams until, like jewels, they coalesced upon the banks forming the golden amber gems and multicolored stones that filled its beaches. These stones would contain the enchantments of the woods and the mysterious magic that would be born of its many sorrows.

The white horse carried Ana out of the river and onto the beach. They then fell upon the sands, exhausted. There they rested from their long journey. But as Ana caught her breath, the mist parted before the tree line beside her. The scintillating rays she had seen from afar beamed down their warmth through the silver ash trees that stood along the riverbank. She and the horse then climbed up through the trees and onto the grassy hillside above the shore.

They were drawing nearer to the source of the shimmering lights which gleamed beyond the wooded hills. Following a densely wooded path, they walked through a windy row of tall trees that grew above them on the hillside. She watched the happy trees bend and dance to the sunny lights, as it flickered through their leaves and limbs.

But as they climbed onto the last majestic rise of the woody ridge, Ana had to cover her eyes from the radiant beauty of the scene that unfolded before her.

THE GLORIOUS GARDEN

Beyond the river the woods grew still, as Ana wound her way up the misty hill. Upon the summit of the lofty height, she hoped to glimpse the glorious light. Past low-hung limbs and whispering leaves, she wound her way through the shimmering trees.

She neared the heart of a most sacred ground, which many had sought but few had found. For beyond the wood's own morbid gloom, a miraculous sight before her loomed. She gazed with wonder upon a realm forbidden, whose peaceful lands from evil eyes had long been hidden.

On the hilltop Ana stood in awe before the dawning view. As the veil of clouds was whisked away, she saw upon a distant hill a towering tree of tremendous size whose shining trunk and limbs were imparted with a golden light. At first she turned to hide from its wondrous glow, as its burning sun was more than her eyes could bear. But as she looked again her heart was stirred with an elevated joy, and moved by its primal beauty.

Below the tree stretched a shining valley, wide and green, peaceful and serene. The forest shade behind her had fallen away, revealing a rich grassland that stretched as far as she could see, down into the great expanse that lay before her. Around the edge of the clearing grew a stand of monstrous trees, towering and white, whose sacred grove encircled the open valley, separating it from the darker woodlands that lay behind them.

But within the valley's midst stood the mountainous hill of the shining tree. Its glorious heights, bathed in the youth of eternal spring, shined down its living lights upon the gently rolling swards below. Upon its slopes lay countless terraced gardens, which stretched forth in endless arrays of flowering growth and blossoming color, casting their showering petals like snow down upon the tender valleys. About the hill spilled forth many shining silver streams, which sparkled like jewels in the glistening sunshine as they wound their way through the emerald expanse.

Above it all, on the hill's very summit, stood the monumental tree. This colossal tree caused Ana to catch her breath, as its beauty was beyond anything she had ever seen. Its shining form threw its radiant light down upon the idyllic scene such that the garden upon the hill and the valley below it glowed forth with dazzling color in the lingering gold of the sweet warm air. For the bark of its trunk seemed to glow with a gold and honeyed hue. Its creamy limbs stretching up into the heights of Heaven shimmered with youthful leaves, which sparkled in the tree's sunny light like molten silver set aflame.

The feet of the tree's mighty roots were wound about a tiny spring upon the hilltop, whose silver waters flowed wild and free, laughing with joy as they poured down from the heights. For since the tree's birth those spirited waters with great mirth and love for it had bubbled up to feed it. Their sparkling essence had then tumbled down through sleepy gardens in countless streams until they had gathered as one about the mound's base. Collecting themselves into a rocky brook, they then poured forth over a cliff beside the hill, down into the cool depths of the valley below.

This was the One Tree that had been born from the Sacred Seed in the youth of the world. Few had witnessed the glory of its beginning or had known the hidden splendor of its long life. For in the sparkling dawn of Phantaia had an ancient seedling risen from the blackened soil, the first of its kind. In the waning light of the twilight world it had thrust its great bulk high up into the shadowed Heavens, struggling to find the nourishment of the divine light promised it by the Great Father who had made the cosmos.

But the divine beams of Heaven that might have fed the young tree were cruelly extinguished by the Endless Night in the unmaking of the world. And the last of the silver traces that yet twinkled upon the Mountains of Heaven the Magra Lords had long ago ripped away in the battle of the seas.

Yet a gentler spirit had come into Phantaia to rest alone in sorrow beside the tree deep within its mound. Her enchanted waters would feed the seedling, her loving sacrifice alone sustaining it. Nourished by her blood, the sapling shot forth into the cold night, beaming out into the Heavens its own life-giving light, giving back freely the life it had been given. So was the One Tree nurtured ever after by the liquid essence of the Secret Spring who slept beneath its roots.

For untold eons had the One Tree's ambrosial almonds, which ever fell from its pale limbs, seeded Phantaia's noble earth with its countless forest-children, so that from its sacred fruit alone had the many woodland wonders in that wilderness come forth. Even Phantaia's most ancient trees had been born from the one loving tree. For it was their undying sylvan father who would grant to them the gift of their own long lives. The One Tree was thus a Tree of Life, the eternal bearer of every seed ever planted in Phantaia, and the forest-father of all that would ever live and die there.

The One Tree appeared like a great white specter to all who saw it. Its tall white trunk stretched up from the top of the hill, high into the inky depths above. Ghostly limbs wound their way out across the starless skies until they disappeared into the gloomy blue heights of Heaven. Upon their boughs shining leaves fluttered with a wondrous spectral light. And its smooth white trunk beamed forth with a radiance that turned about like a thousand suns, cascading out its prismatic sheen far across the shadowed landscape of vast Phantaia, until it set the trunks of its unnumbered children aglow in the distant reaches.

So had the dark Heavens been illuminated by the great tree's fire, its creeping shadows thrown back, and the drapes of night flung open by its brilliant beams. The light of the Spirit Divine, born of his Creative Flame, was thus rekindled by the bark of the One Tree, whose hot flares danced again upon the rocky face of Heaven's blessed peaks.

Beneath the wingless Arch of Heaven was thus made the Amladem, the golden roof, which the One Tree alone had created by the lights of his shining limbs. That life-giving glow would burn bright for many eons within the reflective skies, feeding the many forest-children who had grown beneath the tree's wide-rooted feet, as it spread its gift across the many wooded realms that stretched far and wide before it.

Yet by a mysterious source which none could find were the One Tree's strange lights granted unto it. And this hidden gift the tree would closely guard.

Around the base of the majestic tree had grown a bountiful paradise known as the Gardens of Abrea. Their rolling hills of verdure had climbed up from the wide and radiant valley below, until they had stretched their magnificent growth out into the farthest reaches of Phantaia's rich forests. But within their heart stood the mightiest of their hills—that which is named Abra. For upon the summit of this sacred mound would sit the noble tree. And about its slopes grew the Gardens of Abrea, for which the encircling woods and valleys of Phantavra, and the more distant twilit glades of Avra, were so named.

To some it was called Riabra, the queen of gardens. For the enchanted growth upon its rise was said to be blessed by the hill's hidden maternal waters, whose well lay beside the spirit of she who dwelt within its rocks. For within the Hill of Abra there had bubbled forth the waters of the Secret Spring, and upon whose top the Sacred Seed had been planted long ago.

Upon Abra's summit had formed a tiny pool whose waters had sprung forth from the hill's own depths where the mother-spring had slept within a tomb. Her waters had flowed up and out of the rocks, gathering within its hilltop pool until they overflowed its cup, dripping down about its slopes, feeding the magical gardens below, and embracing the mound itself in its numerous veins of crystalline waters.

Though sustained by her loving essence, the living plants of Abrea's many gardens like the trees were born from the seeds of the great father-tree. For the source of all living things in that realm had first taken root through his will alone. The Gardens of Abrea had thus become the shining center of this world, surrounded by the twilight forests of Phantavra, which encircled its father-tree and gardens in a loving and protective embrace.

About colorful Abrea, like the hub of a wheel, had the dark and colorless skies also turned. For like Phantaia itself, that garden of delight and its honeyed airs were fated to be held apart from the enduring gloom of shadows, the wickedness of savage storms, and the grimmer beings of Oblivion which drew ever nearer to it.

Though many glorious gardens had been seeded long ago upon the most distant fringes of Phantaia's vast arboreal lands, this most ancient inner realm alone had remained bound to youthful splendor. Within Abrea had survived a Land of Eternal Youth borne forth by its living lights, sustained by its glorious gardens, and fed by its pristine waters since time immemorial. For all who came to dwell in Abrea would remain eternally childlike by the strange enchantments of its timeless lands.

This was a winding and twisting landscape of endless gardens captured in a state of everlasting springtime. Its young plants trailed forth in never-ending galleries of bloom and color, down into the depths of the forests in every direction. In that strange garden had lain many hidden glades of flowering trees and bushes bearing fruits of many kinds, each raining down their flowers and petals on their neighboring hills and dales below. But never would those gardens age, though eons creaked ever onward. For the trees and plants nearest to the Gardens of Abrea remained bewitched by that strange curse of youthful vigor, an undying nature which they could never shake.

And so was Ana enthralled from afar by the grandeur of that flowering paradise. For she could see no dying tree, withered plant, or brown blade of grass within its midst.

But it was the magical water of the pool upon the distant hill that truly sustained Abrea. Wherever it flowed, the plants and trees were greenest and appeared almost like young saplings. For the secretive waters of Abrea's well had flowed unceasingly and with great power for many ages atop the shining hill of Abra. Cascading from its overgrown summit, its streams trickled down across the green grassy slopes that stretched beneath the great tree until they wound their way down through soft meadows and lush mounds of growth, into the moist catacombs of misty trees and ferns in the valleys far below.

On the hillside of Abra, beside those strange waters, there had grown great orchards of fruiting trees, endless arrays of blossoming bushes, trailing tracts of shining young trees, and luscious fern-covered sleepy grottos, dark and mysterious. Shaded waterfalls and roaring white cataracts fell about the foot of the great hill, spilling their waters down into the awaiting pools below. Underneath the misty falls had slept shadowy glades of gigantic ferns and bracken-filled grottos, whose wild growth billowed up from the multicolored gravels that sparkled like gems beneath silent pools within their neighboring cool blue-green waters.

In the wide valley that stretched beyond the falls and cliffs could be heard the loud rush of thundering streams as they gathered together in their rocky grottos, before pouring themselves into the river below in a great fury over the lichened boulders. About their banks had grown bright green copses of mossy trees, clustering upon the edges of their many arteries. Beyond these waterways lay a vast floodplain of listless swamps and sleepy bottoms, which in turn were fed by the dripping seeps that lay buried within the rocky hills about Abrea. Thus had the hidden well of Abra by many secretive paths joined the river of Avalyr, feeding the blessed forest that slept beside her until their own essence became one with the river and were carried onward to the sea.

So had this valley become an untouched virginal paradise of living trees and plants, green growth, and flowering abundance beyond all measure known. For the Gardens of Abrea seemed to summon into their lush growth the very spirit of the rich earth and waters that lay hidden beneath their feet. This was a place blessed by the grace of its creator, born into timeless bliss, and bathed in the glory of its creation. For since the birth of Phantaia and its secretive gardens, no hand had yet marred it or scarred its idyllic beauty. Pure, perfect, and serene, it was a place of eternal joy and enduring peace, seeking neither curious visitor nor thirsty eyes to bear witness to its hidden splendor.

Yet within its solemn grandeur, the vital essence of Phantaia had long remained concealed. Alone in Abrea, its spirit had meditated for endless ages within its own quiet mind, free of the curse of time, and divorced from evil and its destructive will. Yet was it conscious of its eventual end. For evil's dark servants had crept ever closer to its beating heart. And Phantaia had struggled to hold apart the eldritch night and the devouring void from its youthful lands. Upon its last shining hill were its soil, seed, and spring still one. And so in Abrea alone the loving light of life still won.

But it was the blessed light of the One Tree that had truly sustained and protected that glorious idyll from the encroaching darkness. Touched by its strange spiritual glow, reflecting upon the upturned leaves of countless trees, the One Tree had sent its loving spirit into Phantaia's virginal wood, feeding its many children, and bending all things born there to its secretive and primeval purpose.

Hidden by the magical glamour of those shimmering lights, darkness had been cast away from its inner woods. For its bright glow had enveloped Abrea, protecting it from the gloom of the darker forest beyond, and chasing away the evil ones that had come to pollute it and corrupt its countless innocent children. Thus, by the light of the shining tree was Phantaia unbound from the dark dreams that had long gripped it and which had ever after sought to possess its last living children.

By the presence of the One Tree alone had the forests of Phantaia been granted protection. Yet, by the powers it granted to its many children, were the trees to transform the dark and violent cosmos into one living land, and by their evolving, ever-blooming, miraculous growth, cover every foot of this dying world in a wild and unbroken wilderness. Such was the secret desire of the One Tree and the true labor granted unto it by the Great Father.

For long ago the Great Father had hoped that through his youngest son a river of life and goodness would flow throughout the world, a graceful garden stand beside it, and the glory of his lights beam out bold and bright to bless all his sons, drawing them as one to this his greatest of creations. For unto his sons would be given this new home and heaven, the wilderness of Phantaia, whose joyous story in this tome of Phantammeron would be told. Only then would his sacred plans be made manifest by the works of the One Tree and be made known to them all, such that the Primordial Ones and their children, dearest to him, would all come to know the full glory and beauty of Phantaia, the spiritual paradise which they themselves had helped make.

But by the evil and destructive deeds of the Primordial Ones had Phantaia's living lands been filled with such dread and terror that only the innermost garden would now remain, closing in upon itself, and shutting its shining gates to all eyes but its own. Yet, by the tree's hope-filled and loving lights that yet stretched their grander beams out into the shadowed woods, had its farthest realms of fallen and forgotten trees still felt its long-held desire for the return of their once-loving brotherhood, though shadows had long filled its most distant paths.

Those trees then drank of its merciful radiance and slept in peace-filled harmony, protected by its rays even to the grim gates of Oblivion itself. Thus from its very beginning, in that youthful age to the One Tree's woody rhythms alone did the hearts of the trees of the world still beat. And as long as the One Tree lived there yet remained an abiding hope in Phantaia that the sacred plans of the Great Father would someday be fulfilled.

The white horse had led Ana up and over the last rise, towards the edge of the grassy valley that stretched before them. It was leading her to the great hill where the shining tree now dwelt. To Ana the white horse seemed at peace in this strange place, as if it were home. And she now understood where she had been led. But she still knew not the reason.

She and the horse walked side by side through the last of the twilight woods that grew about the valley. The last line of trees stood ahead of her, just before the bright valley that fell below. Yet the shadows of the dimmer woods still clung thickly to the trees and earth around her. For this was the last bastion of woody shade which the hands of the Twilight Mist had yet held in his protective grip.

They walked past the thick and warty trunks of hoar hawthorns that stood within the encircling woods, watching for any evil that might attempt to enter Abrea uninvited. They were the most ancient of the One Tree's forest-children—the children of Kum, the aged lord-tree of the hawthorns, who watched over them from his distant meadow. Their brown and bulbous faces, large noses, and red-rooted feet stood out upon their short but wide-girthed bodies.

Of these trees it would later be known to Ana that there were nine. They long held the garden's sacred knowledge close to them, shared only in silent whispers borne by the winds. For they had clamored before the hill of their father-tree in earlier times, seeking to know of the many secrets that lay hidden within his roots. These ancient hawthorns had been possessed of strange spirits, which were bound to the mind and heart of the One Tree and to the hidden spring that lay deep within the breast of his ancient hill. As Ana walked beyond the last shade of the gloomier forest, she could hear the voices of the hawthorns whispering to themselves in the depths of the distant woods that stretched to either side of her.

As she and the horse approached the clearing that fell away into the valley, they entered a short ring of taller trees. They were cast in the purest white, standing in silent grandeur around the upper rim of the valley. These were the mightiest of trees within the woods of Phantaia, the last of its gateway trees. For they guarded the many pathways into the valley of Phantavra. Here, the last of the great elderwood trees of Phantaia rose up from the green grasslands and meadows that lay beyond them. They stood like smooth white obelisks, bright and graceful against the open skies. Thick with dew, their wet woods contained the last trees trapped within the lavender mists that rose each evening to engulf Phantaia.

Yet with their graceful height, their glossy forms rose far above those fogs. Upon each of these slender trees a thousand branches had been born. Their leafy heads and bright foliage bent over the trail, tossed about high above their heads by some celestial breeze that flowed within the azure Heavens. Like the hawthorns, they seemed to talk amongst themselves in a strange tongue, conversing in endless chatter with the mighty father-tree that stood proudly before them. Others giggled with the youthful trees that grew about the hill in the valley below.

This secretive and narrow, white-ringed wood of elder trees was named Breddwynn, the White Forest. For the beauty of this grove of gateway trees stood apart from the dimmer twilit forests that lay before them. Yet to some was it called the Ringwood. For its princely aisles of trees encircled and protected Abrea from the outer evil, while boldly marking the entrance into the vast and shadowed wilderness of Phantaia that lay beyond them.

Yet were the trees of Breddwynn also caretakers of the vast nurseries of Abrea. By their warm reflection of its inner lights, were much of its brighter rays radiated back into the garden, thus feeding it. The trees of the elderwood were the noblest of the sons of the One Tree. And like the rowan, their brethren that dwelt upon the middle realms of Phantaia, they often moved in the depths of the twilight hour from their rooted spots, walking through the mists to encircle and guard the One Tree and his gardens in his time of need.

In later ages many would seek to find these beings, to draw forth their strength and knowledge. But they could be hard to find. For often they would disappear in the darker mists and cluster deeper in the depths of Phantaia, or come to the aid of some sacred glade, tree, or pool whose powers only they understood.

Shadowed by those great trees, Ana and the horse quietly walked through their sylvan meadow unchallenged, then down into the vast green fields that stretched out across the wide valley below. Here upon the slopes lay the wide grassy Glades of Aron, that which encircled the Hill of Abra and the Gardens of Abrea. No trees grew upon this vast rolling turf. Its sweet rich grass breathed a perpetual dew, mingling with the mist that drifted up from the river each night. Its moist blades in the shade of the glades of the towering white elderwood seemed to sparkle like emeralds in the ephemeral air.

As they descended through trailing fields of yellow and white daisies, they entered the final copse of trees that lay before the towering Hill of Abra. In this narrow wooded valley the last of the stately trees of Phantaia grew. Beyond them Ana saw the great hill with its splendid gardens rising just beyond the tops of their leafy heads.

These trees were small in size, bright green, graceful, young, and lithe, with newborn leaves that had not yet fully opened. At their feet lay bright mossy rocks and stones that had tumbled down from the hill above. The exotic beauty of this tiny wood was set aglow by some native glamour whose source her eyes could not find.

As she passed through the narrow forest the trees about her suddenly awoke. In sheer joy upon seeing her they began chatting and laughing amongst themselves like children. With the first bending of their boughs by soft breezes borne aloft and the whistling of winds through their leaves were the voices of the youthful trees thrown upon the airs and shared between them. Ana could not help but laugh herself listening to them.

From these young trees was the secret language of Phantaia first spoken long ago, their voices echoing through the farthest corridors of the woods. Even the haunted trees of Avaras had heard their whispers and learned their songs. Yet, while the wheeling seas roared and the rolling thunder of the storms bellowed forth, the tree's music would not be heard or known beyond Phantaia. And so the song of the trees could not travel beyond the wall of solemn oaks that hung low upon its most distant shores.

But the Twilight Mist had somehow heard their strange whispers upon the seas, calling him from far away. For it was their cries that summoned him from the Dreaming Seas, to return to the Secret Spring who yet wept for him in the depths of her mound. So was that couple's timeless love born anew by the song of the trees, and by their words renewed in their hearts. And so, ever after, would the trees and the burgeoning wilderness that grew beyond them remain hidden by the powers of the Twilight Mist. For he had come to Phantaia to protect them from the sea and storm in return for their great gift of song.

In the midst of that laughing wood, Ana now heard the sound of rushing water trickling down from the flowering paradise above her. From atop the hill she saw several young streams of purest water flowing forth and filled with the scents of the gardens above. Gathering amongst themselves their many dripping springs at the base of the great hill, those waters formed a fast moving rivulet that flowed through the narrow copse that encircled Abrea.

So had arisen the bubbling brook named Lilu, she who had gathered as one stream to her the many laughing waters of Abrea. The trunks of the trees had all leaned toward Lilu, as if the stream's mirthful waters bore some special power. For this was a happy and magical brook, though it contained a hidden sadness. For it stilled the hearts of those whose lips touched its wondrous waters, turning their minds towards deeper reflection upon its secret source and the sorrowful mother within the mound who bore them.

As Ana walked towards the tiny stream, she saw where it was joined by a dozen more that had seeped down and around the hill. Though Lilu's many silver streams flowed apart about Abrea's slopes, they had gathered again beneath the hill as a single rivulet, singing and giggling together in their rush to the river.

Fed by the burgeoning streams that fell from above, Lilu had also taken into her Aron's many rain-fed rills, drawn from the thick clouds of mist that hung in the skies above. She then collected them together as sisters, gathering them before a rocky prominence beneath the Hill of Abra. There they fell over the cliffs as the thunderous white waterfalls called the Falls of Bann. The waters of Lilu then drifted down into soft green pools that lay beneath the falls, joining her beloved sisters to her as one again. They then flowed boldly through the land, carving a rugged course through the rocky alcoves until they poured with great haste into the headwaters of the mighty river of Avalyr.

The sound of that cataract's roar and its rising mists stilled Ana's heart, returning her mind to thoughts again upon her grandfather's words once more—the troubled world he had left behind, of wars continually waged, of her father's cruel deeds, and of the mysterious pool that lay hidden deep inside her. And yet his words for her were also of hope for happier days yet to come.

The waterfall's white spray climbed up and over the trees and hills above her, until their clouds were cast aglow by the miraculous golden light of the One Tree. Their white mists then shed forth a spectacular rainbow, which coruscated its magical lights and colorful rays against the gloomy walls of the distant wood. Ana's heart then leapt for joy at the beauty of that scene, its quiet grandeur renewing her spirit and mind.

She would now complete her journey with pride and yet with hope that some happier and more purposeful fate awaited her. For she had travelled far and faced many fears. Seeing the beauty of this place she felt that at last she had found her true home.

But in the midst of that joyous scene Ana heard a distant and melancholy voice piteously calling up from the depths below. It seemed to be the song of the rushing river. Or was it a girl's voice? She stood still listening to its mournful song, wondering about the meaning of its strange plaintive cry. She then thought about the voice of her mother who dwelt in the distant seas. And she wondered if she would ever see her face or hear the soft beat of her heart again.

But that lonesome call had come from the river. Ana cautiously approached the dark cliffs of the waterfall, looking down where the waters of the falls had gathered in sleepy pools under the shadows of the cliffs. She then saw where they formed the headwaters of Avalyr, the cold river within which the strange girl had appeared. But as she looked in the distance, she saw the tiny Isle of Adda which she had earlier passed, its dark pupil peering up from within the shimmering eye of the river. Just as the mother-stream had encircled Abra, so too had its silver waters bound the lonely isle in her loving arms. The unusual song was then heard again. And Ana knew it to be of the lonely island girl.

The great stallion walked to the edge of the stream before the falls, bending his head and drinking deeply from it. As he drank it filled his spirit with some enchanted power. For his coat shone even whiter, as his golden horn gleamed in the light of the great tree. They then crossed the rivulet above the falls, walking carefully on the dark gray stones. Ana stopped to look down over the cliff. She could barely see the cascading waters as they fell away, into the cool viridian pools that lay far below in the foggy depths. She then thought she saw the snow-white leaves of a ghostly tree, hidden within the mists and shadows of the black ravine.

Ana and the horse wound their way past the white waterfalls and black cliffs of the Hill of Abra, making their way toward the steady incline of the Gardens of Abrea whose green slopes towered above them. A pale mist began to slowly encircle them, bathing everything again in its moist fog.

They had finally come to the edge of the small forest that surrounded the hill. Here the last of the One Tree's young saplings lined the banks before the base of the lush gardens. The trees here seemed ever youthful, their new silver shoots breaking free of the rich soil at her feet. They had remained eternally young as saplings, never aging or dying. For here, on the edge of that mossy underwood, the loving light of the One Tree had shined brightest. And Lilu had graced them with her vitality. These trees alone would remain the great tree's timeless offspring, never aging or growing beyond their youthful state.

The maze of gardens now stood towering before Ana and the horse. But that strange hill had seemed to appear and disappear by the movements of the eerie mist that now flowed up and over their heads. For that fog had moved quickly to wrap the hill in its giant cloud, dimming the glow of the One Tree before their eyes.

Ana was still, moved by the sight of the tree's shining beauty as it disappeared beneath the cloud. She turned to the white horse, climbing onto his back, and placing her arms around his neck. For she felt the nervous anticipation in her heart that they would soon reach the summit and come at long last to the end of their journey. That hopeful and happy feeling drove them both quickly forward, as they climbed through the last trees and into the midst of the beautiful paradise of plants and flowers that lay about the slopes of the Hill of Abra.

They began to climb the hill, twisting and turning, and following a narrow path that wrapped about the hill. The fog became thicker as they strode up into its dense blanket. But as they turned to climb a new rise, something snagged Ana and pulled her off the horse. She became separated from him and was quickly lost in the fog. She called out to him, but he was nowhere to be seen. In a panic, she struggled to pull herself up from the thick bushes of thorns and brambles that entangled the silver drapery that wrapped about her. But, as she looked to the ground, she saw around her a dense thicket of black roses whose dark shriveled and satiny blooms shone forth with a sinister light.

Their sweet scent filled the air with the sickly smell of seduction and sordid temptation, secretive desires, and perverse fantasies, all of which were beyond her youthful mind's comprehension. But their blood-red thorns would not be denied their victim. For they twisted about her body, seeking to pierce her arms and legs with every step she took. Her instinct told her to remain still. And so she froze in the midst of those evil bushes. Fearing the dagger-like thorns now pressed against her arms and legs, she cried out again in the mist for the horse to come to her. But the stallion was nowhere to be seen.

These were the Murgala, the Black Roses of Abrea. And in their terrible thorns lay a cursed poison that filled the mind with many nightmares, binding one to a sleep from which one might never awaken. For many ages those vile bushes had grown unseen within the shadows of the brighter Gardens of Abrea. For their bushes had sprouted in secret from the tears of the Endless Night when first his desired bride, the Sacred Seed, had left him and departed that lonely hill. In the heavy dusk of evening he had walked upon the mound, before even the planting of the One Tree, seeking the beautiful maiden and awaiting her return. But she would never come again to him.

But before the Endless Night departed, he had dripped down upon the hill the dark tears of the Glourun, which he had shed for her. From them grew black satin roses born of the seeds of his darkness, so that the Secret Spring might remember him. He then departed the Hill of Abra, vowing never to return. But the Murgala had remained, a reminder of his cursed and doomed love. And so would those roses lie fallow yet rise up by their own evil will, to entrap and ensnare in their large blooms and thorns all those who might seek to penetrate those gardens and harm the sacred spring that dwelt there.

But upon the birth of the One Tree, its first lights were cast upon the Murgala's dark leaves. And they were burned by them. They then died until only a small patch of the sinister roses remained at the base of the hill. There, under a bluff, they hid in the shadows within a secretive part of the garden. And so had they survived, fed by the darkness and hidden from the light of the tree, waiting until it should wane or die when their evil vines might grow forth again unchecked, stretching their black and tangled stems about the garden and claiming that hill as their own, as they had in ages past.

Ana stopped moving and looked upon the large blooms of the black roses with fascination. For in each blossom lay the wonders of darkest night and the silky shadows of a world she had never seen. And she seemed drawn to those roses in a way she could not understand. For the glamor of the Glourun was contained in them—the dark powers which the Night had made to hide, by deceptive beauty, his own workings of great evil. Something in her desired to pick one and know more of the depth of its seductive scent.

But as she reached to take one of its black blooms in her hands, from out of the dark mist came the white horse, galloping up to her. He pushed the blossom away from her hands with his muzzle. She then climbed upon his back again, and they rode on up the high hill away from the dark garden.

The strange mist had finally broken free again, its shifting shadows departing the hillside, revealing the secret beauty of Abrea's many wonders. About them lay the threshold of a flowering and flourishing paradise, ageless and unhindered by the march of time. As the clouds' gloom was flung apart upon the summit of the hill, Ana saw the colossal tree high above her, the sun-glow of its towering trunk casting rich luminous rays down upon the colorful scenery that lay before her.

Ana and the horse wove their way through the lush gardens about the hill. Travelling up a twisting pathway, they climbed past tall terraces and open arbours of rich green growth, upon whose dangling branches and vines hung great clusters of flowers and fruits of every kind. Soft fragrant winds wafted past the tumbling display, carrying upon its breezes the perfumed scents of a thousand budding blossoms newly born. The great tree's lights wove their many colors steadily into the surface and shadow of every living thing, so that no stem, leaf, or flower was without some enchanted aura, its strange glow forged from the radiant hues cast within and upon it.

As they climbed higher, Abrea's plants swelled up from the rich mulch of the mound in great abundance, overlaying everything with a floral icing of younger buds and blooms. They opened their flowering clusters in a multitude of wondrous forms, shapes, and colors as they walked by.

This was the heart of the garden called Glorianna. A bejeweled bed of great beauty, this sylvan glade seemed to shine like a great treasure chest of gems. To Ana, like flames upon the eye, that garden's blazing color seemed. Rich crimson reds, soft pinks, faded fuchsias, buttery yellows, vibrant violets, hot oranges, and cool whites appeared in the dense growth of the hillside, clamoring about the heights and hollows of the rambling garden. The overflowing bushes and vines, overlaid and underfoot, covered every inch of earth, so that the hillsides seemed adorned with one never-ending bright bouquet.

As they climbed higher still past the mass of blooming growth, about her stretched great clusters of wisteria whose knotted vines, thick and tangled, spread out beside the path on either side. Their grape-like blooms of creamy purple and white, held a magical odor that caused her to stop and smell them. Above them grew wide clusters of honeysuckle, saffron and white in color. Enhanced by their romantic perfumes, these twin vines, entangled together, whispered in the winds the joyous tale of a passionate interlude long held between them on the hillside.

Upon a high spot Ana paused and looked down. The warm colors from above reflected upon the rich green canopy of the trees and laughing streams below, so that all was afire in a wondrous glow. She then heard the sound of water from above. As she looked up, she saw where a small stream had dripped down from the heights. The most delicate of ferns had crowded upon the cliffs in great clusters, drawn to the sweet water as it tumbled down the hillside. Even thicker mounds of vegetation clung upon the elevated rocks about it, stretching their masses of leaves and vines down into the misty valley that fell away before the falls below her. Above the white mist of the falls they swayed in the gentle winds, as if dancing to the song of the glassy brooks that sang to them in the roaring depths.

As Ana and the horse drew near to the top of the hill, the abundant green and flowering growth gave way to vast fields of swaying grasses and shorter growth. Here lay the pale-green grassy fields of windswept Annafar, which had drawn themselves about the breezy top of Abra.

Many hidden flowers of rarest beauty grew upon its grassy slopes, gripping the dark soil in their ghostly roots—blue-budding petunias and pale lavender lilac, coral-colored hollyhocks and tiny yellow hyacinths, beds of jewel orchids and dark violets in many rich shades and hues. Small purpled nettles and pink pansies divorced and dwelling far apart in the sparse valley below had one last time gathered here, wedded together as one, shining out even brighter as they grew united upon the hillside.

Close to the summit, Ana saw delicate blooms of rarest columbine, shining down their lovely faces at her as she approached from below. But as she drew close to the top of the hill, it was the buttery yellow of the daffodils in the soft fields of Annafar that drew Ana down from the horse. She knelt to touch and smell them, and then stood within their joyous crowds in amazement at their beauty. For their seemingly endless fields swayed as one atop the hill, bending their heads up and down to the rhythm of the breezes that flowed past their tops, casting them about in its sway. Her journey had been long and weary. And she felt uplifted by them.

As they climbed the last part of the hill, Ana saw the most beautiful bushes of ruby red roses, small and delicate, spread across the mound about their feet. From high above the violet mist descended from the skies and hovered over them for but a moment, reflecting the roses' sanguine light down about them so that all the vegetation seemed bathed in a mystical crimson glow.

As they walked out upon the summit of the hill at last, Ana looked about her feet and saw tiny gray-green grasses, delicate maidenhair ferns, and tiny mosses all of which fed on the tiny streams that seeped out from some hidden source near the base of the great tree.

As they walked through the maidenhair ferns that grew upon the moist hill, Ana looked up and saw the source of the magnificent lights she had seen shining down from afar. Rising up from the center of the summit stood the One Tree, its shining trunk thrusting up its mighty bulk high into the Heavens above her head. Its white limbs glowed with a golden brilliance, radiating their warm lights down upon the forest below.

Though its trunk shone with a warm white light, from its highest boughs was cast the glitter of shining silver and gold. A million leaves sparkled in the pollen-filled air like the twinkling of stars. Yet was its light cast not in a chaotic spectacle. For the great figure of the noble tree had seemed to order with a lawful touch its own filaments of light as they wafted through the ether, so that no leaf or living thing in the forest below was left untouched by its glorious beams.

Ana walked up to the great trunk to look upon it and ponder its majestic beauty. Above her the tree's great limbs had spread out straight and wide. Luxuriant in its leafy hair, its wide umbrage had stretched out across the skies, filling the Heavens with its dense verdure. Its massive white boughs seemed to curl up into the sky, beyond even the farthest reaches of Heaven's own canopy. Roofed against the sky, the great tree with an almost divine strength seemed to push its mighty form up into the shapeless void, beyond even the Arch of Heaven itself, until the very skies groaned against its weight. Yet in a strange way it almost seemed to her that the skies were supported by this mighty pillar of a tree, as if the central axis of the Heavens was held up by its powerful column alone.

Ana returned the white horse in awe of the spectacular sight, peering up into the tree towering above her. She reached out to touch its outstretched limbs which, smooth and thick, hung low over her head. To some unknown breeze they gently swayed, their leaves, ginkgo-shaped, fluttering in the breeze like bright sparkling saucers. Upon every branch grew bountiful blossoms of purest white with faded crimson within their centers. They opened up ever so slightly as Ana touched them with her hand. Yet she could not see their centers.

These flowers had borne upon them many fleshy fruits, which had hung low upon the tree's numerous branches. Only great blooms now remained upon its golden branches, as if awaiting some momentous event that would send them forth fruiting again. From those fruits would come the seeds of an even greater generation of trees. And so its blossoms had been born to feed and nourish the children of a future time, shedding the seeds of its own shining children back down into the fallen world, so they might shoot forth with new life from the sullied soil.

As Ana looked below the tree, she saw how the broad roots of the One Tree had twisted themselves about the top of the Hill of Abra, sinking their white tendrils deep into the earth. About its feet grew delicate red poppies, which seemed to glow with an odd illumination. She then turned to look down from the hilltop and saw an idyllic scene below her. An endless vista stretched before her through which many veins of silvered brooks now flowed.

Below the gardens lay the wide valley of Avalyr, whose dark river twisted and turned through the blue onyx haze of the humid air.

Beyond the valley lay the cool green of the foggy forests through which she had passed. Those wooded hills stretched far and away into the blue horizon, until even the distant mountains had faded to gray in the twilight gloom. Yet the warm glow of the shining tree still lit the tops of Phantaia's rocky peaks with its golden lights, so that above the purple mists their summits were set aflame, shining like blades of tangerine gold against a turquoise sky. Entranced by the sublime beauty of that spectacular view, it felt to Ana that this fleeting moment would never end.

But as she looked upon that vast paradise, she heard the gentle sound of a bubbling brook coming from the shadows beneath the great tree behind her. She then climbed around the huge trunk. There beside the tree stood a miraculous pool whose ephemeral waters bubbled up from within a small cauldron of rock. It was a tiny well, lined with delicate stones whose bright green mosses shined with a phosphorescent light upon their gray surfaces.

The white roots of the tree had woven their way around the pool, diving down into its water and rocks, drawing into itself the precious waters of that quiet spring. The young waters of the pool seemed to flow forth from some hidden source deep within its rocky depths, first filling its stone container, then dripping down over its lip. In four corners of the tiny pool, the waters trickled out over the small mossy stones, until they formed small seeps that fed the Gardens of Abrea that wrapped about the hill in all four directions.

The One Tree's magical lights danced upon the surface of the pool's clear cool waters, casting up a sparkling spectra of colors from within its depths. Yet no other tree, rock, or plant would reflect therein. This was the Secret Pool that had dwelt under the One Tree since before its own birth. Here the waters of the Secret Spring had first welled up, pristine and pure, carving out from the rocks the receptacle that contained it. So it appeared as an enchanted cauldron of silver whose precious wine had overflowed its cup.

By the motherly grace of she who had dwelt there had those waters first birthed the tree from the fertile soil of Abra. By those waters and her brother's own earth had they together fed and sustained it. Here the Sacred Seed had given his only child, the One Tree, to this world. His brother's children, born of the Immortal Clay, had then sustained it. For they would not let it die. So too had the Twilight Mist, for love of that spring, wrapped his tendrils about the tree, bathing it in his mist's wet dew. And so by their communal love as one family had they bound themselves together to the tree and its fate. For they alone knew its secret purpose.

Ana walked over to the pool. Kneeling down, she looked into its clear waters. Oddly, she saw only her own silver reflection and that of the tree upon its wavy surface. As Ana stared at her face, she appeared older now and somehow different. She pondered the strange appearance of her dark hair, her violet eyes, and the wondrous limbs and lights of the tree reflected therein. In that mysterious picture she and the tree seemed joined as one. As she knelt beside the beautiful pool, she heard its calming sound. And she reflected upon her life to that point. All time seemed to drift away in that silent hour.

For a long time she sat beside the quiet pool, peering at the delicate nature of the brooklime and white meadowsweet that grew along its banks. She saw too that beyond its ferns and rocks grew brilliant red amaranths, whose unfading color and beauty stood out boldly against the deep green ivy that grew about the rocks. The blood red amaranths had been the first flowers to grow beside its magical waters. And so they were Abrea's most ancient of flowers. The amaranths seemed oddly familiar to her. Yet few would know of the blood of the Secret Spring that had made them.

She felt at home here, as she sat beside the pool. She lay down within a small bed of maidenhair ferns, weary from her long journey, looking up into the peaceful canopy of the great tree above her. She then drifted off to sleep beside the bubbling sound of the pool. She felt like she was drifting down into the hill, deep into a secret chamber unseen below, where she could at long last rest there in peace herself for all eternity.

But to Ana had returned strange dreams. She looked down upon her sleeping self as she lay there beside the pool. All of a sudden there stood a figure before her hidden in the mist. It seemed to walk forward, then hover above the waters. It was the figure of a woman, tall and beautiful beyond compare, with long golden hair whose woven braids stretched almost to her feet. Her eyes were darkened and her skin was pale. And her soft young face seemed sorrow-filled.

Upon her head had been bestowed a wreath of green garlands, woven about its crown with tiny white daisies. Her long wavy dress of white, pale gold, and soft green flowed about her as if floating within a cloud. Her dress appeared to be embroidered with bands of fantastic designs and circular emblems of some divine form she did not recognize.

Ana saw that she was weeping. For in her arms was a child which she cradled closely to her breast. But as she reached out to touch the spirit it backed away quickly, disappearing like vapors in the mist as if to hide herself and her child. But as that ghost glided away into the shadows, Ana heard from her lips a strange word she did not recognize. *Phanduan.* She then faded from view.

The white horse had appeared over her as she slept, its large warm eyes peering down into hers. It nudged her from her sleep, as it had done before. But this time it seemed more animated. Ana awoke and quickly rose to her feet, concerned and anxious by its pacing and excitement. The white horse then galloped to the edge of the trunk of the great tree. There it turned and looked back at her. Ana ran after him and stroked his neck, trying to calm him. It looked deeply into her eyes, as if to express some thought she could not fathom. The white horse then turned away, disappearing around the wide trunk of the One Tree.

Ana stood alone at the foot of the tree's winding roots. She thought to herself the horse must be hiding from her in some sort of playful game. She heard the sound of giggling. Then a child's head suddenly looked back at her from behind the thick trunk of the great tree. But as quick as it appeared it was then gone. She climbed upon a root of the tree and looked where the child had been. But she saw nothing. She then heard another sound, as of laughter coming from around the other side of the tree.

As she walked around it, she saw no sign of the voice or of the horse. But as she turned to walk back to where she had stood, an odd boy suddenly appeared. He looked to be about her age and similar in height. But the boy was very strange in appearance. He had skin the color of dark green leaves in summer. But as Ana looked closer at his face she saw within his skin many variations of a bright, leafy green with turquoise combined, which sparkled and shimmered with tiny lights within its swirls. His eyes were a golden reddish color. And his thick, shoulder-length brown hair, filled with streaks of golden saffron, hung about his face like straw. Strange was this autumn boy that had appeared before her.

Ana stared at the boy in complete surprise. But the child being happy and animated only smiled, holding his hand out and introducing himself. "Hello. My name is Ama," the boy said. Ana stood unmoving, still surprised.

"In truth, I already know who you are Ana, and have known you well for some time," the boy said, smiling. "For I am the white creature that has led you from the sea, carrying you—quite painfully—on my back through Phantaia." He then feigned pain in his back, holding his hips and stretching, all the while smiling at the girl through squinted eyes.

Ama laughed, telling Ana, "I only took the form of Phanyan the white unicorn to protect you from the dangers of the woods, and to carry you to these, the Gardens of Abrea, the place upon which we now stand. Besides, four feet are better than two. You agree?" He stood quietly before the startled girl with a slight frown upon his face. For Ana could not speak and was still shocked by his sudden change in appearance.

He held out his hand in the air before her, palm facing out, as if to touch her. Ana looked carefully at the strange boy, until she too reached out to put her hand on his. She longed to touch him, as she was still unsure if he was real, a dream, or a ghost.

But as she touched his hand, his skin suddenly changed pale like hers, his hair and eyes to a rich hazel brown. Ama then stopped and looked at his arms and legs with curiosity. At this miraculous change, the boy then told her, "This appears to be the form which you desire most to see in me. For I change in appearance by the will and desire of the spirit that touches me."

Ana marveled at the young boy's more natural appearance, as he seemed so much like her own. But he was in many ways different from her. For though they seemed the same age, he was a rough and rugged boy with warm hair like the bark of a tree, tangled and wild like its leaves. His arms and legs were strong yet long and wiry, as if made for running and climbing. About his waist he wore a pair of short leggings upon which light green leaves were woven like the tiny scales of a fish. And his tan feet appeared nimble and light.

Ama giggled to himself seeing how pleased she was with his new appearance. He then walked under the shade of the great tree, calling her over to follow him as he stood beside the pool. He danced and smiled as he walked, joy-filled and carefree. But Ama was simply happy to reveal his true self to Ana.

Ana walked cautiously behind him, unsure of his mysterious and odd nature. They then sat down beside the tiny pool. "I know you have many questions for me. But first I want to show you a trick," Ama said. He reached behind his back. "Pick a hand," he said. She picked his left hand, as he looked at her with feigned concern. He then pulled out his left hand and there within its palm burned a ghostly white fire. Ana looked with amazement as she stared at it, hypnotized.

"This is the White Flame of Truth," Ama said, "It burns bright within the great tree. In it is the living spirit of the forest. For it can strike at any time and burn away parts of the forest that are untrue if it desires. The Dark Flame of Lies dare not come into its heart as long as its candle shines brightly. Like the tree, the truth in our own hearts burns within us and shines on, even beyond our death." Ama looked into her eyes with a serious expression, though she knew not what his words meant.

Ana then picked his right hand. And Ama slowly pulled it out, revealing a beautiful ruby that sparkled with a deep red light within its center. "This is the Red Gem of Passion," Ama told Ana with a crooked smile. "It represents the earth beneath the forest, the blood of the rock, and the creative spirit of the body that sustains all things." He then whispered, "It also represents untethered passion, which, guided by true and abiding love, may reach to great heights." Ama's eyes almost seemed to flame up within their depths, as he stared into hers.

Ama then said to her, "The stone always bears the ruddy light that the flame shall eventually cleanse away. For the light is eternal, while the earth is not. And the fire of its light shall reveal all things as they truly are in time. But the stone is the essence of your life. The two are required for you to live Ana, and so are married as one. For they together make up the Creative Flame, which the Creator has placed in all living things." Ana held the strange ruby in her own hand, entranced by its beauty. She then returned it to him.

Ama took both forms in his hands and placed them in hers, slowly closing them. He looked down holding her hands in his. He then shook them, telling her to open them again. And from them sprang many colors of tiny dancing lights that drifted up into the trees. Ana and Ama laughed at the beauty of the lights, until they faded in the canopy of the great tree and were gone.

"What do the lights mean?" Ana asked.

"Nothing more than the many lights of the spirits yet to be born," Ama replied. Ana then looked happily at the boy. But he saw great uncertainty in her eyes. Ama then looked deeply into Ana's eyes and said, "Do not worry. For there is much more I shall reveal to you in time. I promise I will try and answer all your questions when the time is right." Ama then started to walk away.

But Ana stopped him. "Who are you, really?" she asked. "For I was not told of you by the Twilight Mist." Ama then looked at her sadly. He had known of the death of the Twilight Mist. And he knew she had seen him depart this world. He then said to Ana, "I too loved the Twilight Mist, your grandfather. For he had, for many ages, guided me as a mentor in the forest and guarded me from all harm when I was but a tiny infant in Phantaia. From him I learned many truths about the realms beyond this one, the fate of many in this world, and the sad destinies of many others." Ana stared at him again, uncertain of the meaning of his words.

Ama, seeing she still had many questions, pointed to the great tree behind her. "I am the first-born child of the One Tree, which was planted long ago in Phantaia—the tree born of the Sacred Seed and the waters that once sprang up beneath him. My father-tree's first fruit was of both the spirit and the flesh. From that first seed-of-the-forest—that which is named Am—was I born. I lay within its golden egg for a time, hidden in the earth. But it was your grandfather, the Twilight Mist, who had found me and released me from its shell. And by him was I so named Ama, the golden-one, and the son-of-the-seed."

Ama walked over to the trunk of the tree and lovingly placed his hand on its trunk. "Upon my birth, the Twilight Mist had heard me crying in the garden beneath the spring," Ama continued. He took me and raised me as his own. With loving care and gentle guidance he showed me many wonders and strange magics. He shared with me the secret knowledge and history of the world. And so I know your grandfather well, Ana."

Ama had been created by the One Tree and cast into the heart of the forest so that he might go forth and plant his many brothers and sisters, the mighty trees of Phantaia. With the seeds of the One Tree and the help of the guiding winds, it was Ama who sowed the trees and plants about its vast realms. Thus, the first trees of those woods were planted by this golden child, yet nurtured by the rains of the Twilight Mist, his uncle, in the first dawning forest-age of Phantaia.

Ama then walked to the edge of the hill and looked out across the vast forests of Phantaia, as if deep in thought. He turned and looked upon the great tree, saying, "My father and my uncle, the One Tree and the Twilight Mist, have both dwelt here in peace, free of the evils of the outside world for many silent and enduring ages, Ana. Phantaia in time was filled with my countless siblings, the tree-children, many of which I helped nurture. I have grown to know and love them all, and their children, and their children's children, too."

Ama then turned and looked at Ana with fearful eyes. "But I had not allowed them to be harmed until the coming of the Magra, which destroyed many of my brethren in its relentless storms. For this beast had come upon us after the sundering of the seas and the fall of the spirit of the one who once held Vatavandr—the Limitless Void." Ana then walked over to Ama, and sat upon a root of the white tree listening to his story.

For many ages Ama had remained beside the father-tree, standing as a mighty oak himself, looking over the gardens and forests of Phantaia. For he was a timeless being like the One Tree, his father. And as long as the mother waters of the Secret Spring poured forth into that world, he was immortal and unaging like the trees. But Twilight Mist had stayed beside him for many ages in that garden. For he and the Mist were now its sole guardians. But in time the Twilight Mist taught him many enchantments, granting to him power over his changing form, as the Twilight Mist could do. Ama had then taken flesh as he desired, so that he might defend Phantaia against the evil that ever encroached upon its fringes. And so was he its sole guardian.

He had then taken form as the spirit-deer of the wood. In this higher form was he so raised. As the Ebrandeer, the golden-horned unicorn, was he to remain for many ages beside his uncle. And so as horse-of-the-forest was he born anew by the Twilight Mist's own strange glamour. By that spoken name could Ama's spirit transform from tree to horse. And by it alone could he be called, as by a magical summons, in time of need. But to his brother trees, as the forest-guardian named Phanyan, was he freely named. And its word would be spoken many times upon the forest's whispering winds. But Ebrandeer was a secret name tied to the great wisdom of his father and the magical powers of his uncle—a name which he had been given in the youth of the world. With the passing away of his uncle, this name none would now know but him and his father, the One Tree.

In this fleshy form, Ama guarded Phantaia, chasing out the demons that had wandered into Abrea. Many he had banished from those sacred woods and gardens. For his silver hooves and golden horn had beaten back the evil creatures that had come to possess the trees. Indeed, his very form frightened many darker beings from the depths of that twilight land. And so he became Abrea's greatest warden, guarding it and the One Tree from the evils that had slowly crept into it.

Ama, continuing his story, sat down beside Ana on the white roots of the tree. "I had remained in these woods for countless eons of time, engaged in a never-ending war with the creeping darkness that had sought to find my father's tree. But my aging uncle, Twilight Mist, had returned to me upon the end of a weary age, revealing to me that a new being would soon enter the forest. That being, he told me, would be permitted to dwell within Abrea, ever after" Ama said. Ana then gazed with wonder at Ama.

"So, at a chosen time, had your grandfather sent me to the troubled shores of the sea to find you," Ama said. "As Phanyan he had called me once more, to rise again and come to him upon the shores of Phantaia. And so had I rescued you, so you would be safe from harm. For the Oversoul of the Magra that haunts the skies overhead and the demonic trees that creep about Avaras had all risen up from their graves to take you away. But here in Abrea I have chosen to return to the form I most love, as the boy you now see standing before you."

"Do you like my new form?" Ama said, standing up and turning himself around. Ana nodded her head in agreement, though still shocked and confused by the dramatic events of the last few days.

Ama chuckled, saying, "Such a long tale as this is probably more than you can handle right now." He smiled again. He then walked about the trunk of the tree, dancing before it but pausing to watch Ana's reaction. Ana smiled a bit, then looked down, as if in sadness. For she had come through many trials, and many questions yet remained.

Ama, seeing her forlorn, ran back to her and sat beside her. He could see the fear and uncertainty in her eyes. "You must not be afraid, Ana. For the Twilight Mist summoned me long ago to bring you here. It was his desire alone that you should be brought to the lush meadows of Abrea, to dwell beside me in peace and happiness. If there was any other purpose, I was not given that knowledge, Ana. But I loved your grandfather Ana. And I trusted him. He has given his own life so that you and I should be here together." Ama then touched Ana's cheek and felt the tears that came from her eyes.

Ana looked up into Ama's searching eyes. "I have felt an encroaching fear the last few days since the passing of my grandfather," Ana said. "I do not distrust him or you. Nor do I fear this beautiful place. There is another I fear—my father, Agapor. For I faced his black servant, the Shadow, above the falls of the river. He vowed to return and kill me, then destroy the light of the One Tree. He has vowed to destroy Phantaia itself."

Hearing this, Ama slowly stood up. And with cold and unmoving eyes he stared out across the gloomy valleys of Phantaia for a long time. He then turned and looked down at her, peering deep into her eyes, as if wanting to speak but unable to. He then knelt before her, holding her hand. "Again, do not fear for the future, Ana," he told her. "For we have both feared the ever-encroaching darkness for too long. If that dark being seeks to harm the tree, I will face him. With the help of the powerful and unyielding oaks of the woods, I have chased many demons of terror from Abrea in the past. Together, we have faced even greater foes. For those oaks and many others of my brethren have vowed to guard the One Tree with our lives."

Ama then stood and walked about the pool, saying, "In truth, I have known of your father, the Lord of Destruction who now dwells in Oblivion. For your grandfather revealed to me that Agapor, his own fallen son, had slain the Limitless Void. It is Agapor who had summoned the Magra of death, she who is named Yana. It is her storms that now chew upon the trees of Phantaia."

Ama reached out and grabbed Ana's hands, saying, "Ana, if we are forced to face Agapor we shall persevere, as long as we stay together unified as one against him. But we must discover the secret destiny that your grandfather has withheld from us." Ana looked down, refusing to look at Ama in fear of revealing a secret she now longed to keep.

Ama turned away, and looked up at the tree. "The forest is a mighty spirit that shall not die as long as the light of the One Tree shines in its beating heart, and we remain here to defend it. His light alone shall protect us from the forces of darkness and destruction that yet gather in the great gray gulf that lies beyond Phantaia. For no shadow may come here as long as he yet shines."

Ama sat again beside her, holding her hand, saying, "And I shall protect you, Ana. As long as I live, you shall be safe from all harm here in Abrea. This sacred vow I made to the Twilight Mist long ago, and I make it to you now." Ana then put her arms around her new friend and felt comforted by him. He felt warm to her. And she felt secure in his arms. After all, they had endured many trials together. She felt an abiding trust towards him. And the gentleness and kindness of his spirit washed away her fears and doubts.

Ana then told him, "Ama, I am feeling very weak from thirst. The journey has been long, and I am in dire need of refreshment." She then stood up and walked over to the shimmering silver pool. Seeing the sweet waters bubbling up within it, she knelt before it. She then cupped her hands and bent down to drink from it.

But Ama quickly grabbed her hand. "You must not drink from those waters," he warned. "For they are fed by a spring eternal and pure." Ana then quickly withdrew her hands in fear and shame.

"It is the well of all life, borne of the Secret Spring who sleeps eternally beneath it," Ama said, gazing into it. "About that well do the Heavens now rotate. And its waters are promised to the trees and plants alone, the true children of Phantaia," Ama told her, looking into her eyes. "For long ago it was set forth by the well's spirit that those waters would remain untouched and untainted by the flesh." Ana then stood and wrapped her arms around herself as she stepped away from the pool. "I did not know," she said solemnly.

Ama knelt beside the pool, touching the thick white roots that dipped down into its water. "My father's tree was born from these waters. And he is sustained by it still. Even now its waters are drawn up into his mighty roots." Ama then stood and looked out over Phantaia. "No rain falls from the heavenly dews but are born of the waters drawn from this pool. For it is the source that nourishes this land and cleanses all impure things that enter it. Even the flowers of Abrea derive their beauty from its fount. So do all things in Phantaia spring from it and thus sustained by it, Ana. You must never drink from this place." Ama looked sternly at her.

He then looked down with sad eyes, saying, "Should the pool perish, then would the One Tree also die. All living things in Phantaia would then pass away, withering and becoming as corpses, hollow, empty, and dry. By its water's touch are the aging trees young again. For it ever renews the living—a font of rebirth. For those denied its waters shall pass away from this world, while all others live on through the ages, forever youthful and undying. So must it never be harmed."

Ama then told her that many demonic beings had come to Abrea seeking to find the pool, the living source of Phantaia. But they had failed. For evil had seen the magical lights of the One Tree from afar and sought to destroy it. He and the guardian trees had then driven them back. But though the forces of darkness had sought to destroy the tree, none had ever known of its well of life hidden at the foot of the tree. Should they know of it they would then seek to pollute it and destroy it. Then would the tree, the forest, and its children surely die. For though new seeds of new trees might be born, the fallen well that once sustained them would not. For as long as the pool remains shall none ever truly perish in Phantaia.

Ana then came and stood beside Ama, saying, "Ama, I fear that my father now knows of the pool." But Ama said, "Agapor knows only of the light of the sacred tree. But he does not yet know of the spring. For it has remained hidden from his eyes and the servants of darkness and destruction he now commands. And it must remain so, Ana." Ana looked at the grave expression on

Ama's face. Ana then looked upon the strange waters again, deep in thought.

"Is there a well in Phantaia that might cleanse the flesh of the living from all evil?" she asked. Ama turned, and looked perplexed at Ana's odd question. "There is not," Ama said. "Though the trees cannot invite evil into them, the heart of the flesh can choose it. So evil's dark cloak may enter the heart and dwell there unbidden. The wells of all hearts are thus tainted by their owner's will alone."

Ana then asked Ama, "If this well was tainted by the flesh and my father drank of it, would the evil in him be cast away?" Ama looked at Ana in shock. For it bothered him that she would pose such a thought.

Ana, embarrassed, turned away, looking upon the pool seeing her reflection again upon its calm surface. Ama then looked at her again, and with a defiant expression said, "Ana, the pool will not save your father. For no one shall poison the well as long as I live." Ama then walked away to the edge of the hill, still contemplating the terrible thought.

Looking across the gardens down below, he then spoke softly, saying to Ana, "But should he do so the pool would be depleted, fading forever into the rock, as if a thousand sips had been taken."

"But your father would be cleansed of his own darkness," Ama said, turning to look upon Ana's face. "And he would see the world for what it is, the children of the forest for what they truly are, and know of the divine play of the world. And he would know of his truest self, though the world be doomed." Hearing his ominous words, Ana looked with trepidation at the solemn pool.

Ama then looked upon the lonely girl and smiled again. For seeing Ana now with him, he could not remain gloomy in spirit for long. He then laughed, saying to Ana, "You are thirsty. Ana, will you come with me? Follow me down the hill. For in the shadow of the mound dance the sweet waters of Lilu. Though they are not as pure as the source, they retain the spring's life-giving powers, and shall refresh you in mind, body, and spirit. You may drink from those waters safely, the place where the waterfalls cascade into the depths below." Ana smiled, since she remembered Ama drinking from it.

Ama held Ana's hand as he lead her down through the garden to the shining stream below. Ana then drank from the cool waters and was refreshed. Ama and Ana then lay beside each other in the lush green meadows of Abrea that bordered the silver stream. They sat together for many hours sharing stories of their long adventures together, there in the cool of the twilight evening.

THE CHILD OF THE SEED

Ana and Ama had dwelt for a time together in that land of peaceful splendor. Far and wide they would wander, so in time every hill and dale, glade and vale, was known to them as they roamed about their garden home. Never apart their youthful hearts grew ever closer still, as yet they had become more tender, until in time they found themselves lost as one in the blissful valley of love's great unknown.

In this land of perpetual spring, Ana and Ama had dwelt together under the navy arc of the cloudless Heavens, dancing and playing upon the windy slopes of Abrea's trailing paradise. In endless joy they long endured in perfect harmony within the rolling idylls of Phantavra's many glades and gardens. They would sit under the arbours of bountiful blossoms or lay side by side in the green grass that grew in abundance about the slopes and lush meadows of Abrea.

Ama had showed Ana many hidden wonders in Abrea. For it contained an endless array of fruits and nuts, and things of great sustenance which he alone had carefully nurtured and guarded since its genesis. With the dawning of each new day he would bring Ana delicious things to eat. But Ana in time grew curious, so that Ama showed her the many fruiting plants that grew about the gardens and valleys below. And so in time Ana too would know where the valley's wealth of food lay hidden.

Ama also knew of honeyed-ambrosia born of the intoxicating fruits of rare fruiting trees that lay hidden in the depths of the forest. They were fruits born of the sweetest of nectars, their golden husks rich with honeydew and the divine draught of that paradise. He also brought Ana fermented grapes whose time on the vines bore dark wines. They would then laugh and sing as they dined on the intoxicating fruit until they at last fell asleep in each other's arms. They would then lay together upon the green grass at the heights of the hill, their young bodies now covered in the sticky sap of the garden.

Yet when thirst would come upon her, Ana would always return to the tiny stream of Lilu that lay beneath the hill and drink of the cool waters that lay there. Where the stream poured forth into the valley she would gather its precious waters in bowls and cups made of leaves and bark, and bring them to Ama to drink. But she would not draw water from the well upon the hill, as Ama had forbid her to ever drink from the waters that flowed there.

But in the fading light of early evening when Ama was away she would often climb the windy Hill of Abra in secret and sit beside the mysterious pool, listening to the peaceful sound of its waters as they gurgled up from the rocks below. Often she thought she saw the eerie forms of ghosts within its reflections, or strange lights thrown up from its sandy bottom as they cast their many odd colors up into the low-hanging boughs.

The everlasting daylight of the One Tree always seemed to shine down upon their faces, never diminishing, until it felt like the golden day would never end for Ama and Ana. Then upon a strange twilight hour the purple mists of evening would return to fill the valley and wrap about the gardens where they dwelt. Then would fall the solemn pall of sleep upon their fading minds once more. They would then hide deep in the mist-shrouded bosom of Abrea where the eyes of evil, they had hoped, might not find them. In the splendor of their cloud-enshrouded beds they would sleep, deep within the garden's hollows, dreaming of their day's many adventures.

In time they would know to return to the gardens at twilight time. For the fading light of the One Tree, drawn back by that veil of mists, always called them back to the safe heart of its secret beating paradise. But when they awoke each day the mist would melt away, disappearing down into the depths of the river valley below. Then the bright light of the One Tree would cast its yellow sunbeams upon their bodies, warming their faces and brightening their hearts and minds. And so the light of day and mist of night like warring twins would come and go, return and leave again, tied to their own rhythmic flow.

As the twilight fell upon them, Ana would lie beside Ama under a dense tangle of flowering wisteria, deep within the confines of the garden. As their tired minds faded into soft dreams again, she would look into Ama's eyes and hold his hand. A sudden rise of joy would come into her. She was truly happy here with Ama. And she felt he was a permanent part of her life and time in that mysterious place. It was a time she hoped would never end. She often fell asleep beside his warm body. But she often found him again in her dreams.

As they slept in the misty night, the little pool seemed to laugh and giggle on the humid heights of the foggy hill. Ana often awoke in the night, hearing its mysterious and haunting sound, as if it was calling her to it in the depths of some dark dream. But seeing Ama's gentle face as he slept, she would forget the sound and curl up next to him as she drifted away back into peaceful dreams.

* * *

High above the Dreaming Seas, beneath the forbidding dome of the Arch of Heaven, the mighty Shadow had flown on tattered wings. For upon his back the battered wings of his father spread above him, casting their latent darkness onto the silent seas far below. With his father's wings and their commanding shade, he had held dominion over the powers of the nighttime skies and the many winged creatures of the netherworld that had followed him into Phantaia.

But the Shadow had been badly burned by the fierce light of Phantaia. For it had seared his flesh, chasing away the last shadows from his wings, and bleeding him of his father's Glourun, the dark essence which had sustained him.

His vast shadowed armies, like trails of smoke streaming across the skies, retreated back to their homeland in broken and weary lines. They were returning to the safety of the grim Lands of Midnight from whence they had been summoned. They too had suffered a terrible loss at the hands of the Twilight Mist and the dawning of the lights of Phantaia. For their own shadows had been ripped away when their master's great wings had failed to protect them from its golden rays.

The Shadow was now weakened and drained of his own night essence. In a daze he drifted upon his shredded wings through the somber gray skies, striving with all his might to return to his homeland. For he was gravely injured. In his frail state he opened his black eyes once more and saw below him the vast abyss of the monstrous seas. And there bubbled forth into his bleak mind the secrets of the ocean-child named Ana, which he had dared to seek and slay.

He now knew that what had filled the seas now dwelt in her. But as long as she yet lived, so was this world threatened. For he had seen that under the spell of those waters would this world soon fall, the fading night falter and wane. And so had he vowed to destroy those waters at all cost, pledging his life and kind until that savage deed should be done. Driven by his burning hatred of those waters he would gladly die but to see them perish before his eyes.

But the Shadow had now sensed that a strange light was somehow wed to those waters. Should the strange girl who carried them reach her destination, what new curse of light would then befall them? With this terrible question in his mind, he flew on in doubt and despair, his ragged wings carrying his pale body on the cold winds that flung their mighty draft against the pitiless skies. Down into the Lands of Midnight he flew, until he collapsed upon the rocky cliffs that lay before the seas.

There upon a windy ledge the Shadow lay, wrapped in his dark wings alone and dying. But Anissa, the Queen of the Cromwich, had seen his withered form upon the dark precipice and had come to his aid. Seeing him dying from his terrible wounds, she spoke to the Shadow, saying, "Soon shall your dark flesh, born of the Night, fade to gray. Without the black blood of the Night's own essence, you shall soon perish." The Shadow then looked up in agony at the witch, his mouth open, speechless, and with the distant glow in his crimson eyes slowly fading.

With her garnet eyes set ablaze, Anissa looked closer at the seared flesh of the Shadow. She knew that no power could cause such harm to the Child of Night except the Sacred Lights that once burned upon the Mountains of Heaven. Anissa then said to the Shadow, "The spiritual light of the Essence Eternal must have been restored to its ancient lantern in Phantaia, as no other but its hateful flame could burn away the midnight color from your skin with such violence."

But the Shadow laughed, saying, "It matters not, for I now wear the Wings of Night. They once belonged to my father. Have they not protected me from those evil beams? Have I not been spared total annihilation?" Anissa looked again upon the horrible welts and wounds that lay upon the tattered wings that wrapped about him. And a knowing smile came upon her face.

She then stared down at the Shadow with her green glowing eyes, saying to the Shadow, "Only the blood of the Murgala that grows in the depths of Phantaia can save you now. Without them you will surely die, as the Sacred Light has drained all darkness from you. Long ago your father the Endless Night had placed within the roses the last of his tears for this world, so that they might be as sustenance for the Children of Darkness. I will go forth into Phantaia when twilight falls upon the wood, find the black roses, and return with their oily essence. Yet is it a perilous venture." Anissa looked with a grim expression at the Shadow. And he saw great fear buried in her emerald eyes.

Anissa placed her sickly hands upon the dying Shadow's face, like a mother's hand upon an injured son. But her long black nails drew black blood from his lips and cheek. "I will fetch the blood of the black roses to heal you," she said to him. "But I desire a price be paid. I desire the dark ring that lies upon the hand of Agapor. And by no other treasure shall I grant you life."

The Shadow looked with paltry eyes upon the crooked witch, his mind growing weak. The Shadow then said in a failing voice. "If my power is renewed and my darkness restored, I shall be free to seek the girl and slay her. Then shall the light fail and Phantaia perish with it. Only with my earned freedom might I then destroy my master Agapor, just as I slew his father. The ring shall then be yours witch. This vow I make." But a lingering fear of the light that shined in Phantaia still haunted the Shadow's mind.

The witch then drew the blood of the Shadow's cheek into her fist, speaking the words of a strange incantation as she dripped it over his body. Anissa then looked at the Shadow and smiled, saying, "By your own flesh that binds you still to this world has your sacred vow to me been made." And she cackled to herself as the Shadow drifted away into dark dreams.

Anissa climbed onto her great broom of yew and flew off across the Dreaming Seas, seeking to find the Murgala that now lay hidden in the depths of Phantaia's vast wood.

* * *

The Shade had ridden upon the winds of Heaven, weakened by her brother's violent hand. For he had cruelly slain the Endless Night, their blessed father, and stripped him of his powerful wings. She had flown away in fear and desperation, seeking to find Agapor and warn him of her brother's foul deeds. For she had known that her brother would now go to Phantaia and slay the child himself. But she also knew he would seek to slay Agapor, her beloved.

Hovering over the vast catacombs of Oblivion's cityscape, the Shade looked down into the cold depths, searching in the shadows for something. She then descended into the cavernous hollows of the icy city, flying down through a great crack that had pierced the vaulted ceiling of her master's candlelit chamber. But as she floated into the room she saw no sign of Agapor. She called for him. But only his wormy servants came to her.

The Shade then demanded to know where Agapor had gone. They cowered before her, telling the Shade that he had set sail a fortnight ago on an ebony ship of dark timbers made, whose black satin sails were borne by the dusty winds of Yana. To the sandy shores of Phantaia had he gone, seeking the lost child, the blessed one. But they knew not if he had perished on the seas. For it was now an unforgiving, gray, and heartless realm.

The Shade then said it could not be. For he had promised to wait for her. They were to depart this world together, fleeing away into the unknown spheres that lay beyond the ethereal seas that flowed between all worlds. He was in danger now. For without the Wings of Night he could not venture safely into the savage wood of Avaras. Agapor had no knowledge of the forbidden paths that led through it. And the lights there burned all beings not born and sustained by its strange essence.

The Shade in a panic flew up through the hole in the ceiling of the chamber, out across the gray skies, and flying towards Phantaia. She would find Agapor in those haunted woods, risking the searing lights of Phantaia, and facing terrors of Avaras if she must. By her burning love for Agapor she would gladly perish.

After many nights the Shade, riding aloft upon the highest winds of Heaven, flew over the dark ocean, looking through the fog below for a sign of Phantaia's silent shore. But no sign of it came to her. Then she saw a sparkle, as of a distant star floating high above her. She then swung her feathered wings up and above the mantle of Heaven, for but a brief moment. And there above the Arch of Heaven she saw the silver glow of the Mountains of Heaven, whose lonely peaks had lain hidden from all eyes.

She looked with awe upon the beauty of their ancient summits and saw below them where the stars would lie within the dark mantle of night. She thought again upon her father's words. But seeing only an empty Heaven—no stars, suns, or even nighttime sheath to hold them—she turned away, dispirited.

As she drifted below the Arch of Heaven, the clouds suddenly parted and she saw below her the storm-worn beaches of Phantaia. As a clouded vision made crystal clear, they appeared. But as she looked down the beach she thought she saw a strange figure walking from the dunes towards the trees. Slowly she drifted down until she landed onto the white sands of the shoreline. About her the gloomy clouds of the Magra still brewed. And the beach shook with the rumble of thunder in the distance.

She found footprints in the sand. Yet no ship could she see. But as she followed the trail of prints, she saw where they led into an opening in the black and ominous forest. Here the trees had made a tall archway beyond which the shadowed woods of Phantaia now beckoned. The trees beyond the gaping door seemed to call her in strange whispers she could barely hear. But as she approached the opening, she thought she saw the tattered cloak of a being disappear into the grove of black trees.

The Shade then grew fearful. For she had been told by the Shadow long ago that beyond the beaches of Avaras the dark spirits of the demonic dead still crept in the trees and rocks. And beyond that sinister wood the burning lights of Phantaia would scorch all creatures of the night in their baneful beams. But she could not stop now. She had to reach Agapor.

As she approached the edge of the woods, the mists of the twilit wood had descended about her, covering the brighter lights cast from the tops of the trees. Now was the time she could safely enter the wood, as evening had approached. But she must hurry, for soon the fog would retreat and the evil sunbeams shine forth through the trees again.

The ethereal night of Avaras at first comforted her with its deep shadow. But as she walked into the dark door, a sense of deep foreboding came over her. She sensed that something sinister yet stalked those woods. Something had remained there that did not belong. An unnatural presence with a purpose most pernicious hid under every rock and branch. Even the preeternal night of her father had forsaken this primeval forest. For it had been replaced by the penetrating gloom of much older and more sinister beings, whose cursed spirits now seemed to creep under the earth and within the boles of its ancient trees.

The Shade crept deeper into the woods until she could see no sign of the skies above. Only a ghostly fog drifted above the rolling wet earth of the giant trees. Suddenly she heard the snap of a limb, and saw a strange hunched figure fleeing before her in the distance. But as she ran after it she soon became entangled in the mud and mire of the rotting black earth. Thick black roots erupted from the leaf mulch about her, thrusting up from the earth, and wrapping her feet and legs in their woody tendrils to entangle her.

The slippery black arms of other roots seemed to grasp about in the air, seeking her in the darkness.

The Shade grasped for the black soil around her, thinking she was free. But even thicker roots collapsed about her waist and legs, dragging her down into the depths of the moldy earth with a determined strength and force. Bent down and pressed against the earth, she clawed desperately in the black mud, struggling to free herself. She then screamed out in terror.

As she was pulled beneath the surface of the wet mire, she looked up and saw the sinister glowing gray eyes of the witch-like faces of the hazel trees. Peering down at her with their icy stares, they seemed to smile with wicked grins as she took her last gasp of air. But she thought she saw hovering beside the trees the glowing green eyes of a hooded figure, cursing her in her last moments alive.

Down into the cold earth she was dragged and pulled, until strange translucent bodies of men and women suddenly erupted from below, squirming in the bowels of the black wet earth. Like maggots they wormed their putrid bodies about her own until she was nearly suffocated by them. A hundred hands and fingers began to touch and feel her, as if in their endless orgies they had become aroused by new flesh thrown down into their midst. The Shade, crushed by the pulsating mounds of writhing bodies, gasped for air until she screamed out with her last breath in horror.

Then from above she felt a strong hand, warm and alive, pulling her up from the surface by her arms, ripping her away from the foul creatures that groped her in the decadent soil. For they had tried to pull her back down into their erotic masses. Suddenly she was yanked free of the roots and earth, and thrown down into a great puddle of mud upon the forest floor.

Happy to be above ground and free of the demons of that foul earth, she closed her eyes in relief. But in her gasps for air she looked up to see a towering stand of black witch-hazel trees ringed about her, their blood-red eyes swirling and boiling in anger, casting their salient lights down upon the wet pools of mud about her.

She then saw the tall form of Agapor standing beside them, looking down at her with cold and expressionless eyes. She knew he had saved her. Yet it almost felt like she had been cast into some type of new prison made by the malevolent ring of scowling trees.

The Shade, covered in the dark putrid mud of the woods, now struggled to get her footing. Looking at Agapor, she yelled out, "You betrayed me!" But Agapor stood over her, gazing down at the helpless figure saying nothing.

The Shade then saw upon his finger the strange dark ring whose great stone was cast aglow with a dim white light that throbbed and pulsated with glee. Agapor seemed different, changed somehow, obsessed, and determined. Had the evil trees of Avaras changed him, she thought? Or was it the strange ring that he had coveted so closely?

Agapor then approached the Shade, holding out his hand to her, saying, "Where have you been?"

The Shade smiled, struggling to gain her balance in the mud. "I did as you asked. I went to the Lands of Midnight, seeking the Wings of Night," she said, as she struggled out of the mud, standing before him. "My father the Endless Night was there, hidden deep in his cavernous tomb just as you said he would be. He was alive until..." Agapor's dark-ringed eyes then seemed to flame up in curiosity, yet behind them hid some secret.

"But my brother was there. He followed me," the Shade said, holding her hands to her face. "He then slew him and cruelly cut the wings from his back. I then saw with my own eyes that the unending darkness that yet fills the farthest corners of this world would be his, and the last of my father's essence would flow through him. My brother has now increased in strength, as the powers of the Night now dwell in him and within the Wings of Night he alone now bears."

The Shade then looked down. "I have failed you," she said. "The Shadow now has that which he needs to face you."

Agapor looked upon the sad form of the Shade with a feigned pity. He then said to her in a calm voice, "You have not failed me."

He then raised his voice, saying, "You have betrayed me! You chose to share with your brother the knowledge of those wings which you knew he had been seeking. The Shadow now possesses the Essence Eternal's greatest gifts. With them he may now slay the child I seek. With them he may destroy our world."

But the Shade looked at Agapor in confusion. "Surely my brother has come to Phantaia already. Was he not seen in these woods?" the Shade asked. Agapor smiled at her with a curious expression. He then walked away.

But he quickly turned and laughed, saying, "I have recently had an epiphany. You know not the true depths of my plans. For I saw in a vision long ago how I might use you and your brother, as my own father had planned, long ago. As slaves and servants unto me were you and your brother meant to be. For I had known the manacles were meant for me, the Son of Twilight, and that the Children of Night would serve only me. Yet for a greater purpose were they designed, a purpose hidden from me till now. But it matters not to me now. And so I care not for the fate of the Shadow, your corrupted brother. You and your brother shall soon perish by your own evil deeds."

Agapor looked down at the sad Shade, grinning as he spoke. "I sensed your brother would follow you. Taking the wings from his father, he would then try and use them to destroy the child, my father, and the lights of Phantaia. But he would fail in his mission by the wing's own betrayal in his time of need. For he does not understand their true powers or purpose, just as I do not yet understand this foul ring that seems to possess me and the cursed spirit that dwells within its stone." Agapor gazed at the ghoulish ring with a curious confusion.

Agapor looked at the evil trees about him, saying, "The witch-hazels of Avaras saw a great battle upon the heights of the falls. I know by the words of their tree-lords that the Shadow was defeated by my father, fleeing the forest injured and near death. He has failed."

Agapor looked down at the Shade in disdain. Agapor then said to her, "With his own dire acts your brother now disavows his pledge to help me find the child. Freedom shall never be his. Such shall be the price paid by him for his arrogance." And Agapor bellowed forth with an almost maddening laughter.

Agapor then called forth the powers from the black manacle on his left wrist. The Shade then squirmed in the mud before him, falling onto the floor in agony so that her screams echoed through Phantaia. The demonic trees of Avaras stood still, listening with delight to her tortured screams. He then walked forward through the mud and stood over the Shade, saying, "It is strange. You never tried to stop your brother from his warped plots against me. Nor did you turn him away from his cruel plot to harm the child. Why?"

"Had the child been harmed by him," Agapor said with enraged and fiery eyes, "I would have cast you into the very mouth of Yana to be devoured." He stood over her with searching eyes as she slowly struggled to her knees.

The Shade then looked up from the floor of the forest in fear of him. But Agapor stood calmly over her as he lowered his left arm, peering down at the sad figure kneeling in the mud. He then walked over to the feet of the great hazel trees to sit down. As he did, one of the hulking monsters lifted up its thick root to accommodate him.

He then looked again at the Shade, and with a softer voice said to her, "The child I seek is my daughter. I have even known her name. She is Ana, born of An my half-sister who dwells forever trapped in the nightmarish seas. By my own seed was she conceived." Agapor then looked down with distant eyes that bore a deep regret.

Agapor then said, "I know now in my heart that the Shadow did not slay her. For what reason I do not yet know. But she yet lives. My own father the Twilight Mist saved her from him. My father had sent her into these woods so she might be spared certain death by the evil storm that I myself had spawned." Agapor then sat quietly, staring off into the woods, as if contemplating some bleak past or baneful future.

Agapor then looked down at his feet, telling the Shade, "In truth I knew she would be taken from me. But Phantaia is not her final destination. For I have made a vow to the Nothingness that lives in the Great Beyond that she should be given unto him for the endless servitude of the Magra Overlord that now continually wages war upon these woods. I sold the spirit of my own child for Phantaia's destruction." Agapor then rose to his feet, and started walking about the muddy pool.

"But by the strange ring upon my finger, had a greater fate been shown to me," Agapor continued, with an intensity in his voice. "The spirit of the Limitless Void had saved itself, housing itself in the ring's dark crystal. I had foolishly desired to destroy it and free the spirit within it. But by the insight granted unto me, I spared the ring and the Void from annihilation. One of its hidden purposes had then come to light. For with the spirit it contains could I now control the demons that haunt this strange wood, and thus all of Avaras. For the fallen children of Oblivion dwell in these trees. And they serve only him. By the ring would they now help me find my lost daughter." Agapor stopped to ponder the ring on his finger, staring into its crystal now turned gray.

Agapor then looked at the Shade with hopeful eyes, saying, "The Lords of the Hazels that rule these woods have shown me the hidden trail to the place where she now dwells. It is a vast distance. But look how the trail leads deeper into the forest. By the powers of the ring I shall now be concealed by the trees of the forest and hidden from the guardians that watch for travelers in the greener woods." Agapor then looked up at the hulking phantom trunks that towered over them, their large demonic eyes now closed in sleep.

Agapor then said, "I no longer fear the Shadow that has fled Phantaia, or the Twilight Mist that once stalked these woods. The trees have revealed to me that your brother can never return. For the lights of Phantaia have burned his wings and body severely. He was nearly slain. But my father perished at the hand of your brother. And so the time of the powers of the Night, the Void, and Mist have now passed away. The age of the Primordial Ones has now ended." Agapor's face seemed cold and hollow but resolute.

Agapor looked into the Shade's dark eyes, saying, "Ana dwells far from me now. But I have felt her spirit deep in Phantaia's heart of late, near to the source of its great burning candle. With the help of the trees she shall be found. And when I do I shall take her away from this cursed wood."

Agapor then sat down, deep in thought. The Shade then climbed up from the muddy pool and sat beside him. He had become pensive, and seemed to be caught in a trance, as if trapped in the thought of an unsolvable riddle. Yet it was the empty feeling inside him—that his shattered family now seemed so near yet so far from him—that pained him most.

The Shade then said to Agapor, "Unknown to you, I have known the child was yours. But I also know of a darker secret which must be revealed to you. My brother told me in secret that within the girl lay the waters that would be the doom of us all. For haunted waters live within this child. They are the deadly waters of the Essence Eternal of which An and the seas bore against us. They now live in her, my love. Like the Dreaming Seas had inflicted upon you in ages past, under the magic spell of those waters shall this world soon fall should they be released from her." Agapor then stared at the Shade in disbelief.

The Shade then stood before Agapor, saying, "As you yourself have known, it was your own father that released those poisonous waters into the sea. By the same evil waters that live in your child shall this wooded realm soon be entrapped. And much suffering shall soon come of it. You know in your heart this to be true, Agapor. Unless those waters are destroyed, we shall all soon perish. For I sense that the baneful light of the tree and the deadly waters united shall unleash some new horror upon us."

The Shade then held up the right hand of Agapor, saying, "By the powers of the Limitless Void that lies in the ring, you must command the evil trees to destroy these terrible twins." Placing his hand down, she looked into his sad eyes, saying, "With my brother gone only you can fulfill this terrible deed now, my love. Only you were meant to bear this ring, wear the manacles that bind me to you, and find the child who carries these waters. Through the spirit of the Limitless Void you now control, shall the ancient will of Oblivion be fulfilled in this world. And by you alone, is it now destined that the Sacred Water and Light of the forest be obliterated forever from this world."

Agapor slowly rose to his feet. He then began to pace about the pool until he stood angrily before the Shade, saying, "To do this would mean the death of my child. And I shall never lead my daughter to that fate. Nor shall I ever abandon my child, as I myself was abandoned by my parents."

Agapor then raised the ring upon his hand, yelling out the Limitless Void's name. And from the ring was stirred the winds of the woods. The dead leaves upon the trees were blown about in a great cyclone. And by his command the skies grew dark until lightning struck down about them in webs of blue and silver. The threatening trees then backed away from him, as if in fear. The ring now seemed to glow with a ruddy light.

But Agapor looked with fear and anger upon the ring, as he lowered his arms. The winds died back down. And he looked once more upon the face of the Shade in angst and frustration. He then said to the Shade, "If within my child lies the powers of the seas and the curse of this world, then I must take her away from it. I shall take her to a place beyond the Mountains of Heaven where the waters can be safely released from her and poured forth back into the monstrous misty abyss from whence they were born. For this is my father's doing."

But the Shade said in defiance, "Saving the child shall bring the wrath of the Nothingness down upon us. Do you not see what you have done? If this is your plan, we should leave now and forget the child and forsake the struggles of this fallen world. For we are all doomed as long as the child and the waters she carries yet live."

But Agapor looked upon her in deep sadness, saying, "I cannot."

The Shade then reached out and held Agapor's hands, saying, "Please...please let us go from here now, my love. Do you not see the folly of this? Nothing good shall come of it but death and destruction. I beg of you, do not seek Ana. From her I see a terrible fate for you, for this world, and for us. Is the child not doomed to die by your own vow to the Nothingness?"

But Agapor cast the Shade away from him in shame, so that she fell to her hands and knees before him. Agapor then turned away from her. But the Shade said, "Agapor, we must fly away from this place, you and I. Leave the flawed child to her own fate. For if she was meant to die or dwell in the heart of Phantaia, it was for a grander purpose whose true nature only your father had known. Within the child, Agapor, dwells a horrible force, uncontrollable, and a curse to the living. What blessing remains from it will soon be Phantaia's alone. By those waters that now live in her lies a fate meant only for the forest-children to come whose path, good or evil, blessed or cursed, matters not to us. For if it was truly destined to be, no force under Heaven can now stop it."

The Shade ran to Agapor and embraced him, as she had done many times before. But Agapor sternly held up his shining manacles before her in defiance. The Shade closed her eyes, as she knew she would soon be called back into its terrible prison.

Agapor raised his left wrist which held the iron band that had bound her spirit to him. He then summoned the forces within it, so that it glowed with a purple light upon his wrist. But he drew not his anger against her. For as she looked the shackle had dimmed, falling away from his arm, down onto the wet leaves at his feet. Agapor picked it up and tossed it to her. By his face she knew he would not waver from his desire to save his child.

The Shade picked up the manacle and stared at Agapor in disbelief. He looked upon her sad face, and with emotionless eyes whose watery orbs hid a quiet passion he still held for her, he said to the Shade, "You are free from your enslavement to me...free from this poisonous love. And so am I freed from you."

Agapor then turned and walked away. But the Shade now free of the manacles, gathered within her the boundless rage born of her long imprisonment to him and his empty love. She drew forth the darkness itself from out of the earth and sky, so that about them the Heavens grew suddenly quiet and grim, as if a black veil were cast around them throwing back all sound and sight, wind and light. Black wisps of smoke boiled forth from beneath her as she summoned the spirits of the shades that had dwelt under every stone since the birth of the world. She drew them up into her, their sensuous black bodies writhing about her in the air in a wide circle.

She now stood before Agapor as an angry Angel of Darkness, her long fangs revealed and fiery eyes aflame. Her wild ebony hair, streaked with red, swirled like snakes in the stagnant air. And her long black wings unfurled and flowed with strange translucent and ever-changing patterns. Her own shadow now hung about her in a widening cloak, until it had spread throughout the woods about them, the forest itself having disappeared beneath its empty and silent pitch.

Only she and Agapor now stood within the black and hollow depths, their frozen breath billowing out in clouds of icy crystals. She then floated above Agapor, enraged, crying out in a haunted voice, "Leave the cursed children of this vile world to their own pitiful fates. Let them perish in fire or water, earth and wind. It does not matter to me now. Forget the child. Now is our time. Let our own dark and corrupted love rule this hollow world, the Son of the Void and Daughter of the Night, wed as one forever after. Our love needs no others. For together we shall bathe this world in eternal darkness and damnation, so that all shall come before us in the midst of their own peril, bearing witness to our unholy union, and bowing before their consecrated queen and king. But our immortal love shall alone be their example, living on to guide them all while they slowly consume themselves in their own dark and decadent passions."

The Shade then drew her body down onto Agapor, so that he fell into the mud and mire before her. She hung over him, drawing forth her great dark fangs. She could slay her cruel master and do what her brother had long desired to do if she wished.

But as Agapor gazed into her jet-black eyes, he saw behind them the savage fires of her own heart burning bright for him. But as the Shade looked into his eyes, she saw only the cold corpse of the love they once had known, having long ago died in him.

Agapor then whispered into her ear, "I am sorry."

The darkness suddenly faded and the Shade stood as she was, a servant to him, standing in the cold mud of the woods before him. Agapor climbed out onto the bank above her, looking at her one last time. He then turned away, disappearing into the woods above her.

The Shade wept in bitterness as she held the dark bracer in her hands. She then ran from him, down the slope of the dark woods with great fury, flinging her body off the cliffs before the sea until her wings unfurled and carried her away into the darkness. Flying high in the gray clouds, she looked at the cold ocean below, tossing the irons that had imprisoned her for so many ages down into sea. She watched with tears of bitterness as they disappeared beneath the gray waves.

Agapor had in secret looked from the hillside and watched as the Shade flew away. The strange ring on his hand now glowed with a sickly throbbing, white light, as if fulfilled by what had transpired. He then drew his dark cloak about him and disappeared into the woods.

The twilight glow of the mists that once guarded the woods had now faded. Yet there remained an odd, almost incarnate remnant of his father's purple mists about the trunks of the trees. Agapor walked forward and touched his father's mists with his hands. And he thought about his father, knowing he would never see him, touch him, or know of him. For by his own heartless will and desire for vengeance had he caused his father's death. And his own black heart was now filled with this tragic truth.

The grim and haunted trees of that ancient wood had followed him closely. As they had encircled him in the depths of the dark forest, they looked upon him with their heartless orbs. With their eyes cast aglow, they grimaced at him in his hour of loss, unmoving and cold. Their towering and monstrous black forms seemed to try and reach out with their mangled black limbs to grasp him in their long woody fingers.

But Agapor held up the shining black ring before their great smoky eyes in defiance and anger at their futile attempt. The demonic trees were instantly hypnotized by its strange blue lights, desiring the ring and what lay inside. They then gathered about him in their trance, as he spoke to them in their strange tongue demanding to know where the path before him might go. They then revealed to him the secret paths and guarded gates of deepest Phantavra, and the long and dangerous journey ahead for them leading into its heartland.

Agapor then wrapped his cloak about him, and like a dark mist, fled off into the blacker corridors of the forest to find his daughter.

* * *

It had seemed a serene and restful time for Ana and Ama. For in their quiet hours no sounds were ever heard in Abrea save the flowing of the waters from the heights above, and the whispering winds that bellowed forth with the laughter of the trees. But they were no longer children. For they now had grown to fullness in that time of youthful splendor.

Many unnumbered nights and days had passed since first they came to Abrea. And in this strange place, time itself had sped up and yet slowed down. For by some miracle of the garden's springs did its enchanted waters alone decide that they should come of age for some purpose unknown to them.

Ana was now a young woman. And in the changing lights of that strange world, to Ama she appeared bathed in the glow of the breathless beauty of womanhood. Her dark hair flowed down her shoulders in a tumbling display. And the contour of her body was graced with curves and hills like the lovely mounds that rose up about the garden itself.

Ama had also changed. For he had grown strong with broad shoulders and brave face. Yet still lithe and agile he remained. Tall and handsome he seemed to Ana, to have grown bolder and more confident, his swarthy figure bearing the virile cast of manhood, now complete. And so Ana often came to him in times of uncertain fear and foreboding, falling into his strong yet graceful arms.

But though their bodies had matured their minds remained unblemished. For in endless childhood games had they often engaged each other. Ama would look for Ana in the Gardens of Abrea. But she would hide far away from him in the tangled thickets beneath the Hill of Abra, until in his frantic searches for her he would finally find her hidden in some dark ferns in the valley or along the banks of the river far below.

Ana would then run from him in laughter, past tall green hedge rows and over towering mossy bridges made of the tangled roots of plants and trees. Past ivy-covered ledges, which looked down into the foggy forests of the valley below, they would race. Through the hidden cool of quiet grottos and forgotten glades, across grassy meadows, and through fern-filled valleys they would wind their way together until the last fading glow of daylight's gold had been spent.

Then in the cool of the early evening they would climb the great tree that stood upon the hill. Ama would guide her to its base where flowed forth the tree's wide white roots. Ama would then climb up into his great limbs, showing Ana how to run and bounce along them with her feet. The thick limbs would then gather to them the force of the gusting winds and rock up and down, throwing them high into the air as they laughed together.

For many hours they played within the heights of the great tree, looking out across the endless groves of Phantaia that filled the valleys below. Then in the cool of the evening Ama would sit beside Ana on the thick boughs and talk of the many wonders of the woods that lay hidden in the wildest hollows of Phantaia. These mysterious places, Ana told him, she greatly desired to see.

But each evening the dark twilit mist of Phantaia would return, rising up from some unknown place in the valley below, descending down and around them and enveloping them in its strange violet dew. The lights of the great tree would then disappear beneath its gloomy cloak. And so the light of the brighter day was banished from the land each evening by that phantom mist.

As Abrea lay hidden in that strange lavender fog, Ana would look down from the cloudy slopes. And a sudden fear would come over her, a feeling vague and uncertain. Never would she be caught in the dark woods alone when twilight fell and the purple mists had returned, as many unknown things would begin to creep within the shadows that lay about the edges of the encircling woods.

But she had learned this was also the time of sleep. For soon would they return to their garden beds, hiding within the purple shadows of the garden that now bathed the brighter world they had known.

Upon a time the gloomy mists had returned again, surrounding them as they lay in their secret hiding spot. There in the cool of the wisteria's perfumed air Ama first desired to kiss Ana, holding her close to his body and touching her face with his gentle hands. For many nights they slept together in youthful innocence in the rapture of a sacred love most pure and untarnished that had grown between them. So was born in the ghostly catacombs of the misty gardens of Abrea an endless bliss and love which, alone of its kind, would ever endure in that sad world. And by its almost divine will alone would it thus be sustained.

But it was a night like no other, when the mists of that twilight forest were thickest, that there came into Ama's dreaming mind a terrible vision most malevolent and unexpected. For he saw in this nightmare his own death clear and sudden. In that dream he stood before a rocky cliff. About his throat were long and wiry black hands. Into the face of a horrible monster he stared. Yet he could see only fiery eyes in the hollows of their shadowy form. The beast then seemed to turn his head, so that he saw with his dying eyes his own headless body thrown down into a swirling mass of clouds, black and baneful.

Ama awoke in a bath of sweat, screaming out into the night whose gray fogs had curled about them. At first he thought he saw the green glowing eyes of another being looking down at him from the midst of that strange fog. Then he saw Ana's kind face looking over him, soothing him with her gentle hands, and holding him tight through that night of terror.

But as she looked into his eyes, he saw in her something beautiful and profound yet dark and cursed within her bound, which he could not grasp and only briefly glimpsed. But he was pure of spirit and could fathom no darkness or evil in Ana, so that he saw behind her eyes only the loving heart she hid within her deepest depths.

Trembling, Ama then said to Ana, "My dreaming mind has seen many horrors, Ana. For several nights before this one have they come unabated. So have I in secret come to dread sleep and the mist that brings it. I have vowed many nights to roam the woods at dusk like a phantom fleeing before the last lights of dusk so I might escape these nightmares. For I have dreamed of not just my own death but of the death of Phantaia."

Ana comforted him and spoke to him with soothing and gentle words, saying, "Ama, into my own mind has come many odd dreams none of which has ever come to pass or ever will. Be not scared of these ghostly days of future passed. For you are here with me now. And brighter days lie ahead for us." Ama was then renewed in the eternal hope he had for them and the abiding love he now carried for Ana.

They then both saw the morning light of the One Tree coruscating over the tops of the trees. The mist was then burned away, and the beauty of the dawning light of that garden broke through the melting mists of that strange half-light world as they had always done to brighten their hopeful hearts. Its glorious lights then returned to their eyes the beautiful emerald of the dew-covered garden and its trailing meadows. Terror was replaced with the joy of that sacred place once more. And Ama soon forgot his bleak visions.

Ama then heard from afar in the soft whispering winds the voices of the ancient trees from deep within Phantaia. "My brothers and sisters are calling me." Ama said as he jumped to his feet.

Ama began to gather food and to prepare for a long journey, telling Ana, "Follow me to the top of the mound of Abrea." At the top of the hill Ama stood on a large rock. He then stood still, as if listening intently to some music born by the wailing winds. He then smiled, saying, "Ana, we shall now begin a grand adventure. For the time has come for me to share with you the many secrets hidden within Phantaia."

Ana then smiled with anticipation. Before her eyes Ama then took form as Phanyan, the Ebrandeer and guardian of Phantaia. He again signaled for Ana to come to him with the food he had gathered. Ana then climbed once more upon his back. With a wild dash he then carried her across the green swards that ringed about Abrea's hill. Ana laughed with delight as they raced across the green meadows of Aron and up the slopes past the White Trees of the Ringwood, out of the valley, and deep into the mysterious forests of Phantaia

For many nights Phanyan carried Ana with the winds to their back, racing deep into the shadowy depths of Phantaia, and into the arcane wooded realms that lay just beyond the river of Avalyr. Ana saw that from the valley of Phantavra they had descended into a hidden forest that lay between the gentle green slopes of the mountains and the seas.

In this peaceful glen had dwelt many of the secretive ones, those who are called the Chieftain Trees of Phantaia. These magnificent trees ruled the dense and tangled wilderness of Phantaia, where little of the light of the One Tree had yet remained upon the tops of the trees. They alone had long towered over that part of the forest, guarding it from the infringing evil that had crept before the tree-lined gates of Avalumlea. But few could find them. For these Lords of the Trees had used their wood-magic, the Galdar, to obfuscate themselves and their forest-children within the ethereal gloom of Phantaia. By their enchantments were many secrets of the forest shielded from the eyes of evil and the knowledge of the children of the Primordial Ones that had for many ages passed through forbidding Avaras and the fringes of Phantavra's sacred Avalumlea groves.

Phanyan had carried Ana far and wide to speak with the enigmatic trees. And from them she would learn of their rich histories, of the strange sights they had seen, and of the vast knowledge and wisdom they had grown to possess. For there was much they had known of that dark world from its earliest age which they had often shared with Ama in days long past.

Ana had in time conversed with many of these trees and learned of their tragic fates. For Ama had taught her their secret language. Their knowledge was given to her in poems and song, which Ama recited as the trees shared their tales with them. In this simpler and more pristine time in the forest she would remember their whispering words of wisdom, listening to their gentle music and that of their children as the soft winds flowed through their swaying boughs.

These words she would keep within the confines of her heart. For none knew what would become of this brotherhood of trees. They often spoke of a bleaker future that had recently seemed uncertain to them. Ama had known this as well from his dreams, and so had sought to preserve the knowledge of the trees should they be lost. So was given to Ana many dark and mysterious truths which these lords of the forest had kept in secret.

Of the Chieftain Trees there were seven greater and five lesser trees. Of the latter little was known. For their purpose was most mysterious. They grew in woody lairs hidden deep in the outer fringes of Phantaia where few had travelled.

Including the One Tree, their father, there were thirteen Chieftain Trees in all. These had been sent to watch over Phantaia and rule over its countless forest-children by their noble patriarch. Yet each dwelt far apart in distant lands, bound to the earth and water spirits that dwelt among them. All things moved by their design and will in Phantaia. For by their works and breaths, guided by the One Tree, was Phantaia's destiny and design eternally bound.

Ama then told Ana of the seven greater chieftain trees. Their secretive names were given as follows:

Durn - oak
Alcu - elder
Afa - ash
Kum - hawthorn
Esnes - black willow
Iwu - yew
Uyl - apple

These were the true Lords of Phantaia, and the most ancient of all trees that lived in the forest and many that would come later. Some dwelt close to Abrea, like Alcu and his princely white elderwood sons that encircled and guarded Abrea. Then there was Kum and his watchful bardic hawthorns which recorded the music of Abrea's waters in their memories. Some like Afa slept peacefully beside the slow gliding river of Avalyr, glancing down upon his children's reflections that stretched in unending rows about its shores. He listened often to the child of the river whose mournful song echoed up from its depths at the falling of the mists.

Others dwelt far away, like the black willows of Esnes whose grim limbs and leaves hung like witches' hair down over pits and caverns that roared up from the dark underworld of Phantaia. But the dark and twisted oak of Durn had the mightiest and strongest children, the Durnach. For they alone had bravely clung to the farthest fringes of Avaras, where their bold trunks yet stood before the tumult of Yana, guarding Phantaia's children from her endless storms.

Yet they of all the living trees that once had grown there had survived by their constitution and indomitable will alone. For the strong enchantments placed upon them by Durn their father-tree had helped them survive and stay protected from sea, wind, and storm. They loved him and drew ever nearer to his great trunk as the world itself grew more threatening, closing in upon them as the fated ages of turmoil passed away.

Unto each of these proud seven was granted many servant trees. There were eight powerful tree servants given to each, nine in total for each kind. These were spread about the distant fringes of Phantaia and before the many gates that led into its interior. Yet were they ever bewitched by the lights of the One Tree and drawn to its center. For by the shining wings of its spiritual lights in the golden skies of Amladem, floating within its ethereal sky, did the One Tree yet feed their silvered leaves and guide them from afar.

These trees then returned songs of thanks and love to him, which they cast up into the air as faint voices in the dead of night. They then were returned by the many young children of the One Tree that rose up at the foot of the Gardens of Abrea. It is these trees and the voices of the Chieftains that could be heard as one great song for those who listened, calling to each other in a fateful and solemn symphony of the trees, deep and mysterious, within the heart of that primeval wood. And so by the concordant harmony of the voices of the trees was Phantaia ever moved and sustained as one living entity through the seeming eternity of that shadowed world.

Over many nights Phanyan and Ana had travelled the far flung trails of Phantaia, as that forest was a vast and nearly limitless domain. But by secretive paths had Phanyan woven his way between the thick and shadowy trunks of Phantaia, suddenly walking into dark portals within the hollows of ancient trees, and then reappearing in the midst of strange valleys Ana did not recognize.

Through underground caverns, over rocky bridges, through mountain passes and waterfalls they roamed unseen by the eyes of evil, always avoiding the darker parts of the wilderness and wary not to wake the strange spirits of the earth and trees that crept there. They would sleep by night in peace and safety beneath the roots of the towering servants of the Chieftain Trees, encircled by their many sons and daughters that grew along the wooded paths about them.

Ana had come to bond with the trees and know of them by name, as true friends and companions. For in the daylight hours

Ama had taken her to their numerous sacred circles, where they would meet and bathe upon the grassy slopes in the bright lit glow of day together. She often danced and sang with them in their shining vales of green and hilltop fields of delicate flowers. And they were ever happy beside the frolicking young girl that had come to greet them there with such happy eyes.

When she walked in those woods the trees would clamor to be near her. For they saw in her some new hope which their own woody hearts could only dimly sense. They often drew near to her, as within her spirit had grown a warm life-giving radiance that drew them ever closer to her presence, like the promise of some vital spring or essence long denied their thirsty roots. Yet by her kind and gentle nature did they come to know and love Ana. And sad were they when she would depart their lonely copse.

Thus the mysteries of Phantaia's most secretive groves and the spirits that grew from the sweet earth about them were slowly revealed to Ana. Yet some things Ama could not show her. For more curious things dwelt in the distant places of Phantaia, inexplicable things of a much older world even Ama could not comprehend. Yet Ana had in time come to know nearly all the great trees that grew there. And she came to see in Ama a truly generous spirit, with a nurturing and gentle heart much like her own that, by its vast capacity for compassion and caring, had guided the countless children of the many forests of Phantaia.

She saw, like children, they seemed to come innocently to him with love and trust like a father. And so his generous nature revealed a spirit that bound Ana to him, as well. Never again could she see herself leaving Ama or his blessed Phantaia. For the love they had all shown her had grown inside her. And she had vowed in secret, in a quiet moment alone, that she would protect Ama and the woods with her own life if she must.

Upon an evening, in the dark corners of Phantaia, they found themselves on the last of their many journeys. It was there that Phanyan took shape as Ama again, leading Ana to the foot of a wide and girthy tree hidden in the shadowed thickets of a black and lonely wood which light itself had seemed to have forsaken.

She could barely see beyond the black tree line the distant lightning of the storms of the Magra mother as she raged on into the night. And she could sense the icy winds upon the tops of the trees as the blue storms raged upon them in unending battles in the distant valley below her.

Here in this bleak valley they slept for a fortnight under the mighty mossy boughs of the black oak named Durn, the greatest of the Chieftain Trees in Phantaia. About his mighty roots lay numerous acorns cast off from his thick curving boughs. The great oak had unbound the very shadows from the twilight of the forest by his breath and the enchantments he had wrapped about his neighboring woods. And the rich smell of his leaves and bark, and of the child-oaks he had raised, permeated the dense shaded woods around them.

Ana looked up from the giant roots under which she slept, and saw the last rays of the lights of the One Tree thrown upon the tops of its crooked black limbs so that they shined like golden arms in the depths of its thick ebony boughs. Stretching into that winding rocky valley his dark oak armies had protected the woods of Phantaia from the evils of Avaras in the canyons below. For the Durnach oaks were the most powerful of the trees in Phantaia. And the witch-hazels below could not defeat them as long as the light that fed them yet shined from afar, and their oak father stood strong and unyielding among them in its impenetrable heart.

Though apprehensive, being so close to Avaras, Ana felt at peace within the shadows of that mighty oak. Ama then told her that long ago had Durn been birthed from the earliest seeds of the One Tree. So like a brother was Durn to him. So too was Durn and his children closest to the One Tree in spirit. For they had followed even closer to its own secretive purpose set long ago—a purpose not even revealed to him.

Ama then looked upon Ana with sad eyes. "Ana, in the night before this one I had a new dream. In it I saw the colors of autumn fall upon the One Tree," he told her. "And in my dream the garden had grown gray." A look of fear had now appeared upon his face.

"I too, long ago, had this dream, Ama," Ana replied, looking for a long time at Ama with knowing eyes. "But I know not what it means, as I can never see a time when the One Tree should ever die."

"Should the One Tree ever fall I fear Durn and all the Chieftain Trees would also perish. And Phantaia, left unguarded by these oaks, would fall before the malicious trees that now gather below in Avaras."

Durn, the great oak, hearing Ama's voice, opened his dark eyes and wrinkled lips. He looked down with his wide amber orbs at Ama. Then he looked into the eyes of Ana and smiled. Like the sound of eternity itself, in a most ancient and hoary voice, he then said, "Beneath my father, the One Tree, has slept for many eons a silver well, my child. It alone has sustained him. The One Tree shall live until the spring that sustains him perishes. Then shall he wither and die. For the mystical water now flows through him and is one with his spirit. So has my brother Kum and his sons been ever watchful of it, listening to the ceaseless sound of its flowing waters for a time when they should be silenced."

Durn continued, "Phantaia shall exist and all my brothers and sisters with it until the time when, by fate's hand, the waters perish and a new spirit enter it. Of this miracle have the voices of the trees of late begun to speak. But with hopeful hearts we now sleep and wait in the shadows for either our death or rebirth." The tree then slowly closed its eyes as the twilight mists climbed up from the darkest depths of Avaras, swirling about its limbs.

Ana thought upon these mysteries as she fell asleep in the arms of the great tree. But as Ana drifted off into a deep sleep, she thought she could see the dim radiance of two glowing eyes in the dark woods that stood about them. They stared at her for the longest time, and then disappeared.

When morning came they left the gloomy Oak Groves of Durn. Climbing a windy hill upon a mountain slope, they saw the mysterious One Tree shining brightly far away in the distance. Like a burning beacon, heroic yet serene, it seemed to call them home.

And Ana was happy about the thought of returning to the peaceful Gardens of Abrea.

As they rode back home she thought upon the words of the ancient oak and how the strange well had sustained the living trees and gardens of that wilderness through the life of the One Tree. And she thought again upon the encroaching evil that now seemed to creep about the fringes of Avaras in the valley below them.

For many days and nights they travelled, until within a tiny glade of grass that grew within the thicker woods they stopped to rest. Ama had returned to his boyhood form. He then walked up to her while she rested in the warm grass, saying, "Ana, I must tell you something. During our journey the past few days I saw an intruder in the woods. And so I have raced ahead, carrying us beyond its reach. But the nature of that being is unknown to me. I know only that the woods' calls of late have been of war and its preparation. For the coming of this terrible intruder in their midst has signaled some change in Phantaia. This new cry shall bring once more a call to arms and the defense of Phantavra and Abrea from the dark evil that shall soon rise again from the pits of Avaras."

But Ana told Ama, "This must be my father and his servants, Ama. If he has come for me then I must face him alone. For I must spare Phantaia his wrath."

But Ama stood firmly, saying, "I do not think it is your father but a being unknown and with strange intent which none can yet comprehend. For the woods spoke of something more sinister among them, a being that passes freely as if unbound by light, shadow, earth, or void. This concerns me. For not knowing what it seeks has brought even greater fear amongst the children of the forest."

After many days travel Phanyan safely carried Ana asleep on his back to the Gardens of Abrea. He then climbed the great hill in the midst of the twilight air and laid her down onto her grassy bed as he had done many times before.

The next day Ana awoke feverish from a troubled sleep. She turned to grasp Ama's hand but he was gone. In a panic, she roamed about the garden looking for him. But she could not find him anywhere. She then called out to him from the slopes of Abra. She then heard a crunch of leaves and limbs behind her in the dense underbrush. Startled, she turned around to see Ama standing before her and holding the most beautiful flower she had yet seen. While she slept he had climbed to the very heights of the One Tree and there found a large blossom which he had picked for her.

Ana looked frightened for a moment, then angry. But Ama only smiled, telling her, "I have one last secret to show you." He carefully unfolded the blossom. She then saw its elegant four-pointed shape. But looking again she saw within it grew a fifth petal from its center, forming an unusual five-pointed star.

Ama said to her, "The blossoms from the top of the tree have the power to heal all ills in Phantaia. These five petals represent the five Primordial Ones, the sons of the Essence Eternal. For the tree is in fact a symbol of their unity, which long ago was divided, and whose reunion is still the Spirit Divine's greatest hope and desire. This truth he has yet to reveal in many other mysterious forms yet to come in Phantaia. So is his hope our hope, Ana, that this world be healed and sustained by love alone." Ama then smiled as he handed it to her.

He then called the great tree by its secret name, *Celebreava*, telling her, "This is the name of the shining spirit that yet dwells within the father-tree and its blossoms, that which gives it life, and that which gives its children life. Yet it is not the secret source of its light, but of another spirit unseen within. Like my own secret name, Ebrandeer, the name of Celebreava must remain unspoken. For the hidden truth of its name belongs to the trees of Phantaia only." Ana then looked with curiosity at the strange bloom.

"Within this flower also dwells the secret to new life," Ama continued. "From the topmost blossoms shall be born the first seed-bearing fruits for the generations yet to come. Yet the blossom's pollen is meant for another. For the five petals also represent the five Maiden Trees. And this the One Tree sheds for them.

"But these trees I cannot show you. For they are hidden from all eyes except one among them that grows near the garden unseen. The One Tree's pollen is shed and given to them alone, borne by the winds that fill Phantaia's greenest and most distant dales where they dwell. The Maiden Trees bring forth new life into Phantaia, taking into them the golden seeds shed forth and given to them by the father-tree. To smell of his flowers is to know of them. For their dreams of new life are bound together as one in those blooms," Ama told her.

Ama then shared with Ana the history of the noble five, the five Maiden Trees that are the mothers of the forest. He shared how they had given birth to the trees, tending to their needs, and shedding tears for the fallen ones that had perished. And so are made the Glessa, or enchanted amber, from their tears whose sap falls into the River of Avalyr when they weep.

Of the five Maiden Trees, their names are remembered as follows:

Phea - beech
Veddu - birch
Anling - alder
Alum - fir
Lumlea - rowan

Phea is their queen. About her shining silver form are encircled twelve slender beech trees born of her dreams and who are handmaidens to her. To her only do they serve and protect. They will die to protect her. For she is the one true source of the next line of Chieftain Trees. She is the sacred bride to the One Tree. And she brings to him great love and faithfulness in all she does in Phantaia. He celebrates the beauty of her heart, her form, and her spirit by the throbbing of his sacred lights. As the One Tree shines a golden light, so she shines a silver one. And the two as one light united bring forth their bright beauty to Phantaia's inner realms where their beams are forever mingled.

Little is known of the other Maiden Trees except for their mightiest of servants, the Rowans of Avalumlea, whose children encircle the lands before Avalyr. These guard the inner realms from the evil that comes into their woods from Avaras to harm their nurseries. These are the children of the ancient rowan, Lumlea, whose white, knotted, and aged trunk lies hidden beneath the falls of Abrea in a fern-laden copse at the very source of the waters of Avalyr.

She was once the mother of that forest in another world now lost for all time. The grandmother and midwife to the trees of Phantaia, she now guides the children of Phea. In her heart are hidden many enchantments born of other worlds before even the coming of the Essence Eternal into this one. For she is thought to have somehow survived the perils that had destroyed many divine and beautiful forests in worlds prior.

Ama held Ana's hand, guiding her by moss-covered stone stairs down the side of the cliff beneath the white waterfalls of Bann, and into the hidden fern-covered grottos that lay below the falls. He then told her that here alone had the warm earth of the Immortal Clay's spirit spoken clearest to the trees. For his earthly essence had lain dormant there through countless eons of time, untouched and unmarred by the unfolding drama of that world.

In this hidden place the spirit of the Rock Eternal had supported Lumlea by his rich nutrients, hiding her away under his towering cliffs from the eyes of evil which had continually sought her. For she alone carried the ancient wisdom of the forest and many others in her spirit. Hidden in her secret grotto beneath the falls, surrounded by impenetrable rocks and soft maidenhair ferns, aged Lumlea had remained untouched and pristine.

Ana gazed upon the ghostly tree, amazed by her strange form and beauty as the pale mist of the falls floated about her white limbs and leaves. Under her dripping boughs would Ana often come to sit alone, listening to the sound of the waterfall as it fell upon the smooth rocks and roots of the old tree. Ana often heard the sad trees mourning for her rowan children in Avalumlea and the felling of them by the evil agents of darkness. To Ana was granted many blessings from this wise old woman of the world. The tree often whispered to her with its eyes and mouth closed. For that mother of trees knew of the secrets bound to Ana which she had not yet discovered. And yet many of these truths Lumlea had kept from her. For she told Ana that her fate would be revealed to her and made known in time.

So, like her own mother, Lumlea cared for the child and comforted her for many days and nights. Many fears, hidden even from Ama, yet weighed upon Ana that only Lumlea had known. The old tree spoke to her of the nature of the world, the seas, and the hallowed earth beneath Phantaia. And from her Ana learned, though much time had passed, there yet awaited a flourishing age—a glorious new beginning for Phantaia which through her and Ama would soon arise again. But this simple yet hopeful truth alone was all the wise tree would impart to her.

In the depth of the night, in the Gardens of Abrea, Ama and Ana rested from their long journeys in that mystical wilderness. On the slopes of the Hill of Abra they had come to rest in peace together once more, sleeping for many long nights beneath the cool shadow of that misty mound.

But Ana had turned to him before bedtime, curious about the terrors of the lower woods of Avàras where she had seen many wicked and tortured faces upon the darker trees. She desired to know who they were and where they had come from, as they remained a great riddle to her. With reluctance Ama then shared with Ana the secrets of that sinister forest, though his knowledge of Avaras and its many dark histories was limited.

The trees of the darker woods of Avaras had dwelt in a land apart from their sisters and brothers since the time when Phantaia's first seedlings took root. But the darker soil of Avaras had been sundered from the brighter earth of Phantavra long before the evil trees had possessed it. For the spirits that crept there were forbidden by the Rock Eternal to ever enter Phantavra and the lands about Abra's sacred mound, where lay his sister in deep repose. Into the black earth had come many abominable spirits and shadows of things unmentionable and most malevolent—the fallen children of the Primordial Ones whose tortured spirits in ancient times had become trapped there.

For it is in the slimy earth of Avaras that the last of the dark lords of a forgotten land had hid their spirits, when their bodies were destroyed in the last wars between the Primordial Ones. They alone had survived the endless battles that destroyed their lands, hiding from the Nothingness that had consumed their siblings, and fleeing before the violent Dreaming Seas that had risen up to devour them. The trees of Avaras, their own spirits having fled their ancient forms in fear, had then become possessed by the demon-spirts that had come to dwell there in the black rocks and earth that remained.

But the evil trees that had grown there were ruled by haunted witch-hazels of great power, those that are called the Connewe. Though these master trees had been children of the One Tree long ago, they had forsaken his warm loving light for the cold grip of darkness. For in ancient days the hazels were once twins to the twelve Chieftain Trees of Phantavra, their noble brothers, bound as one to them until divided by some strange enchantment inflicted upon them.

Like the Chieftain Trees of Phantavra, they became Overlords of Avaras, being thirteen in number. They, however, had no lord. For in the witch-hazels had come to dwell the shattered spirits of the hateful children of the Limitless Void, those whose ghosts had hid there and escaped their cruel fate at the hands of their heartless father. Those great trees were thus possessed and forsook the loving light of the One Tree, their true father, embracing the forces of destruction, darkness, and death, seeking vengeance on all living things. And so too were they fed by the corrupt soil of Avaras, ever after, sundered from the brighter lands, alone and apart from their nobler siblings, forevermore.

The thirteen Connewe, thus united by their evil, collected even great power amongst themselves. As a great war-band they now strove to gather the trees and destroy the One Tree and all of Abrea. For they hated the greener woods where their blessed brethren now dwelt. And so the Connewe vowed to separate the great tree from his many children, as they themselves, as children of the Limitless Void, had been cruelly abandoned by their own father. Yet in their avenging hearts they ever desired to find the Limitless Void and enact great vengeance upon him. For the paternal wound he had inflicted upon their hearts would not heal, and its pain within them knew no bounds.

But it was known by the living trees of Phantavra that only by the will of their cursed father could those devilish spirits truly awaken again. For their spirits were yet bound to him as slaves. Without their father's presence and the rage he engendered in them, they were powerless to destroy Abrea and defy its magical lights. Instead, they wrapped their dark enchantments about Phantaia like a garrote, so they might slowly suffocate its heart. None could now enter or exit its woods. With their own dark magic and the maligned spirits they summoned from the sickened earth, they now filled the sinister glades of haunted Avaras with horrors to entrap the leery and all those who might unknowingly wander into its muddy midst.

This dark land would become a gigantic wilderness of shadowy woods and night terrors, far larger than the inner realms of Phantavra. For it stretched back into the mists of Time's lonely corridors, into the blue mists of dim and unknown lands, whose crumbling earth eventually fell away, down into the bleak chasms of Wendalia.

Great in age and strength, the witch-hazels of the Connewe had ruled over that dark wood for many ages. By the strange powers and wizardry they now possessed were they greatly feared. To each of these trees in time would be born dual servants, so that there was now three of each. They alone were give knowledge of the secret paths through the woods leading into its hidden interior. They could work great wizardry and evil when they came together, joined in a circle by their crooked arms, and call forth the dark spirits and ghosts of the putrid soil to do their vile work.

But Ama told Ana, "We may never see these malevolent trees. For they now dwell in the farthest corners of those darkened lands, far from the lights of the One Tree which ever burns their crooked branches to cinders. They remain unapproachable, even in their own realms, as they are now protected by malevolent spirits hidden within the blackest catacombs of the rocks and earth, where even more perverse beings yet sleep."

Ama continued, "But the Connewe still hope to rise again within the shadows, marching into Phantavra to destroy Abrea and end the life of the One Tree. Yet it remains unknown to them that only by the destruction of the pool may they extinguish its candle. With the corruption of the pool might my brethren weaken, then fall before them. They would then rule over this land. But to what further end might their baneful spirits might be directed, none may know." Ana then looked with fear about the woods.

"So many mysteries yet remain as to the comings and goings in the dark corners of Avaras," Ama said. "But we should not worry. For their ignoble father, the Limitless Void, has perished. Leaderless, there is no one left to command the Connewe towards further violence. And so they sleep. Yet something new has come into the woods that makes me doubt everything I have said to you." And Ama looked far off into the mist.

Ama then told Ana he had found something odd in the forest. In the last age the children of Esne, the Black Willow of Phantavra, had come to dwell among the Avaras children, forsaking the light of the One Tree, and dwelling in their midst. They had planted themselves upon the fringes of dark chasms, caves, and canyons in Avaras, spying upon the workings of the Connewe, and reporting to the Chieftain Trees of their grim toils in that dark land. But in time had seven of their kind been perverted to evil's will and fled the lights of the One Tree and the mind of Esne, their father, joining the Connewe to serve them and their hidden purpose.

They had seemed drawn to something, having fallen into the deep canyons that lay about Avaras, down into the underworld beneath Phantaia where not even the twilight gloom could reach. In those vast caverns the dark willows grew monstrous, so that in time their stringy roots stretched for great distances through the earth and stone. Like vampiric vines, they sucked the life from the trees and plants that grew above them. These willows they called the Were-Trees, or the Koredlum. Yet none had ever found them in that grim underworld, nor could they be destroyed. For some force not of this world sustained them.

But of all the thirteen Chieftain Trees of Avaras, the most powerful were the Seven Hazels of Evil Thought—the Ephram. For they and the Koredlum had gathered together to do great evil. They had long ago found a dark pit that lay in the heart of blackest Avaras. They had grown around it to draw forth some unnatural power from its inky depths.

In this pit had long slept a force none had ever seen or known except Ama. For the treacherous mind of a dark spirit slept in the bowels of its dark pool and the oily waters which lay hidden within. The knowledge of that pool and its secrets remained unknown to all living things in Phantaia, save to the Ephram and the Koredlum, whose wicked roots clung to the entrance of its black orifice.

It was said the dark roots of the Ephram had gathered about the lips of that pit to drink from its poisonous waters, listening to the whisperings of the mystic spirits that slept within its depths. But from that pit, Ama learned, would come the source of something more sinister yet to be revealed in Phantaia. Born of an earlier world, it contained the source of an unfinished evil beyond all knowledge in this world. Ama then looked upon Ana with wild eyes, which she had not seen before.

Then Ana said, "Of late I too have felt the dread of the trees, Ama. For when we had passed through those woods by the seas, I had seen their evil faces. Its then I saw a dark pit in the earth with many strange figures and forms I did not recognize."

But Ama said, "It is unlikely to be the same place. For there are many such dark places in Avaras. It is a vast realm of many canyons and chasms."

Ana replied, "But I saw the Ephram about a great pit. I saw their eyes. Ama, I am fearful they are on the move again, looking for me. It is me they want."

"No Ana. They only want to destroy the One Tree. But do not fear. For those demonic trees shall never make it to Abrea, as the Durnach that dwell within their ranges alert us of all intruders. Nor have the Connewe the courage to do harm to any living being in Abrea. For the lights of the One Tree would burn them to ashes, as they are made of only evil shadows. So had they turned back before the light and fled in past ages, back into the farthest fringes of Avaras to hide from it." Ana then cuddled closer to Ama, her fears and doubts still lingering. For she knew what she had seen. And she hoped that Ama was right.

As the golden rays of dawn beamed upon them, Ama and Ana rested upon the summit of Abrea, napping within the white roots of the One Tree. Beside the silver pool they held hands and looked into each other's eyes. And they felt as one, closer in spirit and in mind to one another than ever before. As kindred spirits were they now, two innocent hearts beating in unison to the rhythms of nature's ancient melody.

Ama had shared many secrets of Phantaia with Ana and had showed her many wonders of the woods. Ama then spoke to her, saying, "Ana, should anything happen to me, you must remember the knowledge of the trees I have given you and keep their secrets close to your heart. For I have sought not to believe in the morbid dreams that now torture me. In recent days, they have come more often, like some cruel memory of a tortured past. And so I have sought to preserve the sacred knowledge and wisdom of Phantaia in your heart and mind, so that they might yet live on should I leave this world."

This hidden tree-knowledge would be named Breddunar, the forest-secrets. For Ama had hoped they would be kept hidden from the world until their knowledge could be shared with the deserving children of a future age.

But Ana said to him, "Ama, do not to speak of those dark dreams and thoughts any longer. For my heart hurts to see you distressed by such things which do not seem a part of this world but of another foreign to us. I am but a daughter of dreams, born of the mother of all dreams, and to which the fates of all living things are bound unto a timeless loom. But to me is it known by my mother's words that many beautiful things yet shall come to pass. For a hopeful future yet lies ahead for us. We should not follow the uncertain paths of our dreams. From us shall come something joyous, which I have vaguely seen in the shadows of my own heart."

Ama then felt comforted by this daughter of the sea. He had grown close to her and drawn to her. He held her face gently in his hands, and drew close to her to feel her warm breath upon his own. Ana looked into his eyes and felt something new and wondrous awakening from within. Ama then embraced her in his strong arms.

But that violently curling mist, like a rising banshee, suddenly descended upon them, hiding them in its thick cocoon. Ana stepped back, startled by its sudden appearance, as it now seemed gray and gloomy, and not of the lavender color she had seen many times before.

It summoned into her mind a dark memory. And she gazed at Ama with her own uncertainty hidden in her eyes. For she feared in secret she would bring some evil upon him and upon that blessed paradise. And she feared she would draw Ama into her own strange fate, which had yet been partially revealed to her by the words of the Shadow and the Twilight Mist.

Would she bring doom to Ama by her presence in Abrea? Would she bring doom to them both? She turned away from Ama and walked to the edge of the pool.

She now spoke. "For many nights and days, Ama, I have thought upon my mother An, who lies hidden in the depths of that far away ocean. I long to see her again. I feel I must go to her and return to the sea, quickly now. Somehow I feel I belong with her, though I know by the words of the Lavanc I am forbidden to return." But in her secret heart, hidden from Ama, she desired in truth to free him from the darkness she knew now would come looking for her. She did not know what her father would do to her, or of his dark and destructive designs for Phantaia. She feared the evil he would bring down upon them both. And that Ama would be harmed. Her heart hurt at the thought, as she wrapped her arms about herself.

But Ama looked puzzled, hearing her strange new desire. Ana, gazing about the valley, then said to Ama, "I still do not know the meaning of this strange place nor my place in it, Ama. Though much has been shared with me by you and the loving trees, I have nothing to give in return. At night while you slept I have heard the pining of the seas calling me." Ana then ran to him, imploring him, "Ama, please, you must return me to the seas now."

As Ama held her, he saw how lost she felt. But he told her, "Ana, I in truth have no answers to the questions that remain in your mind. For I too know not what lies behind the mystery of why you are here."

"But, I cannot take you to the ocean," Ama said to Ana. "For the Twilight Mist asked that you be brought to Abrea and remain here with me. All I now know the Twilight Mist shared with me in the youthful days of Phantaia. Your grandfather had sought to spare you from some terrible tragedy. For the workings of some evil which dwells beyond Phantaia and the seas would someday come for you, he told me. So have I brought you here to hide you away. And I shall protect you from the darkness should it come to threaten you here in Abrea."

Hearing his words, Ana now knew he had known. And she looked down in greater sadness and doubt, no longer able to hide the truth from him. But before she could speak, Ama walked to her and embraced her, comforting her again. Ama then felt the bold heart of Ana beating within her, but with some strange force and design beyond this world.

Ama stood still, pondering its strange beat. For it had some hypnotic power over him. He then placed his right hand on her chest and said to her, "Something great lives inside you Ana, which I had sensed since your first days here." She then removed his hand. For Ana feared like the Shadow he might see some horror therein, and know of the strange waters she had been told held some destiny, which she did not yet comprehend.

But Ama stood as one in a trance. For the strange music of the waters within her had brought into his mind a memory of a story told to him as a young boy by the Twilight Mist. Somehow it had summoned those memories from its own depths and reminded him of a distant time as a young boy beside his gentle uncle in the Gardens of Abrea. But the stories told to him he had not understood until now.

"I am reminded of a strange tale, Ana, told to me long ago by your grandfather. And in its story I feel may lie the answer to your riddle," Ama told her.

Ana slowly walked away perplexed and sat upon a rock beside the pool. As Ama sat beside her, he told her, "I will share the origins of our world and many others, which had been told to me long ago by your grandfather. From it shall you come to know of the One Tree, my blessed father, and how it came to be. But maybe it too shall reveal your purpose in coming here. For in that story lies the mystery of a fated pool, dark and mysterious, which had haunted the children of many fallen worlds before this one."

As Ama began to tell his tale, Ana looked into the pool at her feet and saw her reflection again upon the surface of its silver waters. She then saw that she had aged. Then in the fog that fell about them, she thought she saw herself as a woman, yet much older. About her feet her children played. And she heard a strange word rising up out the waters, saying only, *Maymee*. The vision then faded away as the fog enveloped them.

The pool lay gray and silent again. The once-bubbling brook now stopped flowing, as the forest below them grew deathly still. Even the great tree's limbs stood unmoving. Its once-fluttering leaves and shining lights turned a brilliant shade of lavender, as if the mist itself and the voice of the boy had somehow changed the One Tree's lights. The mist flowed around the hill, wrapping it in its pale gray color and filling the Gardens of Abrea that lay eerily quiet about them.

Ama sat beside Ana in the rich ferns that graced the hilltop. She lay in his arms beside the pool and listened as he spoke, until his eyes melted away into the dreamy landscape of his haunting tale.

THE FALLEN WORLD

Ama sat quietly, gazing off into the distant horizon. "When I was a young boy," Ama said to Ana, "the Twilight Mist had revealed to me many mysteries of our world and many others stretching back in time. Yet I had not known until now, that in his wisdom he had sought to give me a deeper knowledge, so I might gain some understanding in this troubled time."

Gathering the epic tale in his mind, Ama then began.

Before the creation of Phantaia and the mighty earth that stood beneath it, there was nothing except the emptiness of space and the dust and decay of a dying world. Even before this one was made had many others before it been birthed, born, and died, each destroyed by the evil that had always hid there in the shadows.

But despite evil's destructive will, strangely had the good children that dwelt there been consumed by their own wickedness in the end. For they had struggled for power over each other and the world, until they had extinguished the last living flame that once shined brightly within it. Yet with its last dying ember had always remained an enduring hope that something good would be reborn from its ashes.

A thousand worlds prior to this one had a world been made in which the lights of dawn shined brighter than any other, pure and untarnished by the eternal night that always crept about it. In the youthful grandeur of that ancient world had a magnificent tree of golden splendor grown beside a radiant pool of purest silver, wherein no shade or shadow could abide. More beautiful than our own, its sapphirine waters had been born from the primeval dew of the shining tree that grew beside it, so that the pool's own light was most luminous, like that of the golden tree that fed it.

Yet this pool of light dwelt not apart from the tree, but was wed to it in spirit, such that each was sustained by the other. For the loving union of their lights had cast back the shadows from the gloomy world, beaming down as one white beacon their gold and silver rays into the depths where it lay hidden.

About the great tree had grown a rich forest much like Phantaia, stretching boundless through the valleys of a vast sylvan paradise. But of spectral lights were its trees forged, with leaves of gold, and bark bathed in the light of its polished silver. No darkness could dwell in that lucent wood of gold and silver. For into these gilded trees had the beams of the pool and tree ever shined, unfaded, so that the shining glades and glorious meadows grew tall and grandiose in their prismatic lights.

But though the pool and the tree had blessed that world with their unblemished radiance, no child could be born into that forest or dwell therein. For by its blazing sun was that world oddly cursed by its sterile state of unwavering perfection.

Beneath the forest, she who is named the Evil One had dwelt in the dark depths undisturbed. Through the birth and death of many worlds and continuums she had slept, hidden within the foul waters of a baneful pool whose black waters issued forth from the bottom of a putrid pit. This fearsome sea serpent had slept in the depths of those abysmal waters, suffering alone in private agony. Long ago had the ancient shadows of her broken heart bled away, so that nevermore had she the will or even the desire to cast forth ever again her grim shade into this bright world of eternal sun again.

But the hollows of her dark spirit had been filled, long ago, with the Insatiable Hunger of Hatred and the Unquenchable Thirst of Revenge. And so her vengeance against the light and hatred for the living had grown ever greater within her. With her ravenous appetites she had fed upon the living children of earlier worlds, such that no trace of them had remained. The light of their spirits and the form of their flesh was thus savagely devoured by her, so that never again would they be born again into it. With their deaths did their worlds also perish, immolating into the void, a pitiful destiny most malicious and cruel.

But the pool and tree had been reborn into this new world, yet again, to defy her. Bound as one, born of Merciful Love and

Enduring Compassion, finally united, they had come forth again to wage war against the Evil One for the death of their children in countless worlds previous. For they had sought to cleanse it of that vile serpent's spirit once and for all, that which had lain in wait to poison and pollute their love with its fanged maw.

Seeing their blinding light beaming forth upon the horizons of that young world, the Evil One had risen up from her great gulf to assault the source of it and to devour it whole. But as her great jaws opened up to consume the tree and its sister pool, she was seared by the strange spiritual fire that shined out from them both. For the light of the golden tree and its silver pool united had now birthed the Sacred Light, whose mighty candle now burned pure and bright within them both.

The face of the serpent was then seared, and her form sundered in two by its double-flame. She then burst forth into great storms of gray fog and cloud, releasing her own dark waters from her black heart, down into the world. But from her dying body were spawned twin horrors. For two misshapen abominations had arisen from her black and corrupted womb.

These were the bastard sons, born of the ruin of the Dark Mother's putrid and divided flesh. Greatest of these was the indomitable not-being called the Nothingness—he who eats the spirits of the living, the essence of which was gifted unto them from the One Cosmic Spirit. The cleaver of souls, the Nothingness had arisen from the very root of his mother's immolating heart. But from her decaying body had arisen his terrible twin, the vast storm called the Emptiness—that which consumes the secret form of the Vatar, the flesh of the living and the matter from which it takes shape. And so was born the vile slayer, the eater of the dead, the consumer of all matter, and the father of the frightful Magra Lords.

Her two evil sons, the Nothingness and Emptiness, fed upon their malevolent mother's flesh. They then were filled with her evil appetites and insatiable desires. And so in them was thus born anew the unending hatred of the world, its living tree, and its shining pool. Yet the spirit of the Evil One had remained, trapped in her dark pool of death and decay.

The sinister twins now rose forth from her corpse to wage vengeful war against the pool and the tree, seeking to sunder the source of its blasphemous illumination, and thus obliterate its light forever. But the Nothingness and Emptiness could never approach the light of the pool or tree. For by its beams were their own spirits burned. And so they built for themselves a terrible prison in the depths of the Great Beyond, where even the lights of Heaven would fade in the swirling gray fogs of their mother's mists.

Seeing the source of the Sacred Light unapproachable, the evil twins then sought to divide the pool from the tree, one from the other, so that they might falter and fall away, and their sacred spirits forever after divorced from each other. For by the breaking of the marriage of tree and pool would that world fall again, back into restless shadows and dreadful dreams. And so the dying world would be theirs to consume, once more.

By the act of a servant of midnight, a dark demon most wretched and devious had the source of the pool been found and polluted. As its own light faded, this sacred pool was cruelly ripped away from the earth by the Emptiness, so that it bled forth its silver blood about the mound, crying out in agony. The last of its silver waters were then spilled down into the depths of the pit of the Evil One, where they were devoured by the dark waters of the bottomless well that hid there.

With the waters of the beautiful well now destroyed, the union of tree and pool had been broken. Divided from its other half, the golden tree now wilted, and its leaves turned brown. The Sacred Light that dwelt within the tree then faltered and faded, so that its spiritual flame departed that world, cast away as a shining seed, into the mountains that lay within the heavenly ether. The world then slipped back into the silent gloom from which it was made. And that darkness which had always hid among the rocks and trees, returned once more. Only the umber husk of the tree remained, the last relic of that once blessed marriage.

By their endless hunger and thirst, the evil twins gorged upon the flesh of the world and its unborn spirits until they became bloated and fat. Only the foul breath of the Dark Mother remained, its putrid fog hanging upon the surface of the Black Pool, flowing out upon the corpse of the world left drained by her vile and vampiric sons. And so that distant and forsaken world had died, as had many others. But so too had fallen the Evil One that once had cursed it. And she was never to live again in this world or any other. For her two violent children would rule them all ever after.

But something had remained that was left untouched. Though the tree had perished, the empty cauldron of that pool had yet remained. For its rocks were born of the heart of the One Cosmic Spirit that cannot perish—the Sacred Heart whose essence he had placed within the rocky grail of the pool. For in that dying well had yet remained his undying wish that the courageous spirits of his children should rise again and embrace the divine will found within its waters.

Ama then paused. Ana had started to reach down into the well, pondering Ama's strange tale. "It is time for a short break," Ama said. "But the story shall continue."

He then slipped down the hill and out of sight. When he returned he brought Ana fresh water from the streams of Lilu, fresh berries, and nuts from the gardens. They then gorged together beside the crystal spring, as the dark clouds that gripped the garden deepened around them. To Ana it seemed that only Ama, the tree, the pool, and she were now left in that sad gray world. And so she drew close to Ama as they ate.

Ama stood up and stretched his body, refreshed. Smiling, he bent down, saying, "Ana, may I continue?"

Ana then looked up with her tired, yet curious eyes, saying, "Yes, I am ready, Ama. But I am saddened by the dying tree and its pool in this tale. What became of them?"

Ama then stood before her animated, saying, "There is more to tell. Much more." He then began to walk around the pool, looking into it as if searching for inspiration. He then continued the second part of his story.

Many worlds after that embattled one had also perished in darkness, sinking each time into shadowy ruin and wreckage by the violent acts of the evil that lay in wait there. For they had entrapped the minds of many children, those possessed of their own dark hearts which they could not fathom. And so they in turn destroyed themselves and their own kind.

But in the last world, the one previous to our own, there had been born a much brighter and more hopeful future than any yet known. For within the earliest days of its own glorious beginning, there had remained, yet again, a dark and depleted well. Its hollow cauldron was all that had remained of an ancient pool whose waters had long nurtured that previous world. Beside this dry well now stood the sad black trunk of a fallen tree, whose own mists and dews had departed it long ago.

But out of the foggy gloom had walked a grim and forlorn spirit cloaked in the ephemeral gloom of evening's twilight. It had come from the unknown lands that lie beyond the farthest swells of the Seas of Eternity, where the Great Mother's dreams were forever forged anew, and whose immortal tides flowed on through boundless time and space.

This being had come to kneel beside the ruins of the pool, solemn and unseen. With aged and regretful hands, it had carried the last of the waters of an unknown pool, whose grim past was more fateful than this one. With trembling hands, it poured the last of those waters back into the shattered font, so that it might be reborn and its pool yet live again. That being then wrapped its dark violet cloak about it and disappeared into the mist.

The pool then lit up again with a miraculous glow cast from the essence that now possessed it. Though the tree had died, the pool would yet live again to bring new life to this world. For within its waters hid many unborn spirits. Unlike any well known before, was it made. Of light and shadow, and the realm of eternal dusk and dawn equally drawn, were those waters forged. For the twilight children of that world were those waters meant to serve.

But those waters also bore a curse to all who would seek to harm them. For that pool had been remade, such that never again would it be undone or destroyed by the powers of darkness or of light, evil or of good, without exacting its retribution upon them in the end. Such was its Creator's intent. These strange waters now safely slept, bathed in the dreams of future spheres and damned worlds with doomed beings yet to live, suffer, and die by its unrelenting will, until either its own ominous spirit would be obliterated, or its secret purpose at last achieved.

The twilight pool and the corpse of the tree, born unto their shadowed pasts in the throes of their brighter futures, returned to peaceful slumber as this new world awaited the dawn of its own rebirth.

Beneath the quiet pool and the shriveled roots of the dead tree, deep in the ground had slept a hidden maid. That child had for many ages lain in the womb of the world, dreaming in her stony crypt that lay hidden within the earthen mound. She had been laid to rest there by an unseen but gentle hand, to sleep and dream until the time of her awakening would come at last. But the mysterious waters of the shattered pool above her had seeped into the cracks of the rocks, dripping down upon her face. She then rose from her bed, reborn and renewed.

Climbing from her crypt, she came forth out into the dark forest walking barefoot upon the black earth that lay beneath the undead trees. That strange child had awakened in the youth of the world, wrapped in the shining raiment of her own shade, yet with the shadows of an earlier time glowing forth in her dark eyes.

She then had knelt before the tree and pool, as a child praying before her parent's graves. But seeing the black limbs of the dead tree hanging over her, she knew then she had come too late. Her tears then fell, the safni, first tender rains of the Sacred Waters in Phantaia, dripping down into the dark pool and waking its spirits from their eternal slumber. Her sorrows, now mixed with its waters, had become one with its brooding spirit.

Ama, standing beside the pool, looked at Ana with solemn eyes. "It's strange, but the Twilight Mist told me," Ama said, "that by the sorrows for the dead and the dying are our loved ones reborn in this world." Ama stood silent as Ana thought upon the wisdom her grandfather had given her before his death.

Ama then returned to his tale.

As the tears of the girl-child fell into the dark well, an ebony dew rose up from out of it, until a terrible storm had formed within its cloud, blowing the dust of the decayed world about her. As the hand of night rolled over the hill, great thunder was heard from the sky, as of a trumpet blown, bold and clear. The hollow husk of that tree then trembled as the pool grew still. The girl then ran and hid in the rocks below in fear.

As gusts of wind blew down from the skies and the rains about them fell, a mighty lightning bolt flew down from the heavenly mountains above, striking the trunk of the dead tree, splitting it in two, and revealing its rotten and crumbling core. The shattered trunk of the dead tree then fell upon the hill, divided and shattered before the pool. The storm clouds then fled away into the Heavens. The girl-child then returned and stood upon the edge of its ruin.

But as she looked into the skies the gates of the shining Heavens above her opened up. And a bold but bright voice was heard to say, 'I am the beginning.' But from the depths of the waters of the dark pool came another voice, dark and shadowy, saying only, 'I am the end.' As the skies calmed, it seemed that everything had fallen into silence once more.

A great mist had descended, shrouding the mound in its mid-cloak, and bringing forth gentle rains so that the pool was replenished. But as the clouds cleared away, a small white seedling had pushed its way through the barren earth where the old tree had stood, growing from inside the broken log of the black trunk that had fallen.

The girl-child saw the beautiful light of the frail sapling from afar, as it sprouted from the dark soil. She then pushed away the rotting husk so that the new forest-child might grow forth freely upon the mound. With her hands she then took water from the pool and poured it upon the tiny sapling. And so by her love in time would the seedling grow into a mighty and majestic tree.

Ama then strode to the One Tree, standing before it and feeling its thick white bark, saying. "So beautiful was this new tree, Ana, that its bark shined white with the brightest of light, pure and of a pale fire, like that of the Creative Flame that burns in us all."

This tiny white tree the girl-child carefully nurtured. A new wilderness was then born from this sapling. For she took its many fruits and planted a twilight forest from its seeds. And so like Phantaia, those woods soon stretched back into the fathomless spaces of that world.

The pool and tree dwelt side by side. But apart were they in spirit. For within the depths of the pool had lurked a sleeping presence whose force was born of the very breath of the visiting spirit that had brought it. The pool had immured the tree to its own purpose, so that the tree and the world about it both moved within its sphere. And so by its insidious powers and will was the light of the ghostly tree oddly dimmed by it.

In time, the white tree shone not with a gold or silver light, but of eternal gloaming, with the violet cast of early evening's lengthening shade. For the pool's twilight waters were filled with an ambient glow, endowed with the shade of its gloomier heart. Yet by the earthly powers of that phantom tree was the pool's light also changed from its deepening dusk to a dimmer dawn. And so within both tree and pool burned the pale glow of a moonlight lamp whose ghostly glare cast back the eternal night that crept upon them, drawing up the very shadows of the world into its own lavender cloak, mixing them with the lights of the tree, then casting them back out again in twilight hues more magnificent.

The storms and rains had passed. And the clouds parted above the hill. Upon the mountains high above, a shining son had arisen from his heavenly tomb. He beamed down his many blessings upon that dark world, welcoming a new age of light unto it. For it was his bolt that had shattered the dying tree, awakening its own child to shine again.

This golden child had refashioned the daylight Heavens, the Amandyas, summoning forth many blinking and beckoning stars, placing them in the dark skies above him. For he had fathered many celestial children. Their starlight had blasted away the darkness from the roots of the forest. And they had washed clean the face of the dark waters with their silver beams, until they alone were reflected therein like gemstones of many colors.

Yet by the wise labors of this bright boy was twilight allowed to dwell under the brilliant sunbeams of Heavens in perfect harmony with the somber darkness that dwelt beneath it. The violet glow of eternal eventide shined throughout that wilderness for many ages unchallenged, such that evil could not come into it. So by the dusky gloom alone were the nether ones that dwelt in the infernal abyss soothed into a deep and unending sleep of death yet undying.

With the fashioning of that twilit world the girl returned once more from the woods to the hill where the pool and tree now lay. But she was now a woman, tall and elegant in form. As she approached the pool, she looked into its waters, seeing upon its surface many faces. For the spirits of its children were swimming in its depths.

She then pulled from its waters the Children of Twilight, one by one, whose spirits had been placed there long ago. They then drew forth the color of night into their faces from out of the surface of its bejeweled waters. And there shined within the white leaves of the great tree many lights upon their violet eyes, until unto them was drawn the light of the tree, renewing their shadowy spirits with its loving radiance.

The Children of Twilight thus first came forth to sleep as one beside the tree and pool. And so were they united in brotherhood, dancing as one before she who had made them, their Divine Mother. But they saw the light of the star-children in the skies above, which glittered like diamonds in the Heavens. And they heard the music of the spheres, giving back to them their own joyous songs as tribute. They then felt the loving face of the Divine Father as he looked down from his golden halls in the Heavens above, shining his own benevolent light upon them. But they were most joyful for the gifts of the pool and tree, whose eventide glow filled their hearts with hope and peace everlasting.

In time there were born many beautiful children between them. And the One Cosmic Spirit, whose house had been long divided, was brought together again as one spirit through them. And so came to be the Children of Twilight, the cherished ones, who would come to dwell in that world for many ages.

The Divine Mother had dwelt among them in their faded gardens, in peace and happiness. But he who dwells in the Heavens had seen the fair maiden from afar. So in time the Divine Mother heard the blowing of the horns of the Divine Father, calling her from the heights of Heaven's halls. Its music he had made for her. But she could not go to him. For she was bound to the pool and would not leave it. For therein had hid the last of the children of evening within their waters, whose sleeping spirits were yet unborn.

One night as she sat beside the dark pool a strange loneliness filled her heart. But as she stared into its waters, she saw the bejeweled light of something shiny in its depths. As she reached down to touch it, she saw a single bright beam from an unknown source cast down upon the surface of the waters from on high. She gazed upon the beautiful glint of gold, captivated by it.

She then left the pool and climbed the slopes of Heaven, seeking its source. The Divine Mother climbed up into the heights of the mountains until she stood upon the white alabaster steps of a great hall. There in the depths of his innermost chamber she saw the Divine Father praying before a mighty lantern of gold. He then turned and saw that his love had come to him at last by the calling of its candle. The Divine Mother and Father then held each other in a tender embrace.

Their love grew, so that in time the Divine Mother had come to dwell beside the Divine Father in his shining lands that lay within the Heavens. They looked down upon all the children that they had made and were happy. For they now knew they had been summoned forth to bless the world with their noble creations.

For many ages the great lantern of Heaven had held back the evil that still slept in the shadowy pits beneath the roots of the world. For twilight itself had been cast out of those woods by its radiance, long ago. Instead light and shadow had warred for dominion over it until Time's very patience itself had been tried by their conflict. For it could no longer withhold the aging of that timeless world from that which would come to pass. The immortal trees of that wood had grown tall and wide feeding upon Heaven's glow, until the celestial lights of the Divine Father could no longer penetrate the shade of the trees that had grown about their tangled roots.

With the retreating of the shadows the evil spirits that long had crept there, hidden in the floor of the world, now awoke and stirred within their prison. Their spirits then rose forth again, seeking to destroy the light and claim that world as their own as they had done in many worlds prior.

From the depths was then heard a dark and mournful cry that only the Divine Mother could hear. Its cry was of a forsaken child. And so was she stirred by it in her sleep, thinking it to be the last spirits of the pool calling her to return. In her bed she wept knowing she had abandoned them. And so in the heart of the night she fled the golden halls of Heaven, returning in secret to the misty gardens of her twilight realms.

There in the mists of the perpetual gloom she came to where the dark pool slept. She then looked down into its depths to find the source of its hidden voice. But as she looked upon the waters there was revealed to her an erotic vision, spawned forth from the depths of her most lascivious and secretive desires.

By its strange mirror the face of another, handsome and dark, was shown to her. Then a deep dark voice came forth from the depths of the woods behind her, saying, 'By these waters alone shall your desires be fulfilled. Drink from their dark cup and be free.' Entranced, she bent down and with her hands drank from the forbidden waters of the dark pool.

She fell into a swoon as a dark mist enveloped the hill about her. A black figure then walked forth from the misty forest.

Strong, dark, and chiseled in form was he. She rose to meet the handsome figure, running to him with a passion fully unleashed, and born of great desire for him. They then entered the dark pool together and made love within the throbbing glow of the malevolent pool. She then fell into his dark and muscular arms, back into a troubled sleep.

A dream came into her sleeping mind, of a fate most terrible to behold and filled with many horrors. As she awoke she found herself lying naked and alone beside the pool. She then heard the silver horns of the Divine Father calling her from his house in Heaven. But by her shameful acts she could not face him. And so she ran deep into the depths of the twilight woods. There she dwelt alone among the dark and twisted trunks until in time, from torturous labor, she bore a child.

To the Children of Twilight was this baby most akin. And under their care and love was he raised as a beloved child among them. But they also saw within him a being very different. For it was revealed in time that there had been given unto that child many great gifts. There had entered into him the maverick essence of the Spirit Divine. Yet a hidden darkness lay within him, too.

His body and wings were of silver, bearing the merciful light of the stars in the Heavens. But his great heart was of gold, most pure and kind. In him dwelt the lustrous fires of the Creative Flame. Yet within his eyes glowed a dark and dreary light, born of the weariness of the world. For they carried the hidden spirit of the Ghost of Eventide, glowing with the glamour of midnight whose shadows shined forth like the gloom of impending nightfall.

But so too the children saw that he would soon paint upon the blank canvas of the world the colors of even greater wonders and more beautiful works. And they saw that through him would something great be returned that had been reft from them. This child they named the Maker, as he was closest to them and the creative will of the One Cosmic Spirit, their eternal father.

In time he grew to be a beautiful boy, with eyes of darkest night that could see through the limitless spaces, the mists, and the earth that lay beneath the firmament of the world. His own spiritual light shined forth like the twilight trees set ablaze, yet guided by the strange darkness that yet filled his mind and spirit. So most like the pool and tree of that world in twilight was his light cast. For through him like themselves were the dual forces of light and dark that filled the world brought together again.

Beside the Children of Twilight he then dwelt, hidden from the lights of Heaven, deep in the depths of the tranquil woods. By her loving heart the Divine Mother guided her child until such time as he was old enough to leave her. She then bade her beautiful son go forth and find the Divine Father who dwells in the Heavens, send him word of her love for him, and bear news of her return to rest eternal beneath the sacred mound of the pool. For weary with age, she would now return to the tomb where once she had lain.

With tears in her eyes she kissed her blessed child goodbye, leaving him alone in the dim woods. But she could not look upon the pool. For it brought to her mind painful memories. In her former tomb she returned to endless sleep from which she hoped she would never awaken again.

Bereaved by the loss of his mother, the shining son left the twilight woods, climbing high into the mountains seeking the halls of Heaven. There at last upon the rugged cliffs he found the house of the Divine Father, just as his mother said he would. Seeing that winged child standing from afar, the Divine Father came to him and pondered the strange appearance and origin of the pale boy.

The child then revealed to him the fate of his mother and of her return to sleep. The Divine Father then fell to his knees and mourned for her. But the child came to him and comforted him. For his heart was pure and filled with compassion. Its then the Divine Father took the child in and loved him with the full depth of his mighty heart. He then raised him as his son, blessing the boy with his own wisdom and guidance.

In time that child was granted great powers by his father, as he saw the creative will of that boy would not be denied. He then knew that the twilight child would transform the world with his gifts long after he was gone. For he saw that his Divine Son would soon bring great works of beauty into it for the benefit of the children of the twilight forest whom he still loved.

Ana then stood and came to Ama, asking him, "Ama, I know of the Spirit Divine. Is he not this world's Creator and Lord? Is he not the one which fills all living things in Phantaia with his own spirit?"

"Yes, it is true," Ama said. "For this tale was told to me when I was but a boy and I understood but little of our Creator. But I see now the hidden truth of your grandfather's tale. And so are the Great Father's plans for Phantaia and for us somehow revealed therein." Ama then continued.

When the twilight child had grown and come of age, the Divine Father revealed to his son the last hidden truths of that world. He then was given the full measure of its glory. He was shown the Wings of Night upon which the Divine Father had hung the star-children in the Heavens. And to him was shown the gray Gates of Eventide that the hand of evil itself had forged to hold back the light of the world.

To his Divine Son was then revealed the greatest treasure of all—the Sacred Light of the One Cosmic Spirit. This he had withheld from the world until a blessed time when its full radiance would again be allowed to return unto it. The boy could only gaze in wonder at the majesty of his father's flame as it burned within its golden lantern.

The Divine Son for many days thought upon these miraculous creations within the quiet of his father's house. But he desired most to sit in his halls upon his golden throne, and stare into the Sacred Light whose flame had hung there above the seat of his father. Into the depths of his mind then came a strange voice—a strange calling from deep within his spirit. From the darkest recesses of his heart soon flowed forth a dark desire to possess the light and use it for his own purpose.

The Divine Son then came before his father and said unto him, 'Father, I shall go build a great house beyond these heavenly halls. For my own Creative Flame burns brightly, desiring to share its gifts with the world.'

But the Divine Father had known by the will of that boy that soon would that day come. And he bade him, 'Go forth and make a hall for yourself as you desire, my son.'

But the Divine Son said, 'Father, I long to bring the Children of Twilight as one family under my guidance. For them shall I build a sturdy house to draw strength from. But I have seen the true source of the light of the tree which once burned so brightly, now denied them. So shall I take the great flame of your house, the Sacred Light, and from it build an open cauldron to house it, and a mirror to cast its bright flame upon the world. And in that house shall I keep it so that it shines its merciful light, like a bright shining sun, down upon the children of the world. By its beacon shall I summon the twilight children to my halls so that they dwell ever closer to me, far from the evil that lurks in the lands beneath their feet.

'In those shining halls, shall they sing as one in perfect harmony, like the stars you hath made in the Heavens, far from the cacophony of the wild beasts and dark spirits of the woods. And the skies shall be filled with their loud symphony of voices such that order shall flow into it by their music. And their hearts and that of the world shall be forever brightened. To each shall then be given a new world—a mighty star plucked from the Heavens—which they may remake in their own image. And these, their honorable houses, shining like a million candles within the mantle of the inky sky, shall be more beautiful than any of the stars yet created by you.'

"So had the Divine Son willed a glorious plan to be in that earlier world, greater than any yet conceived under this Heaven or their own," said Ama.

This grand design the Divine Son had conceived in his mind's eye, telling his father, 'By my hand may the Children of Twilight dwell apart from the tree and pool, and thus be free at last. They shall throw away the sad lights of dusk and dawn, fashioning a world as they will, as we ourselves have fashioned this one. But for this dream to be fulfilled, Father, I must take the candle of the Sacred Light that lies imprisoned within these halls.'

The Divine Father looked upon his son with doubt, saying, 'Only now in this world has peace finally reigned supreme. Since the demise of many worlds before this one has it been an unfulfilled desire. Peace has been granted unto us as a gift, yet only after many had perished at the hands of the defiant evil that had hidden amongst us to stir up war.'

But the Divine Son said, 'Had not every world before this one perished by its own darkness? It has always been so. The Sacred Light shall protect us, chasing away the monsters that dwell in the deep holds of the world. This light was meant to be given and shared, not coveted and hidden away. For it was created through the glory of the children of this world, whose spirits were made from its very light. It should be given back to them so they might bathe in its glory. By its guiding light shall the children who dwell in the black and oppressive woods be renewed. They shall then use it to remake the world, kindling the creative will that burns in them.'

But the Divine Father said, 'My son, only by the hiding of the Sacred Light has our long sought peace been won. For should the evil that dwells below see the Sacred Light return to this world, it would be tempted again to rise up to destroy it once more. With its destruction would Heaven fall, and all the children that dwell under it perish again. And so has the withholding of the Sacred Light from the eyes of the Emptiness and Nothingness made that possible.'

But the son said to his father, 'Soon shall evil rise again anyway, Father. For I have seen them stirring in their prisons and calling to me in dreams. I, the children's new leader and lord, must take the Children of Twilight from the evil woods before they rise again. In the safety of my halls shall they be free forever from the dark temptations soon to enter their hearts.'

But the Divine Father said to his son, 'Like that granted unto you, the children of the woods have been given the freedom to choose their own fates, my son. For by freewill alone was this world fashioned. They have chosen to live together in peace in the lands of everlasting dusk. And so it is done.'

But the Divine Son said to his father, 'No Father. They had been denied freedom. Are they not enslaved to the shadows of the Forest of Twilight, hiding in its faded former glory? If they are free then they should be free to choose, to remain in the shadows of the suffering wood or seek the light of truth that shall call them now from on high.' At these words the son left in anger, defiant and proud. But his father remained somber, deeply saddened by the words of his son.

As his father slept, the Divine Son fled away from his house to prepare his own. For his Creative Flame burned brightly within him and would not be denied. But as he was leaving he saw from deep within his father's halls the Sacred Light shining dimly from within. He then entered the quiet halls, stealing the Sacred Light and the crystalline lantern within which its fire now burned. He then fled away like a thief in the night, across the fringes of that shining realm, and into the heights of Heaven beyond the summit of its peaks.

The Divine Son then rekindled the fires that burned within him, building a mighty forge to fashion his creations. He then placed the candle of the Sacred Light within its hot center so that by its fires was molded the golden walls of his great hall. The Divine Son then built many chambers for the children to live in, as his feverish mind had envisioned. Upon the completion of his great house of gold, the Divine Son stood pleased. But he did not rest, as he now sought to reveal to the children of the world its many wonders, so they might come unto him, enter his house, and dwell there.

He returned to Forest of Twilight. And there he found the quiet pool beneath whose dark waters his mother now slept. He looked upon the glory of the twilight tree that emanated so beautifully with its pale cast of silver. Upon the summit of that mound he then blew upon his great golden horn, summoning the Children of Twilight to come to him. He then watched as they came forth from out of the glades and copses below.

As the children came to him, they gathered about him, dancing with joy. They then told him they had for many ages dwelt in perfect peace in the dark forests below the mountains. They brought to him many treasures of great beauty they had made. And they asked him to stay with them and share in the rich bounty of the gardens they had grown. The Divine Son was happy and tempted by the strange tranquility of that twilight place. For it was not as he imagined.

But he saw that they were deserving of even greater happiness than what they had been given in those fallow woods. He then asked, 'Who among you will leave this forest? Who will abandon this dark pool and gloomy tree, and dwell beside me and the Sacred Light that now burns brightly for you in the golden halls I have made? Look up with your shadowed eyes to the shining realms beyond the highest Heavens!' He then pointed to the skies above.

The children then saw the clouds part above them. They then beheld a wondrous house of great beauty and splendor. And they were blinded for a time by its golden light. But its beams shined down so brightly that they began to reflect upon the pool and tree below with a sunny glow. They then cast a golden light down upon the forest so that the trees and garden seemed to blossom forth with fresh life and rich miraculous color.

The children of that world were amazed. They bowed before him, shouting that their Maker had returned with great gifts for them. For they had known long ago that he would return to them someday bringing forth new creations. Some among then said they would go with the Maker, for they longed to travel to the new home promised them in Heaven, and look with their own eyes upon the bejeweled lights that lay hidden there.

But many chose to remain beside the tree and pool, saying that they had desired only the cover of twilight. For the powers of the silver tree and its enchanted pool granted all that they now desired. In them dwelt the mingling of the world's lights and shadows in perfect harmony. And the eternal happiness that had bound them as one yet remained in the Forest of Twilight.

The Maker, hearing their words, honored their free voices, saying, 'To each among you has been given the freedom to choose your own destiny. Do so as you wish. Come with me or stay.' And he looked upon their troubled faces as confusion fell among them.

Some among the Children of Twilight left with the Maker, while others remained behind. On the mountain in great streams the masses followed him, leaving behind their forest brethren, until above the mists of the mountain peaks they came upon the shimmering halls he had made.

In that great house of many rooms they walked with quiet grace among the shining candles that warmed their faces and filled their hearts with joy. There they dwelt in simple beatitude beside their Maker, just as he had planned. And he in time told them that unto each would be given their own world, so that they might each be lords over their own realms. They then bowed in thankfulness to him. Then was shown to them the Sacred Light he had kept hidden in the shadows of his halls. Into their dark forms then came its shining breath, as unto their spirits did its light come to dwell, casting back the darkness from their hearts.

But after an age, some in his halls looked down with sadness upon their brethren in the shadowed world below. And they wondered upon the tragic act of those who had refused to come with them. The Maker then saw their sad faces, so that he too looked down with pity upon their lost brothers and sisters trapped in that half-light world. And he suffered to watch them separated from those they loved.

He then said to the children, he would return to the twilit world below and take their brothers and sisters from that dark place, bringing them to his halls. For many chambers remained empty that he had built. And he told them that his house, without them, was incomplete and forever flawed. They then looked down in deep sadness and shame.

The Divine Son then returned to the somber glades of the Forest of Twilight, calling the pale children that hid there to come to him once more upon the hill. In the garden where he sat the lost children appeared to him grim in spirit, as they too missed their sisters and brothers.

The Maker then said to them, 'My children, my house alone now possesses the last of the shining lights of the world. For unto me has the Sacred Light now been given. In my halls will its spiritual fire always reside. And in my house alone may your gloomy spirits be rekindled. For I too, like you, was once a Child of Twilight.'

They then came before their Maker to touch him and look upon his glowing face and form. But some among them came before him saying that he had now divided their people. And yet the hope of eternal peace and brotherhood still remained within the gentle Twilight Forest, their promised home. For the Divine Mother had willed it be so, long ago. Her promise had been fulfilled, they said, while his had not. If he so loved her then would he return the children that now dwelt in the Heavens back to the forested lands, their true home.

But by their refusal to join him, there was born in the shadows of the Maker's dark heart great anger and malice towards them, their stubbornness, and their rejection of his noble plans. He then asked why they would choose to live in the shadows of that dusky land in misery and isolation. Had they ever been free of the curse of the shadow?

Soon the evil that yet dwells beyond the Gates of Eventide in the depths of the Black Pit of the world would come and seek them out. And by their choosing of the shadows, they would soon be doomed by the dark will placed upon their spirits and the evil which would once again creep into their hearts. So to the innocents was revealed by their Maker the forbidden knowledge of the evil that lay beyond the forest in the pits beneath them.

But hearing of the dark spirits that lay beneath their feet, they ran from the Maker in fear, hiding deep in the forest. The Maker then returned to his halls in Heaven. He then stripped the Sacred Light from the cauldron of his house. And as he tore it away, there was heard a mighty screeching and screaming, and a bloody red light alone remained behind. He then returned with the light to the garden. For he had hoped that by this act the enduring beauty and glory of its light would be revealed to them, and their hearts turn towards it.

The Maker then held the mighty light above his head, commanding it to shine forth upon the forest, and burn away the twilight gloom of the woods. A great radiance then shone out, casting back the last shadows of the woods, far and wide, and turning the twilight forest into a forest of light and color, its trees gilded once more with trunks of gold and leaves of silver.

But as the Maker looked upon the brightened woods he heard the dark and gloomy waters of the pool behind him whispering, as they had done to his mother in ages past. He then went before the pool, as he thought he saw something shining in its depths. Holding the Sacred Light, he reached down into the clouded waters. But as he touched them, they burned forth with a great radiance upon their surface, so that the shadows of its dark waters were now filled with the essence of the Sacred Light. A bright white light was then thrown up from the pool and out upon the mound.

Seeing the miraculous change made upon the water by his hand, he went before the great tree and laid his hands upon its bark. And the Sacred Light came into its form as well, so that it also shone, radiant and white again. The pool and the tree then shot forth their twin lights onto the mountain slopes, so that its streams and valleys sparkled in the shimmering rays.

The heavenly halls of the Maker then glowed upon their summits like a blazing coal, so that they reflected their blinding white lights as a mirror, down upon the tops of the trees. The forests were then blasted with its brilliant beam, as the stars of Heaven were dimmed by its brilliance. And the twilight fog that had clung to it was burned away. The Sacred Light was thus born anew in the tree and pool, so that they cast forth their gold and silver lights again as they had so many worlds ago.

Then was heard a great bellowing and a terrible cry far below. For the light of the pool and tree had melted away the iron Gates of Eventide. And the shadowy beings that had dwelt in the depths in that abyss now screamed out in agony from the illumination cast down upon their formless faces.

The Maker and the children of the forest then listened to the terrible roar in the pits below as it shook the earth beneath them. The Maker then looked upon the Sacred Light in his hand and saw that only a tiny ember had remained. For what it once possessed had now bled away into the pool and tree upon the mound.

The Children of Twilight had fled before the blinding rays, into the deepest shade of the woods to hide. But the children who dwelt in the halls of Heaven looked down in awe and wonder at the scene below. Seeing the glory of the shining tree and pool, they desired to return to the garden they so loved. They then fled the golden halls upon the summit of the mountains, winding their great host through many canyons until they stood before the pool and tree.

There they knelt before the majesty and beauty of the electrum lights cast down upon their faces. And many wept, saying at last had the true powers of the tree and pool been restored.

But the children of that shadowy world had fled away in fear, into the farthest fringes of that forest to escape the light so that the Maker could not find them. Dwelling far away from their homeland, these dark children grew black in spirit and mind, hiding behind the trees and under rocks until their own spirits were filled with vengeful shadows. Their hearts grew hateful toward the Maker. And they desired to destroy the tree and pollute the pool, which ever blinded and burned them. For it was no longer their desire to dwell beneath its sterile fires, or hide in the brighter forests that had grown around them.

Unknown to the Maker, those dark children had sought the help of the monstrous evil that dwelt in the gray domain of the Great Beyond. There the Nothingness and Emptiness had long dwelt in misery. But the dark children came before them with many sacrifices of their own kind. Those terrible beasts of destruction were then freed from their prisons by those vile gifts.

By their forceful guile, the Nothingness and Emptiness then commanded these Children of Shadow to rise forth and wage war against the Children of Shining, their sisters and brothers of light who dwelt near the shining pool and tree. At last by dark magic and unearthly powers granted unto them by the evil twins, they rose forth slaying many of their brothers and sisters, until they came as a great swarm to destroy the shining pool and tree. By their violence they sundered them apart, polluting the well and chopping down the white tree. And so the Sacred Light that had burned within them faded again with their passing.

From afar the Divine Son saw the true horror of what he had done. And he fled in fear, back to his father's house with the last fading ember of the Sacred Light in his hands. But before his father's towering gates he stopped. For in shame and remorse he could go no further. It's then he buried the last flame of the Sacred Light in the rocks upon the slopes before his father's house.

The Divine Son then heard the roar of a great storm billowing up from the depths. As he looked he saw the Emptiness come forth to slay the last of the shining children in the garden below. He came to their defense, descending upon the terrible spirit. A great battle ensued, as the forest about them was obliterated by their scorching conflict.

With great will and strength the Divine Son unfurled his silver wings so that they were ablaze with a burning fire. The Emptiness then fell back beyond the forest in terror of its force. But the Nothingness had risen from his pit with violent and destructive winds, sucking away the spirit of the mountains, tearing down the golden halls of the Heavens, and evaporating the essence of the rivers of the wood with his very breath. And so the spirit of that world was laid to waste by that being.

But seeing the precious spirits of the children of the woods devoured, the Divine Son, their Maker, came before that monstrous force with great ire and anger to wound him. A terrible struggle then ensued between them, until the Divine Son was taken by that beast. For the Nothingness was eternal and could not be vanquished by any power under Heaven, save the Sacred Light.

The Nothingness had finally grasped the Divine Son in his great claws. But as he was about to devour him, he looked into his black eyes and saw his true birthright. And he saw the essence of the cursed heart within the boy, which was like his own. Seeing the seed of evil planted within him, the Nothingness then laughed. For he saw his true origin. He then flung the boy away, down into the abyss below. There the Divine Son fell upon the rocks and lay wounded. For in his evil mind the Nothingness had spared him for a purpose unknown to him.

The Divine Father looked from afar in horror seeing the rise of the evil twins once more. But seeing his son assaulted he came forth to aid him. But the sinister twins had laid a trap for him such that his heart would be tested. And by its breaking would he fall.

The Divine Father then came before the Nothingness with his golden chariot whose lights, like a million suns, shone forth. But the Nothingness spoke with bold words, telling him, 'The Divine Mother betrayed you, shining one. For she gave her love to another. From their carnal union was your cursed son conceived. For he is but a bastard child, born of her sins and of the secretive desire she has always kept in her heart for another.'

'For he is the child of *my* seed,' the Nothingness bellowed. 'And of my shadow and shade is his spirit forever after made. By that child's own hands has this world now fallen. For he was made to destroy it. And he shall rise yet again in many worlds after this one to destroy those as well.'

The Nothingness then came before the Divine Father in his final hour of despair, saying, 'Give me the Sacred Light of Heaven and I shall spare your pitiful life.' For the Nothingness sought to obliterate its radiance from this world forever.

Shattered by his words, the Divine Father said, 'I would rather die than surrender the heavenly light to you. The Sacred Light shall live again to bless a new world and banish you and your brother from it, as it has done many times before.'

The Nothingness then churned in the Heavens with great rage. His black storms then sucked the stars away from the mantle of the night, so that its shadow fell from the skies like great wings, down into the depths of the forest below. The star-children that dwelt there then flew to the defense of their Divine Father. The last daughters of the Heavens then drew themselves around him in a circle. For with their silvered shields and spears they sought to protect him.

But before the Nothingness they were defenseless. And so they were devoured wholly into his mouth. In his last fated hour, the Divine Father saw the supremacy of that evil being. And so with his last breath he called out to the Divine Mother, so that she might hear his calls and awaken once more. For he had placed in her the last hope that his son would somehow survive. But he fell before the savagery of the terrible Nothingness. And with him fled away the last merciful light of that grand Heaven.

In her tomb of cursed sleep, hearing the sound of the terrible cries that shook the earth, the Divine Mother awakened. Seeing around her a mighty storm of death approaching, she ran to the top of the hill. Before her stood the sad remains of the pool and tree. For encircled around her was a deep pit of death and destruction, which the maelstrom had wrought upon the woods and earth.

From the summit of the hill she looked for the lights of her children. But they had been devoured by the Nothingness and Emptiness in the last battles in which the Divine Son had fallen. She then looked down into the last waters of that sinister well of sorrows. And she wept once more for that which she had done. As she looked again upon its clouded surface, she saw only the dying light of the tree reflected therein. She then realized that in that pool had the fate of that world now turned.

The last child of the Maker's shining halls had fled from its ruin. For this lonely one had lost his way, and he alone spared certain death. The Divine Mother then heard his sad cry in the wilderness and called out for him. He then heard her call, and so returned to her upon the hill. But the remnant of his darker brethren had also heard her cries. And so had they also returned to her. Seeing their last shining brother standing before them, their dark hearts were then awakened again to love for their lost brother.

The tree and pool were now dimmed. For with the fading of the lights of the Maker had they returned to twilight's somber glow. The last of the Children of Twilight and the Divine Mother then held hands before the pool, as a dark cloud fell upon them. For the servants of the Emptiness had wrapped their storms about the hill to suck them away into their many mouths. The Divine Mother then commanded her children to hide beneath the roots of the dying tree.

But the children would not flee their fate, and gathered about her feet, taking up arms to fight the black spirits that had descended upon them. For they alone had remained to defend their mother and protect the pool and tree from that remorseless evil.

The Nothingness had descended from the ebony skies overhead. With thunderous words, he told the Divine Mother, 'I have slain the Divine Father upon the mountain. And thy son has been cast down into the pit of the world where he shall perish alone.' She mourned as his cruel words were spoken.

But the Divine Mother stood with courage and looked upon the countenance of that cruel abomination. It's then she knew that it was he that had come to her beside the pool in that lurid and steamy night long ago. And she knew now her son was of his dark and doomed seed. With malicious eyes the Nothingness then stared down into hers. He then bellowed forth with laughter at what he had created. And the last of the cliffs of Heaven trembled with its mighty sound.

The Divine Mother then realized the terror of what she had done and the evil that had befallen the world. She called the last of the children to her and asked if any among them would be her messenger. For she knew in her heart her son yet lived. And she sought to bring to him a message of healing, of hope, and of enduring love so he might flee from that world and to safety.

Then a small child came before her and offered herself up to the Divine Mother. With gentle hands the Divine Mother then held her to her breast and slowly brought forth her own heart and that of the child into a new form. And those two, chained together as truth and fidelity, formed themselves into a gray dove. This was the Dove of Hope, he who was named Hu. This bird she sent forth into the world, flying free through the suffocating night to find her son.

A last valiant battle then ensued upon the mound. The Emptiness had come upon their spirits unseen in the final fatal conflict. For it had sent forth its siren song which no being might resist. Then into its vile orifices were the children ripped away from the hill, as death strips the body from its ghost. But a few yet resisted and fled to the edge of the twilight pool where their mother still stood defiant.

The Divine Mother then came before the Nothingness and Emptiness upon the summit of the hill, so that the last of the spirits of the Children of Twilight could return to the waters of the pool unharmed. The last four children, now of darkness, then shed the raiment of their bodies. Their spirits then walked forth and entered the last waters of the pool, returning to its sacred and protective womb once more.

But one remained who was of the light–he who alone had seen the great spirit of the Sacred Light of the Maker as it once had shined, pure and bright upon that world. He then climbed up into the dying tree and hid in the last blossom that had remained upon its blackened boughs.

Seeing her children's spirits returned to the pool and tree, the Divine Mother called out to the Nothingness, 'Take me in your arms as you did so long ago.' The Nothingness then reached down and took the Divine Mother in his claws and carried her away. She then was thrown down into the pit of his evil lair. He then drowned her in the waters of the Black Pool that had lain hidden there for all eternity in the pit of that world, devouring her sad spirit into him.

The Emptiness then came before the darkened pool, shattering its rocks until its life-blood drained away, its waters dripping down into the illimitable void that slept beneath the ghostly hill. It then devoured them into its great mouth before fleeing away into the depths, full from his gluttony. For like his brother no deadly curse, godly power, or dire fate could stop the Emptiness and his ravenous appetite.

But the dove called Hu had borne the last hope of that world in its tiny beak. For if the Divine Son still lived, he would receive news of his mother by the tiny message it now bore. The bird then found its way to him. For he lay upon the rocks of a great abyss. In his suffering he was awakened by the dim light cast down upon him. For the bird had carried the last shining branch of the tree as a gift from his loving Mother. By that message he now knew it to be her desire that through courage he should rise again.

The Divine Son summoned forth the last of his strength from within his heart and flew to the fading lights of the tree that yet shined in the ephemeral night that braced the world. But seeing the destruction wrought upon the forest about him, he soon gave up hope as he knew his mother and father had perished. He then wept. For he saw what evil he himself had wrought.

He then flew to the mountains looking for his father's house. For he had hoped that the last ember of the Sacred Light yet remained. But seeing no sign of the mountains or of his father's halls he felt great despair. Then he saw a light glowing faintly within the ebony veil. There, under the rubble of the mountains, he saw the faltering ember of the Sacred Light.

He then knelt before it in sorrow. But from below the peaks he heard a distant cry. As he descended the slopes, there upon the rocks lay his father. Near death, the Divine Father lay gray and withered, his body lying as a hollow husk of his former self. For the Nothingness had stripped the Creative Flame from him. He reached out for his son with his shriveled hands.

His son ran to him. And they embraced as father and son again. The Divine Son then said to him, 'Father, I am sorry for all that I have done. I was blind to the truth and wisdom of your words. And so have I doomed the world by my pride and arrogance.'

But his father said to him, 'My son, know that it was the secret will of He that dwells beyond the Seas of Eternity that this world should fall.' The son then saw the light in his father's eyes begin to slowly dim.

The Divine Father removed the argent wings that lay upon his back, giving them to his son. 'Do not lose hope. From these wings shall a new Heaven be reborn. To a deserving child must these wings then be given. A new mantle of night shall then fill the skies, housing the stars of Heaven as they once were, and marking the advent of a brighter world yet to come.'

But the Divine Father looked again upon his son, saying, 'My child, the last of this world shall soon be devoured by the wretched beings that wait in the depths full from their carnage. You must bury me with the Sacred Light in a grave upon the mountain so that the children of a new world might someday find it. Long after my death I shall hold the light close to my heart. And there it shall remain safe from harm.'

The Divine Father smiled, saying, 'You were right, my son. The Sacred Light was truly meant for the Children of Shining, just as you said. Through its candle shall their spirits yet shine again.'

The Divine Father then told his son, 'Go my son with great haste to the garden. Return to your mother's pool. For in its waters still lie the life of the world and the spirit of a new one. Perhaps the children of another time and place may discover some truth hidden within its waters. By their enduring courage and suffering must they come to understand it and what it has long desired, or they themselves shall perish like we have. For it has brought down its will cruelly upon us.'

Father and son embraced one last time. The Divine Son felt his father go limp in his arms. He then carried his father and placed him into a shallow grave in the rocks of the mountain. He then placed the Sacred Light upon his chest, as he covered his grave-mound with stones. But hidden within the rocks shined out the pale light of its flame.

The Divine Son returned to the mound of his mother. There he cried out for her. But she wound not come. And so he fell to the ground, weeping for her. Beneath the dying tree now lay the rocky hollow of her empty well, dry and barren. He then saw where the last of its life-blood had drained away, dripping down into the yawning void that lay beneath its earth. He felt almost grateful it was gone. Made of light and shadow, love and tears, he did not understand how that dismal pool had both blessed and doomed that world. For it had strangely doomed itself in the end.

But as he knelt and looked into its cauldron, at the very bottom he saw a tiny handful of water that yet remained. He bent down taking the last of its waters in his hands. In them now dwelt the last of the life of that world, but so too the shadows of the spirits that hid within it. He then flew away on his silver wings as the last of that world was slowly consumed by the evil that had been unleashed upon it.

None remained who had remembered that sad world, walked its splendid wood, or had remembered the grandeur of the trees that once grew there. The terrible twins had begun to consume the firmament of it into their toothed maws, until even the inky shade that hung upon its skies was obliterated. The very hollows of space then split open the belly of Heaven as it collapsed into ruin before them. And the great earth beneath that world cracked and crumbled, falling away into the sorrowful waste that now consumed it.

Now devoid of trees, stripped bare of earth and sky, the last piece of that broken and shattered world floated alone in the malaise of eternal night. Overhead the circle of a darkened Heaven had slowly turned above the dying tree. The last of its kind, it had yet stood resolute upon the summit of its blackened and war-torn rock. Through eons of silence, unknown and unseen by any other living thing, its massive trunk and gnarled roots, uprooted by the powers of darkness, somehow still clung to the remnant earth upon which it once proudly stood.

Stripped of its bark, its dry husk withered away alone on the edge of that spaceless gulf, while the faceless death of the

Emptiness chewed upon the last of its gallant rock. Floating in the emptiness of the void, its plaintive cry echoed out across the ethereal winds in the depths of its mourning. For it had long resisted that terrible evil, though no spirit would remain to witness its final breath.

Ancient and pale, the broken tree had died. The evil twins then came and ripped away the last of its limbs. Its trunk was shattered into many pieces, until the last remnants of that mighty tree was no more.

But it had held upon its shriveled limb the last of its seed, keeping it close to its spirit until that final fateful moment. This seed the tree had hid from the eyes of the evil ones. For it had filled its only child and seed with the last of its love and life-giving essence. This life no darkness, nor light, nor earth, nor waters could breach. For the Sacred Seed was granted the first flesh and spirit of a new forest—the spirit of the True Tree incarnate and the essence of the Forest of Twilight that yet dwelt within its single shining seed.

Ripped from its limbs, the Sacred Seed was then cast forth by the father-tree, out into the cold and merciless gulf of space and time, across the timeless and ethereal waters that flowed throughout. By its cosmic winds and waves, was it carried in the formless void upon that sea, far from the grim eyes of the dark lords of that former world.

Only a ghostly space remained in the ruins left behind. But into the cosmos had returned the Spirit Divine to reforge anew this world from its own ashes. The seed of the tree had fallen into this world, cast into it by the rains and mists that rose from within it. It had then fallen into the Dreaming Seas, buffeted by storms and waves which could not harm it. Within the arms of the loving sea it was carried, past the blackened shores of Midnight, until at last it was thrown upon the spectral sands of Phantaia.

Ama then said, "So had the seed of the One Tree, the Sacred Seed, come from the ancient tree that had perished in that tragic world."

Ama then walked over and touched the trunk of the tree, saying, "By my father's seed alone has a host of new trees been sown in this world since that distant time, taking root and forming Phantaia, the Forest of Twilight. Know that this paradise was created by the One Cosmic Spirit for love of his children, those who he knew would someday come to dwell therein."

"But the Chieftain Trees revealed a secret to me, Ana. The Divine Son, the Essence Eternal, had returned to birth this world, hoping that the Children of Twilight might return to it someday and find a lasting peace within it. But the Essence Eternal has perished. You see, he has died so that we might live? But though he has left us, his spirit remains in this world, in the trees, and in us," Ama said, with fire in his eyes.

"We alone must decide our fate, Ana. For the Creator knows the truth lies not in him but in his Creation. The fate of the world lies with us. And so I fear we shall destroy this world, yet again, unless we the children can embrace the perfect paradise promised to us by Him." Ana then looked at Ama with wonderment and awe.

Ama and Ana sat together uncertain of their fates in that sad world. Gazing down into the glass-like waters of the spring, Ama said, "But the pool is another mystery to me, Ana. In the silver dews of Phantaia's first shining dawn, the sapling of the One Tree had been planted upon this hill so that he might draw sustenance from this pool. For in the depths of the hill lies the maiden of the spring. She sleeps there now within her tomb, deep underground, wrapped and encased in his roots. But they have not pierced the mold of her flesh nor broken the source of her waters which continually flow from her."

Ana then said, "Ama, I do not understand how this pool with such sorrow could bring life to the forest. Surely it must speak of its own heartache, its nature, or even purpose?"

Ama looked deep into the pool, as if seeing something Ana could not. "Yet the Secret Spring is a gift to us," Ama said in a whisper. "For she has lovingly sacrificed her life so that Phantaia might live. It is a thing of joy. Not sadness." With eyes closed, Ana then thought on this mystery as she wrapped her arms around herself.

Ama stood again and walked to the edge of the hill. "Only the Hawthorns of Kum know of the true purpose of the pool and its maiden. But they will not speak of it," Ama told her. "Yet should the pool speak, would it tell much more of its long life and purpose. But since the birth of Phantaia has it remained silent."

"But it matters not," he told her. "For the pool and the tree are now one. They are inseparable. The Essence Eternal brought them here, joining them together so they might give new life to his creation and guide the children yet to come. That is what its waters would say." Ana then looked at Ama and smiled. But seeing within Ama's eyes the same hidden fear, she came to him.

"But I fear for the One Tree with the visions that have come into me lately," Ama said. "The servants of evil that sleep in the Great Beyond shall soon come forth and try and destroy the tree. For its great radiance calls them to war. I know now that the warm lights you see emanating from it are not of the tree, but of a secretive fire that burns within it. And my sisters and brothers have long known that by its mysterious candle would the servants of evil eventually come to Phantaia to destroy it. Its burning fire calls them. And so I fear that the last fatal age of this glorious land has now come upon us. It shall soon come to an end."

Ama and Ana both felt the cold chill of an autumn wind swirl past them as the gray fog rose and fell over the top of the hill. Its moisture dripped from Ama's face and body. But he stood looking out over the misty valley before him, saying, "But Ana, hope yet lives in Phantaia, even in the hearts of the possessed creatures that dwell in the depths of the darker lands. For your grandfather told me, no heart trapped in the dusk of evil was ever completely free of the light of goodness which had once dawned within it."

Ama turned and looked at her, saying, "Ana, I feel that goodness yet dwells in your father."

Having finished his long tale, Ama now sat back upon the rocks to rest. He now seemed content. But Ama and Ana now looked into each other's eyes. And between them they knew that their time together was fleeting. But as Ama looked at Ana again, he saw sadness upon her cheeks, and many tears which she had hidden.

As Ana turned away, a single tear fell into the pool. Yet it did not stir it. For the water remained still and undisturbed. But her tears were not shed for joy, sadness, or even fear. She had hidden a terrible truth deep within her own secretive heart. And for this had she wept.

THE DYING WELL

Ana had kept a secret long concealed that she had not the courage to reveal. She had spared Ama's loving heart a truth that would tear his world apart. Cruel waters on a crooked course soon would flow with sinister force. For within her heart's corrupted state churned a well born of cursed fate.

And so had Ana wept beside the pool. But seeing many tears on her face, Ama said to her, "Hold my hand." She reached out and grasped Ama's warm hand in hers. He then said, "The shadows of our yesterday are fading fast, while a dimmer and uncertain future draws near. But the light of the present shines brightly upon us, and has not yet receded. This is still our time, Ana, though fleeting as it is. What happened to that dream? Let us hold onto it...and not let go."

Ama, resolute and brave, took Ana by the hand and led her into a secluded land deep within the farthest confines of Abrea. To his hidden glade of love he led her, to the place called Unaranna. Within its high walls of swaying oleander, he took his beloved, where neither the light of the shining tree nor the dark shadows of the wood would ever find them.

Concealed within the verdure of its lush and luxurious growth, Ama laid her down under a dense thicket of red roses and scented jasmine. There they held each other closely in the rapture of their long-held passion for one another. And love's old song, which so few times had sung its sweet melody in that sad world, whispered in their chosen hearts its wise and wistful words: *Forsake forever after the glory of thy former selves. Come together and be now as one.*

So were their hearts awakened to the sweet bliss of love, like the pale blossom of the night that opens up its glorious hues before the triumphant light of a loving dawn. In a passionate embrace they kissed. And to the rhythm of their pounding hearts and breath alone did they make love. Like the flood of a mighty swollen river, their desire for each other flowed wild and free within them, until their hearts like their bodies entwined were bound and wound together forever after, desiring never again to be free.

And so what their hearts had long desired, fate at last had sent them in that fateful hour. But fear of a foreboding future vaguely felt between them had cast a morbid light upon their desperate passions. They had known of the fleeting time they had together. So little of its precious moments yet remained, though an eternity seemed to pass before them in that hot and humid night.

With tears of joy, Ana and Ama drew their warm bodies together under the veil of the mist that wrapped about the hill. As the darkness deepened around them, they looked into each other's eyes and kissed long into the night. They then fell asleep in each other's arms and drifted off into a peaceful sleep in the lavender shadows of Abrea.

But about them rolled a foul mist turned so suddenly morose and gray. It hung upon the twilit garden like the putrid fog that fills a forgotten graveyard as it slowly sinks beneath the relentless rot of a bubbling moor. A ghostly figure had crept about the slimy mist, silent and unseen. About it was a dark cloak drawn, its hooked nose dripping with sweat. Looking about, its sinister eyes were cast aglow in a sallow and sickly green.

Its thin wrinkled lips smiled as it stared down through the fog at the writhing bodies of the naked couple. With its aged gray hands, it slowly reached out through the dewy air to touch the thigh of the boy. Its coal-black nails, sharp as blades, could easily cut him. But it stopped. It then drew its bony hands over the midriff of Ana as if sensing something. It quickly withdrew its beastial hands and disappeared back into the mist again.

It soon came upon the shadowy bed of the Murgala where, with its terrible claws it severed the dark stems of the black roses, and placing them into its leathery bag. It then fled away into the depths of the cold fog that filled the midnight air. But as it disappeared it left behind a trail of dark petals that led deep into the shadowy woods of Phantaia.

As Ana slept, it seemed to her that many restless nights had passed, as if she stood before the doors of sleep upon the threshold of a dream beyond which blinked the dreary eyes of a waking nightmare. For the scent of the black roses had now awakened, drifting out into the humid air that hung upon the hill. Her lungs were filled with its sweet and seductive odor. The peaceful waters of the pool seemed filled with that foul dew. For they dripped down about them, racing through the gardens, and fleeing into the river in fear.

From the depths of the valley where the waters now poured, the sad siren song of the maiden of Avalyr echoed through the twilight woods and into the quiet Heavens. But far away in the depths of that wilderness the mournful melody had been heard by another more nefarious being that had for many nights crept through its quiet mists. And it paused as it listened to the furtive tale bound within the strange poetic words of her song.

Ana had fallen into a new dream. And in that dream she was a young girl again, floating upon the Dreaming Seas, abandoned, and lost. But she was not afloat on her mother's blue ocean, but adrift in a foreign place, wherein the sky was dark like the sea, and the frothy waters white as foam.

In a panic she started to sink beneath that milky sea, when she looked and saw the hazy shore of some forbidding realm in the distance. There lay a pale undead forest, rising up from a black-sand shoreline, bathed in the blood of its crimson shadows. A frozen river tumbling with dark ice appeared beside it. But above it all stood a toothed hill of rock, upon which sat a wilted tree from whose bark a paltry light barely shined.

In the darkness she heard someone shouting her name. She then knew its voice. For it was her love, Ama, calling out to her from the heights of the hill. She came to him, and they embraced. But as she looked upon his face she saw with shock and horror that it was black and charred. And its eyes were red and bleeding. It then melted away, until she saw the distorted face of the Shadow looking down upon her, smiling with its gnashing and drooling teeth of jet.

She awoke from the horror of that visage, crying out into the night. Ama awoke, and seeing Ana she held her and stroked her hair and face. She then fell back into sleep as a more peaceful vision came into her mind. For she now saw the faces of her smiling children walking beside her in the Gardens of Abrea. Yet strangely, the colors of early evening had been cast upon its leaves.

But in that clouded vision she also saw their last days there where, swept by great storms, they were driven from Abrea by the gusting winds of a terrible evil. She feared for them in her sleep. Yet at the end, she saw them reunited. And she was with them in that final time of bliss. From the joy of this vision she felt they were real and no longer images in her mind.

And so, when she awoke, she was filled with happiness and hope. Something beautiful had awakened within her, something she could sense yet not see or grasp. It was something she had not foreseen. She must share it with Ama, she thought.

The mist about her had burned away. The sunny lights of the tree and the deep aquamarine of the skies had returned, beaming their bright colors upon her face again. In the valley below she saw the soft breezes blowing upon the tops of the trees. She then heard again the voices of their leaves as they fluttered in the wind. But the world seemed different. A new contentment had come over her. She looked down at Ama, kissing him gently on his cheeks. He seemed to sleep so peacefully.

She now knew he had awakened in her something bright and new, a love eternal that had always been. But she would leave him now, yet soon return. And so in secret she fled away, running through the deep green verdure of Abrea's sloping gardens and across the streams of Lilu. She needed to know something, desperately. She needed to talk to the trees.

Over the many bridges that crossed through the valley, she travelled, into the shadowed woods of Phantaia. On she ran, through the gloomy woods, until she had wound her way into the twilight forest of Phantavra. There she stopped for a moment, unsure of where she was. For she had sought a passage through a secret yet forbidden door. Ana was familiar with the strange portals that led through the hollows of the ancient trees. For Ama had shown her many dark doors leading to even more secretive places within Phantaia.

But there was one door he had forbidden her to enter. It had lain in the darkest depths of cloudy Phantavra. Of all the tree-doors Ama had shown her this one, he had told her, no one could enter, not even himself. But Ana knew where it would take her.

On she travelled for most of the day, under roots and over dirt trails fringed with luxurious ferns. Under the shadows of knotted logs she ran, jumping over tumbling mounds of mossy rocks, and under masses of entangling vines and roots. Within the gloomy woods there suddenly glowed the bright light of a sunny clearing. Ana smiled knowing she had found the secret door at last.

In the bright hollow of the darker woods stood the husk of a giant beech tree. Its smooth dead trunk seemed to loom ominously before her within the middle of a tiny grassy glade. This strange crooked tree stood like a towering white obelisk in the midst of the sunny clearing, its bent boughs broken long ago by cruel winds from its thick trunk. As Ana crept up to it, its cavernous black opening stood threateningly before her. She would hurry now, for she did not wish to be seen.

But as she walked towards the great hollow of the tree, she heard a distant whisper from the gloomy woods about her. She thought she heard her name spoken in strange whispers within the tops of trees and in the shifting winds. Before the dead tree she paused, looking into the dark woods that encircled her. All was quiet again. She then jumped through the cool hollow of the tree, stumbling through the damp air of its woody hollow, until she suddenly fell out of an even larger tree and onto the bright sward of a sunny hill.

Above her the winds were blowing briskly. And about the wide grasslands were trailing fields of daisies as far as she could see. But there on a great rocky rise above her, shining boldly against the light of the One Tree in the distance, she saw a small copse of towering growth. The massive silver trunks of a great ring of trees stretched up into the skies high over her head like the columns of a monumental cathedral. From a distance it seemed like the trees were delighted to see her, as they shook their leafy heads in delight above her in the crystal blue sky.

Here lay the handmaidens of the Maiden Trees, who for eons had guarded Phantaia's endless nurseries and the seeds and growth of countless trees that yet lived and died in the brighter realms of their forests. But so too had they come here to protect Phea, the great mother of all trees in Phantaia. For about her had they gathered so that no evil thing might bring harm to her or to those for whom she cared.

Ana slowly climbed the rocky and windy plateau where, on its summit, she walked into the midst of a quiet clearing. Here the handmaidens had gathered about a tiny field of delicate grass and flowers. Yet when she looked between the tree trunks, the small glade appeared empty. There in the soft lemon-yellow grass of its meadow she sat down and began to speak to them in the tongue of the trees. For she had come to this sacred place knowing they alone could help her.

But as she began to speak, there appeared beside her a strange presence. Something invisible standing before her began to shine within an argent light. Its then she saw materialize before her the silver form of Phea, the great matriarch of the Maiden Trees. Out of nowhere her towering trunk appeared. Her bark shined like a silver star, clean and bright, unmarred by time's relentless march. And her chartreuse leaves and pliant silver stems seemed to be unfolding before her, and ever-young with the new green growth of an eternal spring.

But Ana saw no face or eyes on her tall trunk. Nor did she hear any sound from the towering tree. For like the One Tree was Phea, both a living tree and yet a spiritual being. Then there came into Ana's mind the sweet notes of a voice, soft and slow. It whispered to her, "Blessed Ana. At last I look upon your kind and gentle face. I am Phea, mother of the forests. It is a gift given to me that you have found your way here. For I had prayed that you would come. Stay with me Ana. And I shall care for you all of your days."

Ana then felt the warm spirit of Phea flow through her, and felt her great face smiling down on her.

The loving words of Phea stayed in her heart. And for a moment Ana felt she could surrender to Phea. Her fears and her burdens had been so great. She could almost give up her life and stay beside the compassionate and loving tree. Dwelling beside her warm presence, she knew she could be eternally happy. But with brave words Ana spoke, saying, "Phea, I am scared. I have seen terrible images in my mind, and have been haunted and tortured by dreams since first I came to Phantaia. I fear I have brought some terrible doom upon this place. And this I cannot share with Ama, the guardian of the wood." The great tree stood perfectly still, quietly listening with careful thought to her every word.

Ana then gathered her thoughts again, saying, "But Phea, I come to you seeking an answer to an even greater mystery that now fills my mind. For last night I saw an image of my own children. And I need to know if my dreams speak of truth, or have been sent to deceive me as they had many nights before."

The sound of a gentle wind began to blow through Ana's mind, carrying the faint notes of a mysterious music she could barely discern. Then there returned to her mind the whispering words of Phea, saying, "Within you, Ana, are the seeds of Ama, the son of Celebreava, who is the shining spirit of the One Tree. His seed now grows in you and waits to be reborn through your loving children. For to you and Ama shall be born twins." Ama then looked at the shining tree with joy in her face. Her visions were true.

"Your children shall soon come into this world with happy faces. And they shall be as lords over our woods, the same as their father. And from them shall come the glory of an even greater creation yet to be revealed. For Phantaia was created for you and your children, Ana, and for those that would come later, dwelling here and calling it their home. This is why you were truly brought to Phantaia, to dwell in peace beside those you love," Phea said. Tears of happiness then began to well up in Ana's eyes.

Ana sat quietly, staring up at the quiet majesty of the mother-tree. She then told Phea, "Then my dreams are true. But I still fear for the future, Phea. For Ama and I have seen many horrors and bleak visions of things yet to pass. Surely if this vision is true, then these bleaker ones are not all phantoms of our minds?"

But Phea said to her, "Have courage, Ana. For some may yet come to pass, while others may not. The purpose of dreams is to reveal choices—two roads you may take. For your mother has given you the gift of freewill so you alone might decide your fate." Ana then smiled, thinking of her mother that lay far away in the seas.

But Ana felt troubled again, saying, "Great joy fills my heart, Phea, knowing of the new life that has been granted unto me. But I cannot tell Ama. For in his mind, he is now preparing to defend us against the darkness that now descends upon the forest." Ana then stood and faced the tree, saying, "The evil he will soon face I have brought, Phea. For I know now that my father, Agapor, has come here for a sinister purpose. And yet inside me has been placed an even darker spirit—something malicious which I fear has been designed to fight the will of my father and his dark servant, as the seas of my mother fought his will long ago. I fear it now seeks to rise up somehow and destroy him again, entombing Phantaia and the world in some watery curse."

Ana then stepped back as the handmaiden trees gathered around her in a tight ring. Phea's delicate branch bent down to touch her heart with its leafy hand. The trees then gathered their own limbs about the trunk of Phea. Phea then saw that within Ana lay something mysterious and profound.

The handmaiden trees looked upon her with happy, yet troubled faces. Phea then said to her, "You must return to the garden and prepare a secret place for the coming of you children, Ana, so that the dark beings that come into it may not find them. For it is your children who shall decide the future of Phantaia."

"But the destiny of the well that dwells within you is unknown to us," Phea said. "We do not know what hides in your heart, as it is closed to us. But the Twilight Mist which once dwelt in Phantaia had planned a hope-filled and happy life for you in Abrea. In this knowledge are we certain. For something good that was lost was meant to return to Phantaia, and thus be reunited with it." Ana looked quietly upon the trees knowing in her heart what she must soon face.

She thanked Phea, hugging her silver trunk, and touching the gray branches of the trees. They then looked down from their heights with sad yet hopeful eyes upon her. And Ana turned to look once more on Phea's fading tree, until its silhouette disappeared within the deep azure of the sunny skies above her.

Ana ran off down the hill, hoping to return to Abrea before Ama awoke. Soon would darkness fall. And she knew she must not be alone in the woods after dark. She jumped through the dark hollow of the great tree from which she had come. Stumbling again through the shadows, she fell, tumbling headfirst through the opening of the great tree trunk, and down into the bright green grass.

But when Ana opened her eyes, the woods seemed different. An odd silence had descended upon it. And the mists of evening had filled the woods, wrapping about Phantavra in its dense lavender cloud. It had returned too quickly, she thought. For it was not yet the time of sleep. Or had she lost touch with the weird and staggered flow of time that had always wavered in those ancient woods?

But a stranger fog had darkened the distant trees with its ghoulish blanket. It was an ominous vapor, the same one she had seen in the blacker woods of Avaras ages ago. On either side of her the spooky mist curled unnaturally about the trunks of the trees, hiding and distorting their true forms, as it drifted among them like wandering ghosts.

But as Ana looked through the murky haze she saw the forest begin to change. Quivering lips and ghoulish faces began to appear then disappear on the trunks of the trees that lay in the distant blue shadows of the woods. Ana then knew that the threatening evil of Avaras had returned to Phantavra.

As she ran through the woods Ana felt the hidden presence of another spirit following close behind her in the mist. She paused to look into the forest behind her. But as she did, she saw nothing there save the quiet trees whose lumbering limbs hung still in the mist high above her head. A dark dew had begun to drip down from the tops of the limbs like a soft rain. It covered her dark hair and face in its sticky sap until she could barely see the path in front of her.

Ana then tripped on a root, falling in a dark bed of moss beside the path. But as she climbed to her feet she saw black rose petals laid upon the ground about her. They seemed to follow the edge of the path then trail off into the darker woods. But as she looked up the trail she saw how the black blooms led straight into the heart of Phantaia.

Suddenly she heard a stick break. Turning around she saw only the mist as it curled like a phantom about the trunk of a nearby tree. Its odd and ever-changing form seemed to tempt her imagination. She then heard a dark voice calling her name, its sound penetrating the haunted air of the forest about her, yet echoing through the inner chamber of her very heart .

Ana then felt a horrible thirst come upon her. It overwhelmed her mind and body, as if she would die if she did not find water soon. But that thirst had come from deep inside her—from the new life she was carrying. It was they who were calling her to return to the garden. In her confusion, she panicked, running quickly toward the warm aurora of the One Tree as its warm light cascaded through a tunnel of trees on the horizon.

In the distance she could barely see the gate of the Ringwood forest, whose shining white trees still guarded the trail leading into the valley of Abrea. But their trunks were closing quickly, as if gathering as one to guard against a dark presence following closely behind her.

Ana ran in desperation towards the elderwood trees. But as she ran the thundering feet of some other being rose up behind her. And she could feel its icy breath close on her heals. She then jumped between the tree trunks of the Ringwood as they closed behind her. She then felt the hair on her neck begin to rise as the long trace of a cold shadow cast upon the ground around her began to fade before her eyes. She did not look back to see what had followed her.

On she ran, through the white forest, until she was beyond the last grove of the elderwood trees. Descending the wide grassy slopes of Aron, she fled across the laughing streams of Lilu until she found herself within the safety of the Gardens of Abrea. But the deep thirst that had come into her was now leading her to the top of the hill of the One Tree. But first she must find Ama.

As she climbed the hill, Ana soon came to the secretive spot on the slopes of the garden where she and Ama had slept together. But he was gone. In a panic she looked about the tangled brush. Not seeing him anywhere, she began running up the hill. Nearing the top, she stopped for a moment to rest upon a windy terrace. Catching her breath, she felt safe again in the glowing verdure of the slopes. For the dusk of twilight had not yet settled about the Hill of Abra. And the warm lights of the One Tree still chased away the murky shadows that crept about the distant tree line.

But evening's eerie mist had begun to float again upon the twilight air, climbing up from the valley below and over the tops of the trees, painting its lavender shade upon the canvas of that once-colorful landscape with its sad and silken brush. Yet it seemed to Ana that it was too early for the mist to return. And Ama would not have left the safety of the garden during twilight time. Ana's mind then raced with dark thoughts and sinister possibilities.

From the hill she stood and called for Ama. Her voice echoed out into the gloomy woods. But Ama did not answer. She knew he was not in the garden. Had he entered the treacherous woods alone looking for her? It's then her great thirst overcame her, driving her onward, over the last rise of the hill.

Ana walked the final slope of the trail leading up to the great tree. She crawled over the giant roots that had draped themselves around the tiny pool. There Ana sat, staring into its waters with her maddening and unquenchable thirst. It had possessed her now, filling her with delusions and strange desires she could not control.

It was the secret pool's waters she had sought. As she stared into the water, she realized she knew something of their purpose. Yet she knew even less about the meaning of that which lay within her own heart. And the perplexing nature of that tragic truth tortured her. Why had she come to the pool? Why had she come to Phantaia?

As she gazed at her reflection in the water she felt the relentless thirst again, growing with an irresistible force with her. The new life inside her was crying for its waters. In a panic, she climbed down the hill again, stumbling through the vines and bushes, trying to resist the terrible desire and craving she felt. As she neared the bottom she fell, rolling down the hill until she lay upon the dark rocks beside Lilu's tiny stream.

She reached down with trembling hands to sip its cool waters. But as she drank from it, oddly she felt no comfort from it. Her thirst felt even greater than before. Piercing pains flowed throughout her body. She then heard a horrible wailing from deep within. It was her own children again, crying out in desperation for the waters of the pool.

Weary and exhausted, she climbed back to the top of the hill where she collapsed beside the quiet pool, out of breath. She felt as if she had come to that strange well in a trance, where nothing was seen or heard, only felt. What had possessed her? Was it a nightmare spawned by some cruel spirit to torture her?

She crawled to the edge of the pool, looking into it with lustful eyes. There she knelt before the mirror of the little spring and reluctantly cupped her hands, slowly drawing forth the water of the pool into them. She stared at the purity of them, seeing yet an odd light hidden within them. She then placed the water cautiously before her lips, as she closed her eyes, ever fearful of it. But her thirst was too much for her to bear. She must save her children.

Ana then drank the cool draught of the spring, until not a drop remained in her hands. Instantly, she felt refreshed and soothed. For the crying within her had ceased. She then drew water from the pool again. Suddenly, she was filled with a feeling of overwhelming pleasure and release. Her mind seemed to have been cleared of all fear and regret, filled instead with a deep joy and contentment she had never known. She felt one with the pool, one with Phantaia.

She felt connected to every tree, plant, and living thing, though the ferns and flowers that grew around her seemed to have changed in color and form. She felt an eternal peace within her mind and spirit. For that elixir of life had stilled her heart and yet strangely replenished it. And the spirits that lay within her and around her were all at peace, joined together with her in some infinite kindred moment of boundless bliss.

She felt a spiritual sensation, as if the *capacity* for unending love and understanding, unburdened by the shade of fear or worry, had filled her completely. As she stood upon the hill and looked about her, the world seemed bathed in a miraculous glamour. For the trees below the hill seemed to have changed shape within the purple clouds that flowed about their feet. They now appeared as young children dancing in great unison, hand in hand, to the rhythm of some distant music rising up from the earth below. The trees of Phantaia had at last revealed their living spirits to her changed eyes. And she now saw the true nature of the secretive forest. For through the waters of the pool were her eyes closed, washed clean, and reopened again to the true joy of creation that had been hidden from them.

But that vision soon drifted away. Ana then returned to the pool and drank deeply from it, yet again. Her mind was then filled again with the visual pleasures of things unrecognizable, the secret knowledge of truths long hidden to her, visions of strange colors, and the secret spirit of the living earth set aflame by its own inner light.

When she closed her eyes, even richer thoughts came into her spirit that seemed vast and unknowable. She started to feel dizzy, as if she would faint. But when she opened her eyes, bizarre images returned to her in even bolder forms.

All of Phantaia itself, as far as she could see, seemed filled with great rows of children stretching off into the distant. With garlands in their hair, they ran in never-ending rows across the boundless landscape. She smiled as she watched them dancing in wide circles beyond the hill, laughing as they ran through the many valleys beneath the mountains.

The trees had all but disappeared, replaced by these smiling and giggling children of the woods. Ana saw the elderwood trees as they truly were, dressed in white, their beautiful young spirits prancing upon the grassy slopes of Aron. Their happy spirits had somehow barred the cursed trees whose empty husks stood silent and spiritless within their rings. Ana stood amazed at this wondrous sight. She now saw in a vision, unimaginable until now, what the One Tree had always seen—his own countless children endlessly playing and dancing about his feet.

The proud Chieftain Trees had stood tall amongst them, clothed in rich robes like wizards, their beards shining like their silver hair and eyes. Their many children seemed to flock about them, hand in hand, with unending laughter and delight in winding and ever-widening rows and circles. She realized that, like Ama, the trees too had hidden spirits beyond the leaves, trunks, bark, and roots that bound them to this physical plane. For they were spiritual beings, each of them blessed with a piece of the loving essence of the Spirit Divine.

Ana returned to the pool again and looked down into it, realizing now what it truly meant. Through those blessed waters Ana had seen with the loving eyes of the trees the true beauty of Phantaia's mighty creation and the glory of the miraculous spirit from which it was made. Phantaia was but one great and loving family, alive and yet ever grateful to its Creator for its blissful state, desiring nothing else but to live free and to be. That is all it ever wanted. Tears then came into her eyes.

As Ana climbed down the hill, a strange sleep had now come upon her. She wandered about Abrea listlessly, seeking Ama in the hollows of their hideaway. But as she dug about the bushes upon the slopes, she knew he was gone. She sat struggling to stay awake in her quiet bed, waiting to see his smiling face appear before her from the thicket. But he did not return. Only a sad mist remained in Abrea to wrap Ana in its icy arms.

The weird waters of the pool had drained her mind and spirit. Its intoxicating draught seemed to have dulled her senses and pushed her into a strange half-awake state, unlike the peaceful rest she had experienced before. And so for many nights Ana tossed about in her bed alone.

Then one evening she awoke in terror, startled by a distant sound coming from the woods below. She thought she heard something crashing about in the youthful trees at the base of the hill. She then heard a rustling in the bushes, something that seemed to lurk within the dark roses that grew above the falls.

The lights of the One Tree then suddenly blazed above her, burning away the frosty mist that hung upon the tops of the trees. The glorious hill was then freed of its shadow so that its rich colors sparkled in the fresh daylight dew. But Ana heard again a rustling of leaves at the base of the hill. As it burst through the trees, she then saw the mysterious figure. It was Ama. He had returned to her.

With great relief and happiness she ran to him. But Ama paused, as if unsure of who she was. Seeing her face he then smiled. And they embraced and kissed. "Ama, I feared some harm had come to you." Ana told him. But as she looked into his eyes, he seemed different. He felt strange to her. For she saw in him the depths of a new fear and anxiety newly awakened. He looked upon her in silence, refusing to speak.

Ama then took Ana by the hand and led her to the silver streams that flowed before the cliffs of Abra. Beneath the Falls of Bann they wound their way down the stone stairway to Lumlea, following its rocky ledge as it trailed off under the cliffs. At the bottom they passed the place where the spray of the falls had gathered in a cool showering mist before collecting into one of the many glowing emerald pools that lay before the many rivulets of Avalyr. Beneath the cliffs lay a secluded alcove that wound its way through the black rocks. As Ana looked in the darkness she thought she saw an ancient set of lime-encrusted steps leading down into the depths of the rocks under the hill.

Below the spray of the falls, rising up from the river sands before them loomed the white tree of Lumlea, still bathed in the pale light of the mist cast about in the sunny air above. She and Ama walked beside the beds of colored pebbles piled up around them as the cool spray of the falls fell upon their hair and faces. "Only in this secret place under the Falls of Bann is it now safe to speak," Ama told her, resolutely, "Like Lumlea, here in this alcove we shall remain unseen and unheard by both the spirits of the living and the dead. And you may safely sleep within the maidenhair ferns that lie thickest within the shadows of these cliffs."

Ama and Ana sat down beside the great bulbous trunk of the white tree. With fearful eyes, Ama then told her, "Ana, on the night you had left I had not awakened, even at the light of day. For I had succumbed to the curse of the endless sleep of the scent of the Murgala. Those roses had been stirred by the hand of something that had crept among them the night before. For I saw with my waking eyes the black blossoms cut by its claws.

"Seeing that you were gone, I had feared you had been taken by that being deep into the depths of the woods. In terror I took shape as Phanyan, riding forth through Phantaia seeking you. But finding that none of the Chieftain trees had seen you, I grew fearful," said Ama.

"But I realized in my search that I had gone too far alone into the grimmer parts of the woods. Soon I found myself alone beside the Black Willows of Esnes, who yet grew upon the dark and stormy cliffs above Avaras. Only those secluded and shadowy trees of the borderlands would know of the darker secrets that others had not. But they told me that they had not seen you in Avaras or along the numerous trails that led down into its wood," Ama told her. Ama then looked about and began to whisper.

"But they told me that a dark figure had come into Phantaia, something terrible that had penetrated the secret door of the fortress of the rowans. Iwu the ancient yew had guarded it from all intruders since time immemorial," Ama told her. Looking down in grief, he then said, "But they told me that Iwu's arms and legs had been ripped from the earth by the evil Connewe that had come upon him in the night."

Ana then said, "It breaks my heart to know the old yew is dead." Ama said, "Ana, I am saddened, too."

Ama continued, "The willows then told me that they had seen the blackened eyes of the Connewe's dark lord and leader. With him had followed a thousand demonic trees. They had risen up again to wage war with Phantavra, as they had in ancient times."

Ama looked with fear again upon the eyes of Ana. "But Ana, the willows told me that another more powerful being had come into Phantaia under the cover of darkness," Ama said. "It was an even greater monster which none had seen, only felt in the woods. For its dark form was unknown to the trees by day. It would only walk as they slept at the darkest hour of twilight, when the shade of its shadow cast a veil over their senses. It then followed an unguarded trail it alone had known. And so had I grown fearful Ana. I then left seeking Afa the father-ash, he who has slept beside the waters for many ages, deep in the valley of Avalyr. There his many soldiers had stood guard along its muddy banks unchallenged. For none had ever crossed Avalyr to Abrea for fear of that river and the strong ash trees that gripped its muddy banks.

"But when I appeared beside the river," Ama said. "I saw where his children had fled before some ominous and violent assault suddenly thrust upon them. Many of the once-mighty trees I could not find. Only their fallen limbs, ripped away from their trunks had remained, scattered along the shores of Avalyr."

Ama then told Ana, "But I fear for our safety, Ana. For just beyond the woods that stand before our lands have opened up many dark gulfs and cracks in the ground beneath Phantaia. They belch forth a foul fog that smells of death and decay, and things born of the undead and the underworld. But I fear something even more sinister hides there. Dark catacombs, which I have never seen before, have formed beneath the blackened earth, belching forth apparitions, strange spirits, and wailing specters never known in our lands. The lost spirits of the ancient world bring word of their suffering to us, yet a warning too. If what once has lain in those pits has now awakened then a more ominous presence shall soon fill all of Phantaia."

Ana stared in fear at Ama's revelations. But Ama told her, "I know not the meaning of these horrible sights, as I have not had time to explore them. But the forces of Oblivion have clearly returned to stir the Connewe of Avaras to war again. Yet something unnatural has entered woods. And it is this presence which most troubles me, Ana."

When he was done with his tale Ana hugged him tightly. Though she was fearful, she was grateful to see him again. She then told him, "Ama, I cannot think about all that you have seen, as I have sought for many tortured nights to see your smiling face and be with you again. I am just grateful that you are alive." She touched his lips with her fingers, for she had missed his kind and confident smile.

She took his hand, and with a knowing glance, led him back to the garden where they embraced once more in their secret hideaway. The bright light of the tree shined brightly as it burned away the last shadows of the night. They then ran down into the depths of the many orchards in the valley, eating of the rich bounty that lay about them in the sunny vales below Abrea. But Ama looked with curiosity at Ana as she ate. Unknown to him her appetite had increased with the new life that was rapidly growing inside of her. But she could only look on his curiosity as a hidden pleasure and smile.

For a brief time they laughed and played together as the young and carefree children they once were. And Ana saw how quickly their fears had flown from their minds. Like careless doves flying carefree upon the wild winds of a departing storm were their joyous spirits free of all worry again. For a brief moment it felt to Ana as if their terrors were unreal, just fading ghosts summoned up by the forest's changing mists, or illusions born of their own minds' clouded imaginings.

That night they both slept soundly within the safety of the alcove beneath the falls. The next day Ana awoke early. But seeing Ama beside her, with much relief, she fell back to sleep again. As the light of the great tree shined on the pools around them, they rose as one. She then walked beside Ama through the maze of the beautiful gardens above. Those idyllic days with Ama, she thought, might never end. But Ama had sensed a change in Ana, and in Abrea, that troubled him. But he had not yet discovered its truth. But as the twilight of early evening came upon their sleepy minds, Ama began to ponder its mystery.

"Ana, you never told me where you had gone the night you disappeared. Did you not enter the shadowed woods of Phantaia and become lost?" Ama said to her.

Ana then said, "My love, seeing that you had not awakened, I did venture into the woods alone. For I had sought in secret the trail to the forbidden ones, the Maiden Trees, which you had feared to share with me. It is only their wisdom that I sought. But as I returned to Phantavra's twilight trails, I too felt the eerie darkness of the woods descend around me. It is then I thought I heard my name called from the depths. But as I ran past the boundaries of the Ringwood, I felt the spirit of a terrible presence there, whose searching eyes seemed to follow me."

Ana then paused. "But Ama there is something important I must tell you first," Ana said. But before she could speak, Ama looked about the hill in surprise, as if a new sound was heard upon the breeze about Abrea. He looked up with squinting eyes at the elderwood that encircled them, as if hearing upon the whispering winds the sound of an intruder.

Ama then stood up and said to Ana, "Something stirs in the woods nearby. It has found the courage to come here at the close of day when the lantern of the One Tree still shines brightly upon the shadowy woods. I must take form as Phanyan and go discover the nature of this bold presence. I must confront it, Ana. For I now know that what was heard in the winds upon the tops of the trees was indeed a dire warning. Listen! A black spirit draws near."

Ama took Ana by the hand and led her quickly through the mossy trees of the river and up the winding stairs of Bann. As they climbed the hill Ama stopped, hearing again a rustling in the distance as the fading light of the One Tree beamed out its last rays across the rising mist. "Soon it shall dare to come even to Abrea where the light shines brightest. I hear its heavy feet stalking the dim glades beyond the elderwood. It brings evil again to this place, Ana. It has summoned the darker trees to rise again against us. A new war with Phantaia shall soon be waged unless I can stop it," Ama told her.

But he looked down in doubt, saying, "It seems impossible to me, Ana, that this should be. For only the spirit of the Limitless Void may command this evil. But his spirit and form passed away long ago." Ama then looked up at the One Tree. "The light of the great tree still burns brightly," Ama said. "Its unwavering glow is still untarnished. And so we are safe here. For no power of sky or earth, void or darkness, dares to enter Abrea as long as the tree and its noble pool still live. For they are married, Ana, their hearts and spirits united as one under this sacred mound upon which we stand. But I must go now."

"Please don't leave!" Ana begged him. "This journey is perilous, as many unknown things creep about the woods. I fear for your safety, Ama."

But Ama told her, "It is my duty to protect Abrea and my father's tree. I shall never forsake my responsibility. The destiny of Phantaia now rests with me alone. I will go and summon the oaks to rise to fight this evil, to defend Abrea before it is destroyed."

He then embraced Ana one more time. But she could not let him go. He then told her, "I shall be gone a few more nights, Ana. Wait for me in Abrea, beneath the falls that bathe the tree of Lumlea. There you will be safe. For that place lies nearest to the secret heart of this hill and its spirit. But do not go into the woods again. For where the light cannot go shall evil dwell."

"I will honor your wish," she said. She watched him ride away from her, winding his through the hills and dales below the falls until in the distance she thought she glimpsed his tiny form beside the fog-enshrouded river, far below. She watched as he disappeared into the tree line, and was gone.

The gruesome gray mist had now returned to Abrea, blanketing it in its solemn shroud. But the new life that had grown within Ana had drained her of her energy again, so that as she slept beneath the Falls of Bann, the great thirst was thrust upon her once more. But this time, she thought, she would resist its tempting call.

She slept for many nights in the maidenhair ferns of the alcove, the sound of the roar of the cataract above lulling her to sleep as it had done the night before. The quiet tree of Lumlea also slept, as if she were trapped in a spiritual realm of her own making. As Ana lay in the farthest corners of the cave, she hoped she would awaken to the sound of the happy footfalls of Ama beside her again.

But as she slept the unquenchable thirst had returned. In the middle of the night she awoke, bathed in a feverish sweat. That terrible thirst had filled her haunted mind with dark illusions and dire visions again. But the more she resisted its call, the grimmer became the strange shapes and shadows that crawled about the rocks and pools around her. Her mind became sickened by it, such that she could not sleep. For every hour she would awaken with great thirst and the relentless pull of the pool that lay high above her on the hill.

But in the midst of that restless night, she rose from her bed like a being possessed, climbing the winding paths that encircled Abrea. In the depths of the night she walked alone through the thick humid air, up the winding paths of the hill, until she stood at the foot of the mighty tree. Climbing over its maze of tangled roots, she found her way to the silver pool that slept there, cold and unstirred in the night air. She then dipped her hands down into its depths, drawing out the magical waters, drinking deeply again as she had before. In a trance she then returned to her bed beneath the falls.

For many evenings she had made her way to the pool to drink, as the days blurred into nights. But with each new dawn she found herself alone and unsure of where she was, or where she had been the night before. But to her and her unborn children had been granted a restful sleep, undisturbed and tranquil, unlike that first troubled night so long ago. And so by Abrea's secret waters was given to Ana many nights of peaceful interlude. Yet with each gray dawn she was still weighed down by the uncertainty of seeing Ama ever again.

Many days had passed and Ama had not returned. Ana often sat upon the rocks below the falls and looked down into the phthalo green pools of Avalyr for solace. But the next evening her troubled sleep had returned. As before she made the ghostly walk from her bed, climbing the hill until she came before the silent pool.

But as she reached down to draw forth its waters she saw that the pool was now empty. She then awoke as from a nightmare, rubbing her eyes, looking in terror at the empty well where the precious waters once had flowed. She then realized the horror of what she had done. For the shining spring's waters had been depleted, and yet had not returned.

Ana ran from the pool in terror. But as she fled down the hill, she saw that the light of day seemed gloomier than normal. She then turned to gaze upon the One Tree and saw that the bright light of its trunk and boughs had greatly diminished. Its white bark had faded to a tawny gray. And its leaves, once silver and green, had yellowed and browned, hanging limp on its many drooping boughs. The light of the dying tree now cast only the sad transient glow of eternal autumn upon the dreary forests and gardens about her.

Ana then saw about Abrea that, unlike most mornings, the mists that would normally burn away had oddly remained about the gardens. The lights of the great tree that once shone so bright in the morning air now hung low beneath the clouds that clung about the top of the hill. A cold wind now flew past her, blowing about the leaves and limp plants of the garden that drooped their dry and withered branches. A somber slate-gray sky hung above her, as if possessed by the long shadow of a distant tempest that had gathered in the horizon beyond her sight.

The gray fog now filled the lonely outskirts of the gardens, replacing the purple mists of twilight time. It began to slither its way about the dark forests in the distance, so that by its thickness no light or darkness could pass beyond it. Like a foul vapor of the dead, it seemed spawned from the very bowels of the earth. But what monstrous pit of horrors coughed it up, Ana dared not imagine.

Yet, with the dimming of the lights of the One Tree, there had returned a mournful, almost sublime state to the inner woods of Phantavra—a morbid spirit which it seemed to have once lost but now eerily embraced. It was as if the trees had willingly drawn about them the solemn pall of their long desired death, returning to the promised peace of the eternal grave denied them by the scourge of their suffering lives. For death like life was once a gift to them, stripped cruelly away. And to its grim summons had Phantaia now gladly surrendered.

Yet the black trees that lay upon the margins of the valley were not the ones she had remembered. They were not of Abrea's youthful trees or of Phantavra's gentler woods. And she gazed in horror as she watched the tops of the trees shift and shake as they moved about in the foggy forest. Ana then saw a faint flash of lightning far away in the gloomy horizon beyond the mountains. For the forests about the mountain slopes seemed to have surrendered themselves to the violent gusts of an unseen storm, bending their great boughs to the rhythm of its cold and calamitous winds.

A creeping penumbra began to glide over the Heavens above, covering the woods with its morbid shade until it reached the edge of the valley and stopped. Only the secluded garden and its great tree had stood apart from the odd shadow. For they possessed the last spirit of some inner font of life that they alone could still draw forth, and which could not be taken from them nor easily fade away. Within their wilted growth they would hold on resolutely and yet with desperation to their own living lights, as if gripped with a vaguely perceived fear, refusing to surrender themselves to the creeping shadows that now invaded their once-shining lands.

But with the disappearance of the water of the pool Ana now saw that the One Tree had begun to die. And the living nature of Abrea had slowly begun to perish before her very eyes with the fading of its once glorious light beneath the clouds. As Ana began to weep quietly to herself in the hidden hollows of the gardenias, its endless blooms began to fall like pale ash, drifting down and about her hair and face.

That night she slept beside the pool and would not leave it, looking down into its hollow rocky cauldron in doubt and fear, yet hoping its waters would return. Yet with each passing hour she would awake again with great thirst, staring into the empty pool, seeking its mercy and forgiveness. For she could not satiate the life inside her that desperately needed the magical waters that now were no more.

Then at a fateful hour, when the distant rumble of the storms began shook the hill, she awoke once more in the midst of a nightmare. As she gazed upon the skies, there in the distance, she saw a slowly-boiling blue bank of clouds, much darker and bolder than the others, rolling its way across the tops of the trees like a great tidal wave upon the sea. Beyond the valley flashed another stroke of lightning, much closer, whose delayed sound echoed forth through the stillness of the frightened air.

Ana stood upon the roots of the fading tree and looked to see if Ama had returned. But as she peered around the garden she saw that an ominous new shade now hung upon the ashen plants and shriveled blooms below her. It was not borne by their shadows alone, but thrown forth upon them from some new darkness that had approached the hill with the gathering storm.

It was an ominous presence. For the dying trees seemed black as coal, filled with a sickening shade that they could not shake. At the foot of the elderwood lay grim shadows whose darkness had killed the once-green grass that lay beneath their feet. Its once-vibrant color seemed stained, not by the shadows of the overarching trees, but from some artificial yet permanent hue of the nighttime skies beamed down upon it, an inky blot which no light could now penetrate.

Some power unseen by her seemed to control that darkness. As the shadows shifted and moved about, they slowly filled every corner of the woods with their deep blues and blacks. As Ana looked at her feet, she saw that the darkness had drowned out her own shadow in its black satin sheath. It's then she knew from whence the darkness came.

In a panic, Ana fled away down the hill and into the dark woods, desperately seeking Ama. She ran across the dry beds of Lilu, until she came upon the slopes of Aron. There she stopped at the edge of the still elderwood trees. She cried out for Ama, her voice resonating through the darkness as she walked cautiously through the wilted Ringwood.

But no answer was returned. Nor was heard the whispers of the winds within the tops of the trees. Only a still silence gripped the shadowy woods that loomed around her. But as she walked along the dappled trail she found that the usual paths she had known were now overgrown and unrecognizable.

Parts of the woods seemed overgrown and impenetrable, as if the dark forest had grown wild and savage, sprouting new sinister growths which had buried the living forms that once had filled it. It seemed as if the work of some gloomier spirit had now possessed the plants and trees, and changed the woods to its own maligned design. She tried to find a recognizable path. But not a single tree or landmark looked familiar.

Time seemed to have sped up in the forest causing the dark plants to explode in size, climbing over each other in a chaotic tumble of thicker, more tangled growth. Translucent, fleshy leaves and evil-looking malignant flowers opened their bloated black shapes and purple blooms as she walked past. Dizzying clusters of tendrils brushed against her legs and arms, their tenuous snake-like fingers reaching out from the rotted earth to snag her.

Massive malicious-looking vines clung to every limb and branch, suffocating the trees in their sheer masses. Tangled and thick, their black ropes had reached out to strangle their neighbors, encircling the trees with their hairy arms, wrapping every bough in their sinewy fingers until their weight bent low the imprisoned trees. The open spaces that had remained about the path were now filled with an unstoppable undergrowth of luminous fungi, sickened mushrooms, and dense spongy spores. It was as if the light of some dead sun had fed them, its wicked black star casting down its ghastly glow from the festering sore of a wounded Heaven. Yet radiating from within their ghoulish leaves and ghostly stalks was a darker gloom cast aglow and nursed by the suffocating night from whose shadows they were truly nourished.

Seeing the odd-looking plants Ana turned back in fear, fleeing through the slimy fog that now poured down into the valley of Abrea. It is then she heard a ghostly voice. It sounded as if the younger trees were whispering to her in the throes of their own death, reciting some terrible curse upon her. But the voice had not come from the woods. It came from the hill. As she stopped to listen she noticed it was a woman's voice calling her from some high place on the summit of Abra.

As she walked across the muddy beds of Lilu, Ana thought she heard the strange voice again, only louder. She then heard a sad weeping coming from somewhere near the One Tree. Ana ran up the hill as quickly as she could, climbing over the dead wisteria and honeysuckle, their dried leaves and limp vines crunching to powder under her feet.

Looming above her, Ana saw the gray trunk of the One Tree that once shined so proudly. And a deep sadness came over her. Yet, with the last of its faded lights she could still see the hilltop in the increasing gloom. But as she approached the tree she saw on the hill, beyond the fleeing fog that hung upon its peak, a ghostly figure kneeling beside the dying tree. Its back was turned to her. Ana cautiously approached the strange figure, thinking it might be Ama.

But as she looked through the haze, there beside the tree stood a young woman. Even in the dim light she was beautiful beyond words, with eyes blue as the shining waves of the sea, and skin white as the foam of the ocean. She was clad in a flowing white dress embroidered with accents of red gold and forest green. And her shining, ruddy blonde hair was elegantly braided as it hung down to her ghostly white feet. Upon her head was a shining garland of lilies and orchids, woven like a crown, framing her graceful face.

She seemed to be a being, not of this world, but from some other time and place. For she radiated a strange phantasmal aura that was filled with an unworldly, yet life-giving glow. She was not of the flesh, but appeared as a vision seen only in the depths of a waking dream. Yet Ana sensed she was a spirit of the earth and a being somehow connected to the hill upon which they now stood.

As Ana drew near to her, she saw that her head was held down, as if in deep meditation. Or was she mourning?

Ana stopped and stood beside her, unsure of the strange woman. The golden maiden then looked upon Ana with happy, yet tearful eyes. She then walked towards her, her small feet almost gliding across the earth. Ana then saw her face up close. It was perfect, peaceful, and soft. Beautiful beyond compare. And yet in her eyes seemed to dwell some mystery Ana could not fathom. For the spectral woman bore a profound sadness upon her face. Her watery eyes looked as if for many ages she had wept alone in silence.

The forlorn woman then spoke to Ana in a ghostly voice, saying, "You have returned to the pool. For this am I grateful."

Ana asked, "Who are you?"

The ghostly woman then said, "I am the Secret Spring who has slept in this mound for many uncounted eons, waiting patiently for the last of my days in Phantaia. From me have arisen the waters of the well that lies before you. And from those waters has the One Tree and the trees of the world been nourished. But the last of my waters have all but drained away now. For what essence of me that yet remained in the pool has now been depleted. So, like my own fading spirit, this precious font I once filled has now bled away." She then looked down, as if in sadness.

But Ana fell to her knees, saying, "No, I am the one who has taken your essence. For a cruel thirst possessed me for many nights." Ana then started to cry, saying, "I have taken that which was forbidden. For Ama told me not to drink from the pool. Seeing the wilted tree with its once mighty lights now diminished, I am fearful for the fate of Abrea. For with the dying of the light of the One Tree shall evil soon come upon it. Left unguarded, both the One Tree and its precious garden shall surely die. Then shall all of Phantaia also fall. Only Ama can now stop the dark spirits that come to destroy them."

Ana looked up at the spirit for mercy, saying, "Noble Spirit, Ama disappeared into the woods and has not returned. He must have known of my evil deeds and fled away," She then held her hands to her face in shame, pleading, "Please forgive me for all that I have done."

But the Secret Spring knelt beside her, saying, "Ana, you should not be sad. Nor should your heart be troubled. For these are things that have come to pass which I long ago had foreseen. At last has my own time in this world finally run out, like the golden sands that once poured with vigor from the Hourglass of Time. But the essence that once flowed through me had begun to fade long before you came to Phantaia, as it was made and meant to do. And so have I known that the waters of my life would someday perish, and all things sustained by them also die. For everything that has a beginning must also have an end, Ana."

Ana then looked once more upon the falling leaves of the dying forest and turned away in despair. For it seemed with each passing moment the colors of autumn, red and gold, had deepened, enveloping Abrea and all of Phantaia in the hues and shades of its failing spirit. And she saw in the great tree's death a tragic end to the world of which she had played a part.

But the Secret Spring saw her suffering and touched her face, as she smiled warmly, saying, "Do not fear the future, child. Soon shall new life be born into this world. For I like you came to this marvelous realm with fear until I found love. Yet strangely, unknown to me, I discovered I was brought here by a higher power, so that my own waters might someday nourish the young spirits that now grow in you." Ana then looked in confusion at the spirit.

The Secret Spring said to her, "To you, Ana, has been given a great gift. Soon shall come the time when your own children are born into this world, blessing it with their many wondrous creations and gifts."

But Ana said to the spirit, "How could it be that the pool and tree must perish so that my children live?"

The Secret Spring said only, "Ana, this is the great cycle of life the Essence Eternal, our Great Father, set in motion long ago."

But Ana cried, saying, "If I had known what would become of Phantaia, I would never have come here. For I love Ama as I do the very trees of Phantaia. I never sought to harm them."

The Secret Spring looked at her with understanding eyes. "Through your love for Ama shall the spirit of the seas and the trees now be united. From your love shall the spirits of the Children of Shining be born anew in this world. For it is the secret desire of the Essence Eternal who willed it that this be so," said the Secret Spring, smiling.

But as Ana looked into the compassionate eyes of the Secret Spring, she saw a profound sadness borne upon her gentle countenance. The Secret Spring then said to her, "But one task remains for you." The Secret Spring held Ana's hand, saying, "You know now what you must do, Ana. For you have known it in your heart for many nights in Phantaia, even before you came here. Within you sleep the Sacred Waters of the world—the *true waters* promised Phantaia before its very creation. You must make a choice soon. It is yours alone to make, as no other may decide it for you."

Ana stared at the Secret Spring, who smiled down upon her with kind and understanding eyes that looked deeply into her own.

The Secret Spring then turned away, walking back to the foot of the One Tree. There she looked up at his dim lights, which had now faded to a somber gray. She said to Ana, "My time in this world has passed away. I must soon depart it. For with the last of my waters now depleted, I shall soon perish. With the death of the pool, the last of my essence has now been spent and sped away. My spirit shall soon sit beside my father, the Immortal Clay, who dwells in the Lands of the Afterlife where all spirits of the dead shall soon safely rest."

As the Secret Spring looked down at the base of the tree, she told Ana, "But I am saddened still, Ana. For the spirits of many others that I love dearly must remain behind in Phantaia to assist in the making of this world and another yet to come. They vowed long ago to help the children of the twilit forest. I am most sorrowful for the fate of my brother, the Rock Eternal. He shall stay behind to guard the sacred earth of this world until its final destruction by the evil that hides in the depths. When the last spirit of the last child has departed shall he too be granted his freedom, sojourning forth to greet his many fallen sisters and brothers once more in Avredd."

But the Secret Spring smiled, saying, "My brother has many beautiful gifts and treasures yet to be revealed in this world. With his glad and happy heart, he forges these treasures, even now, under the earth. Someday they shall awaken and be found by the children of the world. But the flesh of their bodies, which shall surround their hearts and minds, he now treasures most of all the things he has made for them. For this worthy task my father had decided his son should do without family or friend to guide him, until such time as his works within this world were completed."

The Secret Spring paused, as if entranced by some deeper thought. She pointed to a place beside the One Tree where its roots had left a small hollow in the rock. There the poppies had grown, bright and red, within a small plot of earth. Ana then walked over and stood beside her, looking down at a small pile of tumbled stones from which the flowers had grown.

The Secret Spring said, "It is here that I buried my daughter Phanduan." She then walked over and sat beside the small grave that lay at the foot of the great tree. She showed Ana the tiny stones she had placed over her body, like a shrine, in the midst of the white roots.

"She died long ago when the world was young. I wrapped her tiny body and buried her here beside the tree where she would not be forgotten. Here she has remained in the cold earth alone yet near to me, her loving mother. For I have slept beneath her in my own tomb, deep underground, keeping her close to my heart, always. In this sacred plot shall the light of the heart of my daughter remain, close beside my own," said the Secret Spring. She then paused. And a tiny golden tear fell from her eyes.

With sorrowful eyes the Secret Spring looked up at Ana, saying, "I shall soon leave this world. And it is forbidden for me to speak of my child's death. But by my undying love for Phanduan I feel compelled to tell you of her sad fate, before my own spirit is forced to forever leave my graveside vigil."

Peering down with solemn eyes at the small grave, the Secret Spring spoke again. "I found my daughter's body in the dark roses that grow at the base of the hill. For as a young child she often played among their satin blooms, seduced by their dark beauty. But I had forbidden her to touch them, knowing that *he* had left them there to harm me and my children. By their savage thorns was she stuck and poisoned, and so had perished in the Gardens of Abrea.

"But after I buried Phanduan, her spirit returned, telling me that she had not perished from the dark roses, but had died for the love of the children yet to come into the world. For by the sorrowful song of the seas' own tides had she come to know of their grim futures," the Secret Spring said.

"My daughter then told me that she had left the Sacred Light she had been given in the depths of her grave so that the children yet to be born into the world might find it," said the Secret Spring. "For a time would come, she said, when they would need it. And so would they be destined to discover it buried upon the hill and use it to bless this world with its glorious light. By its spiritual fire would it then take wings again, chasing away the shadows of darkness and the storms of destruction that would come to fill it. And by its hope-filled nature would it replenish the lights of their hearts, and so stay the evil that has always sought to dwell within us all unbidden.

"My heart still aches, Ana, after all this time, knowing that nevermore shall her loving face and fair form walk this earth. Nor shall she ever know the blissful journey of a long and endearing life. For fate hath cruelly stripped her from that gift. But it brings my heart some solace knowing she has died so this world may live," the Secret Spring told Ana in sadness.

The Secret Spring stood up and turned towards Ana. Holding her hand, she said to her, "I must now leave this world." But as the Secret Spring turned away, she looked back again at Ana. Turning around to face her again, she held in her hand a strange ghostly goblet of silver and gold which reflected its wild prismatic lights upon the scenery about them. A great cauldron it seemed to her, beautiful and beyond belief, wide yet thin-brimmed, with pearls and gems, and covered with many cryptic symbols she could not discern. Its electrum waters glowed with a warm light, much like the tree's. Yet of the fires of a sacred forge, bound to another place and time, was its cup fashioned.

As Ana looked into its waters, she saw upon its frosty surface dancing lights and drifting shadows, and the faces of people and events alien to her and unrecognizable. Ana then became scared, as she had seen parts of this vision before in a dream.

But the Secret Spring spoke to Ana with a calm voice, saying, "You must now summon up great courage, Ana. For these images are of no other but the lights and shadows of your own spirit that you must now face. But within this cup flows the destiny of our world and the fates of many others that shall come from it. This I now give to you."

The Secret Spring then offered the glowing cauldron to Ana. Ana hesitated. But at last, she reached out and took it from the Secret Spring. She then saw that the face of the Secret Spring now glowed with a peace she had not seen before. The cauldron then suddenly disappeared into vapor before her eyes. And the suffering thirst she had borne for many nights was gone.

The Secret Spring gathered her dress, wrapping it about her. She then smiled, kissing Ana upon her cheek as she said goodbye. As Ana looked she saw the Secret Spring walk forth towards the One Tree. Within its trunk a dark door opened forth, as a blue mist billowed out of it. Ana looked with curiosity at the strange door. For it seemed different than all the others she had seen in Phantaia. The Secret Spring then turned and looked upon Ana with hope-filled eyes. She then stepped into the smoky door of the One Tree and was gone.

Ana stood quietly on the summit of the hill as the dark mist rushed past her. She walked silently to the pool and looked down into its dry bowl. She stood for a long time, uncertain and frightened, thinking of the words of the Secret Spring and those of her grandfather, which alone comforted her.

She then heard the sound of loud footfalls coming up the hill. It almost sounded like that of a wild beast storming through the garden. But before she could hide among the rocks, bursting through the clouds, Phanyan suddenly appeared before her. But he looked different. He was weathered and muddy. And his golden horn was dark and tarnished. The color of his once-splendid white coat was no longer white, but mottled and gray.

Before the blink of an eye the great horse had changed his appearance, back into the figure of Ama. Seeing him again, Ana was overjoyed and ran to embrace him. But as she approached him in the mist she saw to her surprise that his youthful appearance had changed. He was an old man now, with a wild shock of hair filled with streaks of white and gray. Upon his face a short but graying beard had grown, coarse and tangled like the tops of the trees that grew about the darker woods.

But he had wild and frightening eyes. She then saw that he had backed away from her in terror, as if he didn't recognize her. Some madness had come upon him. For he seemed to be delirious and in a state of shock. Ama stared from afar at the empty pool, walking cautiously up to its edge. As he peered down into its hollow container a look of horror came into his weathered face. Then Ana saw many tears well up into his eyes.

Ama looked at Ana in disbelief, saying, "This cannot be." But seeing her reaction at his appearance, he raised his hands to feel the grizzled beard and hair that lay about his wrinkled face. He then looked down at his aged hands, holding them before him. In a frenzied and crazed state Ama ran away, down the hillside until he found a tiny pool of dark water that yet remained at the base of the mound. As he crawled upon the rocks about the muddy pool, he looked into its dark water struggling to see his reflection.

Ana came chasing after him. But seeing him weeping before the stream, she ran to help comfort him. But seeing Ana again, he quickly jumped to his feet, backing away from her. "What have you done?" Ama yelled, falling to his knees and holding his face in sadness. She knelt beside him as he wept. He then slowly looked up, saying, "At last has come the time I have feared. For the pool is gone. Soon shall my father perish and all of Phantaia with it." He then looked up into the air as the brown leaves of the dying tree drifted down and around them. A cold autumn wind then grabbed them and tossed them about, throwing them high in the air above their heads again.

Ana then touched his wrinkled face. Like the aging tree on the hill above, she knew now what her terrible act had done. And she clung to his frail frame, weeping and hiding her face in shame. But feeling again the love of Ana, Ama's heart was awakened, drawn so near to her own. His senses returning to him, he held her chin up and gently kissed her cheeks, saying to her, "What was done is now complete. All is settled again in my heart, Ana. For we are together again. And for that am I most grateful." And they embraced.

But Ana looked upon his aged eyes, struggling to tell him what she had seen. For in that vision of the Secret Spring had hid some last truth and hope that the curse of the pool's death might not be in vain, and all that had fallen was not lost but would somehow soon be lifted up again.

"Ama, a spirit of the pool came to me bearing strange news," Ana said. "The time of the birth of our children draws near, my love. For it is I who tasted the waters of the spring so that they might live. And so by their unquenchable thirst has the pool perished. But the spirit of the well told me that its waters had been made for them, and that the pool had perished so that they might live." Ama then placed his hands upon her belly and felt the life that lay within her. Ama looked into her eyes with tears of joy as they embraced again. For that knowledge centered him, all uncertainty and fear now flowing away from his spirit.

But seeing the last lights of Phantaia now fading quickly, he looked up with sorrow upon the wilting of his father's tree. He then told Ana, "Soon the father tree shall die and I with it. For without the waters of the spring, we are now doomed. Without the tree's shining lights Phantaia shall soon wilt and die as well, and the forces of darkness and destruction free to roam the forests and gardens unchallenged. But now is not the time to mourn. Our time in Phantaia has run out, Ana. A great evil shall soon come and devour Abrea. But I no longer care as your welfare is all that matters to me now."

Ama then sat upon the rocks, looking off into the distance, his mind lost in the thought of some horrendous event. "But something sinister roams these woods, Ana. I fear it comes for us. When I left you I had travelled deep into Phantaia. For many nights I sought to find the trail of the black spirit that freely crept about the forest. But as I approached the borders of Avaras I found upon the lonely corridors of the woods the black petals of the Murgala. It was then I had known the truth of that evil and its purpose. For only a servant of the Endless Night would place them there. The Murgala were planted in Abrea long ago so that the Children of Darkness might find their way to its shining glades and bring their own shadow into it. But these petals had been left there so that some other being of great evil might find its way to us.

"I had followed the strange trail of roses through the black woods of Avaras. However, I soon lost its path, as the spirit had traveled without rest, as if possessed by some terrible and unstoppable desire it could not satiate. After many restless nights in those phantom woods I had finally slept beneath the towering husk of an old oak, whose hollow trunk was all that remained of an ancient friend. But I awoke to the sound of thunder overhead, and the strange glow of large eyes that blinked all about me in the dark. It is then I knew that the Connewe had risen again. I then fled away into the dark gate that lay hidden in the hollows of the forgotten tree.

"After I jumped through the portal I saw that I stood within a dead and blasted landscape, one destroyed by the winds of the Magra. Upon a hillside I watched the fading of the lights of the One Tree from afar. I then felt the weariness of age suddenly come upon me. My father was dying. I then knew the powers of darkness and destruction had returned to Phantaia to obliterate him. Yet strangely, they had known its end would come, not by their hand, but by the hand of another," said Ama, staring at Ana in curiosity.

"I ran with great haste on my four feet, racing to get to Abrea. But in the midst of the trees, I heard the feet of the dark creature crashing through the woods like a thundering giant. It seemed to be following me, tracking me. It was then I had known that creature had not been sent to harm Abrea, but to destroy me." Ama said, animated.

"Fearing for my life, I raced through the woods until I came before the rushing river of Avalyr. I then turned to confront the monster. For I had planned to cast him into the cold currents and let the river carry him to the seas. I then saw crashing through the trees a dark shape. Like a great serpent it appeared, born of purest darkness and evil will. It was like no other monster I had seen in both power and strength. But before I could face it, I felt the riverbank give way beneath me, and I fell headlong into the swiftly flowing river of Avalyr, travelling towards my doom at the falls before the seas.

"I had struggled against its flow. But as I swam against it I saw the lonesome Isle of Adda appear in the fog. And so I swam to it with all my might. I then climbed the hill of the island until I reached its summit. As I looked back, I saw no sign of the beast that stalked me except the rustling of the tops of the trees about the riverbank. But as I climbed the golden mound of Anadelling, I saw beside me the mysterious apple trees growing about the hilltop. There I stood before the ancient apple tree of Uyl, whom I had not spoken with for many ages.

"The aged one then spoke to me, telling me of his sister tree which lay within the twilight realms, beyond the farthest boundaries of Phantaia. In this land it said that I could hide and be safe from harm for all eternity, dwelling in the Lands of Mist within which grew the sacred glassy groves of Nemedd. For no evil had ever haunted those crystalline woods. It is then he showed me the secret Doors of Evening that lay upon their aged trunks. These portals they said could take me there, to the lands of your grandfather. For the mists of twilight time had flowed from them, their great gates opening only at the time of early evening's own tide. And so was the great mystery of the evening and of night in these woods revealed to me," Ama said, looking up at Ana with hopeful eyes.

Ana then said, excitedly, "Ama, I have seen this sister-tree, Kurtavla the tree of the white apples. And I know of Nemedd, the Lands of Mist. For my grandfather took me there before his death. Oh, it is a beautiful place indeed. For the children of the crystalline trees yet sleep in its wood, waiting to awaken when their own lands shall be reborn again. But so too is it a mournful land, destined to fade like the twilight itself. For sadly, he that rules it is no more." Ama then looked down in silence.

Ama told Ana, "That ghostly land is our only salvation, Ana. For I fear that with the death of the light of the One Tree, the evil of the woods shall soon come into Abrea to destroy what remains of the tree and the gardens, slaying what few living things remain here. Phantaia itself shall then plummet into an infinite night that never ends, forever after enslaved to its own immortal shade until the evil twins should come forth from the abyss to devour what remains."

A crash was then heard in the trees beyond the dark elderwood. Ama turned to look in the direction of the sound. "The beast has returned! It watches us from the woods. It is stalking us just beyond the Ringwood trees in the distant hills. For I feel the shaking of its great footfall and the breaking of limbs beneath its clawed feet," Ama said, his eyes wide and wild looking. "But it is searching for me. I feel its red eyes upon me even as we speak. But I sense it hath not the courage yet to enter Abrea. For the tree yet shines its last feeble light upon its face."

Ama then turned to Ana, saying, "I must confront the beast before it finds you. You must flee to the safety of the Isle of Adda. Soon comes the time when the Doors of Evening shall open up." Ama pointed to the One Tree, saying, "Look! Twilight time draws near, for the light of my father is fading fast!" And Ana saw the sad form of the One Tree as its faded trunk cast its dying umber glow down upon the valley about them.

Ama then said to Ana, "With the last light of day, evening shall come upon us quickly. But when the last light falls the tree shall shine no more, Ana. When its last beam dies, darkness shall descend upon us and embrace us forever after. Evil shall then freely enter Abrea and devour it in its iron jaws." Ana then ran to Ama's arms in fear.

"Go quickly to the river's crossing below the falls," said Ama. "There you shall see upon the heights of Adda the shining blossoms of Uyl, the ancient apple tree that grows upon its heights. You must wait for me on that shore. I will soon join you by the river's bar. We shall then cross it together. For I alone can carry you across the river safely. We shall then climb the hill of Anadelling that lies upon the Isle of Adda. There within the trunk of the apple trees lies the secret portal to the Lands of Mist. For the Doors of Evening soon shall open upon the crest of the isle. Beyond their gates our salvation lies," said Ama. Ana turned to look at the great tree as its last light began to fade to a dark amber.

Ama looked again at his withering and aged hands, saying, "I must go to my father's tree. Soon old age shall overtake me. I must climb to the top of its highest limb and take its last fruit. From its seed now rests the last hope of a new world. With his seed we shall plant a new tree, hidden in the Lands of Mist, and far from the prying eyes of evil. There in that undying land shall the True Tree of the world grow again in peace, cared for by our children, and far from the dark spirits that shall soon destroy this land."

The winds began to howl around them as the great storm grew near. Ama was about to leave when Ana grabbed his arm, saying, "My love, I have withheld from you a terrible secret. By the words of the Twilight Mist was it revealed to me that the Sacred Waters of the world lay hidden in me. These my mother had placed within me so I might carry them to Abrea unharmed. For it was the desire of the Essence Eternal that they be brought into this world for some strange purpose I could not comprehend."

But storm's winds began to swirl around them, throwing dust and leaves about, as Ana shouted, "But Ama, I know the truth now. For I was born to bring them here so that this world would be renewed and the forest reborn. They have since remained inside me, waiting to be released at a time only my heart would know. That time is now, Ama."

She then held Ama's arm, pleading with him, "Let me go with you to the hill, Ama. Do not leave me in this final hour. For my place is with you. Yet my heart is with Phantaia. I will not abandon her in her time of need. For soon I must complete the sacred task that has been given to me."

But Ama said to her in anger, "What would then become of you? What would become of our children? Those waters cannot be undone from your flesh. They are a part of you now and inseparable. Though you release them into this world, nevermore may you dwell therein. For you would surely perish. This you surely see, Ana?"

Ana then said, "I would risk everything to fight against the bane of evil and the uncertain future that stands before us in Nemedd. For the Sacred Waters were meant to be here, to grant something wondrous I have seen and known in the very depths of my heart. We shall all die if I do not make this choice. Phantaia shall die, as shall the world."

Ama pulled her arm away from her, saying, "I shall not let you perish even if our children should live. Nor shall I permit your spirit to leave this world, even if the destiny of a thousand worlds depended upon it. For I love you truly."

But Ana stood in defiance before him, saying, "I shall go to my death alone then and do what I must for the blessed children of the forest. For at the spring I saw them dancing about the hills and valleys. Do you not see that your sisters and brothers are dying, Ama? Do you not hear their sad cries? The children of Phantaia must be saved. It is the will of the Twilight Mist and the One Tree it be so!"

But as Ana marched up the hill, the winds died down as the skies grew still. Ama then said in a calm voice, "Then go and do what you must. I shall go and confront the dark figure in the woods. And though we both perish and our children with us, shall we at least have had but a brief moment alone with our pride and with the glory of our fateful sacrifice to comfort us in this final hour. Goodbye Ana."

But Ana stopped and turned to look upon Ama with sad eyes. Ama then walked up to her and took her in his arms. "Phantaia's time has passed. Do you not see the dying tree and the woods about you? Nothing more remains for us here," Ama said to Ana with dreary eyes.

Ana felt all joy leave her spirit. For she knew Ama was right. And soon would a malicious and unstoppable force come into it to destroy what remained. Then was heard from afar a great roar and gale like no other, falling about them from the Heavens, and burning their faces with its frosty breath. Ama pointed to the skies, saying, "The light of my father's tree is now gone. For the Magra draws near!"

As they gazed into the Heavens they saw a black cloud approaching. A frothing storm had suddenly appeared above them, its colossal vortex a force most terrible to behold. In the distance it slowly began to turn about the apex of the distant mountains. And the earth beneath their feet began to rumble and shake violently from its thunder.

"We will surely die if we stay here," Ama then said to Ana in the tumult. They saw its great mouth open above the horizon, sucking up the trees in the distant glades of Avra. Soon would the monstrous spirit come unhindered into Abrea itself, devouring the Hill of Abra and the One Tree, who now stood lifeless upon its summit.

"Will you go forth to the river and wait for me?" Ama asked. "I will," Ana said. Ama drew Ana to him in a last tender embrace. They kissed again before they parted, not knowing if it would be their last in that doomed world.

Ana watched as Ama walked away. She watched him as he climbed the gray Hill of Abra, making his way towards the trunk of the sad tree. She then looked away. With careful steps Ana climbed through the dried brambles that lay thick about the base of the mound. She was with child now and so walked carefully. Tired as she was, she wound her way through the dying stands of trees that once had sung so beautifully about the streams of Lilu, passing on across the muddy plains of Aron, then towards the river in the distant valley below.

But she had turned back briefly. For she thought she saw the last of the lights of the once great tree still shining from some hidden place about its base, like a tiny star hidden behind a cloud. It quickly disappeared in the black vapors of the flowing fog that now encircled Abrea. But oddly, as she looked up at the tree she saw no sign of Ama.

Ana had walked out onto the dismal fields of Aron. Where bright fields of green grass and daisies had once grown only a wide swath of muddy earth now remained. The lights that once shone pure and bright upon the white bark of the elderwood was now gone. Only a blighted ring of leafless trunks now remained. A pervasive melancholia had crept into her mind as she walked through the vast fields of dead grass and brush, making her way through the rolling hills that wound their way to the river.

From out of the black woods behind her flowed an inky fog. Ana stopped and stood in fascination as its snake-like arms drifted out of the forest, onto the slopes above her, and across the valley, enveloping her tiny figure in its smoky cloud. Suddenly, she felt alone and lost. And this uncertainty began to drain her once-hopeful and brave spirit.

Standing still upon a low hill, Ana was unsure of which way she should go. Closing her eyes she thought about Ama and the promise they had made. This time she would not falter. She then hurried through the putrid fog, running down the hill towards the still waters of the river below.

Between Ana and the river lay a dense thicket of drooping ash trees and dry brush. As she drew nearer to the thicket she heard from the fog behind her a strange voice calling her again. It was very faint at first. But in her isolation, alone in the trees, its sound felt somehow comforting to her. She thought for a moment, it must be the wind in the trees. For she could hear the storm gathering in the distance. She then heard her name spoken again and turned about to see who it was. Had she heard that voice before?

The shadows created by the flowing fog seemed to move around her and encircle her. Frightened by it, Ana stopped again, hoping to hear the voice again. For she had convinced herself that it was Ama. It then became a comfort to her. Even if it was not Ama, anything was better than the emptiness of the heartless night that now surrounded her in its cold dark grip.

As Ana approached the thicket she closed her eyes and plunged into its depths, climbing on all fours through the dense leaves and crumbling logs, feeling her way through the shadows cast by the trees, and towards the shoreline of the muddy riverbank below. As she made her way through the dense vegetation, she saw that the once magnificent and towering ash trees about her looked barren and dead. Their broken logs lay strewn about the forest floor like the huge limbs and legs of giants, ripped from their sockets.

In the blindness created by the darkness, Ana found herself suddenly tumbling out of the woods and down the riverbank. She had rolled down through the mud until she at last lay beside the cool waters of Avalyr. She gazed upon the mysterious Isle of Adda as it stood proudly above the clouds that hung low upon the surface of the glassy river.

But as she struggled to regain her footing in the mud, she heard a terrible scream. Had it come from somewhere behind her? Then she heard the scream again, like the sound of someone in terrible pain and suffering. Was it Ama? In her exhausted voice she called out to him. But there was no answer. Only the creeping fog had remained, silent and soulless as it drifted ominously through the trees above her.

Ana looked through the clouds, past the broken line of ash trees, and up into the black forest that encircled the valley of Abrea. There in the distance, beyond the Ringwood, she thought she saw a strange black form watching her from the edge of the tree line. But as the gray fog passed over the valley again, it disappeared back into the shadows of the ominous woods.

THE SACRED POOL

"Ama is it you?" she cried, as the dark figure disappeared into the woods.

But Ana heard nothing save the onerous silence of the suffocating night. For with the fading away of the light of the One Tree, a deepening and permanent darkness had fallen upon Phantaia so that nothing that yet lived dared move within it. Only the cold fog remained animated, its wavering sheet of gray drifting down and around her until it covered the valley in its morbid shape and shadow.

She heard again the crack of thunder. And she saw overhead the gathering of black storm clouds as they billowed down into the valley from the mountains beyond the tree line. Long fingers of blue lightning streaked across the skies of Abrea overhead, lighting up the tops of the trees and hills with flashes of white. The storm was quickly approaching.

But as she stood along the muddy banks of the river, Ana heard again her name called out from the depths of the woods around her. It was louder and closer than before. The voice echoed through the forest and across the sandbar, originating from a place just beyond the edge of the tree line. Yet the deep and sonorous sound had filled every part of her fragile mind with its haunting and memorable sound.

She turned to see where the voice was coming from, but saw only where the gray mist had parted before a stretch of trees that lay above the riverbank. As she looked into the gloomy woods she saw a tall shadowy form suddenly step out from behind a tree. Standing in the shifting mist it looked down at her with its black and penetrating eyes. Ana walked towards it but stopped, for she was uncertain of it. Was it Ama?

She ran through the wet sand of the riverbank, desperately trying to reach the gloomy figure in the mist. Nearly out of breath, she stumbled through the cold mud, frightened and desperate. But as she clawed her way up the muddy bank, the odd figure quickly disappeared back into the woods.

She struggled up the riverbank, until reaching a high point she fell forward, tumbling down into the thick bracken that bordered the tangled wood. An eerie silence seemed to pervade the forest. Overhead she heard the crackle of thunder, louder and closer than it was before. Its crisp white light flashed upon the damp trunks of trees and logs about her, which made them look like the bleached bones of fallen giants.

As the lightning lit up the forest again, she saw a large figure walking away from her, disappearing into the hollows of the woods. The strange figure then reappeared from behind a tree in the distance. It stared at her with strange reflective eyes that shined like gold saucers in the shadows. She stood up to run towards it. But it was gone.

Ana then heard the chilling voice again echoing through the trees. Dark thoughts and doubts then flooded her mind. She thought to herself, it must be Ama. He was hurt. As she stumbled over numerous logs, she cried out to him. But as she made her way deeper into the forest, she thought she heard the loud breaking of limbs about her in the shadows around her. Something else was there, encircling her, observing her. It was the trees. The whole forest was now alive and moving as one mass.

Lightning flashed all around her, as she dashed past the animated trees. Thunder shook the leaves and earth beneath her feet as she wove her way deeper into the forest. Beds of large mushrooms glowing with purple, yellow, and orange heads, cast an eerie glow as she raced past them. They had grown along a faded trail, lighting a tunnel through the black woods for her to follow. On she ran, following her chosen path as it wound its way to some unknown destination.

Suddenly the lightning flash brighter than before, revealing a clearing up ahead. But as she looked through the trunks of the trees, what she thought was an old stump in the clearing was really a dark figure. Was it Ama? As she cautiously approached the entrance, she saw the ominous trees gathering in the gloom behind her. But each time she turned to gaze at the slithering shapes, they suddenly seemed to disappear in the midst of the fog.

Ana walked cautiously into the clearing. A sudden gust of wind then blasted through the trees about her, blowing away the mist that had filled it, and throwing great clouds of dust and debris into the air. As she looked through the blowing dust at the strange figure, she saw that it was gone. She stumbled about in the windstorm, holding her hands to her face, trying to find Ama. For she was sure she had seen him standing there just moments before. She then screamed out, "Ama...Ama! Where are you?"

A strange man then stepped out from behind a large tree at the edge of the clearing. He was tall and dark-skinned, with a thick black cloak that wrapped about him. He had broad features, aberrant and demonic. For his damaged face and form had been worn and weathered by endless ages of violence and war. Yet he bore the sad aura of a spirit tortured by his despair, tormented by his own depravity, and terrorized by the impending death of the world.

Ana felt a chill come over her. For his great cat-like eyes had opened wide, glowing with a gold and ambient light, as he looked upon her face for the first time.

The tall figure walked towards Ana as the lightning from above flashed upon his weathered face, casting nightmarish shadows upon the deep recesses of his cheeks. She saw the horrible hollows of his black-rimmed skeletal eyes as they looked down into hers. Ana trembled as she saw within them the rise and fall of an angry fire.

Yet strangely, Ana saw within him a being like her, proud and determined, yet conflicted. For she saw in his face something restrained yet stained by his evil. It was a countenance that reflected the hidden pain and anguish of something long denied yet ever hoped for. She saw, that despite his terrible appearance, in him dwelt a sympathetic spirit. In her heart she felt a sudden rush of sadness and pity for him which she could not understand.

She stared into his eyes with great curiosity. For it seemed to her they still held a small piece of something she had seen in the eyes of the Twilight Mist. That something also dwelt in him. For as the raging fire within their orbs now dimmed she saw a delicate violet much like her own return to them.

The strange man smiled at Ana, staring down in wonder at the muddy girl who stood before him. He then offered her his hand in assistance, speaking in a deep crackling voice that shook the air around her, "Ana do not fear me." But she stood unmoving. Weak from exhaustion and still unsure of him, Ana backed away to the foot of a nearby tree that sat at the edge of the clearing. But the dark figure did not move.

Oddly there stood about Ana a ring of trees almost impenetrable. Seeing no exit, she began climbing up the wild roots and knotted trunk of one of the trees. But as she did, she saw upon its dark trunk the glowing amber eyes of the witch-hazel she had seen long ago in the depths of Avaras.

She jumped back down into the clearing, as the tree scowled at her with its black and hoary face. Bravely standing before the dark figure again, she said, "I demand to know who you are. Where has Ama been taken?" For she was certain she had seen him just moments before.

The dark figure did not move, but said in a deep voice, "I know nothing about your Ama." He then walked around her slowly, peering again into her eyes as he did. He walked towards her and lifted a finger to touch her cheek. But she turned her head away.

He only smiled, asking her, "Do you not know in her your heart who I am?"

Ana then looked closer at his face. She backed away a few steps from him again, wrapping her arms around herself. Shivering, she hung her head down in sadness. "Are you not my father?" she asked.

"Yes. I am Agapor, your father," he said, smiling. Ana could only gaze at her father with an icy stare, gathering her thoughts and feelings, still unsure of who or what he was.

"I have traveled these lonesome woods from a faraway land, enduring many struggles and trials to be with you, my daughter," Agapor said. "But I thought you were lost for all time. Come. Let us embrace as father and child." He held again his dark hand before her. Ana looked upon his black-nailed fingers and saw the strange dark ring as it vaguely shimmered and shined. Seeing her unmoving, Agapor lowered his arm to his side again.

Agapor looked upon Ana in frustration, saying, "This is not the way for a daughter to act before her beloved father." A darker expression then came upon his face. "You must come away with me," Agapor said, "far from these tragic woods of doom and gloom. For soon an unstoppable force shall come into the forest, desiring only its dying spirit, and consuming the last of its fallen trees. You too shall fall prey to its ravenous hunger if you stay here."

But she walked boldly up to him, saying in anger, "It is *you* who have brought doom upon Phantaia! For the monster that has for ages chewed upon its farthest cliffs was sent by you. It is you who command the evil hazels to rise again and bring war upon us. Father, you are cruel and heartless like the evil you command. I shall never leave Phantaia. I shall never go with you." And she turned her back to him.

But Agapor expressionless said to her, "Look at the forest, Ana. It dies a pathetic death by the hand of some evil unknown to us both. For by its own attrition, the living light has faded since first I came into this wood. That which sustained it, its own life blood, has bled away from the very trees and earth—as if consumed by its own children. It is not my desire that Phantaia should perish so. But the evil spirits that now creep about in the depths of the world have come to destroy it. The Magra were made to destroy it. In the end they have always won. But it is true, my child. The great storm of Yana was sent by me to pursue the Twilight Mist, my father, and drive him from his hold. For by my own devious will was I duped into summoning her." Agapor paused, looking at his daughter with deep sadness. He then walked about the glade quietly as if deep in thought, his heavy cloak encircling him.

Agapor turned to his daughter again, saying, "Do you not sense in your own spirit that you are like me?" Ana paused, uncertain of the meaning of his question. Agapor then said, "Our two hearts are as one, Ana, for we are of the same fallen seed. Though you deny it, you are a child of the Limitless Void. The power of its devouring spirit yet dwells in you. I too feel it. It creeps in you and hides in you, this will to destroy, to devour, and to drink of life itself. This one truth is inescapable, my child. This you can deny if you choose. But you cannot change it," Agapor said proudly. "For you are born into it." Ana looked down, hiding her secret shame. For she saw he was right. Its will had allowed her to destroy the pool. She had consumed it just as Yana now consumes the forest.

But something more filled her troubled and confused mind. Ana then began to shake as the cold winds of the approaching storm dipped down into the hollows of the glade and the boiling black clouds overhead poured over the tops of the trees. Agapor took off his great cloak and walked forward to drape it around her. But as he did Ana backed away from him in fear. Agapor looked at her with a pained expression on his face.

Ana then said, "Do not come near me, Father. I do not want anything from you." She then screamed out, "You sent the Shadow to slay me! Your own servant would have killed me if your father had not saved me. It was you that had abandoned my mother, just as the Shadow had said. Did you not send the servants of the evil twins to destroy her, as you now use them to destroy Phantaia? How could you do this, Father?

"You never loved me. You never loved my mother. You never loved anyone or anything!" Ana then held back tears as she looked bravely at her father. "You have now taken Ama from me. And so have you sought to harm the only one I ever truly loved," Ana said, heartbroken.

Agapor then looked away, stunned and hurt by her brutal words. But he turned about, his dark cloak flying about him, enraged, saying to Ana with eyes aflame, "These are all lies told to you by the Twilight Mist. For it was he that sought to fill your mind with these cruel lies so that you would turn against me, your own father, who has come to save you from the evil that now descends upon the woods."

"I loved your mother," Agapor told her. "For I have sought to save her from her tortured sleep within the cruel prison of the seas which your grandfather made for her. She is still trapped by its curse, even now. Like her, I was deceived by the selfish powers of the Primordial Ones, which have now used me to destroy the world and all love left in it. Have the ancient ones not succeeded in their cruel plans to divide us and destroy our love?" Agapor asked, whipping his cloak about him and turned away from his daughter, hiding his own tears and pain from her.

Agapor looked down in sorrow, saying to his daughter, "But none of my past, my mistakes, matter to me now. For the shining tree upon the hill is dead. And the living spirit of Phantaia has departed. Yet it was not my intention or desire that Phantaia should perish, Ana, or its light fail. I have come for you, my child. You are all I have left." It's then Ana looked upon her father in pity.

Agapor then looked into Ana's eyes again, saying, "Soon the beast in the heavens shall come to devour all of Phantaia. Even I cannot stop her now. So has the Nothingness that hides in his prison deceived us and won. For this reason I feel pity for the terrible fate soon to befall Phantaia. For the trees shall be ripped from the soil and their earth obliterated from this world. Darkness shall then creep upon the firmament that remains. A thousand soulless ages of night shall then rein here, until the Nothingness and Emptiness return from the Great Beyond to claim their prize once more."

Agapor looked upon his daughter with earnest eyes. He then said to her, "In your heart you must see that I came here to save you. In you, Ana, now rests the last hope and light of goodness that still burns in me."

Agapor then held out his hand one last time. "Please come with me, Ana," Agapor said. "Come with me to the timeless lands that lie beyond the Seas of Eternity. There may we dwell in peace. For a curse lies upon this sad world. The forest of Phantaia was created to eternally bring destruction and war upon itself. It is a doomed place. That is the tragic truth you cannot see. It shall ever after awaken the vile hatred of its immortal enemies that hide within its own shadows, until it is annihilated by them, again and again.

"Do you not see this? This world has fallen like so many others before it. It is time to leave it behind. Soon even the seas shall be sundered from the world. I shall then be free to take you and your mother away from here. You see, I have sought only to bring my family together, Ana. That is truly who I am and what I seek," Agapor told her.

Hearing these words, Ana was moved, seeing in her father a different spirit, driven not by a sinister purpose but something worthy and true. She then looked upon her father with kinder eyes, saying, "Father, I want to be with you. And I desire with all of my heart to see my mother's face again. But I cannot leave Phantaia. My place is with Ama now. For the hope I feel in my heart for us has not yet died. All I want now is to see him again and be with him. For this reason, I must remain behind in Phantaia."

But Agapor grew angry again, saying, "Where is this deceitful being, this Ama, in your time of need? Are you not alone in the world? Soon the face of an evil whose power you cannot fathom shall look down upon you with its cold and pitiless eyes and laugh. In me now is your only hope." Agapor looked up into the skies as the lightning flashed around them. "In the Heavens now descends the mighty maelstrom. And it comes for you," Agapor cried out as the winds blew about them.

A great burst of wind began to whip the nearby trees, blowing them about, and tearing the tops of their limbs away. Feeling its blast, Agapor struggled to regain himself. Then another great crash of lightning flashed before them, striking one of the black trees at the edge of the clearing. The towering Connewe screamed out in agony as the bolt sheared it in two, sending its shattered trunk flying back into the forest behind them. An opening had appeared in the circle made by her father's war-like trees.

Ana looked into her father's face, saying, "Father, I am sorry. I will not go with you. For my fate and that of my children remains here in Phantaia. Unlike you, I shall never choose the darker path.

By aligning with its evil will, you have brought a curse upon yourself and your family. You alone must now go forth and face the horror of what you have done—face the final act of your fallen fate. I love you, but my heart remains here in Phantaia. And I would rather die than be without her." Ana then fled away through the gap in the evil trees. Agapor stood quietly as he watched his daughter disappear into the shadowy woods.

Ana ran as fast as she could, her heavy breath casting billows and clouds in the frosty air. The woods about her now appeared bathed in the cloud of a thick blue shadow. Its bent trees with their crooked limbs were all that remained of the once-beautiful forest. With the death of the One Tree and its life-giving light, not a single green leaf grew upon the trees and plants. For the greener growth had been destroyed by the evil witch-hazel that now crept about in the far corners of the foggy woods.

Bright blue flashes of lightning lit up the forest floor around her. But as Ana looked within the slithering mist that poured up from the earth, she saw that the evil trees appeared to be creeping towards her. Their giant eyes glowed with a vengeful blood-red color. She saw upon their distorted faces that they all bore downturned mouths. For within them lay a sinister desire to do her great harm.

As she hid behind the dead trunk of a tree, they shuffled about in the shadows to surround her. Their black bloated roots writhed and curled like snakes in the mist as they rushed upon her from many directions. They slithered through the fog, trying to grab her with their long wooden fingers. But she jumped between their trunks and under their roots, fleeing on foot out into the wider hollows of the darker woods. Only ghoulish carpets of blue-green fungi remained to light the forest floor about her.

As she ran, she cried out for Ama in the darkness. Then from the depths of the forest behind her she heard Agapor's distant voice, as it echoed around her and through the trees. He was calling her to return to him, to leave Phantaia. But Ana knew that he had sent the terrible trees to grab her and bring her back to him. And she knew that soon there would be no escape. Without Ama, they would soon find her.

Ana bravely stumbled on through the blue haze of the nighttime forest, over logs and through great piles of leaves until in her confusion she realized she was lost. Alone in the woods at night, she was frightened more than she had ever been. She did not recognize the trees in this part of the forest. For an evil shadow had replaced the twilight mist that once filled it. It's then she saw a pair of green eyes glowing faintly in the shadows of a tree in the distance. It was the same eerie eyes she had seen many nights ago.

She struggled through the darkness, following the mysterious eyes. But they always stayed several steps ahead of her. She stopped to catch her breath as the thundering storm raged on in the distance. The voice of her father had faded away. And she was alone again with no light or sound to guide her. As she looked around she did not recognize this more forbidding part of the woods. Had she roamed into the dreaded lands of Avaras?

The dense umbrage of the canopy of the trees had gotten taller and thicker until it hid the flickering lights of the thunderstorms far away in the distance. Oddly, the demonic hazel trees seemed to have disappeared, as if in fear of this part of the woods. What few trees remained here stood far apart, like great towering titans not of this world but of another more ancient one. For they were monumental in size and height. Yet they seemed almost spiritless, sucked of all life, undead.

The green-eyed creature had suddenly appeared again beside a great trunk, glaring back at her as she plodded on. But the landscape had started to change, and she began to stumble into puddles and shallow pits of mud and dark water, becoming cold and wet. Exhausted, she struggled to orient herself as she walked slowly through thick beds of dark leaves and under logs that hung over the faint trail she had been following.

She then saw that the soil under her feet had changed. Beneath the rotting piles of moldy leaves and detritus, great cracks in the black earth had appeared. Staggering onward, she soon found she had to jump over large crevasses and narrow chasms, which opened up at intervals within the uneven forest floor around her. Thick masses of roots and logs draped themselves down into the cavernous openings that lay in the soggy soil beneath her feet.

She stopped and turned around. She must go back, she thought. She must find a path back to the river, or to any familiar tree or trail she might remember. "Ama..." she cried.

Suddenly, she felt her foot trapped by a tree root that hung upon the lip of a wide and sinister-looking pit. It had appeared in front of her, as if out of nowhere, blocking her path forward. As she struggled to get free of the root, she saw on the other side of the chasm the ghoulish figure, its eyes burning bright with a sickly green as it stared at her. The root then tightened around her ankle, so that she fell forward into the dark opening in the earth. But she caught herself from falling, grabbing onto the rotten roots of a nearby tree that hung down into the pit.

As she climbed up the tangled mesh of slippery roots and black limbs that hung down into the pit, she looked down into its dark depths and saw the enormous size of its opening. Lying in the midst of that wicked and wasteful wilderness, she now hung before an immense and yawning chasm. A putrid vapor carrying the foul odor of rotting and decaying flesh belched forth from out of its dark and decadent mouth. It was a truly pit of death. And Ana became scared.

But as she looked about her she saw around its rim a cluster of ancient willows hanging half-dead and unmoving, their drooping roots and limbs bending themselves down into the darkness, as if seeking the source of some dark nourishment in the depths below. As she peered down into the shadows she saw that their large gray roots had clung to the walls of the pit, diving down into its farthest depths towards some unseen source of water.

Fearful of what lay hidden in the darkness below, Ana began to climb up the roots that dangled around her, trying to reach the forest floor. She would find a way out of this netherworld of death and decay, and face the evil witch-hazels that had sought her. For she would rather face her father than die in this awful place.

But as she began to pull herself up from the edge of the pit, the rotten roots gave way around her. Into the darkness of the black orifice she fell, falling faster and faster, until she landed into a great pile of dirt and leaves at the bottom. A waterfall of refuse then rained down upon her from the forest above, burying her in a grave of debris and earth. Ana then fell unconscious, her mind drifting away into an empty but peaceful place. Her spirit had surrendered to the darkness at last. She would give herself up to her grave, drifting off into the eternal sleep that is death.

She thought she heard the ghostly voice of Ama, calling her from some unknown land of the dead. She could see his smiling face aglow in the shining light of that new spiritual realm, looking down upon her on some forlorn beach, where silent silver ships sat waiting, ready to carry them to the spirit-lands that lay beyond its ghostly shores.

Ana felt that she was but a phantom adrift upon a silent sea. But she had awoken, as from a horrible dream, back into a frightful place of infinite darkness. In a panic, she began to climb forth from the cold earth, gasping for air and clawing her way out of the dirt and rot that had fallen from the heights above. Erupting from the mound, she struggled to orient herself. But as her eyes adjusted she saw she was at the bottom of a great pit deep beneath Phantaia.

High above her Ana could still hear the faint thunder of the storms that were now ravaging the woods of Phantaia. Its howling winds barreled down into the depths of the pit, whose rocky walls stretched high above her head. She then saw a massive rotting stone stairway that spiraled up and around the walls of the pit, as it wound its way up to the surface high above her.

But a dim light had been cast from some unseen source hidden in the darkness behind her. It seemed to throw its unnatural colors about the walls and floor like the moving reflections cast by water. Ana crawled down from the pile of earth and leaves. But as she did she saw the floor of the pit was filled with the skulls and bones of strange beings and beasts of some other place and time.

Frightened, she ran to the stairs hoping to make it back to the surface high above.

But as she began to climb the stairs she heard a ghostly voice. She stopped and turned back to see what it was. As she left the stairs of the pit, she saw that she stood at the edge of a giant cavern that stretched far and away into the shadows of the underworld. Odd phosphorescent growths clung about its roof and walls in sheets and masses, throwing their eerie colors about the cavern. They appeared almost sickly in hue—of washed-out pink, white and gray, acrid orange and deep violet. A pale vapor writhed about in the still air, lit up by the morbid colors cast upon it, until its wisps dissipated within the cavernous heights above her.

A thick layer of dust lay upon the carved stone of the ancient floor. As Ana crept into the cavern, its foul dust billowed with the slightest footstep. She then heard the crunch of dried bones, and saw at her feet the black crust of countless layers of shed blood splattered about the floor and walls. The dried corpses and shattered skulls, broken weapons, and battered armor of slain creatures and figures lay piled up in its farthest corners. She saw that untold violence and conflict had been committed here, undisturbed since time immemorial.

But in the middle of the great cavern she saw an even stranger sight. For in the middle of the cave lay a large pool, dark and foreboding, its slimy black water lying stagnant and still in a stone basin carved within the center of the floor. From within its poisonous waters ghostly vapors had arisen, swirling upon its oily surface like a potion of dark enchantment. It cast an eerie glow as the shining fungi reflected their colors upon its dull black surface.

To Ana the dark pool seemed ancient beyond all knowledge, older still than the well of Abrea. And the smell of death and decay seemed to hang above its quivering, almost gelatinous water. It was as if some terrible being had perished there, its sinister essence now sleeping alone within its slimy depths. For she felt the presence of some ancient spirit hidden within—something hate-filled, vengeful, and maligned towards both the living and the dead. Its radiating malevolence seemed to pervade her own heart and spirit such that she began to feel nauseous and ill.

Yet something inside Ana drew her towards the dark water. She crept cautiously up to the edge of the pool. As she gazed into its clouded waters she saw strange murky images bubbling up within it, as if by her presence alone they had been unleashed from some nightmare of the mind. Many haunted visions and horrors flooded into her imagination, things born of distant worlds, conflicts ancient and indescribable, heroic beings, magical beasts, enchanted relics, strange events, lost causes, victories, and fabulous histories stretching back in time. She saw people filled with the joy of their happy lives, dancing as one together with their many children. But others she saw cruelly slain in the prime of their youth, falling in desperate conflicts borne up by the dreadful cataclysms of endless and tragic wars.

As she looked down into its brooding depths, she became entranced by its strange tale of woe, desiring to know more. A part of her spirit felt drawn to the tragic faces that appeared before her in the water. She felt pulled into their plight by a force uncontrollable that crept within the pool itself. Like the seductive wine of a forbidden goblet, she desired it—a perverse desire for something that lay corrupted and foul, lustful and salacious within it and within her.

Ana stood before the pool, her eyes turning dark. She would undress herself before it and enter it, letting it take her. Her body desired it, to dive into its black waters, to return to it and reunite with the manly forms that she saw spread before her. She would embrace the strongest among them, the handsome one she saw hiding within its erotic depths.

But as Ana began to slip her raiment from her body, the oppressive stillness of her muddied mind was broken. For something more sinister began rising up within the pool's depths as it began to bubble violently. All of a sudden it stopped. For the waters seemed to arrest themselves, resisting and lying still again as its dark images melted away from her sight.

Ana then saw the faint glow of a bright star rise up slowly from center of the pool. The face of an elegant dark woman then appeared upon its shimmering surface. She seemed to be a beautiful queen, a mother of darkness bathed in shadows. Her hair and eyes were darker than the darkest night. And she wore a magnificent tiara of jet with a black veil partly covering her face.

The ghostly woman held out her hand to Ana, imploring her, as if trying to tell her something. Ana saw her lips moving, but her voice seemed muffled by some force beyond her own control. They were words of something forbidden, mysterious, and yet unresolved. She seemed to be longing for something long desired and disturbingly profound. Yet the vision seemed unreal, even less a dream than an illusion of her mind's inner eye.

But as Ana reached out to touch her hand, she felt something powerful break the surface of the pool in a violent fashion. Ana fell back as a great tower of dark water burst forth from within the pool. A boiling column of blood-red water then gushed up from below, shooting high up into the cavern. But as the spray fell about her, the pool returned to calm again. It lay still, simmering and seething in its own blood with a perverse delight.

But from out of the middle of the pool climbed a monstrous form whose horror her worst nightmares could not have fashioned. A great amorphous cloud, ghostly and gray, filled the air above the water. Like an ever-changing storm born of flesh and mist, it seemed to be writhing and wrestling within itself, crying out in the torture of its own suffering existence. It struggled at first to form itself, as if some other being was battling it from below. It then broke free of the pool, taking the form of a boiling tempest from which sprang tendrils of cascading red lightning that cast about the cavern, blasting and shattering the carved and crumbling stonework around her.

Hovering in the heights of the cavern, the monstrous spirit took shape as a bulging blob, its many eyes opening at once, staring down at the small girl. But it began to shift again, massing itself into different shapes as if searching for one more desirable. At first she saw in the cloud a great white hawk, its pale wings outstretched. Then she saw a demon, dark, bat-winged, and vile. It then took the white bird and black demon, merging them into itself and forming them into a mighty dragon that shined with scales of gold and silver. A being born of great musculature and strength, it had a golden crown upon its head, with many sharp horns and mangled teeth that seemed to grow forth and crowd its fanged mouth.

But this form it also quickly abandoned. As she looked on, its boiling shape had shifted again into the head of the terrible Shadow, growing larger and larger until only its wide warped face looked down on her own, smiling from the heights of the cavern with its long wiry teeth. Changing quickly again, she saw before her a spinning wheel that swirled and twisted faster and faster over her head like the storms of the Magra. Its throbbing vortex thrust itself down to swallow her. Ana then cowered on the ground, covering her face in terror. But the maelstrom had slowed and stopped until it had dissipated in the air overhead. The cavern then lay quiet once more.

The great cloud then reformed, slowly gathering its many appendages back into itself, swirling them about its hot center until a familiar figure began to take shape. Drifting over the waters stood the figure of her mother, her soft countenance staring down at her as the drapery of her ocean dress flowed behind her. She stood with arms outstretched for her child. But Ana looked away, for her heart could not bear the pain of seeing her image.

But hearing her mother's voice again, she reached out to her. But knowing in her heart it was an illusion, she turned away again. Gathering her courage, Ana then stood before the vast cloud, saying, "Who is it that has come forth with my mother's face? For I know not the meaning of this strange place or perceive the purpose of the strange visions summoned up to haunt me."

A booming voice then came into the image, saying, "Does this form please you?"

Ana said, "I know not why you torture me so with false images of those I love."

The being then spoke in a commanding voice, saying, "I have taken the shape of that which dwells in your earliest memory, that which you trust most. I am the ancient child of the Evil One, whose broken spirit is no more. I am that which sleeps in the pool you see before you, and in the darkest depths of the world."

Ana stood upon the slippery slabs of stone that lay beside the pool, saying to the gray spirit, "You are not of this pool or this world. I know who you are. You are the devouring spirit of the Great Beyond, that malicious being who hides in the bowels of the world like a coward. You are that which devoured the flesh of your own mother. And you are that which has destroyed countless worlds like this one, consuming the living spirits of the innocent children that once had filled them.

"You are the Nothingness!" yelled Ana, as the waters of the pool quivered in the darkness.

The Nothingness stared down at the girl, gathering its malevolent spirit and mind into itself. It then said, "You have been a most inquisitive child, knowledgeable and wise, but naive. For many questions in your mind yet remain unanswered, dark truths yet to be revealed to you. I am indeed the Nothingness. Yet am I a mystery to many. For my true purpose is unknowable. Though I have devoured the spirits of countless worlds, in the end have they been destroyed by the sins of their own children. My brother and I have fed upon their lifeless corpses. But we have not destroyed them. They have destroyed themselves.

"Even this world shall eventually consume itself. For its own children shall be the source of its demise in the end." The image of her mother then grinned. "Such is the nature of the cursed flame that burns within them. For their own Creator placed it there. I have not stoked its fire nor fed it, but let their own villainous ways—their greed, their corruption, their perversions, and their murderous ways—rage within their doomed hearts, letting the fires of their own desires burn them to cinders." the Nothingness bellowed.

Ana's heart grew heavy as she looked at the stagnant pool. She then saw how it boiled and bubbled red and thick with dark blood. The jet black eyes of her mother's image then stared down at her, cold and unfeeling. The Nothingness then said, "Yes, you see the blood. In the pool is the blood of the dead, the countless fallen from many worlds who, by their malevolent acts, had given themselves up to me. Their blood now courses under the very rocks of Phantaia, filling its underground rivers with the liquid essence of the dead. It flows endlessly into the mouth of my brother, the Emptiness. For he is the vampire that drinks from it, never satiated, sucking its ever-increasing streams into his wide belly."

But Ana now stood bravely before that being, saying, "You are but a maligned spirit filled with many tricks meant to entrap me. For Ama revealed to me your true purpose in this world. You are a deceiver and a liar, sent to pollute the minds of the innocent just as you polluted my father's mind, corrupting it to your own end."

The Nothingness smiled, saying, "If you desire, Ana, I shall reveal many truths to you. It was my hand that parted the waves of the sea so that your father could sleep with your mother. And it was I who sent the bolts of lightning upon the trees so that you could escape the Magra. For I desired that you be spared an early death at the hands of your father's servants until your own evil deeds could be fulfilled. And so have you done so, just as I had planned."

The Nothingness then suddenly grew dark, his cloud taking a red and horned demonic face. He then drew his great cloud down upon her, shouting in a violent voice, "It is I who fathered the Creator, the Essence Eternal that spawned this world, whose very spirit now lives in its children. They are my children, all of them. My dark seed lives in you all!" A hot blast of wind from the breath of the Nothingness blew down upon Ana's face, casting back her dark hair from her shoulders. But she stood defiant and unmoving before the foul spirit.

The Nothingness then gathered his storm about him, taking shape as the proud face of the Twilight Mist, smiling down at Ana with his sadistic eyes, saying, "Like your grandfather, were you born to fulfill my secret will. And so were you made to follow its twisting course wherever it might take you. The well of the Secret Spring that fed the One Tree was destroyed by you. But it was my will alone that it be so. And so have we together slain the great tree and its cursed light."

The Nothingness then slowly transformed his face to that of her father, saying, "Even the heights of your father's own evils are not fully known to you. For long ago your father vowed to give up your life to me, Ana. He willingly sacrificed his own daughter so that Phantaia might fall, betraying his own child so he might slay his father." The Nothingness smiled, as he looked upon the pained face of Ana.

The Nothingness then rose up again, taking the shape of a great blood-red dragon, saying, "By your father's oath are you now mine to slay, if I desire. Only by your death shall your father be released from his solemn vow to me. How much love hath you for him now, Ana? Show me this love so I might devour it." The Nothingness then shook the dark cavern with the roar of his great laughter, as Ana's mind became clouded and confused. She began to lose herself, lose her purpose. And she fell into a deep despair.

But Ana said to the Nothingness, "Though I love my father, I know not who he truly is. Yet my heart tells me he would not knowingly make such a vow. For you are a vile and sinister spirit, cursed with many lies and untruths designed to imprison the wary and the trusting. Unlike my father, I am neither of those things. So I will not be deceived. If my heart is evil and corrupt as you say, then I have truly fulfilled all that you have asked of me and my task in this world is complete. You could slay me now if that were true." Ana knelt down, weary of all she had heard.

"It matters not to me whether you live or die, succeed or fail," said the Nothingness. "I may spare the world your death so you might have the pleasure of watching its slow and torturous demise by your own hand. But in truth I need not your help, for your own children shall destroy themselves and the world soon enough. Then shall they come before me in submission, begging for death's sweet oblivion. Know that I shall wait on them as a loyal servant, serving up death to them all."

The Nothingness then gazed into Ana's eyes, his own face changing into her own. "In you, child, flows a part of something greater," said the Nothingness. "It is a sinister force that even I do not understand. Yet I sense that within its waters lies the limitless source of an undying curse, that which has doomed the children of countless worlds before this one. Soon it shall be unleashed again into Phantaia and into this corrupted world, inflicting its poisonous and hateful wrath upon you all. For this world was conceived by its enduring will. And by its curse shall this world soon perish. So have I spared you, Ana, so that your last terrible task may be completed." The Nothingness looked down with an evil grin. Ana then watched as his great gray cloud slowly faded away in the air above her.

Ana looked down, unsure of all she had believed since she first came to Phantaia. She no longer knew what the truth was. For that spirit had placed the seeds of doubt within her. Ana knelt beside the pool, forlorn and sad. The vile spirit was gone. But she was left alone to her uncertain destiny in Phantaia.

Ana sat beside the pool, thinking about Ama's fate and the sad and tragic plight of Phantaia. And she thought to herself whether death was now her only friend. She stood up to leave, when she felt a presence behind her in the shadows of the cavern. She then turned and saw Ama standing beside her. He seemed young again as he smiled down at her. But Ana felt conflicted and confused. His eyes were his own, yet something black had filled them.

Ama then said to her, "Ana, I have returned. Do not worry about me any longer. For I am with you now." Ana reached out to embrace him, but pulled back feeling something strange about him.

Ana then said to him, "Ama, my heart aches as I have missed you dearly. But I am unsure of this place, or of who you are. My mind is now clouded with many delusions. And many dark things have been shown to me I had not seen. I am doubtful of the future, of you, and of everything."

Ama brushed her hair with his pale icy hands. "I could not tell you," Ama said in a hollow voice. "But this dark place is my true home. And the spirit that haunts it, my true father." Ama then took Ana's hand, leading her to the pool. "Come with me and spare the world its doomed fate," Ama said.

But Ana resisted, stepping away from him in shock at his words. With deep black eyes staring into her own, Ama implored again, "Do not hesitate, Ana. Come away with me now." He then reached out his pale hand to her.

Ana hesitated. Then feeling again her deep love for him, she looked into his sad eyes, saying, "If it is true that within me dwells a horror unseen by me, then I would rather perish. By my death shall I spare the world its curse, and save my father from his terrible vow that binds his fate to my death. But most of all I wish to be with you, even in death, Ama. I have longed for it as much as I have longed for you. I will go with you." Ama and Ana then walked together to the edge of the dark pool, which simmered and boiled with a dark red color.

But as Ama reached out to take her hand, she ran towards him. And with all of her might, she pushed Ama into the foul waters. A shrill scream of pain was then heard echoing through the cavern, as the form of Ama tossed about in the water. But as Ana looked, she saw him change shape into strange forms of beasts and monsters most hideous. Its then she saw the true form of the gray Nothingness tossing about in the waves.

"I will not let you deceive me as you deceived my father," cried Ana. "The Sacred Waters of the world shall be restored, and the children reborn into this world, forever after living in peace and harmony by its essence. The lights that burn in the hearts of my children shall rise again to defy you and the evil seeds you have planted in this world!"

The agonizing screams of the Nothingness echoed through the cavern. But the dark spirit of the pool had come forth from the depths to claim that being. As it writhed and twisted in the black water, the pool's dark arms wrapped about the cloud of the Nothingness. The spirit held again that being in its grip, like a mother holds her child. It then dragged the great form of the Nothingness down into the depths to drown it in its blackened waters. Ana looked down into the depths of the pool with pity for the creature, until she saw only peaceful water resting again upon its tranquil surface.

Ana turned away from the dark pool and began climbing the stone stairs that spiraled their way out of the pit. But as she did a strange white light was thrown about the cavern walls behind her. And a haunted voice could be heard, saying, "Return...return to me." Curious, Ana crept back down the stairs and walked towards the pool to find its odd source.

The face of the dark woman then reappeared upon its surface. She reached out with her dark hands, imploring Ana not to leave. But as Ana crept closer to hear the dark queen's words, a cryptic vision appeared again. Ana saw a dark young woman dressed in black satin, standing beside a pale young man whose hair shined like gold. Before them lay a shining fountain of shadowed waters. And above them a white tree, free of shade, unspoiled, and pristine. But upon the young woman's hand lay a dark ring in which shone the lavender colors of twilight.

Suddenly, a great angry cloud thrust up through the water with great violence, shattering the serene vision. The pool's waves lashed angrily against the violent gray fog, as if to assault it in a defiant display. The cloud curled within itself as if being torn and rent by the water, until finally escaping its brutal assault once more, the thundering storm billowed forth again into the cavern.

Ana ran for the stone steps, as she saw its dark black cloud fold itself into great black hands to grab her. She ran up the slimy steps of the pit. But parts of the spiral staircase crumbled under her feet so that she slipped, almost falling back down into it. She crawled up the last steps on her hands and knees, out of breath as she struggled to reach the surface. But from below she heard a hideous cackle coming from darkness below.

Ana then heard its terrible words, saying, "Return to Abrea...return...return. Return to the pool and your fate. There you shall find Ama. There you will find him...return...return..." And with a blast of hot air, its sinister laugh bellowed up and out of the pit.

With the last of her strength, Ana walked up the last steps of the rotten stairs. She then fell onto the cold mud of Phantaia, grateful to be above ground again. She felt the loud crash of thunder in the chilly air. Frequent flashes of lightning lit up the dark woods about her, bleaching the boughs of the trees in a bright blue sheen.

The center of the violent storm seemed to lie just beyond the trees to her right. She then knew where it was heading—the Gardens of Abrea. There the storm would be gathering its forces to finally destroy it. She must hurry, race against the storm before it is too late. But as she followed the flashes of lightning, she heard again, roaring up from the depths of the pit behind her, the insane and tortured laughter of the Nothingness, echoing through the forest around her.

As Ana fled into the woods, she saw within the dark horizon that stretched before her an almost treeless vista. The world seemed bathed in the fog of a deep blue night, beneath whose empty skies lay endless fields of rocks and dirt, heaped and piled up in rolling black mounds around her. What few trees that remained were now only burnt stalks, their trunks blasted by lightning, their boughs ripped away by the violent winds that billowed overhead.

Only a ghostly fog now clung to that sad earth. The land seemed to be but a lifeless wasteland of rotting logs and debris flung far and wide by the ravages of the Magra. Seeing the state of Phantaia, Ana's spirit now sank. Yet, she had resolved to get to Abrea. She must reach the hill of the One Tree before the storm and no matter what terrors she might face.

As she ran on through the mounds of mud and leaves, she came to a barren hill devoid of all grass and trees. But something yet remained upon its highest point that looked familiar. As she climbed to the top, Ana saw the wreckage of Durn, the great oak, his battered trunk still standing boldly upon the blasted hill. His limbs were torn from his trunk. And his leaves stripped away from his shattered boughs. She saw only a pair of closed eyes upon his weathered trunk. Yet his face seemed to move with some faint spirit of life that remained deep within him.

As Ana approached, he opened his large eyes. But as he looked upon her, he seemed unable to speak. For his grief was great. Ana wept beneath his great roots, begging his forgiveness for what she had done. She then placed her hands on his great trunk, saying, "Great tree, I need to find Ama. Is he alive? Do you know anything of his fate?"

The great tree then slowly opened his wide mouth. With a creaking and dying voice, he said, "I am happy that you are alive, Ana." His great face then turned morose, saying, "Many of my children have been slain by Yana. Others have fled into Avaras to battle the evil hazels that now rise up to fight them. With the return of the spirit of the Limitless Void that lies in your father's dark ring they may now haunt Phantaia freely again. But many have perished, Ana. Yet they lived happy lives knowing that this day would come."

He then smiled at Ana's tear-filled face, saying, "My spirit shall soon leave this world, too. For the hope of a new forest promised us has now been lost. The time of renewal has almost passed. The powers of destruction have won. They shall soon come and finish the destruction that the Connewe had begun. My own spirit shall soon leave this world and return to the father tree that bore it."

But the kind tree looked again upon the face of Ana, saying, "You have had great courage in your heart and have faced many trials to try and save us, Ana. Thank you. Leave me now and go forth to the Isle of Adda. There shall you be safe from harm. For the last waters of Avalyr that wrap about it are filled with the Sands of Time, and so are feared by the darker powers. Soon the Magra and the Connewe shall destroy the last of the living spirits that remain in Abrea. For the heart of the Rock Eternal alone remains in Phantaia. For he has been secreted away there."

He then looked with sad eyes at Ana, saying, "Ana, I know not of the whereabouts of Ama, except that his spirit has not been seen or felt in Phantaia for many nights. This worries me, for the spirit of my brave brother has always been known to me wherever he might roam in these woods. Take with you my love and the enduring hope that now rests with you and your children." The withered tree then closed his eyes in a deep and knowing sadness.

Ama then hugged the old oak one last time. And with tears of parting, she said goodbye.

The storm billowed overhead, its tall blue and gray thunderheads crackling with lightning. Ana rushed down the hill. But she had not taken the old tree's advice. She would make her way to Abrea. She then saw the old trails that Ama had long ago showed her. The winds began to blow about her as the skies grew blacker and the charcoal gray clouds above her filled every corner of the brighter heavens that had yet remained.

Torrents and sheets of rain and hail soon fell from the clouds that streamed overhead. As she neared the gardens, the tempest had increased in power as if fed by the large swaths of earth and wood it had consumed into its wide mouth. Its wild cyclonic winds slung the dead and decayed logs of trees about her, until to Ana it seemed as though the storm was trying to block her path.

Ana saw what was left of the splintered and bent trunks of the elderwood as she approached their groves. She placed her hands on the shattered remains of their once living trunks. But as she gazed upon the towering Hill of Abrea, she gasped. For beyond the stumps she saw what remained of the beautiful Gardens of Abrea. What had once shined so bright and green was now a black mound of dirt and death. Brown and burnt, its withered plants and bushes were now reduced to a few dead stalks. All about the hill was a muddy ruin of decaying leaves and rotting logs. And the savagery of that wreckage was more than she could comprehend.

But Ana held her mouth from screaming as she saw upon its summit the splintered and blackened trunk of what was once the One Tree. She was too late. For its great bushy head of leaves was gone, so that only a few shriveled boughs had yet remained on its great trunk. Its hollow body looked as if a great hand from above had ripped its leafy head from its trunk, yanking it up from the earth. Its gray roots bulged from the broken earth in tangled masses. Yet the stump and roots of the once great tree still clung desperately to a ball of dirt, standing proudly upon the summit of the hill as if it had bravely resisted the violent hand that had sought to tear it away from its sacred earth.

Ana stood for a time and looked with trepidation upon the wreckage of the once-majestic tree. She then saw a faint glow from deep within the dark hollows of its bole. Its last golden lights had somehow remained, cascading out its rare beams like an evening star alone upon the cold horizon.

Ana descended the slopes of Aron, determined to make her way to the tree upon the hill. The rain and winds had died down, so that everything seemed calm. She gathered her courage and walked quietly through the valley. As the black storm twisted and turned about her head, she walked on towards the once green and bountiful hill.

As she approached the Hill of Abra, she saw the true violence of the destructive winds that had battered its slopes. For the plants of the gardens that once grew there had been torn away from the rich soil that once sustained them. Heavy rain had then flooded the mound, so that the base of the hill was but a slimy mass of mud and refuse. The youthful trees that once ringed the hill now lay in decaying piles of rotting limbs and leaves, washed down the valley by the torrents of water that had poured from the hill above.

As she climbed the slippery hill, Ana saw about her the dark limbs of the once-great tree strewn about the slopes. They appeared to have been shattered by the storm. As she climbed the hill, blue bolts of lightning crashed down in the woods around her, while above her the black mouth of the Magra slowly turned. Yet, by some unknown force, the storm had paused on its final destructive path, arresting its final wrath, as if waiting for some final command from an unseen master below.

As she struggled through the piles of timber that lay strewn about the hill, she saw that the black roses growing at its base had nearly consumed the garden. As she climbed the slopes of the mound, their sharp thorns tore at her gown, so that her arms and legs were covered in scrapes. And she began to feel dizzy from its poison as she clawed her way up the muddy hill.

As Ana neared the top of the hill, she fell on her hands and knees, exhausted. She then looked up and saw the sad state of the great tree, its splintered remains standing before her. She wept knowing the time to save it was now past. It was gone forever. With tears in her eyes she looked down in horror at the ravaged world below her. And she wondered if her children would ever know of the beauty that once existed in Abrea.

Seeing the magnificent tree destroyed, she climbed to the top of the hill where its broken form now stood. She reached out to touch its dark wrinkled trunk. She then held her head down in sorrow. But, as she looked down, she saw under its roots the rocky place where the Secret Spring had buried her child, Phanduan. Under the stones of her grave she saw a strange golden aurora. There among the rocks, hidden and unseen for countless ages, glowed the Sacred Light of the world.

But as she reached out to touch it, a tall black figure walked out from around the trunk of the tree. Its great leathery wings unfurled themselves from around its frame, blowing back behind it like a black sail. The beast then slowly opened the savage slit of its wide mouth, baring its jet black teeth at her. Its wicked red eyes burned bright with hate, as it looked down at the frail girl.

The Shadow had returned.

Ana shuddered in horror as that monster of the night stood before her. The malicious Shadow smiled with an evil grin that dripped with the drool of his long-held enmity for her. He looked mightier and more powerful than she had remembered. His muscular black arms and chest bulged with tremendous size and strength. And his own darkness seemed immersed in the depths of an abyssal night, such that its black vapors fumed from his face and body, filling the air and dyeing the earth about him with the ink of midnight's pitiless gloom.

What little light that yet remained had been sucked into the dark guise of his broad wings, as they unfurled over her tiny form. As he stood over her, Ana thought she could hear the rustling of the black roses as they crept about the hill, curling their dark stems about her feet and ankles. They had grown with great vigor, nourished by the Glourun cast by the Shadow's wings. Fed by the dark essence, they blossomed around her, their large blooms shimmering like black satin in the cold rain's dark dew. The Shadow bent down and picked one of their dark blooms, admiring its rich scent as his sinister lips curled up in disgust at the sight of the girl.

The Shadow then looked down at Ana with his glowing red eyes, which bulged from his sallow and sunken ebony face. With a sinister grimace, he said, "At last we meet again. Yet joyless it seems. Let it not be like a tragic family reunion, one wrecked by endless disappointments and regrets. Let it be renewed, this kinship we share. I was such a fool to have left you on the very eve of our initial date. For I had so many things to share with you. Forgive my errant ways, my coarseness, and my crudity. I can only offer you this rose, as I seek your forgiveness." The Shadow reached out with his dark claw to hand her the black bloom. But Ana backed away, cowering in fear of him.

The Shadow then looked at her, smiling. "It is no matter," he said, his eyes now blazing forth like dark red coals. "You are indeed your father's child. You have destroyed the pool, as I have the tree. Like two sickened lovers drawn together by their perverted passions, wed in secret to each other through pleasurable purpose, we have defied the will of the better world by our acts. Have we not committed crimes together, sundering the union of the tree and pool by our own degenerate desires? For the malevolent mind of the evil that yet dwells in the Great Beyond planned these acts long ago. By its own dark seeds has its evil will now been sown in Phantaia through us, its fallen children."

He then shouted, "A new age of darkness has now been planted. And by the fruit of our savage acts has its dark deed now been done!" A terrible laugh then bellowed forth from the Shadow's wide jaws.

"But I have returned again without fear of you, but with the knowledge that I may slay you, if I wish," said the Shadow. "For I have contemplated, since last we spoke, the act of ripping out your heart and drinking the blood from its pool. Would they satiate my thirst as this well has satiated yours, I wonder?" The Shadow then bore his long glassy teeth at her. And an evil grin came upon his face, as he watched Ana crawl away from him in terror.

The Shadow said, "But I need not lift a finger. For your weak heart shall break soon enough." The Shadow then reached for something dark that lay hidden at the foot of the fallen tree. Ana fell back in dread. For in his hands was that which she could not bear to see. She gazed in disbelief as the Shadow held in his claw the bloodied head of her beloved Ama. Ana then screamed in horror at the sight, crying, "No...no..."

The Shadow held the severed head before the dark and threatening skies. He then looked up into the Heavens with his wild eyes of madness and cackled with glee. "The son of the great tree is dead!" he shouted, his deep voice bellowing through the icy air.

The Shadow then held the dark head of Ama before her, as the blood from its gouged eyes and mouth dripped down into the grave that lay at the foot of the tree. Then was heard a faint sound of something breaking.

With a gratified look upon his face, the Shadow said, "I had heard of your great love for the guardian of the woods. And so I brought his head as a gift to you, so that you might love him still." The Shadow laughed as Ana recoiled in fear. Hiding her tear filled face from the terrible sight, she wept knowing her love was gone forever.

Gazing into the dark Heavens, the Shadow said calmly, "After strangling Ama at the foot of his father's tree, I carried him far from here, casting his headless body into the gulf of Wendalia. Yet, you should know he fought bravely. Like the burning light of the father-tree, nevermore shall the shining son haunt these forlorn woods. Oh, how tragic..."

But looking down and seeing her absence, the Shadow flung the head of Ama down the hill in frustration. The head of Ama then rolled over the dripping Falls of Bann, disappearing into the river below. He then stormed down the hill, seeking Ana. For she had secretly crawled away.

His great clawed feet crashed through the dried brush that lay upon the mound, as he called to her in his thunderous voice. But Ana had hid in fear beneath the roots of the dead tree. There she saw again the fading glow of the Secret Light that lay hidden beneath its roots. And its merciful flame gave her heart hope in that dark hour. But as she reached out to take it in her hand, she paused. For she saw where the tree had wrapped its loving roots around it, as if seeking its nutrients. It had given its light freely to the tree so it might feed its children, the trees of Phantaia. And she knew then of the light's loving gift, its power, and its true purpose.

But the Shadow saw the glow from afar, and descended upon her secret hiding place within the roots of the tree. He then dragged her out by her feet, throwing her down before him. But as the Shadow looked upon her in anger, Ana had gathered the strength of will that still shined within her. She then stood bravely before him, closing her eyes, trusting herself.

The Shadow, surprised, stood still as Ana placed her tiny hand upon his great chest. As she listened to the sounds of his beating heart, she heard something strange that dwelt within. She then said to him, "A vision comes to me. And I see you as you truly are. But in you dwells a terror, some nightmare of the netherworld. That which once cursed your father now lives in you. You are but a vassal to it."

The Shadow stood still, as in a trance, Ana slowly removed her hand. The Shadow then awoke. "What trickery is this!" yelled the Shadow. "You take me for a fool? I am the Lord of Darkness, the master of my fate." Ana backed away, falling to the ground amongst the sharp thorns of the dark roses, as the Shadow came at her with his sharp claws.

"Come to me, Ana," the Shadow roared. Enraged, he reached out to grab her. She then screamed in terror as he snatched her up from the ground. But as Ana looked upon the Shadow's horrid face, his expression suddenly changed. His deadened eyes now had an icy stare. Fear had returned to his sullen face, as he stared at something behind her.

Ana then heard a familiar voice, powerful and strong. "Back away from the child," said Agapor. The Shadow then stood up slowly, gazing at Agapor with uncertainty. As Ana looked behind her, she saw her proud father standing at the base of the hill. His great cloak was wrapped about him, but his right arm was exposed, revealing the black manacle he still wore. His face was filled with some long-buried and simmering hatred for the Shadow. But as he looked into her eyes, Ana felt his abiding and undiminished love for her. His eyes were resolute. He had returned for her.

She then saw again upon his right hand the strange glow of the black ring. For its great stone of jet had cast a morose moonlight glow about the hill as it throbbed. As Ana looked about the forest she saw the woods begin to shift and change, moving towards them slowly, as if drawn to its glow. The trees had come alive. But as Agapor looked at her, its weird light had begun to fade again. And with the ring's dying light the vast armies of trees began to back away from the hill, slowly creeping into the shadows of the Ringwood from which they had come.

The turning and churning tumult of the Magra had also retreated. Its once-boiling black and angry storm clouds had calmed, parting in the skies above the hill. The dark clouds born by the Magra then drew themselves back beyond the horizon of the trees, until only a few ghostly clouds now drifted quietly about the Heavens. And all lay calm and quiet as it once had been.

But Ana now saw the true scope of the powers her father possessed, and the true horror of what he had done. For Yana's storms had nearly consumed Phantaia. And she looked away from her father in shame. The Shadow then looked with a cautious eye to the skies, as the foul maw of the Magra fled away before them.

Agapor gazed upon the Shadow, staring him down as he held before him the enchanted bracer of iron. It glowed with a bright light as he commanded its strange powers to stir. Ana then saw the Shadow grimace as a sharp pain filled every part of his wracked body. He backed away from her, stumbling on the hill and holding his heart, as if his spirit and flesh had returned to some infernal dungeon of unending torture and pain.

Ana cried out, "Stop it, Father! Stop his suffering! He is but a servant to a greater evil. He knows not the source of the foul spirit that possesses him."

But Agapor looked upon the writhing Shadow with vindictive eyes. He then said to his daughter, "He is a servant to me. But he was doomed long ago, not by that which lies within him, but by the evil path he has chosen." The Shadow then backed away into the rose bushes atop the hill.

"Ana, I have come to take you away from Phantaia and the dark powers that shall soon obliterate it," said Agapor. "There is nothing left for us here. Only evil remains. For it has come to do you great harm. Ana, let us leave this cursed world now." Looking around and seeing the destruction her father had wrought, Ana looked down in disappointment.

Agapor then walked towards her, saying, "Ana, you can choose to hate me for all that I have done. But I love you still. Could you ever trust me again?" But Ana looked at her father, doubtful of everything he had told her.

"I shall not leave without you. I shall not leave you to perish here. If you stay in Phantaia the Shadow shall come looking for you, until the very end of his days. And he shall not stop until he kills you and your children. For this task alone was he made, Ana. Your life shall forever be in jeopardy if you choose to remain here. Ama is dead. Nothing remains here for you now."

As Ana pondered her father's words, she saw a strange darkness rise up from the hill. The black roses about the hill had begun to move about as the Shadow stretched his great wings across the height of the hill. Defying the tortures his master had unleashed upon him, through strength of will, he had drawn to himself the vile essence of the Murgala into his great wings. From out of the roses he drew up into himself their inky essence—the Glourun of his father which for so long had been denied him.

The deepest shades of night then suddenly fell upon them, such that the outer woods seemed to disappear behind a dark curtain. The skies then became black as pitch, so that it felt as if they were standing alone in some deep abyss at the bottom of the world.

A hot crimson mist flowed up from the black roses about the hill, filling their senses and emptying their hearts of all feeling. Its strange red tide flowed up and over them, until all was bathed in a bloody mist. Its luminescence then cast aglow the nightmarish monsters, abominations, and undead that erupted from the bloody earth.

Yet, they were horrors of the mind, creatures of the night that had always been, slithering within the corners of their shadowy dreams, unseen by their inner eye or waking spirits until the mists of their imaginations had unveiled them. Horrific screams, murderous voices, and vague sounds of agony arose from the darkness, as they drew themselves up from the ruddy shadows around them. Ana cried out to her father as they swarmed around her, trying to pull her down into the darkness.

Ana then heard her father's calm voice, "Close off your mind and heart to the Shadow. You must concentrate. For he has placed within your imagination the terrors of your mind's own creation." Ana closed her eyes. She strove to erase the horrors that now seethed within her fragile mind. The sounds then stopped as the terrors of her mind faded away, like the morning mist.

Ana opened her eyes again. All was as before. But seeing his dark enchantments dispelled, the Shadow looked down upon Agapor in rage. The Shadow then wrapped his great wings about him, gathering the shadows of the black roses and the dark woods into him again. His wings, imbibed with the forceful Glourun of the Endless Night, began sucking in all darkness into them—the very shadows of Phantaia itself—until a black mist began to seethe around him in a wide whirlwind. Before their eyes, the Shadow began to change and transform into a more monstrous form.

A colossal, dragon-like serpent now rose before them, with black scales as hard as diamonds, and jaws filled with dagger-like teeth. His thick bat-like wings beat the air violently about him, as hot steam flew from his wide nostrils. His long black body, snake-like, coiled itself around the top of the hill. The great wyrm then thrust his great scaly neck into the sky, as he stretched forth his massive jaws of iron, dripping with drool.

The black serpent then turned its thick head towards them, looking down at Agapor with a malicious stare. It then said in its slithering tongue, "In this child now dwells the woe of the world. For polluted and poisonous waters yet flow in her. But they are not of the light or of the darkness. For they were forged by the will of the malicious spirit, thy twilit father, who hath sent them here to curse us all. The child must die, Agapor. Even you know this to be true. You have made a vow. Now you must fulfill it." Agapor held his head down in sorrow.

Ana then looked upon her father's face, saying, "Father, is this true? Tell me it is but a lie which evil hath conjured up to deceive me from every quarter." She stood as one frozen between the serpent and her father.

The Shadow then shouted out, "Agapor, tell her! Just as the pool and tree have died, she must die. When she is dead shall the waters also perish, and we both shall be free. This world shall be free. Slay her. Slay her now! For you have made a vow before the Nothingness that dwells in the Great Beyond to surrender her spirit to him."

"The Nothingness was right," Ana said, as tears welled up in her eyes, "How could you?" Ana then looked away from her father in dismay.

But Agapor looked upon his child, saying, "Ana, soon the sinister twins shall come to destroy us all. You must trust me. We must flee this world. Forget Phantaia. Come to me, Ana." Ana looked with anxious eyes at her father. She then ran to him. And they embraced as father and daughter. Agapor then felt within his own heart the love for his only child made whole at last, that which he had sought for so long.

But as father and daughter embraced, Agapor felt the strange beat of the heart within his child. And its mystery weighed upon his mind.

Ana looked up the hill at the monstrous creature. She then gazed upon the black and broken tree that stood defiantly upon the hill. The faint glow of the Sacred Light still beamed out from beneath its roots. It then cast its warm light upon her face. Ana then realized that a tiny piece of Phantaia had refused to die—refused to give up hope.

Ana turned to look upon her father's face one last time. She then stood before him with tears in her eyes, saying, "I shall always love you, Father. You must know this. But I cannot go with you. For I love Phantaia still. I belong here beside the tree and its garden. My children belong here. Please Father, stay with me in Phantaia and live here in peace with us. We can fight the Nothingness. There is goodness yet in your heart, for the light of hope yet lives in you. I feel it. And my mother, the keeper of the destinies of the living, long ago revealed to me in a dream that you would someday stand and defend Phantaia against that darkness."

Agapor cried out to her, "Ana, do not to do this." But Ana could only look down in sadness as she walked away from her father.

But the shadow-serpent, seeing her alone, flew down upon her and wrapped his dark coils about her. As Ana struggled to get away from him, his great leathery wings beat the ground with such force that great cyclones of dust flew up and about them.

But Agapor rushed the beast, striking his jaw with his great fists, so that Ana fell away from the serpent's clutches. The black wyrm then wrapped his thick body about Agapor to suffocate him. He then bit down on the shoulder of Agapor, so that great streams of blood poured out of him. Agapor then turned to Ana and said, "Run Ana. Go to the top of the hill. Save Phantaia!"

Weak from loss of blood, Agapor stretched forth his right arm, summoning forth the dark powers of the mystical manacle once more. The bracer glowed with a hidden fire as the great serpent, feeling its torment upon him, fell to the ground, coiling about himself in agony. Yet he stared up with a vicious eye at the shackle upon his master's wrist. And the words of the Twilight Mist then returned to him.

Agapor called to Ana as she ran up the hill. She then paused to look back. But as she did, she saw the massive head of the dark wyrm rising up behind Agapor. The great beast bared his toothed maw, dripping with drool, as he looked down upon the unknowing Agapor. As Agapor turned, Ana saw a look of dread upon her father's face as he saw the open jaws of the monstrosity that loomed above him. Agapor then held his right hand before the creature, commanding his dark spirit to obey.

But the serpent came down upon him with his mighty mouth, biting off the right arm of Agapor, and swallowing it down into his great belly. So was the black manacle that had enslaved the Shadow ripped away from its master. But so too was consumed into him the dark ring that lay upon Agapor's hand.

Agapor cried in agony as he fell before the beast, his blood pouring forth from his arm. But as he collapsed to the ground, he turned and looked upon his daughter, as she stood upon the slopes above him. His life was now quickly draining away. And he desired to look upon his daughter one last time.

The dark ring was now lost. And the spirits of the forests and skies began to stir. For without their master those spirits were now set free. But within the dark bowels of the beast was that evil relic now held. It then began to glow within the shadow-serpent, as a great ringing was heard in the skies. The black wyrm then roared and writhed in agony as the hateful ring burned deep within his belly.

With the cries of the ring, Yana was now unleashed from her prison in the skies. The gates of the storm-filled Heavens were then opened wide to the mighty mouth of the Magra mother once more. Her great vortex began to hover above the great hill of the tree. As she spun about in the Heavens, it seemed to Ana that the whole universe now revolved around Abrea. Down upon her then poured a great blast of wind from the storm. The muddy ruin of Phantaia then began to lift up around Ana, rising up into the mouth of Yana.

Into its great orifice was flung large logs and limbs from below. Huge hunks of the earth below the hill were then sucked up into its cloud. It drew forth the soil from under her feet, so that as Ana neared the hilltop, she felt herself begin to slip downward. A terrible rumble and roar was then heard all around as the very earth seemed to groan and quake. Ana knew the end was near for Abrea.

"Go Ana!" Agapor yelled. "Death draws near. It shall soon take us!" Agapor then collapsed on the hill, where he lay dying from his wounds.

Ana approached the top of the hill, as the dust and debris from the Magra swirled about her. Great billows of leaves and limbs began to spiral about the hill below, forming a thick cloud of brown dirt and debris.

The Shadow, having taken into his belly the source of his slavery, roared in the chaotic gale with exhilaration at his new freedom. The serpent then looked down at his fallen master as he lay weak and near death. "I am now free of my enslavement to you!" he cried. The Shadow then bent his dragon-like head down to devour Agapor.

Seeing her father in peril, Ana screamed. The serpent, hearing her cry, then turned and gazed at Ana. But seeing her close to the top of the hill, he became enraged. For he knew now what she would do.

With his mighty clawed feet, he stepped over the fallen form of Agapor. As Ana climbed out onto the summit of the hill, she crawled on her hands and knees, over the scattered roots and rocks until she lay beside the rocky ruin of the pool. She slowly climbed to her feet, not knowing if she had any more to give. As she staggered to the edge of the empty well, she closed her eyes, summoning up the last of her courage from deep inside her.

She then felt the icy breath of the serpent behind her, blowing down her back and across her shoulders. As she looked down at the ground, she saw the shadow of the dragon-like head of the serpent looming over her. Ana watched in horror as the shadows of his black jaws slowly opened above her.

Closing her eyes, she gazed down into the empty depths of the pool. She placed both hands upon her heart, trusting that everything she did from that moment would be as she imagined—a calm and peaceful journey.

The serpent reached out with his hooked claws, as his black head rose up to devour her. He then thrust his giant jaws violently down upon her. But Ana was gone.

THE WINGS OF NIGHT

Ana felt herself falling, farther and farther, into the silent depths of the pool. She seemed to be floating, almost weightlessly, as she drifted down into the darkness of that seemingly endless pit. It felt as if she was in a perpetual state of rest and calm, as she fell deeper into the earth. And so she was not fearful.

A feeling of endless peace had come over her. For an eternity had passed since she stepped into the well. She then saw in her dreaming mind again the glowing faces of her children. They appeared before her, bathed in the light of a shining new age which she had known would someday arrive. Their smiles and laughter now sustained her. Yet strangely, three faces did she see.

Ana then felt the gentle arms of some being holding her body, slowing her fall, and suspending her in the shadows of the cold earth. The living roots of the One Tree had reached out to hold her. They had wrapped their soft roots about her small frame as they carried her downward. Cradled in their many arms, she felt herself embraced by the tree's loving spirit.

Deep under the Hill of Abra lay the forsaken tomb of the Secret Spring. Upon a sacred slab of enchanted stone the roots of the tree laid their precious cargo. Within the rocks of the hill would Ana lie for all eternity, and like her mother bound to infinite sleep in timeless dreams encased. And so was the fate of this sad world now woven and wound within the tangled webs of the visions of Ana and An.

The tree then sent forth its thick roots around her frame, wrapping Ana in its cocoon. They then pierced the Sacred Heart of the Luffa she had long held within her chest. The Sacred Waters then burst forth from her breast, flowing down and around the cave of her tomb in a great flood.

Only the tree could release the waters from her flesh. And so was Ana left unharmed. The tree had drawn her spirit to him with abiding love and care. And so were they bound as one beneath the Hill of Abra, renewing, by their loving matrimony, the dying spirit of Phantaia.

With the releasing of the Sacred Waters into the well, the Sacred Heart of the Luffa had fallen away beside her bed within the tomb. As a bejeweled brooch of woven gold and silver inlays was it made, with four faces of the Primordial Ones bent outward. But its inner shape was of the tree, sitting atop a circular cauldron that swirled with the tragic waters of life. This treasure would remain hidden in her tomb until it would be given to another even more deserving, and its enchanted powers summoned forth again. For it had been made to carry the wild and relentless waters of the pool into a new world.

Those waters had been imprisoned within her heart. But freed, they would not hide in the darkness of her lonely crypt. Rising swiftly from the rocks below, they swirled through the cracks and crevices of the dying hill. Rushing up into the empty pool, jubilant and free, they rushed forth with great vigor into its earthen cauldron, filling its deep cup, and flowing over its brim.

The virginal waters, pure and chaste, then spilled over the lip of the pool that held them. They laughed as they fell about the gardens, until their waters had replenished Lilu's barren streams. With a joyous and frothing display, they then rushed headlong over the Falls of Bann and into the awaiting arms of Avalyr. The river then sparkled with many lights and colors, greater than before, refreshed with the radiance and life of the loving waters.

The cauldron of the pool had swelled with the spirit of the Sacred Waters, drawing them continually up from their undying source. The unspoken language of their dancing reflections sparkled with a thousand suns upon its trembling surface. Its mirror then cast its spectral beams upon the ravaged tree and gardens, as the first tender lights of a happy spring awaken a frozen and forlorn winter world.

Thus was reborn the Sacred Pool of Eternity in this troubled world, as it had been remade in many worlds prior.

The wounded spirit of Phantaia was then revived and healed. The roots of the great tree then drew forth its nourishing waters from the well, renewing its heart and spirit, until the One Tree's battered boughs and leaves began to stir again. The shining spirit of Celebreava was then awakened once more within its great trunk. The living tree then thrust up from the mound, bursting forth from the black bole that imprisoned it. A new trunk now grew forth as the old one fell away. Yet it was not a new tree reborn from the old, but the old tree resurrected.

Shedding its former skin, it stretched its thick white limbs into the skies, reaching new heights even greater than before. In the ecstasy of its youth, its new leaves and limbs beamed out with a perfect light, shining forth with a new brilliance, chasing back the shadows of the night that had come to possess the sky and earth. The ghostly trees that had descended upon the nearby woods fled before its golden beams, back into the farthest fringes and darkest haunts of Avaras, where the shade and mist that crept there had long shielded them from its former sun.

Atop the Hill of Abra, the Shadow had returned to his original form, having shed away his scaly skin. He then stood upon the edge of the pool, looking into its hypnotic waters, seeing again the haunting visions of his own forbidding future.

He watched with fascination and yet horror as the Sacred Waters that Ana had borne within her now filled its cauldron. And the dread of them filled his mind again. It was then he saw the One Tree grow upon the mound, its great lights shining forth from its mighty trunk to blind him. Before the burning glow the Shadow cried out to his father, begging for mercy as he fell to his knees.

But with the return of the waters of eternal springtime, the tree had cast its vengeful fire upon that vile Child of Night. The Shadow then flew forth with haste into the skies, trying with all his might to escape its searing flame. For his dark wings were filled with the powers of the Glourun, the essence of the Endless Night, which he thought would shield him. But against the mighty beams of the Sacred Light, fed by its enchanted pool, were those powers defenseless. For as he flew from the top of the hill, the tree's great fires burned away his face. And he cried out in agony as his black body began to smoke before its radiance.

Its light scorched his flesh, burning away his mighty wings, igniting his body, and casting it aflame. Agapor watched as the Shadow exploded in a ball of fire, falling through the sky like a comet burning bright in the Heavens. The smoking ruin of the Shadow then fell to the earth as a molten mass. Its hot embers, like a shower of sparks, were thrown down upon Abrea, into the dark roses of the Murgala that lay about the hill. And so from that which is of darkness made would yet come light. What was left of the Child of Night then disintegrated into coarse ash, which blew about in the winds as its dark sands sifted down into the earth, becoming one with the Gardens of Abrea.

His bat-winged servants and spirits of the night that had come from the Lands of Midnight were chased back into the depths, fleeing in terror before that blazing sun. But so too were heard the shrieks and howls of their master's tortured spirit as it fled away into the blacker woods of distant Avaras.

* * *

Agapor lay dying in the midst of the tangled thickets beneath the hill. His mind began to fade as he thought upon all that had come to pass. But he smiled knowing his daughter's wish was fulfilled, and that her sacrifice for Phantaia would not be in vain. He gazed upon the wondrous light of the new tree as it stretched its white limbs high overhead. And he marveled at the odd changes taking place around him in Abrea. For the plants and trees, like their father, began to grow again.

But the manacles that were once his to command now were gone. And the dark ring that lay on his hand was lost. Yet, the servant of darkness was no more. And the dark trees of the Connewe had fled away, back to the darkest corners of Avaras. Powerless, Agapor was free. But the storms of Yana had raged on around him. The Magra had now begun to seethe and boil with malice, seeing its enslaver near death.

The great storm of Yana began to turn again in the skies, until she spun about in the Heavens overhead, peering down with her evil eye upon Abrea. Her cold winds blew down upon the hill, buffeting the limbs of the great tree. And she cast her evil shadow of death upon it, as her great mouth drew nearer to the summit. The silver leaves of the shining tree were then stripped from its boughs and sucked into her wide maw. Yana then began to slowly pull the shining tree from his rocky firmament as it had done before.

But the Magra soon cast her eye upon the vulnerable pool, its waters like a tempting wine now hers alone to drink. Her cyclonic cloud then dipped down its wide mouth onto the hill, sucking up the magical waters of the pool into her great gullet. And deep she drank from its cup.

But the Sacred Waters were not of this world. For they were created by a force and intellect beyond her own, a power unyielding, never-ending, and relentless. For nothing that dared harm them could ever escape their wrath. For those wild waters would fill the world if they could, against the forces of evil and good, light and dark, which might unite to destroy them.

As Yana drew forth the Sacred Waters, her belly filled with its fateful essence until it became bloated and full. She then burst forth in the Heavens like a great rainstorm. The cursed waters of the pool had consumed her, the imperishable one, as the Dreaming Seas had once done to her sisters. The thunderheads which had stretched out across the sky now imploded, bursting forth with violence across the Heavens.

Long gray rainclouds stretched their strata across the skies in great streams, pouring down the life-giving rains of the Sacred Waters into the forest. With her death, the evil Magra had released the sweet waters of that enchanted pool back into Phantaia's living earth. And so was her secret labor in that world now complete. And those which she had selfishly taken—the innocent spirits of the forest—were given back again, their seeds released into the ripe earth, fed by her rains, and then sprouting as new plants and trees within the boundless woodlands of Phantaia.

And the oaks and the yews, and the gentle ash, and the mighty rowans were all renewed by her storms, their spirits returning to the loving forms they once knew. Phantaia, rejuvenated by both light and water, grew with great vigor again, its wild wilderness alive and fresh in the blissful dews of its triumphant rebirth. And so ended Yana, greatest servant of the Emptiness, she who had perished by her own foolish avarice and thirst.

But with the sundering of Yana's spirit from her form, there was released from her womb a thousand stormy children, each bound to their mother's ancient design. These storms then fled away upon chariots of thunder and lightning, riding the bands of wind and rain beyond Phantaia's timeless shores.

Seeing the annihilation of their mother, they had fled away in fear, back into Oblivion and the Great Beyond. Others escaped into the underworld, hiding in deep holds and catacombs, cowering within the shadowy rocks and cliffs beneath Phantaia. But some of Yana's spawn still hung upon the fringes of Phantaia as their mother had done, forming great thunderheads in the Heavens, tearing away at her cliffs, and assaulting the remnant oaks that still clung to the earth of darkest Avaras.

Others simply remained in the skies over Phantaia as storms, boiling with clouds of gray just beyond the horizon, ever-threatening the woods with their bright bolts of lightning, sending down their sheets of rain and hail, and harrowing the tops of the trees with their ceaseless gales and cyclones. For those bestial storms, ever after, would seek to avenge their mother's cruel death. But long would they wait for that time to come, if ever it would again, when the tree should wither and its light fade. Then would they return, seeking to finish that which their mother had not.

The blazing light of the One Tree had burned fiercely, like a mighty star, ablaze with the twinkling lights of a great golden sun. With the One Tree's light renewed, the shadows and the evil that had come to destroy it had fled away, into the pits and hollows of the earth, the woods, and the skies. And so had the reunion of pool and tree, water and light, justice and goodness in Phantaia brought down its full vengeance against the powers of darkness and destruction.

The Chieftain Trees and Maiden Trees, near death, grew forth in even greater glory than they had known before. As their beautiful spirits returned to their bodies, they then turned their thick trunks to look upon the wondrous new tree and its magnificent lights. For it had christened them with its love and compassion again. The gardens about Abrea now grew forth with even greater beauty, unfolding new leaves, buds, and blossoms.

But the Murgala that had wrapped themselves about Abrea had been burned savagely by that light. And so had they slithered away, hiding their diminished kind within the valley below. Only in its deepest glades were the shadows dark enough to hide them and covet them away, until they could entangle the young, the naive, and the innocent again.

But the blazing glory of the One Tree was short-lived. For though it had been reborn, brighter than before, so had the color and glamour of its candle begun to change and transform, fading quickly into the colors of twilight time. No longer did it bear a golden hue, but was now fast bound to gold and silver lights intermingled. The bright sun of the One Tree's burning spectrum had now dimmed to a more subtle shade.

With the return of the Sacred Waters to the enchanted pool, the ruddy light of the One Tree had been cast away. For that pool had now stained it with the phantasmal shade of its own twilight. Therein were light and darkness equally contained. And so was the tree renewed again in this world, yet forever bound in equal proportion to dusk and dawn, cursed and blessed by the somber light of eternal evening.

The One Tree and the Sacred Pool had thus come together to cast a mighty twilight glow over all the world. Phantaia had truly become a Forest of Twilight, embracing the darker dreams of sleepy mists, half-awake, half-alive, yet bathed in its own shadows. Dark purples and rich lavenders now painted its greener woods in their haunted shade. And it would be, forever after, cursed with that phantom glow, guarding its light yet worshipping the night, trapped in a world between two worlds now tainted and forever stained.

The leaves of Phantaia's living trees would still sparkle and glow with deep greens and warm silvers. But its glistening trunks and slippery boughs would cast forth a pale violet color upon their bark, still bathed in the dew of its own strange haunting mists. Yet the Gardens of Abrea still glowed with rich color. For its secret spirit had somehow survived, bearing within itself the remnants of that golden light of old. For the Sacred Light within the grave of Phanduan still cast its warmth upon it and the valley below. Yet it was no longer bound to the One Tree as before. And this strange truth would await those who dare awaken its sleeping spirit in future days.

The Sacred Waters of the pool were now released into Phantaia, flowing down and around its warm green mound. In those waters was now held the hope of new life—the loving children that had been promised Phantaia by its Creator long ago. For that twilight well had been made for the children of the world so they might live there in peace. With the promise of providence and paradise it now bore, and the undying nature of its secret purpose, was it so named the Pool of Eternity.

The pool's shining waters had flowed forth and overrun the earthen cup that had held them. Spilling down in a great torrent, the Gardens of Abrea now burst forth with new life and new bounty. Glorianna's green growth blossomed forth in great abundance, as the rich grasses of Annafar and Aron danced once more in the winds. And so had the Sacred Waters blessed that land, as the One Tree shined forth its lavender lights, casting aglow the resplendent gardens that now grew at its feet. Yet would Unaranna, the loving glades of Ama, remain coldly silent.

Deep within the tomb of the hill, Ana now slept. But the spirit of the Rock Eternal had appeared beside her bed. As he looked with merciful eyes upon the sleeping beauty, his manly form held her hand in his, saying to her as she slept, "Ana, your gift to us shall be forever cherished and long remembered. But from this sleep divine you shall never awaken. As your mother is bound to the seas, are you pledged to the fate of the forest. For you alone now sustain the One Tree and these lands with your undying waters, and shall do so until the end of the world." And a tear fell from his eyes.

But Ana in dreams heard her visitor's voice. And she spoke to him through her visions, whispering into his mind, "Spirit of the Earth, I have but one wish. I desire to walk again in the beautiful Gardens of Abrea, taking flesh to dwell beside my young children until such time as they no longer need me. For I long to see them, to love them, and to be with them."

The Rock Eternal looked with gentle eyes upon the sleeping Ana, saying, "This one desire I shall grant you." His form then departed from her bedside. But in truth the Rock Eternal would never leave her. For his earthly spirit would ever after sleep beside the lonely lady of the pool, watching over her spirit within the hallowed halls of the earth of Phantaia, which he alone commanded.

* * *

There had returned to the Gardens of Abrea another being, dark and dolorous. The Shade had hid in the depths of the woods, watching the destruction of Abrea from afar. But she had watched in horror as Agapor had fallen before her terrible brother. And she heard his cries and felt his suffering from afar, waiting till the light of the One Tree should dim.

She then came to him when the dews of the twilight mist were thickest, his pitiful cries having ceased, seeking his dying form hidden within the tangled vines of the garden. With her dark feathered-wings unfurled, she reached down and took Agapor in her arms. She then flew from Phantaia, carrying him far from that cursed wood, drifting upon the ethereal winds of Midnight, beyond the Dreaming Seas, and into the deepest pits of icy Oblivion.

There she laid him upon a bed to rest alone within his candlelit chamber. She then lovingly tended to his wounds. But he would not awaken. For he tossed within the nightmares of his own mind, haunted still by his loss and yet the horror of his own vow still unfulfilled. His daughter was gone, his family destroyed. And he had lost all power over the Realms of Oblivion. For both the iron manacles and the dark ring had been taken from him. And so a sickness of mind and spirit soon crept over him.

But the Shade loved him truly and would not abandon him in his time of need. And for a time her love alone sustained him, though it was itself doomed. She stood beside Agapor many nights as he struggled to stay alive. But the poisonous wound of the Shadow would not heal. Yet the Shade would not let him perish. So she bled forth her own essence into his mouth so that he would yet be saved. Weakened, she remained beside him and cared for him, night after night, until he at last awoke.

Agapor cried out in agony. For trapped in his madness, he saw only the dark face of the Shadow. He then collapsed back into a cruel and torturous sleep, so that even in his dreaming mind he had sought death. The Shade then held him to her. When he was asleep again, she left him. In the midst of his dark laboratories, she then summoned his alchemists to her, commanding them to fashion a magical potion to heal his madness and clear his mind.

But when the Shade, triumphant, returned with her enchanted brew, she saw that Agapor was gone. In desperation she sought to find him, racing through the shadowed halls of the underworld, crying out for him. She then saw dark trails of blood on the cavern floors, leading forth into the darkness.

She followed their dark traces through many winding and twisting tunnels, until she had come to a great cliff that fell away into the gray depths of the Great Beyond. There upon a ledge stood Agapor alone. The Shade then looked in terror at the abominations that lay waiting for him in the abyss below.

The Shade stood in shock as Agapor walked to the edge of the cliff. But hearing the presence of the Shade, he turned to look upon her. "I made a terrible vow to these spirits for the life of my daughter. But never again must evil threaten her, or her children. And so must I fulfill my vow. I will surrender myself in return for her life, so that she and Phantaia may live, undisturbed and unharmed, ever after," said Agapor.

The Shade ran to him. And he held her again as they kissed, one last time. Wiping tears from her face, Agapor then said to the Shade, "My love, you must return to the land of your father. For something there yet remains for you to do." Agapor spoke again, as he looked into her tear-filled eyes, "Complete the will of your father. This you must do for the children of the world." Agapor looked into her eyes one last time, as he let go of her hand. He then fell backwards, falling away, disappearing in the mists below. Agapor was gone. And like his mother never again would his form or spirit be known in this world.

The Shade then fled away from Oblivion, never to return.

* * *

Flying on her ebony wings, the Shade wound her way through the lonesome corridors that lay beneath the Lands of Midnight. She had returned to her father's lands. Down into the catacombs of his labyrinthine halls she flew, until she arrived at his massive tomb. But as she stood before her father's empty grave, she heard a distant voice coming from the depths below.

She then walked forth and down the great steps to the place where she had heard the pitiful cry. Like the wailing of a lonely specter haunting a forgotten grave, its lonesome sound had risen forth from the strange sewers below. There the dark waters of a mysterious stream had once flowed, pouring forth from some undead well of the underworld that once had fed it.

As she searched the sewers, she saw floating in the black water a lonely figure. It was her father, frail and wounded, yet somehow alive. He had called her from afar. But seeing his daughter again, the Endless Night reached out to her.

Pulling him from the dark water, the Shade knelt beside her father, holding him in his last fateful hour. The Endless Night then said to her, "I have waited for you, my child, holding on to the last light of hope that you would return to me. For my life is almost spent."

As he looked upon his daughter's face, he saw within her eyes a secret sorrow she had hid deep inside herself. He looked into her heart and knew then of her love for Agapor. "I had hoped that love would find you. For so little of it has been given in this world," he told her. He then touched her face as her tears fell upon his hand.

The Shade then said to her father, "Father, your son took your powerful wings and tried to destroy the child called Ana. For in her dwelt some mysterious water whose purpose he alone had understood. But he has failed, Father, for Phantaia yet lives. And the pool that died has now been reborn. She has given Phantaia new life. For the great tree that grows there draws forth some strange new light from its well. It now bathes the world in everlasting twilight, Father."

The Endless Night smiled. He then asked the Shade if her brother yet lived. "He is gone, Father. For the light that shined briefly in the tree has burned him to ashes."

The Endless Night then looked away, saying, "Your brother had come under the powers of a terrible spirit, one which I had spawned. Yet strangely in the end, he had embraced its evil rather than resisting it, his heart filling up and brimming with deep hatred for the world."

He then looked upon the Shade with fearful eyes, saying, "Though your brother is dead, I yet hear his spirit calling. Do you not hear it?" The Shade looked at him in doubt.

He then asked, "Does the witch yet live?"

The Shade said, "I do not know Father, as she has disappeared. I fear this creature, as I feel she has betrayed my brother."

The Endless Night then spoke with introspection, saying, "Her spirit came to me, long ago, from a dark place beyond this world that none might ever find. I cared for her, and she for me. But I had discovered too late that she lived for a purpose most devious that she would never reveal. And yet I spared her life from the destruction of my brothers. For I loved her truly." The Endless Night then looked down, deep in thought again. For he could not tell his daughter a painful truth.

The Endless Night was near death. And he looked into his daughter's eyes with great love and admiration for her. But she saw a deep sadness yet in them. He then said to her, "My daughter, long ago I defied the Essence Eternal, my Father. And so had I destroyed this world, seeking to gain power for myself, driven by greed, desire, and pride. You alone, my child, must go and redo what I have undone.

"Soon a blessed child shall be born into this world, one who, by his vast creative powers, shall place within the Heavens the Star-Maidens. By the lights of these Children of Heaven, bound to the mantle of the night, shall be made known a new message of hope for those yet to come. With the remaking of the Sacred Pool, once again, shall a new generation of children, more joyous and at peace, soon enter this world. For them alone have our many works and labors been granted by Him," said the Endless Night.

He then said, "The time has come for my last labor to be completed. Return to my tomb and shatter the dark crystal of my thrown. Hidden inside it lies the Wings of Night. For I had kept them there safe from all evil until the time when you would return. These wings the Essence Eternal had given to me, left over from a fallen world, so that you my daughter might reforge the Heavens anew."

"Go with haste!" said the Endless Night. "With the Wings of Night you must form the midnight mantle of the Heavens. By the shade of those wings shall the night skies then be remade for the star-children to dwell therein. Under their guidance shall the Children of Shadow and the Children of Shining someday dwell in peace in Phantaia. The beginning of this new age shall be heralded by their beacons. And so must the mantle be made so that the shining splendor of their hope-filled lights endures."

"Father, I shall fulfill your wish," said the Shade. The Endless Night then looked upon his daughter's compassionate face. His heart was now at peace.

She held him close to her in his final hour. The Shade then wept for him and all that she had lost. The Endless Night then passed away in her arms, crumbling into a dark dust that fell through her fingers. But as she looked up into the heights of the cavern, she saw his silver spirit flying free, gliding with great gossamer wings upon the night winds, until he disappeared in the darkness high above.

The Shade came before her father's massive throne in the great tomb where he had lain. She then shattered the black crystal of that mighty chair, tearing away the rocks with her bare hands. There, within the stone, lay a pair of small silver wings—the mighty Wings of Night given to her father by the Essence Eternal.

They shined out with a divine radiance, yet drew unto themselves her dark and silken shadows. Within their shining feathers shone the promise of a million sparkling stars and worlds, yet unborn. The Shade then drew them forth, gazing with reverence at their transcendent beauty. With great humility, she placed them upon her form, opening them wide before her. Something miraculous and purposeful then stirred within her heart. She now understood all that had been given to her, and all that had been lost. And she felt the divine grace and mercy of the Spirit Divine, and his secret purpose for her.

The Shade flew out beyond the Veils of Night, soaring upon the cold night winds. On her black wings she soared, high up into the sky, until she reached the Arch of Heaven. There she untied her silken sashes, letting the sails of her argent wings unfurl. She stretched the Wings of Night wide before her, until their bright cloak had filled the skies. They then changed from light to dark. And the true nature of their nighttime sheet was revealed to her. The Shade and her mighty wings were then drawn up into the Arch of Heaven. And there she became one and inseparable with it.

The heights of the Heavens were thus remade and bound unto the Shade, whose spirit forever after held its dark mantle in her loving arms. The children of Phantaia would often look upon her beauty and wonder, gazing upon the stars she held so dear to her and their star-children yet to come. But with the darkening of the skies to perpetual night were the Gates of Heaven forever closed to them. Never again would the children of Phantaia see the grandiose Mountains of Heaven that towered beyond the Arch, nor speak of the mysterious Lands of Mist which lay beyond them.

And so was the first age of the forging of the world now complete. The Anakra, first Dreamtime of the Great Mother, had now passed.

* * *

Below the nighttime skies, the Gardens of Abrea had flourished. As gentle rains fell from passing storms, the forest of Phantaia returned to its former glory, bathed in the jeweled light of its magical dews. Yet the gloom of the twilight mist had returned to haunt Phantaia, unfaded and undying. Pouring out from the Doors of Evening, it wrapped its great cloud about the hill of the tree and pool. And so the three became one in purpose and design.

No being had yet walked within this mystic twilit paradise. But upon an evening, the gray fog had returned once more, drifting out among the purple boughs and blossoms as a fiendish creature crept about its gloomy gardens. With her glowing eyes of jade, the witch Anissa now stalked about its silent corridors. She had returned to creep among the black roses that grew there, seeking that which was promised her long ago.

With her long black nails she dug about the mound each evening, searching that which was thought lost for all time. She would then depart on the eve of each twilit dawn, only to return again in the cool of the evening when the dusky tree's lights burned dimmest.

Anissa had returned to the base of the hill in the depths of its eventide. She then found the Shadow's remains buried within the Murgala where the roses grew thickest. With cautious hands she turned over the black soil with her nails, until at last she found the black ring of jet promised to her long ago. And so, with the finding of the ring had the Shadow's deadly vow been fulfilled. Anissa then disappeared into the woods, never to return to Abrea.

* * *

The river of Avalyr now flowed wild and free with the rebirth of that eternal spring. But into its sleepy river had fallen the grim head of Ama. It had rolled down over the waterless cliffs and into the quiet river below. There it floated on the still waters as it made its way to the seas. But the gentle hand of the river-child named Atar had rescued it from the waves. Seeing the head of Ama, she held it in her arms and wept. For she loved him as a brother. She then cared for it, placing it upon the Isle of Adda, deep within the tomb of Anadelling. There it would remain. But whether it spoke to her, none would ever say or know.

As the glorious garden within Phantaia grew forth in living splendor again, the darker destiny of its sorrowful past seemed almost forgotten. A happier and more peaceful age of innocence and youth was once more upon it. For within the twilit garden were heard the cries of children coming from the heart of Abrea. They had come unexpected into that place, calling out from the top of the hill where the Sacred Pool now bubbled forth with bold jubilation. Two loving hands then reached down into the depths of its silver waters, pulling forth two beautiful children whose happy eyes shone with the sparkling joys and hopes of a new dawn.

The End

FAMILY TREE

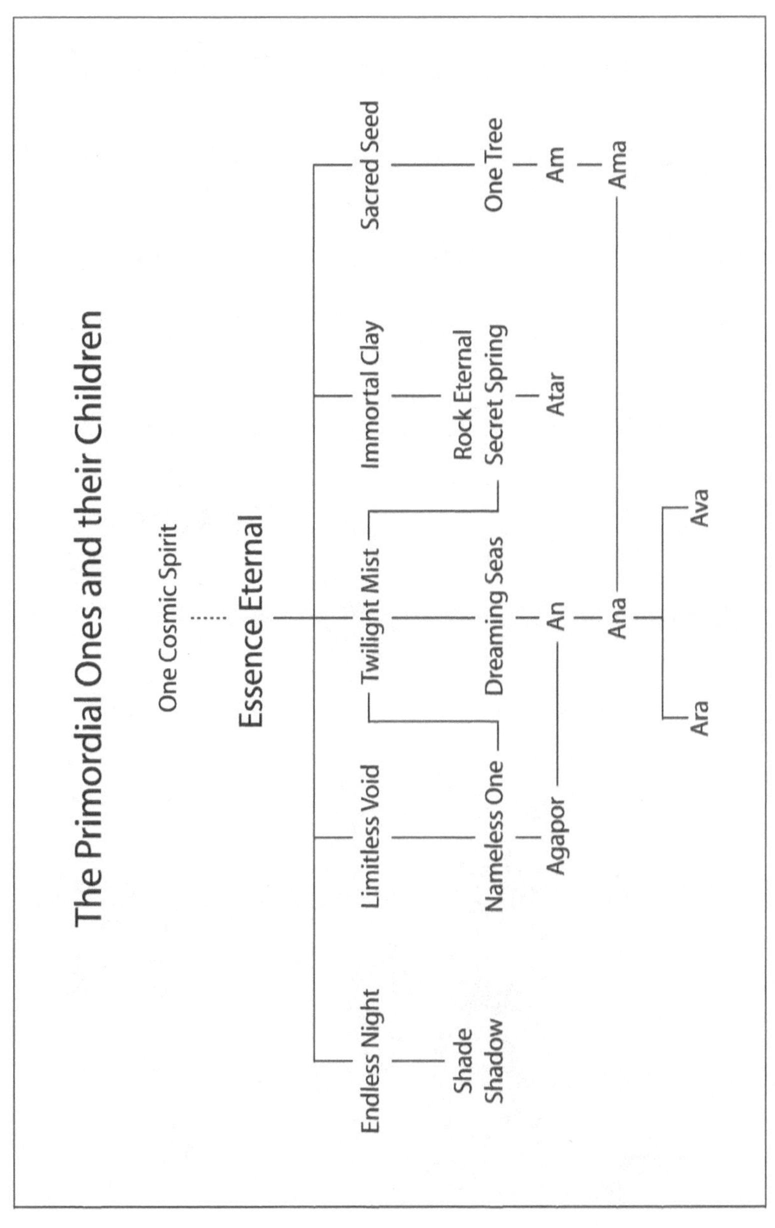
The Primordial Ones and their Children
One Cosmic Spirit
Essence Eternal
Endless Night
Limitless Void
Twilight Mist
Immortal Clay
Sacred Seed
Shade
Shadow
Nameless One
Dreaming Seas
Rock Eternal
Secret Spring
One Tree
Agapor
An
Atar
Am
Ana
Ama
Ara
Ava

LEXICON

Introduction

Most of the languages and names used in the Phantammeron were based on a casual study of the Insular Celtic languages of Ireland and the British Isles (Irish Gaelic, Welsh, etc.). However, in researching ancient languages, I found I was often more interested in their appearance in ancient Indo-European philology and fairy tales than in the more general study of linguistics and the construction of artificial fantasy languages from them.

Many of the fantasy names used in my books originally used elaborate accents, umlauts, etc. to guide the reader in their correction pronunciation. But after careful consideration, I removed them in an attempt to simplify the words and avoid printing errors. In my notes, however, exist my original word designs, accents, and inflections. The new names were then redesigned to make them as easy and as intuitive as possible for the reader to pronounce. It was then my hope that newer words constructed from earlier forms would use rules the reader could easily understand and build upon, deriving meaning from more complex names built from various roots and stems. In that sense, I tried to build languages in my current books using ordered constructs that readers could easily build on in pronouncing words used in future Phantammeron books. But I also wanted readers to sense their hidden meaning, and find deeper connections between the characters, places, and events these names represented.

Because the Phantammeron books represent a written mythological history spanning a great deal of time, the names used in Book One had to be loosely constructed from future languages that evolved in later books (for example, the world of Anatar). Yet, as Book One covers the initial cosmology of the Phantammeron series, primitive names given to early divine places and beings in it had to form the basis for more complex derivative names used in later books, as well. This pattern, I felt, reflected how ancient mythological names have been used in our modern world. For that reason, the simpler names used in Book One were carefully designed to fit a more ordered mythology and comprehensive evolution in both their meaning and influence over later languages, stories, characters, and books of the Phantammeron, even though those languages and the races that used them had yet been born.

But it is still my hope that you will find more value in the hidden spiritual meaning, inner connections, and carefully constructed purpose of these languages in representing the often irrational, spiritual, and emotional nature of the mythopoeia found in the Phantammeron, and less value in attempting to portray the ordered and coldly logical artifice of fantasy linguistics and language construction.

Core Pronunciations

I have included some core elements from the various names used in the Phantammeron, which should help you in their pronunciation in this book and later ones.

a - most often a soft 'ah' in sound, as in Ana ('ah-nah')
c - almost always the hard 'k' sound, as in Celebreava ('kel-e-bray-ah-vah')
ch - can be a traditional 'ch', as in Cromwich ('krom-ich'), or hard 'k', as in Durnach ('dur-nak')
dd - same as 'th', as in Breddwyn ('breth-win')
i - often used as a hard 'i', as in 'high'. Examples are Lilu ('lie-loo') and Iwu ('eye-woo'). Use the 'ee' sound at the end of a word, as in safni ('saf-nee')
u - often 'oo' in sound, as in Koredlum ('kor-ed-loom')
w - more often pronounced as hard 'w'. But sometimes silent, as in Cromwich ('krom-ich')

y - often pronounced 'eye' (hard 'i'), as in Amandyas ('ah-man-die-us'), but also soft, as in Avalyr ('ah-vah-lir')
aia - pronounced 'eye-uh' when at the end of a word
ea - pronounced 'ay-uh' when at the end of a word
ia - pronounced 'ee-uh' when at the end of a word
ua - pronounced 'oo-uh' when at the end of a word

Special Pronunciations

Phantammeron - pronounced as 'fan-tam-ur-on' (or like fant-hammer-on)
Phantaia - pronounced 'fan-tie-yuh' (same as Gaia)
Iwu - pronounced 'eye-woo'
Uyl - pronounced 'oo-il'
lyr - pronounced 'lir'

Index of Names

A - 'essence, Great Spirit, heart, one, all' (Ah), the One Cosmic Spirit, essence of all things, creator of the Spirit Divine, father to the Essence Eternal
Abra - 'spirit-hill, heart-of-the-earth', the sacred Hill of Abra, earthen mound in the center of Phantavra on which resides the Gardens of Abrea, the One Tree, and the Sacred Pool
Abrea - 'spirit-garden, flowering-heart', encircling gardens that lay about the Hill of Abra in central Phantavra. Also, a general term for heart of Phantaia. See Riabra
Adda - 'spirit-island', the river isle of Avalyr, once an ancient hill from a prior world, much like Abra. Also, alternate name for the world of Anatar that came later
Afa - great ash tree, one of the seven Chieftain Trees of Phantaia
Agapor - son of the Twilight Mist, father of An
Alcu - great elder tree, one of the seven Chieftain Trees of Phantaia

Alum - great fir tree, one of the five Maiden Trees of Phantaia
Am - 'seed-of-the-forest, wood-spirit, father, male, golden', first seed sown by the One Tree in Phantaia
Ama - 'son-of-the-seed, heart-of-the-forest, father-like, boy, golden-one', guardian of Phantaia, born of Am of the One Tree, first child and son of the Sacred Seed
Amandyas - 'father-sky, heart-of-the-heavens', the shining gold and silver, star-filled heavens
Amladem - 'golden-roof', the daylight heavens created by the golden light of the One Tree above Phantaia
An - 'queen-of-the-seas, water-spirit, mother, female, silver', daughter of the Dreaming Seas, mother of An, weaver of the fates of the children of Phantaia upon the Loom of Time
Ana - 'daughter-of-the-ocean, heart-of-the-sea, mother-like, girl, silver-one', daughter of An, mother of Ava and Ara, keeper of the Sacred Pool
Anadelling - 'queen-of-mounds', golden hill that lay upon the isle of Adda
Anakra - Dreamtime of the Great Mother of which there were two ages: Anakra I (story of An and her child in Book One) and Anakra II (story of Ana and her children in Book Two)
Anissa - 'fallen-mother, witch-queen', Queen of the Cromwich, her witch-sisters from the Lands of Midnight, daughter of the Endless Night
Anling - great alder tree, one of the five Maiden Trees of Phantaia
Annafar - 'flower-mound', the grassy flowering hilltop of Abra
Atar - 'river-daughter, heart-of-the-world', child of the Secret Spring and the Twilight Mist that lived in the river of Avalyr
Avalumlea - 'rowans-of-light', sacred groves of rowan trees that grow within the farthest fringes of Phantavra. Includes the outer ring of rowan trees that form its gates
Avalyr - 'river-of-light', the encircling River of Time that flows from Abrea to the Dreaming Seas, fed by the Sacred Pool in Abrea
Avara - 'twilight glow, shining mist, of-light-and-dark', the purple lights and fogs given to the Twilight Mist by the Essence Eternal

Avaras - 'land-of-twilight, lightless realms, Lands of Darkness', the darker evil woods of Phantaia that encircle the brighter inner realms of Avra and Phantavra

Avra - 'half-lit land', the misty forests that lie just beyond the fringes of Phantavra, and that stand between Avalumlea and darker Avaras

Avredd - 'half-lit underworld, Lands of the Afterlife', the three ethereal planes of the dead beneath the Dreaming seas, ruled by the Immortal Clay, their Lord

Breddunar - 'forest-secrets', the hidden tree-knowledge of the living trees of Phantaia, given to Ana by Ama

Breddwynn - 'White Forest', the encircling groves of white elderwood trees that guard the inner realms of Abrea and which make up the Ringwood

Celebreava - 'shining-spirit-of-the-tree, pale-one', the spirit of light bound to the One Tree, his secret name, father of Ama

Connewe - 'witch-hazels, Overlords of Avaras', the thirteen possessed witch-hazel trees of Avaras that ruled over the dark trees in that land

Corridors of Darkness - the towering black hallways that led through the underworld beneath the Lands of Midnight, connecting that realm to the haunted Halls of Time

Cromwich - 'witch-coven', the witch-sisters of Anissa that were summoned to the Lands of Midnight from the dark waters of the world

Dreaming Seas - the mother-seas made by the Twilight Mist, mother to An

Durn - great oak tree, one of the seven Chieftain Trees of Phantaia

Durnach - 'strong-grove, oak-clan', the black oak groves and tree-children of Durn which stood before Avaras

Ebrandeer - 'unicorn, great-horned deer', the white unicorn form of Ama, his secret name. See Phanyan

Emptiness - twin and evil brother to the Nothingness, devourer of the flesh of the world, child of the Evil One, born of the spirit of the Insatiable Hunger of Hatred

Endless Night – first-born son of the Essence Eternal, a Primordial One, Lord of the Lands of Midnight, and bearer of the Wings of Night

Ephram - 'evil-thinkers, Seven Hazels of Evil Thought', the seven most powerful witch-hazels of the thirteen Connewe of Avaras

Esnes - great black willow tree, one of the seven Chieftain Trees of Phantaia

Essence Eternal - the Great Father, Spirit Divine in living form, the Creator

Evil One - the dark queen and mother to the Emptiness and Nothingness, destroyed in an earlier world

Galdar - 'wood-magic, secreted', the secret enchantment used by the trees to hide parts of the forest of Phantaia

Glessa - 'tree-tears', the magical amber of Avalyr made of the sap of the Maiden Trees of Phantaia

Glorianna - 'hidden bloom, joy-of-my-heart', the beautiful blossoming hillsides of Abra and the Gardens of Abrea

Glourun - 'masked-by-darkness, hidden', the shadow-powers given to the Endless Night by the Essence Eternal

Great Beyond - the gray misty void that lies beyond the Realms of Oblivion and all worlds, prison of the Nothingness and Emptiness

Great Mother - ancient undying mother of the Seas of Eternity that washes all worlds clean, past, present, and future

Halls of Time - the endless gloomy hallways that stretch forever from the Lands of Midnight into infinity

Immortal Clay – fourth-born son of the Essence Eternal, a Primordial One and lord over the Lands of the Afterlife given him by the Essence Eternal

Iwu - great yew tree, one of the seven Chieftain Trees of Phantaia

Koredlum - 'black willows, Were-Trees', the seven black willow trees, dark sons of Esne that ruled the underworld of Phantaia

Kum - great hawthorn tree, one of the seven Chieftain Trees of Phantaia

Kurtavla - 'twilight-fruit, dragon-breath', the aged dark apple tree of Nemedd, the tree made of the breath and spirit of the twilight dragon that guards that realm

Lands of Midnight - the gloomy region between the Dreaming Seas and the Realms of Oblivion that is filled with the Corridors of Darkness and guarded by the Veils of Night

Lavanc - 'sea-creature, great-fish', the messenger, servant, and guardian of An and the Dreaming Seas

Lilu - 'laughing-waters', the silver streams which encircle Abrea, which are fed by the waters of the Sacred Pool upon its heights

Limitless Void – second-born son of the Essence Eternal, a Primordial One, Lord of the Realm of Oblivion, and bearer of the shining spirit-sword Vatavandr

Luffa - 'heart-of-the-pool, grail-of-the-waters, Sacred Heart', the secret receptacle that held the Sacred Waters carried by Ana

Lumlea - great rowan tree, one of the five Maiden Trees of Phantaia

Magra - 'storm-servant, Gray Ones', servants of the Emptiness, ruled by the Oversouls, their leaders

Maymee - 'alone-child'

Murgala - 'rose-of-darkness, Garden of the Black Roses', the ebony roses born of the tears of the Endless Night for his love of the Secret Spring

Nameless One - mother of Agapor, created by the Limitless Void

Nemedd - 'crystal-forest, Lands of Mist', mysterious realm of the Twilight Mist that lies hidden in the dark valleys beyond the Mountains of Heaven

Nothingness - twin and evil brother to the Emptiness, devourer of the spirits of the world, child of the Evil One, born of the spirit of the Unquenchable Thirst of Revenge

Olybana - 'bejeweled-waters', the bright sandy shoreline of Avalyr

phan - 'tree, bole'

Phanduan - 'forest-daughter', child of the Secret Spring, she who was given the Sacred Light

phanta - 'forest, wilderness'

Phantaia - 'Forest of Twilight, woodland-realm, paradise', the vast wilderness that exists beyond the Dreaming Seas, the forest-heaven of the Gods

Phantammeron - 'Book of the Forest', the mythical written history of the the Children of Shining (Fey) and their enchanted paradise, Phantaia

Phantavra - 'Forest of Light', the encircling woods and valleys that encompass the inner realms of Phantaia, from Abrea its heart to Avalumlea its outer lands

Phanyan - 'forest-guardian', the forest-name of Ama as the white, golden-horned unicorn. See Ebrandeer

Phea - great beech tree, one of the five Maiden Trees of Phantaia

Realms of Oblivion - the dark lands between the Lands of Midnight and the Great Beyond, ruled over by the Limitless Void

Riabra - 'queen-of-gardens'. See Abrea

Sacred Seed – fifth-born son of the Essence Eternal, a Primordial One and the seed that held the One Tree, the father-tree of Phantaia. See Celebreava

safni - 'first-tears, tiny-rain', tears shed by Ana into the pool of Abrea

Spirit Divine - a form of the One Cosmic Spirit that is contained in all living things, that which was given to the children of the world by the Essence Eternal

Twilight Mist – third-born son of the Essence Eternal, a Primordial One, creator of the Dreaming Seas, Lord over Nemedd and Phantaia

Unaranna - 'secret-place-of-love, hidden-in-the-heart', the secret spot where Ama took Ana in the Gardens of Abrea

Uyl - great apple tree, one of the seven Chieftain Trees of Phantaia

Vatar - 'flesh-of-the-earth, clay-made', the body that was made to house the spirit

Vatavandr - 'flesh-cleaver, spirit-sword', the shining sword given to the Limitless Void by the Essence Eternal, used to sever the spirit from the flesh

Veddu - great birch tree, one of the five Maiden Trees of Phantaia

Wendalia - 'not-world', the bottomless chasms within the Realms of Oblivions that lead past the Gates of Eventide to the Great Beyond

Wings of Night - the shining wings given to the Endless Night by the Essence Eternal to form the dark mantle of Heaven

Yana - 'Death', storm-servant of the Emptiness, the Faceless Form and Magra Oversoul, Queen of the Gray Ones summoned by Agapor to destroy Phantaia

www.ingramcontent.com/pod-product-compliance
Lightning Source LLC
Chambersburg PA
CBHW051207120726
47905CB00004B/1014
* 9 7 8 0 9 9 7 0 3 7 5 1 7 *